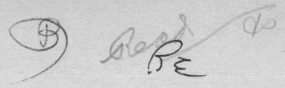

Abruptly, before she could escape, he pulled her to him and kissed her,

a bruising kiss that left no doubt about the magnitude of his anger. As Rand's mouth lingered, her lips parted of their own volition and instantly his tongue was inside her mouth. His arms tightened, until she thought she couldn't take a breath, until her senses reeled from the sensations he wrought in her.

When he released her, Leilani would have stumbled backward but for the sturdy door behind her.

"Think about that, Leilani," he told her harshly. "And consider what it is I care about."

Then he was gone. She went into the quiet house, suddenly trembling so that she had to grasp the banister as she walked up the steps to her bedroom.

Dear Reader,

Hot off the presses, the February titles at Harlequin Historicals are full of adventure and romance.

Highland Heart by Ruth Langan, another title in her popular Highland Series, is the story of Jamie MacDonald, a continuing character in the author's tales of sixteenth-century Scotland. And from Donna Anders comes *Paradise Moon.* Hawaii during the turbulent days following the end of the monarchy is the setting for this fast-paced romance between star-crossed lovers.

For those of you who enjoyed Sally Cheney's first historical, *Game of Hearts,* don't miss her second. *Thief in the Night* is a humorous tale of a British detective and a pretty young housemaid who may or may not be a thief. The author's quick wit and delightful secondary characters make her a wonderful storyteller. And readers of Westerns should be sure to pick up a copy of Jackie Merritt's *Wyoming Territory.* This well-known writer's first historical is a sensual romance between two headstrong neighboring ranchers.

From your cherished favorites to our newest arrivals, take a look at what our writers have to offer you this month. We appreciate your support, and happy reading.

Sincerely,

The Editors

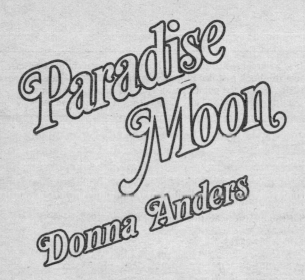

Paradise Moon

Donna Anders

Harlequin Books

TORONTO • NEW YORK • LONDON
AMSTERDAM • PARIS • SYDNEY • HAMBURG
STOCKHOLM • ATHENS • TOKYO • MILAN
MADRID • WARSAW • BUDAPEST • AUCKLAND

Harlequin Historicals first edition February 1992

ISBN 0-373-28713-5

PARADISE MOON

DONNA ANDERS

delights in every aspect of writing, particularly the re-
search. Her explorations have led her to some pretty
strange situations, like being stranded in a remote area
of Mexico and spending the night at the only lodging
available—the local brothel. She is an enthusiastic
reader of just about everything, but her first love has
always been historical romance. In addition to her
historicals, she is the author of short stories, children's books and various works of nonfiction. When
she isn't conducting writing workshops, working as an
office administrator or, of course, writing, she loves
to spend her treasured free time reading, painting and
taking long walks.

For Lise Wilber,
A Friend Forever

Chapter One

Honolulu
May 1898

Flushed from her headlong flight down the sidewalk through Chinatown, Leilani Kauwe welcomed the afternoon breeze off Honolulu harbor that cooled her cheeks. *Damn! I'm late,* she thought, and pushed back a wisp of long black hair that had slipped free of her chignon. She'd promised to help Dr. Pete in surgery but had been held up by the serious condition of the bedridden Puntis woman she'd just visited. Fearful for the old woman's weak heart, she'd waited until a son came from the cane fields, but she still wasn't sure her instructions had been understood, as the family's was a Chinese dialect so different from the one she understood.

"Say, girlie!" a sailor cried. "Want a good time?"

"Yeah!" his companion chimed in. "We hear you Orientals know how to treat a man right!"

Intent on her own worries, Leilani paid no attention; she was oblivious to the stares and comments of the men on the street. She had long since ignored the possibility that her work with the doctor to treat the poor was dangerous for a young woman of twenty-three. Heedless, she went among the shacks and humble businesses, through the narrow alleys to tend the sick, and because she expected proper respect from undesirable people, she usually got it.

Even the Kauwes, the Hawaiian couple who'd adopted her as an infant, saw no harm in her work. But then they trusted everyone, Leilani thought with a fond smile. She paused at the corner of Beretania Street to allow a buggy to pass, then several farmers who trotted after it, their shoulders bent forward from backbreaking loads of taro on bamboo carrying poles.

Once the street was clear she started off again. The doctor's office was on the outskirts of Chinatown near the waterfront, in an area of gambling dens and saloons, and as she headed toward it, a couple in the next block caught her eye. With a start, Leilani recognized the brightly dressed girl, Kini Chin, daughter of a poor Chinese produce vendor and his Hawaiian wife. Kini, the oldest of nine children, and barely sixteen, was being led into a fan-tan hall and brothel, a saloon where opium might even be sold. Appalled, Leilani broke into a run. Kini was beautiful, trusting and innocent—like many Hawaiian girls of mixed blood. And she had no business in such a place!

"Kini! Kini!" Leilani called, recognizing that the girl's escort was a *haole,* a white man, and the son of one of the rich shipping families in Hawaii.

The girl didn't hear her. Instant anger flashed through Leilani as the couple disappeared through the swinging doors of the establishment. She knew the *haole* wouldn't dream of taking a *proper lady* into such a place. He was up to no good— and Leilani meant to stop him before he ruined Kini's future. She didn't stop to consider her own safety, or that Mama Kauwe would only shake her head and cluck her tongue at her adopted daughter's impulse to protect Kini from unsavory influences. "Lani, Lani!" she'd say. "Time you forget old secrets. Time you stop trying to save all the mixed bloods like yourself. Find husband and have fine family."

Again Leilani was brought to a sudden stop, waiting as workers carrying supplies from a wagon into a store blocked the sidewalk. For a second her thoughts lingered with her kind Hawaiian parents. Mama and Papa Kauwe, unable to have children themselves, had taken in the infant left on their doorstep, believing the old gods had answered their prayers for a child. Leilani knew she was a quarter Chinese, that her fa-

ther had been a *haole,* because of a carefully printed note
pinned to the blanket by an ancient Chinese cloisonné pin.

Her hand automatically felt for the pin, which hung from a
chain under her bodice. Her long lashes swept down, narrow-
ing her gaze as the old frustration filled her, the sense of having no real roots. She'd often speculated on what might have
happened back then. Perhaps her mother had been a girl like
Kini, and was seduced by a *haole* who wouldn't marry her
when she became pregnant. In any case no one had wanted the
infant Leilani, even though money had been placed anony-
mously in the Kauwe account each month until Leilani reached
twenty—money that had enabled her to get an education and
ultimately her job as Dr. Pete's assistant. Upon reaching
adulthood, Leilani had tried to discover the name of her bene-
factor, but had failed. Someone had gone to great lengths to
obliterate the past.

The workers cleared the sidewalk and Leilani rushed on toward the saloon. She meant to save Kini from becoming the
next victim of prejudice and scorn. The *haole* might promise
the moon but the reality would be with Kini forever—and with
the unwanted child, if worse came to worst.

Although Leilani had never been inside a brothel, she was
aware of what happened to the women who worked as pros-
titutes: disease, opium addiction and dishonor. That the place
was the favorite of the *haoles,* and owned by the infamous
Madam Silk Stockings, a mysterious old woman who, rumor
said, wielded great power in Chinatown, didn't stop Leilani.
She went into the big front room without hesitation.

But the crowded saloon gave her pause, the wide sweep of
her black-and-white-plaid skirt stilling against her dusty shoes.
She could no longer see the bright red of Kini's gown, or the
top hat of Kini's escort. For a moment no one noticed her, a
young woman dressed in a prim, white shirtwaist with a turn-
down collar, gathered puffed top sleeves and attached cuffs,
incongruous among the skimpily gowned women with their
rice-powdered faces and rouged lips.

Then a short man in a black lounge suit turned from the bar,
his eyes under bushy brows immediately on her. Surprised, he
lifted his whiskey glass in a salute, and the gesture attracted

more attention to Leilani. The next second brought several men to her side to compete for her favor.

Ignoring the men, Leilani moved around them. She'd caught sight of Kini, and headed toward her on the other side of the long room. Instantly, one of the men grabbed her arm.

"Pardon me," Leilani said crisply, then shook him off and continued to weave her way through the crowd. She closed her ears to the lewd remarks, keeping her eyes focused straight ahead, and tried not to acknowledge the men's bold appraisal.

As she approached, Kini glanced up from where she sat at a table, an untouched glass of liquor in front of her. It was all Leilani could do to keep her temper in check. How dare the man seduce an innocent girl!

Embarrassed, Kini jumped up, suddenly disconcerted. "Oh, Miss Kauwe, I—uh—" She broke off and her long lashes fluttered nervously while color suffused her cheeks.

"Do your parents know you're here?" Leilani asked, and managed a calmness she didn't feel. Kini's response was a deepening of her blush and a lowering of her gaze. Leilani went on quickly, her tone firm but not unkind. "I think you'd better come along with me."

Embarrassed, Kini's dark eyes widened at Leilani's directness, and she was once more the schoolgirl being chastised by an adult, not a worldly woman like the others in the saloon, who watched the scene with amusement on their painted faces.

Then the girl's escort jumped up, his round face flushing with anger. "See here," he interrupted, his voice raised, his watery blue eyes alight with indignation. "Kini is with me." His gaze raked Leilani. "I don't recall anyone giving you the authority to speak for her. She's staying right here!"

The man stepped closer, dismissing Leilani in his superior manner. He knew the woman confronting him was Dr. Pete's nurse, that she was well-known for her pluck, as well as for her exotic beauty. But it was also rumored that she came from a questionable background, and he'd be damned if the likes of her would order him around. "Leave Kini the hell alone!" he told her coldly.

"Please, Tom," Kini said nervously, aware that she was the cause of a scene. "Maybe Miss Kauwe is right. I—I shouldn't be here." Her pretty face was strained, and her eyes pleaded for understanding. She wanted to please him, but Leilani's words had brought her up short, made her think twice about what she was about to do.

A new wave of anger flowed over Leilani, but she suppressed her retort to Tom out of sympathy for Kini. Leilani knew very well how infatuation could cloud the senses. At eighteen she'd fallen in love with Elwood Benton, son of another leading *haole* family, and he'd given her up because of their disapproval. Leilani had come to see that girls of mixed blood, like her and Kini, were often seduced and then cast aside. Luckily she'd escaped with her virtue intact, and she meant to see that Kini did as well. If Tom had serious intentions, then he'd concede to her the same proprieties he'd expect for his own sister.

"Hey, Tom!" a man cried. "You gonna be bossed around by a slip of a girl, a half-breed *pake* at that?"

The taunt brought more laughter as everyone waited to see what would happen next. How would Leilani react to being called *pake*, the insulting word *haoles* called the Chinese? Tom's lips tightened with determination; he wasn't about to let this troublesome girl ruin his plans. To back down now would mean a loss of face. The seductive Kini was staying—and he vowed to have his way with her before the day was over.

Watching his expression, Leilani guessed his thoughts and felt like slapping his face. But she controlled herself, knowing she'd only gain more hoots from the men and lose her chance to save Kini. She concentrated on keeping her composure and getting them out of the saloon.

"Come on, it's time to go." Leilani spoke calmly despite her growing apprehension. Then she took Kini's arm and would have started for the door, but the men crowded closer; she was unable to take a step. Then Tom moved between the two women.

"Get out of the way!" Leilani cried, her gaze flicking between Tom and the joking, raucous men. Beyond them Leilani caught a glimpse of an old woman, elaborately gowned and coiffured, her face so white from rice powder that it resembled a Chinese mask. She sat on a dais at the end of the room, like a sentinel, much as an empress would sit on a throne in China, Leilani thought suddenly. For a brief second, their eyes met, and an odd expression flickered momentarily on the painted, powdered face.

Quickly Leilani glanced away, knowing she'd just made contact with the infamous Madam Silk Stockings. Her gaze was caught by the tall man next to the madam. Although he was white, his black hair and eyes denoted Hawaiian blood in his lineage. He, too, watched, and something about him reminded her of his pagan ancestors—men who once made human sacrifices to their ancient gods. When he sprang from the dais and headed toward her, Leilani was spurred into action. Somehow she felt more threatened by him than by the drunken men surrounding her.

"Not on your life!" Tom retorted finally, his eyes filled with outrage. "*You* get out of the way! Kini stays." He turned to the girl. "That right, Kini?"

Kini lowered her lashes, hesitant. Leilani saw that she wanted to please him but was fearful as well. As the girl hesitated, Leilani grabbed her arm, taking the decision into her own hands, and started for the door. When a sailor tried to block her way, she kicked him in the shin. The next man to try received an elbow in his ribs. Finally they reached the exit, the enraged Tom only steps behind them. They plunged through the swinging doors only to crash into several more men about to enter.

"Whoa!" a bearded man in *paniolo* garb cried. "What have we here? Two little fillies trying to stampede into the street?"

"What's the hurry?" another cowboy added. "We'll buy you both a drink, show you a good time!"

"Let us go!" Leilani cried when the newcomers took hold of them. "How dare you detain ladies!"

"Ladies!" The first man snorted. "Ain't never seen a *lady* come out of a brothel!"

A work cart and horse were tied to a hitching post within arm's reach, and Leilani grabbed a whip and brought it down across the man's back. Because her arms were confined by his, she wasn't able to put power into the blow, but her action gained her freedom and brought an oath from the man.

"Spitfire!" he cried in fury. Before Leilani could grab Kini's hand, the man twisted the whip from her, then slammed her body to his chest, his action so violent that it knocked the wind out of her. "When I'm done with you, *pake,* you'll know how to respect your betters," he ground out between clenched teeth.

"You—you bastard!" she cried, incensed. Then Tom joined the confrontation, pulling Kini from the other cowboy's grasp.

"She's my woman!" he told the man, who immediately backed off, intimidated because he recognized the wealthy young man. But when Tom indicated he didn't care about Leilani, her captor's fingers tightened cruelly.

Struggling, Leilani knew she was fighting for her virtue if not her life. She glanced around wildly. There was no one to come to her rescue. Even if some of the Chinese people wanted to, they didn't dare; the *haole* always won when it came to the law. It was up to her to free herself. She kicked and bit and squirmed, and her hair fell from its pins to spill down her back to her waist. Instantly the cowboy twisted his fist in the long shimmering black strands and pulled so hard that her head was yanked backward to tilt to his. Whiskey breath gagged her but she didn't lower her eyes; she knew her contempt shone openly at him.

"By damn!" His hands stilled on her although he didn't relinquish his hold. "A *pake* with eyes the color of sapphires!"

He drew in his breath sharply, suddenly unsure. All at once she didn't look Chinese at all. Come to think of it, she was taller than an Oriental, and her flawless skin was too fair. But then he realized that her large eyes were almond shaped, after all, and knew he hadn't been mistaken; she was part Chinese. And her exotic beauty excited him!

While he hesitated, Leilani suddenly twisted out of his arms and whirled around to rescue Kini. But it was hopeless. More men had followed Tom out of the saloon, and the two girls were surrounded once more. For the first time a cold finger of fear touched Leilani's spine. Anything could happen. But before she was grabbed again, a gunshot rang out over the din, and instantly there was dead silence.

"Leave the women alone!" a deep baritone voice commanded.

Then the man who'd been with Madam Silk Stockings pushed his way through the crowd to Leilani's side, his smoking pistol still in his hand. As the men fell back, the stranger put the gun back into a shoulder holster under his frock coat. But that was a mistake, for a drunk sailor pushed through the men and made a grab for Leilani.

"She ain't your woman!" he cried. "And you have no say over us!"

The stranger didn't hesitate, knocking the sailor backward into the crowd before Leilani hardly blinked. The suddenness of his action precluded more defiance, but he stood poised on the balls of his feet, ready if another man wanted to try. His lean, handsome face was set into hard lines and planes, and his dark eyes glinted dangerously. Within seconds the crowd broke up, and Leilani suddenly released her held breath. It was obvious that the stranger was known to the men, that he commanded respect.

"And you, Tom?" the stranger asked coldly, his thick black brows lowered in a forbidding line above hooded, equally black eyes. "Want to reconsider detaining the girl?"

Tom glowered, and his eyes accused Leilani of spoiling his fun, but he didn't dare express his feeling aloud. Finally he shrugged, and after a glance at Kini, turned away. "Hell! I was looking for a good time, not a damnable fight!" A moment later the saloon doors swung shut behind him.

"Yeah, it ain't worth getting shot," a *paniolo* grumbled. "Too many willing women to fool with uppity *Celestials!*" he cried, referring to the Chinese blood in both Kini and Leilani. As the man spoke, his voice was joined by the murmuring of the disgruntled crowd of men who were now dispersing.

At that moment Dr. Pete hurried across the street to join them. "Rand! Thank the good Lord you were here. I saw what was happening and couldn't get through the throng in time."

He glanced at Leilani, his bright blue eyes looking concerned behind his round spectacles. "For God's sake, Leilani!'' he cried, and pulled a handkerchief from his pocket to mop his forehead. "What am I to do with you? You've got to stop getting yourself into dangerous situations, or one day there'll be no one to rescue you.''

"Leilani?'' The stranger's attention shifted back to her abruptly, holding her eyes prisoner by the intensity of his glance, making her aware of the thickness and length of his lashes that hooded his stare. He boldly took in every inch of her. With a suddenness that took her breath away, his well-defined lips curved attractively, and his whole expression softened. *"Leilani Kauwe—Chinatown's angel of mercy?* I should have known!''

She'd stepped next to Kini right after the gunshot, and placed her arm around the trembling girl. Now the man's unexpected words disconcerted her. Was this Rand paying her a compliment, or making fun of her? But her retort remained unsaid, for her mouth had gone dry and her heart was suddenly pounding in her throat. Leilani was aware of his amused gaze, that he didn't miss the fact that her clothing was rumpled, that her hair was flying free of its pins and that his continued scrutiny had fired her face with heat. He was the most attractive man she'd ever met—and the most devastating to her equanimity!

"You all right?'' he drawled, and something about his casual tone—when she suspected he knew he'd unsettled her even more than the men who'd accosted her—kept her from uttering her thanks. When she didn't respond, he continued, "Doc Pete is right. You were asking for trouble when you went into a saloon.''

Irritated by his superior bearing, Leilani found her tongue quite unexpectedly. "And you?'' She managed to bring up her chin in a gesture of disapproval. "Is that why you were in the saloon—*looking* for trouble?''

But instead of angering him, she saw his grin broaden in a flash of white teeth against his bronze skin. She had a mental flash of ancient Polynesian men garbed in loincloths and robes of bright yellow feathers. Men who *took* the women of their choice.

The afternoon sounds faded into the soft whisper of the wind off the Pacific Ocean, and Leilani was suddenly too conscious of his appraising look, which flickered from her face to her feet, and back to linger on her mouth. Something warm ignited in his eyes, something that sent shivers rippling over her skin, a sensation that seemed to stir even the tiny hairs on her arms and legs. Then their eyes locked, and it was as if they were the only two people left on the street.

"So you know of Leilani, eh?"

Dr. Pete's voice shattered the strange moment, and Leilani pulled her gaze from the compelling dark eyes to glance at the doctor. She sensed her rescuer's smile and was annoyed, though more with herself for reacting to him. Yet, even as she thought about it, she knew that her response had been spontaneous, beyond her control.

"But I don't believe you've met Randolph Walsh, have you, Leilani?" Dr. Pete went on, seemingly unaware of the attraction between the two.

"No." She shook her head. "I've never met Mr. Walsh." She hesitated, pleased that she'd recovered her composure. "But I, too, have heard of him."

"Nothing bad, I trust?" Rand Walsh drawled with infuriating calm, as if he weren't aware of the strange undercurrent between them. He combed his fingers through his crisp black hair, and she found herself contemplating its texture.

Quickly, she took herself in hand. Only her lashes fluttered ever so slightly as she again met his fathomless eyes, thankful that the cadence of her tone was in perfect balance with her words. "I've heard you practice law here in Honolulu, that you're one of the few lawyers who'll defend *haole,* Hawaiian and Oriental alike." She hesitated. "And I've heard that you're fair." Leilani didn't add that she'd also assumed that the lawyer she'd heard so much about was much older, not a man barely thirty, whose very presence was a threat to her composure.

The corners of his mouth twitched, as though he guessed the part of her evaluation she hadn't stated. He realized she was part Chinese, part white, maybe even a little Hawaiian, and the combination made her the most beautiful, most exotic woman he'd ever met. She possessed a mystique, he thought suddenly. Though fearless and daring, she was also feminine and vulnerable—and Rand felt aroused all at once. He quelled an absurd desire to take her in his arms, right then and there. He hadn't felt that fire in his blood for a long time—had even hoped it would never return. As he felt himself pulled into the brilliance of her blue eyes, he was jolted by yet another perception. In an indefinable way Leilani Kauwe reminded him of his late wife.

When his expression hardened suddenly, Leilani misunderstood. *He disapproves of me!* she thought, and the return of her anger brought a strange sense of relief. She could deal with anger, but not with the reaction of being emotionally shattered simply because he watched her, stood too close. Those were confusing feelings that upset her normally cool, no-nonsense manner. So she allowed her anger to grow, knowing intuitively it was her only defense against him.

"Thank you, Mr. Walsh, for coming to our rescue." She glanced at Kini. "We're both grateful," she added, but her tone was stilted because her discomfiture was growing under his level gaze. She just wanted to be away from the man. She turned to the doctor, who'd watched the interchange thoughtfully. "I'll see Kini home and then meet you in your office for surgery."

Dr. Pete nodded, but before he could reply, Rand Walsh spoke instead, and her traitorous gaze shifted back to him.

"Stay out of dangerous places, Leilani Kauwe. Next time you might not be rescued in time." His knitted brows lifted, as did his voice when he turned to speak to Kini. "You remember that, as well, young lady. You almost ruined your life."

Even though Leilani agreed, something about him gave an impression that he disapproved of her.

"I appreciate your concern, Mr. Walsh," she said stiffly, and there was an edge to her tone. "But where I go is none of your business." She contrived a brief smile. "I'm perfectly safe. The incident in the saloon was an exception."

"Exception, hell!" he retorted. "Every part of your job is dangerous, and the run-in with the sailors and *paniolos* was a good example. You're asking for trouble!"

"Come on, Rand," Dr. Pete interrupted before Leilani lost her temper completely. "You're right to a point, but Leilani is right, too. Up until now she's been perfectly safe. Everyone knows her for Chinatown's angel of mercy, as you yourself said a minute ago." He paused, realizing Rand's criticism included him for allowing her to work among the sick. "She's performing a needed service," he stated emphatically.

Before Rand could answer, someone called from the balcony overlooking the street, and they all glanced up. Madam Silk Stockings stood looking down at them, and as she continued speaking, her Chinese words were directed to Rand. Leilani was even more surprised when he replied in her Hakka dialect, agreeing with whatever the old woman had said.

Again he'd astonished her. Even if he did have Hawaiian blood, he was the first *haole* she'd known who spoke fluent Chinese. But Leilani didn't dwell on her new perception of him. Instead she used the interruption to take a tighter grip on Kini's arm, and started off down the sidewalk. The girl went mutely, as though she now realized the enormity of what her misguided action had caused.

Leilani was glad of her silence, for her mind whirled with new thoughts. Maybe Rand disapproved of her for other reasons, like the one that had forced Elwood Benton to give her up. The observation jabbed her with fresh pain. One day she'd learn the truth of her past, she vowed.

Someone knows, she reminded herself, and she'd find that person one day. Her lifelong quest for the truth was part of her reason for working among the poor Chinese, that and a genuine desire to help.

Let Rand Walsh disapprove, she fumed. She didn't care! He lived a privileged life and was where he was by choice. Not like her.

But she did care.

"That's it." Dr. Pete straightened up from where he'd been bandaging the cut hand of the local butcher, a *haole* who'd been in the Islands for twenty years, and whose customers included all the leading families. "Just keep it dry until it begins to heal," he instructed.

The man was the last patient of the day and Leilani was relieved to be going home soon. The butcher had heard about her earlier confrontation at the saloon and the doctor was filling him in on Rand's part. Leilani listened in silence, and learned that Rand came from Maui, where his family grew sugar, that because his older brother now ran the plantation, he was free to practice law with Lee Chun, the son of the Walshes' field manager and his friend since childhood. She was impressed to hear that the Walsh family had paid for Lee Chun's education in San Francisco, while Rand studied law at Harvard.

"Mr. Rand believes the future of Hawaii depends on a blending of all races now that the Islands have been annexed," the butcher said as he stood up.

"He's the man to see to it, if anyone can," Dr. Pete replied. "But it'll be a tough job. Hawaii could well lose what's left of its cultural background in the process."

"I agree with Rand Walsh on that point," Leilani added. "The future of Hawaii is for all of us regardless of our backgrounds."

"Too bad Rand'll never remarry," the butcher went on. "You know how these Hawaiians feel about the old beliefs."

"Nonsense, pure nonsense." Dr. Pete turned to wash his hands in a bowl. "Because he lost his wife in a freak buggy accident two years ago doesn't mean the pagan gods were exacting some sort of revenge. The old taboos that forbid outsiders to live on land that belonged to Polynesian kings are now viewed by most as quaint superstition."

"Perhaps Mr. Rand doesn't agree with you." The butcher shrugged. "After all, he and his wife had only been married two weeks when she died. True or not, the taboos have bedeviled the *haole* families for years, even those with Hawaiian blood, like Rand and his father-in-law."

Leilani's hands stilled on the doctor's instruments she'd been clearing away. She hadn't known Rand Walsh had been married, or that he'd been widowed only weeks later. It was tragic.

The doctor looked thoughtful. "That poor girl was an only child whose mother was already dead. Now her father has no family—except Rand."

The talk drifted into other channels and several minutes later the butcher was gone. Amid talk of tomorrow's schedule, Leilani finished her chores and got ready to go home. Dr. Pete, his thick gray hair looking windblown as usual, his plump face and blue eyes hidden behind glasses and a bushy beard, stood at the door as she started off down the street. She turned to wave from the corner, knowing he would watch her out of sight, then headed out of town toward the road to Nuuanu Valley, and Mama and Papa Kauwe's small taro farm.

She sighed as she hurried along, suddenly hungry. Her Hawaiian parents, the doctor and his wife, and her two young stepbrothers were the people she loved most in the world. Mama and Papa Kauwe, big people in stature as well as heart, had taken in their two young nephews several years after adopting her. The boys had lost their mother to childbirth, and a year later, their father went to the leper colony on Molokai after he'd been diagnosed with the disease. Leilani wanted the best for them all, and part of her wage each month went to help support the family.

But as she walked toward the mountains, her thoughts lingered with the events of the day, and Rand Walsh. Even thinking about him brought a quiver deep inside her, a sensation she'd never felt before, not even for Elwood, the boy she'd once loved.

As she rounded a turn in the road and approached the farm she came to an abrupt stop, her gaze fastening on the crowd of Chinese men in the yard. Even from a distance she could hear them all talking at once. Suddenly fearful, she broke into a run, and as she approached Mama Kauwe glanced up and saw her.

"Oh, Leilani!" she cried, her words dragged out in a low wail. "Something terrible is about to happen!"

Chapter Two

"What's wrong?" Leilani cried, her gaze on the half-dozen men who stood in a circle around someone they'd stretched out on a blanket in the yard. Even as she spoke, she was already elbowing into their midst. The man, obviously a field worker, lay moaning from pain, his clothing in tatters and covered with blood. "My God!" she cried, and then concealed her horror as she bent to examine him.

"A bad *luna*," Mama Kauwe murmured over and over. "Boss man is cruel *luna*. Poor Chinese work hard, don't deserve such torture." She wrung her large hands, and the folds of fat on her arms and neck wobbled as her body rocked back and forth, her ample skirt swinging around her legs.

"*Luna* punish him for resting. His pigtail tied to horse tail, then horse slapped by *luna* into a gallop," explained the man who crouched next to Leilani, in halting English. "He not able to keep running—horse drag him until we stop him. Then we bring Chock to you. You fix?" he asked, his small eyes anxious.

She recognized the speaker as Hoy, a man who was industrious, worked long hours in the cane fields, saved his pennies and was learning English from the schoolmaster who'd started classes for the Chinese. But she also saw the anger behind his usually inscrutable manner, and a glance told her that the others felt the same way toward the *luna*. She just hoped they didn't retaliate, because the Chinese workers had no rights and would be treated harshly by the authorities. But there wasn't time to deal with that now; the man on the ground was seriously hurt, could possibly die. He needed a doctor immediately.

Quickly she instructed them that they must return with her to Dr. Pete's office, that they could use the blanket to carry the man, four men each holding one corner to keep the injured man lying flat. Hoy, who understood her own broken Hakka, saw to it at once.

"Yes, go—go," Mama Kauwe said. "Dr. Pete will fix up. Then you come home, Leilani, help fix little brothers, who are being picked on by their mean *haole* teacher."

Unable to linger, Leilani couldn't question her mother further, although Mama Kauwe's announcement sent a shiver of alarm through her. The teacher was getting worse, had even made fun of the little boys because their father had died on Molokai from the *mai pake* disease, leprosy. A severe disciplinarian, the man had no sympathy for the two young orphans, and Leilani guessed the reason was they were Hawaiians attending a mostly *haole* school.

When they reached Dr. Pete's office, she left the workers and went to fetch Dr. Pete from his house behind the office. Once he returned with her and took a look at the patient, he quickly took command. In seconds he had the worker inside his surgery, issuing orders to Leilani. The others waited in the outer room, and Leilani tried not to think what would happen if their friend died. She'd understood enough of their conversation to know they were planning retaliation against the *luna*. She must convince the men that revenge would only cause them trouble; they might perhaps be shipped back to China without their wages.

Finally Dr. Pete looked up from bandaging the man's legs and arms. "I think he'll be fine. It looks much worse than it is, because he's so cut and scraped up. We'll just need to watch for infection, maybe a concussion."

The man on the table had opened his eyes, and as Dr. Pete cleaned the wounds, he winced from the pain. He watched Leilani and the doctor, his gratitude expressed in his eyes if not in words, and she wondered how much he understood of their conversation, for the doctor had responded with anger when she related what had happened.

"There's only one person who can help these men with that overseer and stop the brutality," Dr. Pete stated emphatically. "And that's Rand Walsh. He's helped with their rights before, settled a number of disputes to the benefit of all involved."

Leilani lowered her lashes so that the doctor wouldn't see how the mere mention of Rand's name unsettled her. "I'm not sure that Hoy and the others would allow Rand Walsh to intervene. They'd be fearful of reprisals after he was gone."

Dr. Pete glanced at her over the top of his glasses, and his blue eyes had never been more serious. "It's the only way to straighten out that *luna*, Leilani. If he knows that someone like Rand is aware of his cruelty, and the plantation owner knows, too, then he won't dare continue such horrendous deeds."

"Perhaps you're right," she said, but she wasn't convinced. Although many plantations were fair to the workers, she knew that the Chinese usually bore unjust treatment in stoic silence, patiently waiting for their five-year contract to expire so they could either work their own land, or return to China with their savings.

"Hell! I know I am!" Dr. Pete retorted, and Leilani knew the anger edging his tone wasn't directed at her. He was one of the few *haoles* who felt the future of Hawaii would include Orientals, Hawaiians and *haoles* alike. "Talking to Rand will save these men more trouble. I think you should see him tomorrow morning, get him involved before something worse happens."

He hesitated to reach for another bandage. "I'd do it myself only I don't know when I'll find time." His blue eyes flicked to her momentarily. "Besides, the workers came to you for help, Leilani, because they've watched you work among them. *They trust you!*"

As she watched him finish up, Leilani was thoughtful. She'd known Pete and his wife, Esther, since she could remember. He'd doctored her when she was small, saw to it that she stayed in school and later trained her in the art of nursing. He and his wife were almost family, and she valued their advice. But fearless as she usually was when it came to helping the Chinese, her stomach swam when she thought of going to see Rand Walsh.

"I'll think about it," she replied noncommittally, and then went to wash the instruments the doctor had used. As she worked, her sense of fairness asserted itself, and she realized her feelings shouldn't stop her from doing what was right for the workers. It was abominable that anyone could treat another person so cruelly. She would go to Rand's office first thing in the morning, she decided.

When she turned back, Dr. Pete had already motioned the other men into the room, and was explaining the patient's care to Hoy. Within seconds they had the man back on the blanket and were starting for the door. Leilani detained Hoy long enough to caution him about taking the law into his own hands, that she meant to speak to the *haole* lawyer on their behalf. When he looked suddenly alarmed, she reassured him that nothing would be said to the *luna* without Hoy's being consulted first.

With a deep bow, he thanked her, and promised no retaliation—this time. Then he followed the others into the street and disappeared. After a few more words between the doctor and Leilani, he went back to his cold supper and she locked up before starting home for the second time that day.

So preoccupied in thought about seeking out Rand tomorrow, Leilani suddenly realized she was almost home. Slowing her steps, she calmed her nerves, annoyed with herself for being so affected by a man she'd only met once. But she recognized that she found him attractive for all he disturbed her peace of mind. With resolve she turned her mind to the next problem she must deal with; the situation with the teacher who picked on her little stepbrothers.

As she moved toward the door of the Kauwe cottage, Leilani suddenly had another thought. Since she was to consult Rand about the workers, she might ask his advice about the teacher, too.

"I'll think about it," she decided, and bracing herself to cope with two upset little boys, she went into the house.

* * *

"I believe I can take care of this," Rand said, and glanced up from the notes he'd taken as she related the incident concerning the worker and the *luna*. "The man won't get away with that kind of treatment, no matter what the workers did to make him mad."

His words rang with outrage, and Leilani, sitting across the desk from him, suddenly realized why he commanded such respect. Although he worked for peaceful settlements, it was clear that he would be a formidable opponent if crossed. The thought didn't help her emotional state, although she managed to hide her intense awareness of his male attractiveness behind a calm facade. Being alone with him in his small office made her even more nervous than she'd expected to be. And that astounded her. He was the first man to make her feel all fluttery inside, and she willed herself to concentrate on their discussion, confident that she looked quite proper—and businesslike—in her baby-blue skirt and jacket.

Leilani had gotten up early so she could bathe in the iron tub before the others were awake. Her night had passed in a series of naps, her mind too preoccupied to sleep. Not only were the Chinese workers in her thoughts, but also her stepbrother Wile—Willy—who'd been eliminated from a spelling competition by the teacher, who claimed he'd cheated.

"But I didn't, Leilani! Why would he say that?" Willy had cried, his bottom lip trembling.

Even though Leilani had managed to calm him, the unfairness stung her with outrage. Willy, like his younger brother Paulo, was an excellent student, and so in awe of being in a *haole* school she doubted he'd dare misbehave. Now Willy was discouraged, and, at ten, was already talking about dropping out of school.

"What's the use?" he'd asked her, his dark eyes bright with unshed tears. "No one likes us anyway."

All during the night her anger had gathered momentum. In the morning she took extra pains to pin up her hair into a sedate coiffure, and dress in her best bell-shaped skirt, its tiny waist and wide hem flattering to her slender form, the blue color a perfect foil to her eyes. She tried not to dwell on Rand Walsh and add to her upset.

"What'll you do?" she asked now, her scattered thoughts returning to Rand's remark. "I promised Hoy that you wouldn't jeopardize them further with the *luna.*"

Though his expression didn't betray his feelings, Rand was completely aware of Leilani sitting so close to him. Since he met her, she'd come into his thoughts more than he cared to admit. It was hard for him to concentrate when she regarded him so directly. He'd never seen another woman who came close to her in looks, unless it was his late wife, he reminded himself. He realized the resemblance between the women was more in expression than features, and in similar gestures. Amazing, he thought wryly. Some said a man was attracted to the same type of woman over and over. Rand gave himself a mental shake and reined in his thoughts abruptly. He had no intention of falling in love again. He couldn't risk such pain twice.

"I assure you," he began, reverting to his best business tone, "I wouldn't do anything to make matters worse. I'll talk to Hoy first, and then to the plantation owner, whom I know, by the way. I'm quite sure the owner doesn't know what his *luna* is doing."

His voice faded into a sudden silence, and Leilani glanced down at her clasped hands, aware that his tone had cooled. Again, as it had during their first meeting, his manner had altered abruptly. This man was an enigma, she decided. Maybe doing business with a woman of mixed blood was distasteful to him, she thought suddenly, even if he did champion equal rights for men of the same group. But she put such thoughts aside, thinking instead of her humiliated little brother.

Gathering her resolve, Leilani raised her long lashes so that her gaze was direct. She tried not to think about how handsome Rand was in his stylish lounge suit, and his white shirt that accented his darkness, and reminded her of his Polynesian forebears, who'd crossed thousands of miles of ocean in open boats to claim Hawaii as their own. She suspected this man was a throwback to those ancient, primitive people.

"I have one other matter to discuss." As his dark slanting brows arched in a question, Leilani went on quickly. "It's about my brother—uh—my young stepbrother," she corrected. "And of course I wish to pay whatever fee you charge should you decide to intervene on Willy's behalf." To her chagrin, her words sounded stilted, unnatural, as she rushed on. "I appreciate your not charging a fee from Hoy and his coworkers."

Again there was a subtle change to his expression as she spoke, for the corners of his mouth twitched with a suppressed grin. *Damn him!* she thought, annoyed because her display of pride amused him, and frustrated by the turmoil he created in her. She'd have gone elsewhere for help, but that was the problem. There was no one better to handle Willy's problem than Rand Walsh.

"And just what is this situation?" he drawled lazily. Taking a cheroot from his pocket, he lit it and blew smoke that obscured the odd little lights in his eyes. "How can I help young Willy?"

She willed herself to keep the tremor from her voice, the flutter from her lashes, but she couldn't stop the blush that touched her cheeks with fire. Nevertheless, she plunged in, and, as she explained about Willy, her concern for everything else faded away, at least for the moment. When Leilani finished, sudden quiet fell over the room.

Abruptly Rand snubbed out his cheroot, his expression furious all at once. He stood up and came round the desk. Leilani stood as well, facing him, uncertain.

"You bet your life I'll take the case," he ground out. "Damn! Will things ever change?" He sucked in his breath angrily, remembering how even he, from a prominent family, had suffered on occasion because of being part Hawaiian. But he didn't say that aloud. Instead, he took her arm in a casual manner, directing her to the door. "It's the first thing I'll do today. That boy can't face the other students until the incident is cleared up." He hesitated before opening the door, and turned her so that he looked directly into her face, shaking his head. "If everything you say is true, then the schoolmaster is

discriminating against a Hawaiian boy in his own homeland.''

"Of course it's true!" she bristled unreasonably. "Willy
doesn't lie—and neither do I!"

His finger on her lips stilled her protest, and even after he'd
removed his finger, her lips felt as if they'd been seared by his
touch. "Of course you wouldn't lie," he agreed at once, and
his tone softened. "I'm quite sure that Chinatown's angel of
mercy wouldn't even tell a fib." His comment brought a return of humor to the set of his handsome features.

Before she could determine whether or not his last remark
was meant to mock her, he'd opened the door and she found
herself stepping into the beautiful morning, breathing the sea
fragrance that had turned shoreward on the breeze.

"I'll let you know what happens," he told her. "And as for
the workers, I promise not to make matters worse."

His final words, coupled with a jaunty grin, sent little sensations rippling over her flesh, and a jolt of flutters into her
chest. Once the door closed she hesitated for long seconds,
until her breathing slowed, and the wind cooled her face. Then
she began to walk.

Dear Lord, she mused. What happened to her when she was
with that man?

Quickening her step, she didn't allow herself an answer.

"So you really didn't catch Willy Kauwe cheating." Rand
pinned the tall, gaunt schoolmaster with a look that he meant
to be intimidating. "You just *thought* he had to be cheating to
get an A? How is that, Mr. Morrison?" he asked, his tone deceptively calm.

The teacher glanced away, unable to hold his eyes steady,
infuriated that Rand Walsh was questioning his integrity, and
in front of the principal. "I, uh, assumed that a boy of his—
uh—limited background couldn't possibly surpass the whole
class," he stammered, his thin voice discordant. Then as his
sense of duty reasserted itself, his calling to teach on a hea-
then island thousands of miles from his New England home,
the teacher pursed his lips and straightened his narrow shoulders, every inch the injured party. "Indeed, you're familiar

with these natives, Mr. Walsh. We *know* they aren't overly bright."

"I tend to believe the opposite, Mr. Morrison." Rand's voice was low and controlled, because he leashed his anger by sheer willpower. He itched to grab the man by his skinny throat and throttle him. "I believe you're the ignorant one, not Willy." He stepped closer to the man. "And a prejudiced clod who hides his own inadequacy behind a false superiority."

"Did you, or did you not catch this boy cheating on the test?" the principal interrupted sharply.

His face blanching, the teacher tried to hedge, but neither the principal nor Rand gave ground. Finally he admitted that he hadn't actually caught the boy cheating, and began to repeat his earlier assumption. He was brought to a stop by the principal.

"The purpose of this school is to teach, not humiliate students, *any students.*" Then the principal turned to Rand. "Be assured that this matter will be taken care of, Mr. Walsh. There will be a public apology to clear this boy's name. And you can be sure this will never happen again."

Rand shook the principal's hand, then after a curt nod to the teacher, left them. Little Willy would be exonerated, and the teacher wouldn't dare a repeat performance. He felt a surge of pleasure to know that the principal was a fair man, and concerned for the feelings of a young boy. He hurried back to his office, his mind already on his next case, the abusive *luna.* He meant to settle that problem by evening.

He grinned to himself, pulled a cheroot from his pocket, then went to the window overlooking the harbor. Tomorrow was Saturday. He'd ride out to the Kauwe farm on Sunday, he decided. He'd tell the family—and Leilani—personally, that the school matter was resolved.

As he went to his desk to begin work, he dismissed the real reason he wanted to visit the Kauwes. Leilani.

"Leilani take boys to swim," the beaming Mama Kauwe told him, having come outside to stand in the shade of a mango tree as Rand reined in his horse. "In the forest beneath the falls."

He hesitated, uncertain. "Do you expect her soon?" he asked, pricked by disappointment.

She shrugged, and her voluminous form quivered under her flowing dress. "Home by suppertime. You stay?" Her dark eyes invited him, too. "We want to thank you, all of us, for your kindness to our boy Willy. Willy happy now." She spread her arms, as though she could embrace the whole world. "We happy now. Please us mightily if you stay." Her smile broadened. "Please Leilani, eh?"

He couldn't help returning the kind woman's grin. She was old Hawaii, one of the generous, unselfish natives who, as a people, were fast disappearing. His hesitation gone, he nodded, thanked her and then dismounted.

"You go meet them," she suggested, and pointed to a path that led into the forest of lush greenery. *"Aloha,"* she said, and turned back to the house, fully expecting him to comply.

Her suggestion gave Rand pause, but he brushed aside his reservations. It was business, after all, he told himself. Then he started off, heading up the valley toward the mountains. As Rand walked, the serenity of the island settled around him, and he suppressed all thoughts of why he shouldn't be there. Eventually he came upon the stream that flowed into the valley to irrigate the Kauwes' taro crop, and followed it up the sloping land toward the sound of a waterfall.

The trees opened before him, and Rand came to an abrupt stop, his gaze on the little pool beneath the falls. Birds twittered in the branches above him, and the music of the waterfall crashing on the rocks to bubble into the pool was a masterpiece of nature.

But he only took in the grotto of shade-dappled foliage, the heady scent of wild blossoms and the absolute peace of the secluded spot in passing. His gaze was fastened on the huge boulder where Leilani sat, like a wood nymph in her short native dress, her long black hair shimmering over her bare shoulders, her long shapely legs dangling just above the glassy surface of water. He stood as if frozen, unable to move or call out, enchanted by the unexpected paradise... and by Leilani's uninhibited beauty. Her two brothers were nowhere in sight, and he suddenly knew he was intruding on her privacy;

it was obvious that she'd been in the water, that she wore nothing under her skimpy bathing garment.

As though she sensed his presence, she turned and saw him before he could quietly back away. Their eyes locked, hers reflecting shock. Although a short distance separated them, Rand could see the color rise into her cheeks, her lips part from surprise, and her full breasts, where the nipples were molded by her wet dress, tremble from a sudden acceleration of breath. His arousal was instantaneous; he had an overpowering urge to go to her, kiss her mouth and breasts . . . make love to her. Her sudden dive into the pool broke the unspoken connection between them.

When Leilani came up, only her head and shoulders were exposed to his gaze. The cool water had brought back her equanimity—and released her anger. How dare Rand Walsh watch her in the privacy of her secret place! And how had he known where she was? Too distracted to worry about proprieties, she confronted him instead.

"Please!" she cried, her tone accusing. "Be a gentleman and turn around so I can come out of the water!"

Startled by her censure, and unnerved by his own desire, Rand put up his hands in a gesture of surrender. "I'm sorry," he began. "But I didn't expect—"

"I asked you to look the other way!" she cut him off.

Sheepishly he turned, and Leilani, her gaze never leaving the back of his blue shirt and black riding pants, eased out of the water, then darted to grab her clothing before heading behind a bush.

"I promise I won't peek," Rand said, carefully casual, aware of her embarrassment and still coping with his own wayward thoughts. He reminded himself that he'd vowed never to get involved with another woman, never to fall in love again.

"I'm dressed," Leilani said several minutes later. "You can look now."

Slowly Rand turned, his eyes immediately on Leilani, who stood completed clothed in a pale pink cotton dress. Although her shoulders and legs were now covered, in his mind's eye he saw them naked. Determinedly he put the image from his mind, aware that his desire was barely under control. As he walked across the lush carpet of ground cover to her, he managed a friendly smile, one that hid his real feelings.

"I didn't mean to startle you, Leilani," he said. "Your mother said you were here and suggested I come out to meet you—and your little brothers." He hesitated, and in the silence that grew between them, Rand busied himself with lighting a cheroot. "I came to report on business, of course. Then your mother also invited me for supper, so I accepted."

His information was disconcerting. It was just like her good-hearted Hawaiian mother to invite him, she fumed. Mama and Papa Kauwe were so happy for Willy that they would have invited the whole island to a celebration feast if they'd had the means. But her consternation had deeper roots; how long had Rand stood in the deep shadows of the foliage observing her? The question brought another rush of blood to her cheeks, but she didn't avert her eyes from his. He was too attractive, she decided, too sure of his maleness...his superiority? Whatever he was, she knew it affected her dramatically.

"We appreciated what you did for Willy," she replied finally. "And Willy, and his brother Paulo, will be delighted to know you'll be our supper guest," she finished weakly.

He closed the space between them so fast that she'd only considered stepping back a moment before he was right in front of her. "And you, Leilani? Will you also be delighted to have me?" His voice had fallen to a whisper. "Or will I upset you—more than you are right now?"

Her eyes widened, and her delicate features froze in shock that he would ask such a thing. "I—I'm not upset," she stammered. "I was simply surprised to see you here, a place no one ever comes."

"Not even the *menehune*," he drawled, and took another drag on his cheroot. "This seems the perfect place for the little elves to dance in the moonlight, eh?"

Her long lashes fluttered, yet still she managed to hold her gaze steady. But when his eyes lowered to her lips, and lingered, she glanced away in confusion, because she suddenly wondered how it would feel to have him kiss her. Even the thought sent strange little shivery sensations into the pit of her stomach.

Time seemed to pause, suspended by the growing tension between them. Abruptly, he took a final drag on his cheroot, then tossed it into the pond where it caught the current, was pulled into the creek and disappeared downstream. Within that space of time Rand moved forward, took hold of Leilani and pulled her into his arms. For a brief moment their eyes met, and then his face lowered and his lips claimed hers.

At first she struggled, but his arms held her secure and she found herself pressed tighter against his hard male body, breasts crushed to his chest. And then, as his kiss deepened, her resistance waned, replaced by tentacles of heat that tingled into her limbs, and into the warm folds of the place no man had ever touched. Her body began to respond, even as her mind rejected the sensations. A primitive instinct that came from the very core of her being was suddenly awakened, and she feared what was about to happen, even as her resistance to stop it was slipping away.

"Oh my *ipo*," he crooned against her lips when he lifted his mouth briefly. "It was inevitable that this happen."

"No, Rand, we must stop," she whispered faintly.

"Shhh," he murmured. Then his lips were on hers again, crushing, his tongue thrusting into her mouth, demanding more. His hand moved into her hair, his fingers stroking its silky strands where it grew next to her ear, and his light touch seemed to trace fire along her flesh. His other hand caressed her side next to her breast, and she felt the nipple harden under her dress.

He'd called her "sweetheart," and then his touch had driven her growing passion even higher. She knew it was madness, and somewhere in the back of her mind was a warning that told her they must stop, now, before it was too late.

And then the matter was taken out of their hands. They both hesitated at the same time, a pause right at the moment when Rand was about to lower Leilani to the soft earthen blanket at their feet. The voices of her brothers approaching along the path jolted them back to their senses. Just in time they stepped away from each other.

Then the little boys saw them, and when they heard the man was Rand Walsh, their hero, there was a babble of questions and thanks and little-boy talk. Over their heads she met Rand's amused gaze, and was strangely annoyed. His expression held no hint of the fact that he'd just made passionate love to her—that he would have gone even further had the boys not returned.

She turned away, suddenly upset and uncertain about his motives toward her. But she knew one thing for sure; something had happened between them and she couldn't pretend it didn't exist. As they started back to the cottage, Leilani was pleasant, but aloof, allowing her turmoil of feelings to subside. She wondered how Rand could seem so unaffected.

The thought lingered all through supper, which she helped to serve. It wasn't necessary for her to contribute to the conversation, for the boys kept up a steady stream of questions, obviously in awe of Rand, and even more so when he told them that he, too, was Hawaiian, if only half. By the time he left, Leilani felt wrung out from the strain of acting normal when so much lay unsaid between them.

"Thank you, thank you!" her family cried in unison as he went outside to his horse. *"Aloha!"* Mama Kauwe said from the doorway behind Leilani. Then she gave Leilani an unexpected shove that propelled her out the door behind Rand. "Say goodbye," Mama whispered with a sly grin. "Say come back soon."

Then Leilani was left alone with Rand as he mounted. He looked down at her; a last ray of sunlight was caught in his eyes, giving them the look of molten gold, a look that started the sensations again deep within her. But she quickly suppressed her traitorous feelings; she held his gaze and waited.

The wind caught a wing of his hair, and as he sat in silhouette against the purpling sky, she suddenly thought of his pagan ancestors. The breeze was cooler all at once, and she shivered. Was he going to sit there all night watching her? she wondered crossly, and resolved to wait him out.

"I'll see you soon," he said finally, his tone so low that it seemed to vibrate on the air currents. "I think you'll agree that we have new business to discuss."

Despite her hold on her nerves, his words jolted her. He hadn't forgotten their earlier meeting. In fact she could tell from his slumberous expression that he was remembering each detail.

"Perhaps," she evaded.

His brows slanted and the corners of his mouth quirked, but he controlled an urge to grin at her sudden primness. With a salute, he clucked at the horse and yanked the reins, and was soon disappearing down the track to the road. Leilani went inside. She didn't want him to turn and see her watching him go.

But his lean handsome face didn't fade from her mind as she helped Mama Kauwe clean the kitchen. Even after she was in bed her thoughts churned with him, and the things she'd learned about him during supper. While discussing his work in Chinatown, and how he'd taken care of the *luna,* he'd casually made reference to Madam Silk Stockings, who was also his client. The comment had surprised Leilani at first, until she remembered that she'd first seen Rand at the madam's establishment.

It was only his sense of fairness that allowed him to have clients like Madam Silk Stockings, she told herself as sleep began to encroach on her thoughts. He would never do anything that wasn't legal and proper.

And she wouldn't allow herself to believe he would play with her feelings either. *Because,* she admitted in the darkness of her room, *I'm attracted to him.*

And then she slept a dreamless sleep until morning.

Chapter Three

She'd hardly knocked when the door swung open and Rand stood framed in the doorway. His shirtsleeves were rolled up and his hair was mussed, as though he'd been deep in his work and had absentmindedly run his fingers through the crisp strands. Even his forehead was furrowed at the interruption—until he saw it was Leilani.

One black brow shot up in a question. "To what do I owe the pleasure?" he drawled, and smiled suddenly, revealing a flash of white teeth against his bronzed skin.

All set to pass on Hoy's thanks, Leilani was suddenly disconcerted. She couldn't understand it, but she'd braced herself for the reaction, and it still hadn't helped. No one had ever affected her as Rand Walsh did, not even Elwood Benton.

"I only stopped by on my way past as a favor to Hoy." She managed a cool smile, and declined his offer to go inside. "He wanted to thank you. It seems that everything is better for the workers, and the *luna* has been given another job." Leilani hesitated, noting the twinkle in his dark eyes, his awareness of her prim-sounding tone. "He came by the farm last night to report on his injured friend, and asked me to express his thanks, and those of the others he works with," she went on with a rush.

"Tell him he's welcome," Rand replied, equally casual, but his eyes were still alight with amusement. "I already knew about the *luna* being transferred, as I'd followed up on things with the plantation owner," he added. Although his manner remained nonchalant, there was an intensity about him as his eyes took in Leilani's short-sleeved, simple lavender gown, its cotton skirt slightly wrinkled and smudged with soil from her morning in the surgery. His appraisal brought a flush to her cheeks.

"I'll tell him," she replied, appalled that her lashes fluttered her nervousness. "When I see him this evening at a meeting." Leilani was suddenly anxious to be away from Rand, and his strange power over her. She inclined her head and would have said her goodbyes, but his hand came down on her bare arm, lightly restraining her.

"So you're going to a meeting?" he began, and his thick lashes suddenly screened his eyes. "As a guest—or adviser of Chinese rights?"

His censuring tone took her even more off guard than his question. Annoyance flared within her but she controlled it, instead replying with her own question.

"Why would you ask that, Mr. Walsh?"

The afternoon sunlight slanted down from a bleached sky, striking his face with a brilliance that was caught in the depths of his eyes, that gave his skin the cast of a bronze statue. She saw him control his own annoyance.

"Because it's dangerous for you to be involved in the political intrigues of the Chinese worker." He drew in his breath sharply, as though her coolness frustrated him. "It's one thing to help nurse sick Chinese families, quite another to be involved in a secret-society meeting where they air grievances, and expect someone like you to help."

"They don't expect that at all!" she retorted, forgetting to hold her temper behind a ladylike manner. "But they need to be heard if they're in the right—if they're being mistreated!"

"Everyone doesn't mistreat them, Leilani, and you know it. Some planters are more than fair, although they expect the workers to fulfill the original agreements they signed before being brought from China to work."

He was right, but she'd be damned if she were going to tell him so. For some reason they always seemed to disagree on something or other. And all she'd meant to do was stop by with Hoy's words of appreciation, because she hadn't been able to refuse the grateful man's request. She took a deep breath and willed herself to disregard Rand's superior attitude. She suddenly realized that each of their conflicts had been rooted in some aspect of her work among the poor in Chinatown.

"You're right," she said finally, speaking as patiently as she would to her young brothers when they were upset. "Many of the planters are true to their word." Then she tilted her face and looked him straight in the eyes. "But that doesn't change the fact that they have no rights, that the law isn't on their side, and many other people take advantage because they know a Chinaman can't retaliate without risk of being arrested, or worse."

"Be that true or not," Rand began, and made an effort to sound as composed as she was, "it's not up to you to champion their cause. Because not only are you part Chinese, you're a woman as well, and your own rights are limited if you get in trouble." He gave a brief smile, conscious of a stiffening of her features, that she was more than annoyed with him. Yet he felt compelled to warn her. She could find herself in a dangerous position without anyone to help her out of it. "Come on, Leilani, you can help the sick, but you can't change the social structure of Honolulu all by yourself."

"Perhaps you're right." She contrived a smile back, having realized the conversation was deadlocked. Arguing wouldn't help, or change either of their minds, and knowing that, Leilani changed the subject. "I'll let you resume your work, and I'll get back to mine," Leilani said, her tone unnaturally light, as she stepped back.

He inclined his head, knowing she was the most stubborn female he'd ever known, and the most damnably attractive. Hell, even as he watched her thoughts shift away from the topic, he had an urge to pull her into his office, lock the door and make passionate love to her until she obeyed him. He gave himself a mental shake, knowing he was treading on dangerous ground, and allowed her to make her retreat.

The wind caught at her hair, flaying it around her shoulders, and the sunshine silvered a sheen onto its silky length. She lowered her long lashes over the brilliance of her eyes, obscuring anything he might read there, as she turned away.

"Again, Hoy's thanks...and mine," she tossed over her shoulder with a sidelong glance. And then she made her escape, and felt his gaze follow her until she turned the corner.

Only then did she slow her pace, and expel her breath. He's a devil, she told herself in an attempt to place his effect on her in perspective. No, she thought. He's an unholy pagan, a descendant of the Polynesians who sacrificed beautiful virgins to the volcano goddess.

Oh God! she thought as a tremor of heat jolted tingling sensations through her. What made me think of that? But she suddenly didn't want an answer to the question. She wasn't ready to face it...yet.

The next day was Friday again, and Leilani was anxious to be home early, as she'd promised her brothers to take them swimming before supper. It was midafternoon when she made her last house call at one of the shacks off a narrow alley in the worst area of Chinatown. The young woman, her patient, was just getting over childbed fever, and Leilani wanted to make sure she didn't have a relapse. About to knock on the door, she was startled by a scream from inside the dilapidated shanty.

She knocked, but the commotion beyond the door precluded anyone's hearing her. The screaming pierced the alley, scaring a scrawny cat from a pile of garbage. Even people a few yards away on the main street paused, their questioning gazes on her. Leilani tried the door, but it was locked. Soon a little crowd had gathered, and people gestured and muttered in Chinese. One old woman said, "Her man beat her. Mean husband, hurt her bad this time."

The woman's singsong words galvanized Leilani into action. She was about to have two men break down the door when it burst open instead, and a wiry man ran into the street. Behind him was the woman Leilani had come to see, tears streaming from her eyes, and blood from a cut on her cheek where she'd obviously been struck by her husband.

"Stop him!" Leilani cried, and instantly two men grabbed the husband, restraining him by his pigtail when he tried to struggle free. But when they understood that he wasn't a thief, only involved in a domestic conflict, they let him go.

Leilani went to the trembling woman, who wrung her hands, chanting over and over again, "Please—please." It was obvious that the woman was more frightened that her cruel husband had been detained and humiliated before his neighbors, than with her own cuts and bruises. "Wrong you command men to grab husband," she told Leilani.

"Don't worry," Leilani soothed. "Everything will be all right. But your husband must stop beating you. Even if you are his wife, he has no right to hurt you."

The woman's eyes brimmed with more tears, and she trembled uncontrollably as her husband tossed verbal abuse in rapid Punti dialect at Leilani, stepping closer with each word, his manner threatening. From his enraged expression, Leilani guessed she was now the focus of his fury.

She faced him, resolute. She wouldn't back down. He was wrong and she wasn't about to let him get away with beating her patient, a woman with a new infant to add to her brood of six. The man could easily harm his frail wife seriously, and Leilani couldn't allow that. The husband had to be shown he was wrong.

In her halting Hakka, she quickly explained to the onlookers, men who automatically aligned themselves with the husband. Undaunted, she went on to remind them that this was Hawaii, not China, and it was against the law to beat anyone. They listened impassively until one of Hoy's friends stepped forward and interceded on her behalf.

But even Hoy's friend wasn't a match for the husband's rage, and his intent to save face by confronting Leilani. Regardless of her being part Chinese, in his opinion she was mostly *haole*—like the *luna* who worked him from dawn to dark, as if he were a dog. This was one time he wouldn't back down, not from a mere woman.

A chill ran down Leilani's spine when she saw the determined glint in the husband's black eyes as he advanced on her. Suddenly she knew she was in danger of bodily harm—and for the first time since working for Dr. Pete, she was in real trouble. With sheer willpower, she managed to keep her eyes level, unwavering. It wouldn't help to show fear. Her only hope was to hold her ground, and maybe reason with him. He moved closer, and she saw the sun glint on something in his hand. Her stomach knotted in fear. A knife.

"Enough!" A man, head and shoulders above the smaller Chinese, pushed through the crowd to step between Leilani and the man. Her instant relief almost buckled her legs when she recognized Rand. "Go about your business!" he ordered the onlookers, and his authoritative bearing boded no refusal. After some hesitation, they scurried off, leaving only Leilani's patient and her husband, who made no move to obey.

Leilani's relief was short-lived. Although she'd never been so glad to see anyone, even though the dangerous glint in Rand's eyes precluded her saying so, the threat wasn't past. She'd never seen Rand look so angry, and she suddenly wondered if his anger was directed at her as well as at the husband who faced him defiantly. She didn't dare distract him with words, and for a minute she didn't know if she could speak, for she'd begun to shake alarmingly from delayed reaction. She'd almost been stabbed!

"You heard what I said," Rand snapped, his eyes never wavering from the Chinese man, or from the knife. "I meant it. You might get away with beating your wife, but I'll have you arrested if you take one more step toward Miss Kauwe."

Still the man hesitated, measuring his opponent's determination to back up his words, whether an unarmed man, although much bigger, could really stop a knife attack. His small eyes flickered between Rand and Leilani, and then his wife gathered her courage and began pleading with him. After a few more seconds, reason asserted itself, and the man put his knife away, but his final glance at Leilani was malevolent. Then, muttering in Chinese, he took his wife back into their shack, and slammed the door behind them.

About to thank Rand, Leilani opened her mouth, but before she could speak, he had hold of her arm and was propelling her toward the street. The hard set to his jaw, and the angry glint in his eyes told her that he wasn't in a mood to hear a protest to his high-handed assumption that she'd go with him without a word. At the street she yanked free, bringing them to an abrupt stop.

"Now see here, Rand," she managed shakily. "I appreciate you coming to my rescue, and I know the man meant business, and I was frightened but—"

"Later," he snapped, interrupting her. Before she could go on he had hold of her again, this time in a grip that wouldn't allow her to pull free, and continued their flight down the sidewalk, scattering vendors and shoppers as they went. Her protests fell on deaf ears, and she hesitated to create a worse scene. But her own anger was mounting. How dare he treat her in such a manner!

They reached his office where he hardly broke stride as he opened the door, led her inside and then locked it after them. When he let her go she stumbled backward, so upset that her thoughts whirled faster than she was able to speak at the moment. The sudden quiet of the room was an anticlimax, and Rand, infuriatingly sure of himself, moved to his desk where he found a cheroot. The match striking wood brought her gaze to him, and she watched as he lit the tobacco—and his hand trembled slightly.

But Leilani discounted the possibility that he was even more shaken by her narrow escape than she was. Her outrage wouldn't allow it. "What's the meaning of this, Rand?" she demanded, and once she started speaking, she couldn't stop the flow. "I know you saved me from that crazy madman, but what in the world will people think, now that they saw you yanking me along the street like—like a trollop! You had no right to treat me with such disrespect!"

Throughout her tirade he only stared at her through smoke-veiled eyes, his expression darkening with each accusation she flung at him. Then, as she gulped a breath and whirled away toward the door, he moved with lightning speed, stopping her hand on the knob.

"Not so fast, my little angel of mercy." He pulled her into his arms and put out his cheroot in an ashtray almost in the same motion. "You're going to listen to a few rules first, and—" He broke off, and she could see the fire in his dark eyes, even though he spoke with icy calm. "And you're not leaving here until you agree to obey them."

"I'll leave when I say, not you!" she cried defiantly, and tried not to think about how close his mouth was to hers, or that his arm had tightened, pressing her body into his. "You have no right—"

"I have every right, my sweet," he said in a low tone. "I won't stand by and let a woman—any woman—do dangerous work, not when I know about it and can put a stop to it before people get hurt."

"That man was beating his wife, Rand!" she retorted. "I couldn't let him get away with it—because he might have killed her. It was wrong."

"Wrong or not, that woman was his wife, and there's a certain point where you can't interfere." He loosened his hold and she took a step backward, although his arm still held her. "Do you realize you could have been killed instead, if I hadn't heard the commotion and investigated?"

Again she noticed how affected he was by the incident. And suddenly she realized that his anger was only a veneer over his concern for her. *He'd thought she was about to die.* And knowing how he really felt diffused her own anger. Her lashes fluttered nervously, and without her anger as a shield, she was suddenly so aware of his arms around her, his hooded eyes taking in every inch of her face, that she couldn't hold his gaze. She glanced down and found her eyes level with the strong brown column of his throat.

"You're right, Rand," she began in a low tone. "I was just so upset because the woman was my patient, and she's not strong, and I—"

Her abrupt change surprised him, and he wondered what had brought it about. With two fingers, he tilted her chin so that she was again looking into his face. He read sincerity there, and an understanding of his reaction to her danger. Somehow her grasp of his motive made him even more aware of her femininity, her mystique. She was always doing the unexpected, and he found himself thinking about the last time she'd been in his arms. At the moment he wanted to make love to her more than he'd ever wanted a woman. But he controlled himself, and instead led her to the sofa, where they both sat down.

For a moment neither spoke. Then to break the sudden awkwardness between them, he smiled, and watched in pleased silence as a blush rose into her cheeks. But it intensified his desire to hold her. Again he resisted, and managed to speak in a normal tone.

"I'm glad you understand, Leilani. My heart almost stopped when I thought that man was about to stab you," he said smoothly, as though he were only a concerned friend. "And if I was that affected, and I'm not even one of your loved ones, then think how your Mama and Papa Kauwe would feel if you'd been killed," he added, trying to get his point across now that she was calmer.

She nodded, knowing he was right. "I'd never want to do that to them. I misjudged the man and I was wrong." She spoke softly, the magnitude of what could have happened washing over her. "I only meant to help, not cause more grief."

"I know, but sometimes we must think before we act." He took her hand in his, and gently raised it to his lips, softening his mild reprimand with the gesture. Then he slanted another smile, a friendly smile that didn't quite conceal the impression that a fire burned in him, banked down by sheer willpower.

"You see," she continued quickly, concentrating on the conversation and not Rand's overpowering presence, "I can't stand a bully who picks on someone who is weaker, and I have to help if I can."

"Within limits, Leilani," he corrected, as she fell silent. "You can't take on the whole Chinese problem." He hesitated, then asked something he knew was none of his business. "In fact, I've wondered why you're so inspired to work among the poor. I can't believe a pretty and intelligent young woman would really want to."

"I do have another reason." She glanced at him, and instantly her gaze was caught and held. "Above my genuine need to help my people."

Something flickered in his expression. Surprise?—or concern? She couldn't tell and went on quickly, before she lost her nerve. He came into contact with many people in Chinatown, and it was possible he knew something that would help her in the quest to learn about her past. "You don't know anything about me, Rand," she began, and faltered. Taking a deep breath because discussing her past was painful, she continued. "I was abandoned as an infant, and only know my birth date and that I'm part Chinese. I've tried to uncover my background—and I believe someone in Chinatown might know something." Her throat tightened but she kept on. "One day, through my work, I believe I'll find a clue—because it's very important to me that I do."

To her embarrassment, tears welled in her eyes. She blinked and glanced away, and hoped he hadn't noticed. He didn't say a word, but when he drew her head against him, she knew he'd seen her distress. Oh God! she thought. Instead of directing the conversation away from her awareness of him, she had taken herself into deep water. Suddenly she wanted nothing more than to cry, and realized that she was having a delayed reaction to the attack. She felt safe in Rand's arms, and every muscle and bone and cell in her body longed to stay there.

Gently, Rand wiped her tears away with his fingers. Then, unable to help himself, he tilted her face and looked into her brimming eyes. Outside the day was waning, workers on their way home. But Rand couldn't let her go now. He kissed her lightly at first, tasting the salt of her tears. She didn't try to stop him, her mouth pliant under his. When her lips parted, he was lost in the sudden passion that flared between them, stronger than he'd ever felt before.

Within seconds they had slid lower on the sofa, so that he was arched above her. Her breath accelerated, her breasts rising and falling with each rapid heartbeat, and when his hand slid over her bodice to caress their soft mounds, her nipples hardened under his touch. He groaned and pressed her closer to him, the urge to undress her so strong that his fingers were on the buttons before his mind registered the command to his hand.

Leilani felt drugged, unable to break the connection to him, or hold back the great lethargy that was spreading from her limbs into the moist place between her thighs. She wanted to stop, but for the life of her she couldn't. He was a fire in her that was consuming the last shred of resistance she possessed. "Mmm," she murmured against his lips, and with the slight opening of her mouth, his tongue found its way inside. And then she was kissing him back, passionately, unable to control the urgency within her that clamored for relief.

Then a buggy rattled to a stop beyond the front door, and even though it was locked, Rand lifted his head. He watched as Leilani's long lashes lifted gracefully from where they rested on the upper curve of her flushed cheeks. Her wonderful blue eyes were brilliant with passion. But there was also an innocence in their depths, and a trust that he wouldn't harm her.

The insight unnerved him, because his thoughts were anything but trustworthy. He was about to take her maidenhood, regardless of whether or not there was love between them. He suddenly knew his need wasn't enough, because he was unsure of his feelings. He'd never wanted any woman as he wanted Leilani, not even his wife. It was a sobering thought that tortured him, because his need was sheer agony. Finally he mastered the savage urge to take her at any cost, and sat up. Then he set her aside, looking away before she saw his naked desire to possess her.

His action was abrupt, taking Leilani by surprise. He turned his back on her even as she throbbed for him, and her desire screamed a silent plea for him to come back into her arms. Then, his rejection hit Leilani, and her whole body went hot with humiliation. Quickly she stood and adjusted her clothing. She couldn't speak, and in the back of her mind a new realization was growing. She could never face him again. She'd been wanton, had fallen in his arms like a whore—like one of Madam Silk Stockings's girls, she thought hysterically.

She started for the door, but he was there ahead of her, his demeanor composed as he looked down into her shattered face. And when he spoke his voice was calm, as though it was his practice to seduce young women. No, she corrected herself as she met his enigmatic eyes, not any woman. Only a self-confessed Chinese girl of questionable background—one who didn't count.

"Look, I'm sorry. I only brought you here to lay out the rules," he said, and his tone sounded stilted after all—from suppressed feelings?—or sudden distaste for her? she wondered. "For your own safety, Leilani, stay out of marital conflicts, and secret meetings, anything that doesn't pertain to nursing with the doctor." He took an uneven breath, unsure in the face of her closed expression. "If you get in trouble the authorities won't help you—you'll be as vulnerable as anyone else here in Chinatown."

When she didn't respond because she didn't trust her ability to speak, he went on, and his tone was sharper than he intended. "Because of being part Chinese yourself."

Her anger was unexpected, and welcome. She understood. Her background was an issue to him just as it once was to Elwood Benton when she was eighteen. "I quite understand, Rand Walsh. And I'll remember your warning, and why."

She twisted the knob and flung open the door, oblivious to her unpinned hair and high color and eyes glinting like priceless gems. "I know that the *pake*—the hated *Celestials*—are the most discriminated-against people in Hawaii." She twisted around to face him one last time. "Believe me, I will never allow another *haole* to take advantage of me!" Her gaze raked him from head to foot, leaving no doubt in his mind as to what she meant.

Then she fled into the ebbing day, leaving him standing uncertain, suddenly aware of how badly he'd insulted her—because he'd suppressed his hot passion under a veneer of coolness. But he didn't go after her to apologize. He didn't dare. Rand couldn't trust his feelings. Watching her go, he wanted her more than ever.

As Leilani ran, the evening breeze off the Pacific Ocean enfolded her with the cool touch of approaching night. Gradually she slowed to a walk, and her skin cooled, if not her feelings of outrage and shame. Was she so wrong to have let her feelings for Rand grow? Dry-eyed, she kept on, headed up the valley toward the mountains. She'd never felt so upset inside, and knew the feeling wouldn't go away soon.

She was devastated. Because she cared how Rand Walsh viewed her. She cared about Rand.

Chapter Four

The door to the surgery opened but Leilani was so engrossed in writing up a patient history that she didn't even glance up, expecting Dr. Pete. Footsteps paused just inside the door, and she suddenly felt eyes on her. She looked up.

"Am I disturbing you?" Rand drawled, taking in her startled expression, the instant rise of pink that touched her face with a flattering glow, and her black hair gilded by golden sunlight that streamed in through the window behind her desk.

He stepped into the room and closed the door, but his eyes never left hers. In passing he noted her prim high-necked waist, its pale blue percale that seemed to deepen the sapphire color of her large eyes, and accent their long sweeping black lashes.

Disconcerted, Leilani jumped up, suddenly too aware of Rand, who now lounged against a cabinet, looking long and lean in his black cotton morning jacket and formfitting trousers. His starched white, high-collared shirt emphasized his sun-bronzed skin and the darkness of his eyes, which had caught the light from the brilliant day beyond the window.

For long seconds neither spoke, their gazes caught, both aware of the palpability of the silence. For the life of her Leilani couldn't think of anything to say, her feelings in sudden turmoil. The last time she'd seen him she'd gone home shattered by his criticism. She still felt the sting of anger and humiliation, but she also felt attraction. Somehow her body seemed to know what she wouldn't admit. I'm not falling in love with Rand Walsh! she told herself firmly. And the thought broke her inability to speak.

"The doctor isn't here, Rand," she said, her tone level, relieved that her voice didn't give away her discomfiture. She came out from behind the desk, more confident that she had herself under control. "But I expect him at any moment. You're welcome to wait." She indicated the straight-backed chairs lining one wall, vacant now because there were no scheduled patients.

"I'm here to see you, not the doctor." Instead of taking a chair, Rand closed the space between then, so that he stood so near Leilani's composure was threatened again.

Her lashes fluttered nervously but she managed to keep her gaze from dropping before the sudden intensity of his eyes. She quelled an urge to step back, to flee from him and from the uncertainty that had flooded back stronger than ever. Instead, she held her ground and faced him, waiting with a facade of calmness she was far from feeling.

"I came to apologize," he went on, and the lines and planes of his Polynesian face seemed anxious. "I believe you went away from our last meeting thinking I had insulted you." His thick black eyebrows lowered as he frowned. Before Leilani could digest his latest unexpected action, he took her hands, as though he were really sorry for any upset he'd caused her. "I was only worried about your safety, Leilani," he said softly, and somehow he'd moved even closer, so that she felt his breath on her face. "I certainly wasn't criticizing you for being part Chinese." He drew a sharp breath. "I, too, have blood in my veins that isn't *haole*."

Of anything she might have guessed he was about to say, an apology wasn't one of them. Again her gaze was held while her mind whirled in a flurry of broken thoughts. Finally she licked her lips and thanked him, and was horrified that her words sounded stilted and ungracious.

"Perhaps I was overly sensitive," she added quickly in a friendlier tone.

"Whatever the case, I wanted you to know I meant no slight." He didn't add that he hadn't been able to get her stricken face out of his mind, that he'd been haunted with feelings of guilt. The last thing he'd wanted to do was hurt her more.

She nodded, but her lashes swept down, so he couldn't read her eyes. He'd noticed that she was distant at first, and felt an even stronger need to make things right between them. He grinned suddenly in a attempt to lighten the mood, and cocked a dark slanting brow in a completely masculine manner, so that Leilani's breath paused in her chest. "And now that we have that settled," he said, "I'd like you to accompany me to the plantation where Hoy works, not to see the Chinese, but to a dinner party."

Astounded by his unexpected invitation, Leilani felt her eyes widen, and was even more disconcerted. Rand had a way of putting her off balance, and she wondered why he would ask her to a party of his friends. She gathered her refusal, but before she could voice it, he went on instead.

"Since you have a poor impression of the plantation, of the plantation *luna* anyway, I'd like you to meet the owners, the Carsons, so you can see that they're well-intentioned toward their workers."

Running her tongue over her lips, she managed to keep her surprise from her reply. "I understand, Rand. And I appreciate your help on behalf of the workers, but it isn't necessary to invite me out socially. I believe they want the best for Hoy and his friends, or they wouldn't have taken care of a bad situation so quickly." She didn't add that it was one thing to have Chinese workers, quite another to invite them to their party. Leilani was pretty sure that her going wouldn't be acceptable—that the owners probably weren't aware of Rand's intentions—a complete departure from acceptable conduct in the polite society of Honolulu.

He watched the play of emotions that crossed her face, and understood her hesitancy. She was so damnably proud, so defensive about her background, that she couldn't concede that she might be liked for herself. Rand was determined to not take no for an answer. As she opened her mouth to speak—say no—he placed a finger over her mouth, stopping her refusal.

Taken aback, Leilani would have moved away but for the desk behind her and Rand in front of her, so close that their clothing touched. Then he cocked both brows and grinned lazily, as though in supplication, as though he took it for granted that she wouldn't disappoint him.

Then the door opened again and the doctor rushed into the room. "Lordy Lord!" he cried. "I'm running behind schedule, as usual." After a greeting to Rand, and quick instructions to Leilani, he disappeared into the surgery.

Rand plopped his hat back onto his head, and his eyes were immediately shaded by the tipped-down brim, so that when he strode to the door, turned and gave a farewell salute, she could no longer read his expression.

"I'll come by the farm for you on Sunday at three," he drawled, and before she could utter a sound, he was gone, the door closed behind him.

Her legs shook with sudden reaction, and her veins hummed from the jolt to her nervous system. How dare he assume I'd go! she fumed. And even if she hadn't seen his expression, she'd heard the humor in his voice. He'd manipulated her!

But as she went to join the doctor, she admitted to herself that he hadn't been laughing at her, only amused that he'd prevented her refusal.

Yet as she worked beside Dr. Pete, Leilani wondered why Rand wanted to escort her in the first place. Suddenly she didn't care. She wanted to go, despite her fears. Her thoughts shifted abruptly to her wardrobe, and what she'd wear.

She wasn't about to embarrass herself by looking anything but her best. She certainly wasn't trying to impress Rand.

"Beautiful—really beautiful!" Mama Kauwe clapped her hands gleefully, her round face beaming a smile.

She had come into the bedroom just as Leilani finished dressing and was about ready for the party. Rand would arrive in a few minutes to escort her to the Carson plantation. Leilani tried to hide her nervousness behind a brave front, but she knew that her mother suspected her apprehension. So she turned away to walk to the wall mirror, her gaze on her image, examining herself carefully.

Would Rand realize her organdy dress was homemade? she wondered. Leilani twisted to the side, checking that the waist fitted snugly, the sprigs of blue and green pattern on the cream background matched at the seams. She'd managed to finish the garment only that morning, and it was too late now to change her mind about what to wear.

Her gaze met her mother's in the glass. "Do you think the short sleeves are too skimpy, and the neckline too low?" Leilani knew she sounded uncertain, because she was. Mama Kauwe wasn't one to dress in anything beyond her best Sunday cotton, a simple garment with only four seams and a scooped neck. Although Leilani always managed the current styles, it was only because she had an eye for fashion and was a good seamstress, sewing for the whole family when time permitted. She'd even made her white ruffled curtains and bedspread, creating a bedroom of contrasts with its dark koa wood paneling, floor and furniture.

"No, just right," Mama said, nodding with enthusiasm, her words lilting in the Hawaiian cadence. "Look beautiful, more Hawaiian today than Chinese or *haole*." Her grin broadened. "Mr. Walsh fall in love today, I think."

"Mama!" Leilani saw the flush creep into the face of her mirror image, and she tried to ignore it. Instead she altered her scrutiny to her swept-up hair, the confection of swirls and waves she'd fashioned so that she'd look as proper as any woman present at the party. She'd only applied powder and a little lip rouge, for her dark lashes and brows needed no charcoal, and the natural pink in her cheeks didn't require additional color. Satisfied, she turned away from the mirror. It was the best she could do.

Her mother had gone to the bed where her blue satin jacket, trimmed in the same organdy, lay on the spread. "Very nice," she pronounced. "You'll be the prettiest girl at the party."

The sound of buggy wheels approaching on the driveway brought all Leilani's apprehension to the surface. For a second her nervous system was in danger of collapse, and she feared she would panic, and be unable to walk downstairs to meet Rand after all. Once she knew she was going, she'd occupied herself with sewing her gown. There'd been no time to dwell on the event, or her feelings for Rand. But now it hit her. She was going to her first party at the home of rich *haoles*. She suddenly wondered if they knew whom Rand was bringing, if they'd approve once they met her. Her fears spun in her head as she hesitated, uncertain.

"It's all right, Leilani," her mother said, again anticipating her daughter's upset state. "Mr. Rand will be with you, and he won't let anyone be mean." She picked up the jacket and helped Leilani into it, then propelled her back to the mirror. "See," she said. "You look—elegant." The last word rolled off her tongue slowly, it being one that Mama Kauwe didn't often use.

Leilani studied herself, and realized she'd never looked nicer. The jacket with its big, puffed sleeves finished at the waist, and drew attention to her slender figure without diminishing the fullness of her breasts. She shot her mother a fond grin before placing her straw picture hat atop her upswept hair, adjusting it so that the blue ribbons trailed down the back. Then she pulled on her long cream gloves, grabbed her chatelaine bag and was ready to go downstairs.

But she hesitated again when she reached the steps, hearing Rand's deep voice blending with those of her two young brothers. Her mother had gone ahead and was already joining the others by the time Leilani had gathered her courage and started down the stairs. With each slow step she wondered why she was going, why she was placing herself in such a vulnerable position. Somehow she hadn't been able to refuse Rand, and hadn't been able to send him a note of regret either. Leilani knew she might be setting herself up for heartbreak—because she was attracted to him. And she knew he didn't intend to remarry, and even if he changed his mind, he probably wouldn't consider a part-Chinese girl.

But, she reminded herself, hesitating midway down the stairs to smooth the organdy over her hips, she wasn't in danger of falling in love with him. Wouldn't she know if she was? Besides, her going to this party was a step in the direction of the Chinese people being accepted into Honolulu's social circle one day. With that resolve, she continued down to the hall, knowing Rand hadn't noticed her yet.

But Leilani was wrong. Rand had seen her from the first second she came into view, and although he'd kept up a lively conversation with the boys, his eyes had never left her. Even as he talked, he'd wondered how he could sound so normal with Leilani approaching, breathtakingly beautiful and as regal as a queen.

His mind flashed on how she had looked half-naked, sunning herself by the waterfall. Rand knew he wanted her, had from the first, although he feared what that meant. He also remembered his pledge when his wife died—that he would never make another marriage commitment. A moment later when she stepped into the hall, he had himself firmly in control. Just because he wanted to make love to her didn't mean he was falling in love, Rand told himself sternly. And it didn't mean he couldn't escort her to social functions, enjoy her company, because she intrigued him in a way no other woman ever had.

"You look lovely," he said, his eyes taking in her gown, lingering on the upper curve of her breasts.

"Thank you," she managed, suddenly aware that her neckline might be too low after all.

Then, after goodbyes to the Kauwes, he took Leilani's elbow and led her outside to his waiting buggy, where he helped her up onto the seat. Seconds later he leaped up beside her, took the reins and soon had the bay horses on the road to the Carson plantation.

They rode in silence after their first spurt of small talk, and Leilani was grateful. Never before had she considered that riding in a one-seat buggy was intimate. But now, her shoulders brushing his navy waistcoat, her skirts crushed to his cream trousers, which molded the ripple of muscles under the fabric as he drove, she'd never felt so conscious of a man . . . and his body.

Darting a glance from under her long lashes, she noticed his soft-fronted shirt was pleated, the high collar starched and snowy white against his brown throat. His own quick glance caught her unaware, and when he grinned, she thought her heart had taken wing and was about to fly from her chest. But she managed a return smile and looked away.

"This should be an interesting gathering," he said casually. "Everyone will be talking about America's war with Spain and if we were wrong to declare neutrality, and thus align ourselves with the United States." He glanced again, and even though his tone and topic were perfectly normal, his dark eyes, their lashes lowered from the glare of the sun, spoke of other feelings—that he, too, was aware of her.

Although she had a strange trembly sensation within her, Leilani followed his lead, and was able to reply in an equally ordinary tone. "But our position in Hawaii has brought a new understanding to American politicians. Because of the war they've realized our importance as a way station for troops. Which means opposition to annexing Hawaii will melt away."

He nodded, but she noticed the quirking at the corners of his mouth. He was trying not to grin!—because she had an opinion about politics—and was a woman? Annoyance surged within her. She couldn't stand pomposity in a man, and if she hadn't been riding in his buggy, she'd have told him so in no uncertain terms.

"I wasn't laughing at you, Leilani," he drawled lazily, and slanted her a glance. "Don't be prickly. I was only thinking that more women should take an interest."

He did grin then, but she saw admiration in his eyes, and as quickly as her anger had come, it was gone. Oh dear God, she thought wryly. The man kept her on a seesaw of emotions. And right now, as she felt a rush of pleasure at his compliment, she wondered what was happening to her. Never before had anyone ever managed to affect her as Rand Walsh did.

"Thank you, Rand," she said finally. "I am interested in politics that have to do with Hawaii—and annexation. One day that will make all the difference for people like the Chinese or the Japanese and others."

Again he nodded, this time seriously. "That's very true. It's also important to the Hawaiians, even though they lost the monarchy." He hesitated. "Perhaps our royal family will rule again, but under the governing power of America. The passing of our history isn't an easy thing to swallow."

The afternoon was exceptionally beautiful, the air fragrant, and the land they passed through as they skirted the mountains held Leilani in the timelessness that was the mystique of Hawaii. Even the wind that had turned inland off the ocean seemed to whisper of other times, other people who'd loved the Islands too. For a moment Leilani was pierced with sadness for all the old Hawaiians had lost, even if the gains for the future were great. Rand seemed to sense the same haunting mood of the past, and for the next mile neither spoke, riding in companionable silence, held suspended somehow by a power they felt but couldn't see.

He patted her knee lightly, reassuringly, as the plantation house came into view. That Rand sensed her rising tension at meeting some of the island planters and their wives, didn't surprise her. He always seemed to know her fears, but for now Leilani put that disturbing thought aside, and concentrated on keeping her composure instead. She didn't want to shame herself by stammering or blushing, because she was equal to anyone, she reminded herself firmly.

Obeying the signal on the reins, the horses turned onto a long lane that bordered a cane field, and headed toward the rambling white plantation house that sat among sweeping shade trees and brilliant flowers. Beyond the elegant grounds Leilani noticed brown huts clustered together at the edge of the fields, quarters for the Chinese field workers, a striking contrast to their master's splendid mansion. As the buggy drew up before the wide veranda, Leilani put aside thoughts of the field hands, determined to be congenial despite her misgivings.

Then the buggy slowed to a stop, Rand jumped down, threw the reins to a Japanese servant and helped Leilani step to the ground. For a second longer he held her, his gaze on her face, trying to read her expression. He knew she was nervous, but no one else would guess from her manner. She was completely in control of her emotions, although there was a tenseness about the set of her shoulders, in the very way her eyes didn't waver. God! he thought, she had no idea how damned beautiful she was. Whatever the circumstances, she stood out above all others.

Within those heart-stopping seconds he held her, Leilani thought she'd lose her hard-won composure after all. Didn't Rand have any idea what his presence did to her?—or did he? She couldn't read his thoughts, for the direct sun was behind him, backlighting with such a brilliance that it was almost blinding. Then voices greeted them and he stepped back so that they stood side by side to acknowledge their hosts.

"Welcome to our plantation, Rand, Miss Kauwe!" Roger Carson, a portly middle-aged man dressed in a white lounge suit strode from the veranda to meet them.

"Yes, we're pleased to have you join us today," added his wife, a plump, graying woman. The smile on her round face included Leilani, and it looked genuine. "We've been looking forward to meeting you, dear," she rushed on. "Ever since you helped us become aware of what our *luna* was doing."

Returning her smile, Leilani relaxed. Mrs. Carson was plain, but her brown eyes shone with kindness. In her high-necked, long-sleeved mauve worsted gown, she looked more like a farmer's wife than mistress of a rich plantation. For the first time since accepting Rand's invitation, Leilani's fear of not being accepted slipped away. She felt Rand's smile but didn't dare even a glance, for she knew looking at him would shatter her balance once more.

There were several other couples, all middle-aged and pleasant, and Leilani felt even more welcomed. Perhaps some of her fears about rich *haoles* were unfounded, after all, she thought many times during the next several hours. Conversation over cool drinks on the veranda was pleasant, as it was during a tasty, many-course supper that was served on silver and fine china in the elegant dining room. While the crystal chandelier caught the setting sun to dapple prisms of color over the diners, Leilani sat next to Mr. Carson, and was soon involved in new conversation topics. She listened with interest to views on annexation, the war with Spain and the upcoming celebration to welcome American troops on the first of June. But Mr. Carson's next remark was meant for her ears alone.

"I appreciate what you did for the workers, Leilani," he said, his blue eyes serious behind his gold-rimmed spectacles. "If you hadn't intervened, taken the problem to Rand, who knows what might have happened? Perhaps the workers taking revenge, and then the whole situation would have been out of hand." He took a swallow of water. "Mrs. Carson is appreciative, too. We both told Rand to invite you out here, so we could thank you in person." He grinned then, oblivious that Leilani's smile had gone stiff, that her fork had stopped in midair.

"Thank you for the compliment," Leilani managed in an equally pleasant tone. "I, too, hate to see trouble when it can be avoided." She glanced down and rested the fork on her plate. When she lifted her long lashes, her eyes were direct. "And I also hate to see the Chinese workers treated cruelly. Most of them are honest and hardworking, even if they do seem different and speak another language."

He nodded. "I've found that to be true."

She hesitated, knowing she was on dangerous ground. "It's gratifying to know there are fair and honest plantation owners such as yourself, Mr. Carson. And I'm sure that has more to do with the workers not causing trouble than anything I did."

"My dear," he said kindly. "I don't know that I deserve such a compliment—" he grinned suddenly "—but I can certainly see why you have the title of angel of mercy in Chinatown. If anyone is fair and honest, it's you. And as I said, we're very happy you could join us today."

She'd hardly smiled back at his unexpected words, when he'd turned away to answer another guest about the celebration to greet the troops who were on their way to the Philippines. In passing she heard that schools would be closed, elaborate decorations would be everywhere, and huge crowds were expected on the waterfront when the troops came ashore for the festivities. All Leilani could think of was the reason Rand had invited her—because the Carsons had asked to meet her, *not because it was his idea.*

Coffee in the parlor was served, and a short time later Mrs. Carson entertained them with piano pieces, including "Hawaii Ponoi," the Hawaiian national anthem. But Leilani's enjoyment had gone flat. They were all so nice, but would they have invited her under different circumstances?—such as being formally escorted by Rand?

When the party broke up, Leilani and Rand said their goodbyes and thanks, and were soon on the road back to the farm. Although it was dark, there was enough moonlight to illuminate the road. Rand had placed a robe over their laps to ward off the night chill from the ocean, creating an intimacy Leilani didn't welcome. She didn't need to feel even more attraction to Rand, for her emotions were already reeling with uncertainty, her plight since first meeting him.

Again she felt the soothing silence of the land, broken only by the whispery sea wind on its way up the long sloping mountains to the domain of the long-dead Polynesians. Leilani shivered, remembering tales of the Night Marchers, *alii* ghosts whose flickering torches might be seen high up on the peaks. Some Hawaiians still believed in the old myths, as did some *haoles*—like Rand and his former father-in-law, who both had native blood. The thought was even more disturbing. Would Rand really stay single because of the old taboos?—because he believed they were responsible for his wife's accident? Leilani shivered again, as another touch of wind feathered her skin with goose bumps.

This time Rand felt the slight tremble that went through her, and taking one hand from the reins, he tucked the robe tighter around her. She glanced and caught him looking at her. Something in his look, even shadowed as it was by the night, ignited a fire in her that wiped the chill of the night from her mind.

"Cold?" he asked, and his tone was low, almost hoarse, as though he, too, was affected by her.

She shook her head, suddenly not trusting herself to speak. Unable to maintain her gaze, Leilani looked beyond him where the moonlight shimmered on the distant ocean.

"Then what's wrong?" he went on in the same soft voice. "Didn't you enjoy the party? I noticed you were a little quiet after supper." His voice gathered volume. "The Carsons didn't say something to upset you, did they?"

"No—of course not," she replied at once. "Everyone was very nice. Mr. Carson complimented me concerning the issue with the workers." She hesitated despite her resolve to sound normal. "He said he'd asked you to invite me." Her words faded into the quiet night that seemed to move closer.

The bays pranced in rhythm with the wheels, a steady sound that filled the pause in conversation, and Leilani was startled when Rand suddenly brought the buggy to a jolting stop. Before her thoughts completely shifted to why he'd do such a thing, she was in his arms and his lips were on hers, passionately. The kiss caught her by surprise, and her mouth opened under his, deepening their embrace even more.

Abruptly, he lifted his face, but only barely. When Rand spoke, his breath was an erotic tickle on her lips, throbbing now from the urgency of his kiss. "I invited you today because I wanted to invite you, Leilani." He broke off to take a ragged breath, as though he controlled himself by iron will. "Did you believe for one minute that I would do otherwise?"

"Of course not," she lied, but her faint tone gave her away, and she lowered her lashes, unable to hold his eyes, which glinted with a passion that both thrilled and scared her at the same time.

With a flick of one finger he tilted her chin, so that Leilani had no option but to raise her gaze back to his. And then he surprised her again. His arms, which had tightened with his question, relaxed, so that when he pulled her closer he did it gently, as a father would hold a precious child. But his kiss wasn't fatherly; it was a lover's kiss, long and tender and infinitely satisfying. And it did strange things to Leilani, tantalizing her in yet a different way, one that promised even greater sensations of ecstasy than she'd imagined before.

When he raised his head he was already looking into her face before her eyes fluttered open. "There, Leilani. That ought to tell you something." He grinned suddenly, and playfully kissed the tip of her nose. "And when you're safely in bed tonight—" his whispered voice grew husky "—you might dream of me, and know why I restrained myself just now."

He took back the reins, signaled the horses, and they were once more on their way. Then he glanced at her, his eyes as dark and mysterious as the tropical night that enfolded them in all its pagan rustlings of ancient promises.

"I'll show you why, my little angel of mercy, soon."

And then she was taken home.

"The island of Oahu fits its name today!" Rand cried, his voice raised over the din of the crowd. He glanced down at Leilani, his handsome features relaxed by the excitement of the day. "It's certainly 'the gathering place.' From the look of the huge crowds, everyone in the Hawaiian Islands must be in Honolulu today."

About to answer, Leilani found her words were swallowed up in sudden cheering and clapping, as more American troops came ashore from one of the three transports anchored in the harbor. She only grinned back and joined the clapping. But she was aware of Rand's dark eyes watching her, his muscular, lean body pressed to hers by the crush of the crowd, and his arm around her so that they weren't separated.

Concentrating instead on the celebration, she watched as more uniformed men came ashore to be taken to the palace grounds for an elaborate meal. Hawaii was really being hospitable to the troops on their way to the Philippines, she thought, pleased, because if the Islands proved a valuable way station in the Pacific, annexation would pass in the American Congress. Then some things would begin to change, like the Chinese being granted citizenship sometime in the future.

"Glad you came?" Rand bent his head so she could hear his question.

She turned to answer, unaware that he was so close, and her cheek brushed his chin. Their eyes met, hers in alarm, his in amusement as he straightened back. For a second she forgot what she'd been about to say, too conscious of his dark pagan face, still too close for comfort. Her whole mind was filled with him: his white lounge suit that contrasted so attractively with his bronze skin, the jacket cut away from its one button just above his trim waist, and his fawn-colored bowler hat that shaded his suddenly hooded eyes.

"I am," she managed finally, and glanced past him to the banners waving in the breeze above the crowd. She was aware that he assessed her, too, and wondered what he thought of her yellow cotton dress, with its tiny waist, its wide sweep of skirt and its short sleeves with a wide overlay of white lace ruffles that were duplicated at the neckline.

The people all around them, dressed in their own finery, and their children, who were more delighted to be out of school than watching history, laughed and shouted and clapped. But Rand couldn't take his eyes off Leilani. She wore her hair free of constricting pins under her straw hat, and it flowed down her back in soft black waves. Although she was sedate, he wasn't fooled; she was as excited as anyone present. And he had an urge to take her somewhere where they could be alone, and make passionate love to her.

For a moment longer he indulged himself, drinking in her beauty and femininity, the way her breasts, straining against the delicate fabric, gave her emotions away by trembling from accelerated breathing. Rand forced his gaze away, and his mind from dangerous thoughts. He reminded himself of his resolve concerning Leilani—his decision to keep love and friendship separate. But that didn't mean he couldn't enjoy being with her, even if he must keep his growing desire under control. He dismissed the notion that he was only fooling himself.

The final boat from the ships landed amid another round of crowd reaction, and someone near Leilani shouted that twenty-five hundred men had come ashore. She glanced at Rand and grinned. The crowd was breaking up, going to other functions, and it was time to go.

It was bittersweet to her, for she wanted to be with him, but it was also a relief that the afternoon was over. Since he'd seen her home after the party with a sedate good-night kiss on the cheek, climbed back into his buggy and then tossed off the statement that he would escort her to the troop celebration, she'd been in a state of nerves. He hadn't given her a chance to refuse, and she'd been angry at first, but then she'd gone into the house, climbed into bed and dreamed of him—just as he'd told her to do. By the next morning she was again pre-occupied by what she'd wear. Mama Kauwe had only grinned knowingly, and helped her alter yet another dress.

"Well, shall we go?" Rand asked, his arm tightening around her as he led them through the surging people to the street. "We'll catch the tramcar over on King Street."

"The tramcar?" Leilani stopped short. "But the tramcar doesn't go out to the farm in the valley."

He grinned, a completely masculine expression that told her he was in command of their day. "I know," he drawled, his thick black lashes again screening his eyes, but not before

Leilani saw the glints of humor in their depths. "We'll take it out to Diamond Head. I made supper reservations for us at the Sans Souci."

"But I didn't know—" She broke off, uncertain. "The family will be—"

As was becoming his habit, he placed a finger over her lips to stop her protests. "Your mother knows." Her eyes widened in disbelief as he went on. "So they won't expect you until later, at which time I'll drive you home in my buggy." He took her shoulders and turned her so she faced him directly. "I thought it would be a nice ending to a glorious day. Will you go, Leilani?" He asked her now, but didn't elaborate on why he hadn't mentioned it earlier—because he'd been afraid she'd refuse, the very reason he'd manipulated her into going with him today.

Her sweet smile was sudden and it jolted Rand, although he didn't let his reaction show. She was so beautiful, so untouched, and his desire for her made itself known in his loins. Goddamn, but he needed to get a better grip on himself. Surely he could have a platonic friendship with a desirable woman, he told himself sternly.

"I'd love to. I've never been to the Sans Souci, and according to what I hear, Robert Louis Stevenson thought highly of the place when he stayed there during his months in Hawaii."

"If the eminent Mr. Stevenson says so, then I, too, recommend the food. Let's go!" Rand's brows quirked, his lips threatened a smile, and his eyes danced with the humor she heard in his words. Then he took her arm again and they started along the sidewalk to the tramcar stop.

As they walked, people nodded and smiled, and Leilani's spirits soared. She felt a rush of pride to be with Rand, walking with him for all the world to see. She was suddenly optimistic about everything, although she didn't care to examine the wish that sprang unbidden to the surface of her mind. It was enough to be with Rand—as though she were the most important person on earth to him at that moment.

Chapter Five

The three troop ships departed Honolulu three days later but a second convoy of transports came into port on June 23, amid excitement that Hawaii was almost annexed to the United States. By July 7, the resolution passed Congress and word reached the Islands six days later. After the settling of an immigration dispute with Japan, which had delayed final annexation by the United States, preparations were under way for the formal ceremony to be held at noon on August 12.

During the weeks between the celebration for the troops and Annexation Day, Leilani had seen Rand on only a few occasions, his work having taken him to Maui and the other islands. He'd again escorted her, and her two young brothers, to the Carson plantation for a picnic, and had stopped by the farm on a Sunday afternoon to visit, joining the family for supper when Mama Kauwe insisted.

His invitation to the Carsons' picnic had put her fear to rest that he'd only invited her the last time out of obligation. But she didn't see him before he left Honolulu, although he'd stopped by the doctor's office twice when she wasn't there. Leilani had enjoyed his company, but the thought crossed her mind that he avoided being alone with her. She was glad they hadn't been alone, as it gave her an opportunity to know him better without all the turmoil of being so aware of his presence that she forgot everything else.

Now, as Leilani stood in the guest room of the doctor's house, waiting for Rand, who was escorting her to the annexation ceremony at noon, she gave herself a final appraisal in the mirror. Again she'd swept up her hair in a chignon that fit under her straw picture hat. The ribbons and ruffle had been changed to match the pink and green satin trim on her white organdy dress. She turned sideways to examine her small waist, because she hadn't worn a corset, it being so hot and constricting under all the other undergarments. The upper bodice of the dress was sheer, as were the long sleeves, although the material over her breasts was covered by ruffles, and the bell-shaped skirt fell in graceful folds to a wide sweep just above her shoes. It was an attractive dress, Leilani decided, if not overly formal.

Her gaze shifted to the elegant ball gown that hung from a wall hook next to the mirror. Tonight she'd be wearing the most beautiful confection of diaphanous blue silk and satin she'd ever owned. Both her mother and the doctor's wife, Esther, had insisted that she go all out for the occasion, and both women had given opinions on what style dress to sew. Leilani grinned at herself in the glass. Since meeting Rand she seemed to fill all her spare time sewing new dresses.

A knock sounded on the bedroom door before it opened and Esther stepped into the room. A plain woman whose kindly face was deeply lined by years of hard work, she, like the doctor, was fond of Leilani, they never having had children of their own.

"My dear," she said, moving into the room. "You look so lovely I can't help wishing I was young again and being escorted by an eligible bachelor."

"But you aren't ready, Esther," Leilani protested after giving her an affectionate hug for her compliment. "It's almost eleven, and the ceremony begins at twelve sharp."

Esther wiped her hands down the sides of the huge white apron that almost covered her gray housedress. "The doctor and I won't be there. He has patients and I'm going to assist."

"But that's my job," Leilani said, suddenly stricken with guilt that she'd left the Petersons in the lurch. "Because I'm going, you can't. I know Friday is one of the busiest days of the week. I just assumed we wouldn't be open."

"No, dear, it's not true that we're staying home because of you." She hesitated, and her blue eyes suddenly filled with tears. "Neither of us could bear going." She dabbed at her lashes. "Although the doctor and I both know annexation will be good for Hawaii eventually, we were born here of missionary parents, and we're sad at the passing of the culture we once knew."

Her voice broke, and Leilani felt her own throat tighten. She understood, and although she was in favor of the change, she often wished that it could have happened without the kindly Hawaiians losing their monarchy, after hundreds of years of being an independent people. She wondered about Rand's feelings.

"But I forgot," Esther said, as though she'd given herself a mental shake. "Rand is waiting for you in the parlor and I only came to fetch you."

At the mention of his name Leilani's serenity vanished completely. A week ago when he'd unexpectedly come into the surgery and asked her to accompany him to the ceremony, then later to the reception and ball, she'd been so flustered that Dr. Pete had spoken up and said he thought it a wonderful idea. But Leilani, after she'd regained her equanimity and her nerve, had been direct.

"It's—uh—unseemly for you to escort a Chinese girl—if only part Chinese—to a ball in the queen's former palace. I believe it would be considered improper," she said, horrified when her voice caught on the last word.

"Nonsense!" the doctor cried, interrupting as though it were his business. "The annexation is for all Hawaiians, not just the *haoles*," he'd ended dryly.

She'd caught a glint of amusement in Rand's eyes, but he'd kept his voice in perfect control when she'd had no option but to agree, and then after tipping his hat and explaining that he'd be at the other end of the island for the next several days, he'd left them. Later he'd sent a note concerning the time he would come for her. In all, she'd been left even more confused about his motives. Nevertheless, she looked forward to the day.

"You look lovely," Esther repeated, interrupting Leilani's thoughts of Rand. "Just perfect for the occasion." She took

Leilani's arm and directed her to the door. "We're keeping Rand waiting, dear. And he needs to be at the palace early, as you'll be sitting with some of the dignitaries."

They went downstairs, and Leilani quelled a new wave of nerves. She'd expected to watch from the crowd, not be up in front. But one look at Rand, and the sudden flash of pleasure when he saw her, put her apprehension to rest. She went forward to greet him, not realizing that her feelings were obvious on her face as well.

The Petersons exchanged glances. It was apparent to them that both Rand and Leilani had serious feelings about each other—even if they might not have admitted the fact to themselves yet.

Leilani stood on the small upper veranda, her cotton wrap covering her silk underthings. As arranged, she was to spend the night at the Petersons after the ball. She'd returned from an exciting afternoon of watching, with tears in her eyes, as United States Minister Harold Sewall read the annexation resolution, then President Dole gave a speech, yielding the sovereignty of Hawaii to the United States.

The Hawaiian National Guard and American warships in the harbor fired salutes, then the Hawaiian Band played the national anthem, "Hawaii Ponoi," for the last time as an independent nation. When taps sounded and the Hawaiian flag was lowered, many people cried, including Leilani. But as the notes of "The Star-Spangled Banner" flowed over the hushed crowd, and the American flag was raised, Leilani was pierced with hope for the future, and her tears stopped.

Many Hawaiian faces were missing from the festivities, and Leilani decided that Mama Kauwe's words summed it up for the whole race. "It's too sad. We are no more. But we will never leave these islands, for it will always be the home of our gods, and for all the Hawaiians who once lived here. No one can change that, even if they change law."

Now, as Leilani gazed out over the city, the setting sun threw its own banners of crimson, purple and pink across the island, shadowing the mountains with mystery and the ocean with the spectacle of another day sliding forever into the night.

She swallowed hard, and knew it was setting on a way of life as well. From deep within her, she felt a stirring of something timeless, an understanding of those ancient Polynesians who'd crossed thousands of miles of ocean to claim their islands. Today they'd lost them.

Moving back into the bedroom, she was determined not to dwell on what was, but to think about the possibilities for the future. And the future meant going to the ball, with her head high, despite her trepidation. And she needed to complete her toilet if she were to be ready on time.

Already bathed, she sat down at the dressing table just as Esther came into the room, her hands full of little bottles and boxes.

"I thought I'd help you, dear," she said with a smile. "Not that you aren't beautiful already, but I believe this special occasion demands special touches."

Then to Leilani's amazement, the woman who never wore powder and rouge opened her containers to reveal those very beauty aids, together with charcoal for the eyes. "I know you already have black lashes, but a little emphasis on the eyelids will accent the brilliant blue of your eyes." And then she proceeded to apply her creams and powders with the flair of an artist.

"Oh, I don't know," Leilani began, hardly recognizing the face that stared back from the mirror. Her eyes seemed more almond tipped even as they appeared larger, their long thick lashes giving them a mysterious quality. Her high cheekbones, accented by rouge, were a lighter tone than her lips. Her image in the glass was beautiful, and Leilani was suddenly hesitant.

"Perfectly acceptable for formal occasions, I assure you," Esther said, moving Leilani's stool so she could step around it. Then she began on Leilani's hair, brushing it until the strands gleamed under the electric lights she'd switched on in order to see better. A short time later Esther finished, and turned Leilani back to the mirror to view the results.

Leilani stared, unable to believe the confection of curls and waves, more elaborate than any style she'd ever worn. Yet it was also relaxed, so that some of the curls trailed down the back of her neck, and others fringed her forehead and ears, framing her delicate features with their blackness, and accenting her beauty. Her blue eyes had never been more vividly blue, her skin more porcelain perfect.

But Esther wasn't done yet. She insisted upon a corset. "It will enhance the curves of your figure in the right places," she stated in a matter-of-fact tone, and Leilani suppressed a smile. The doctor's wife was full of surprises, and so different from her Hawaiian mother, who felt her daughter was beautiful without any artificial help.

Rather than argue, Leilani complied as the older woman produced a tiny, strapless corset, and explained, with a wry smile, that she'd once fit into the thing. After the corset was fitted over her chemise and laced and hooked, Leilani stepped into her lacy drawers. Finally the silk gown was lowered over her head and adjusted into place. Only then did Esther allow her to view herself in the mirror.

The vision in the glass took Leilani's breath away. The silk gown fit to perfection, although its plunging neckline revealed the top curve of her breasts, which had been pushed upward by the corset. Her waist was so small it would easily fit into the circle of a man's hands, and the skin of her arms could be seen through the gauzy lace of the full sleeves. The gown was deceptively simple, its only adornment the deeper blue satin ribbon that circled her tiny waist, and trimmed the wide hemline and fitted wrists. The splendid material, which shimmered with a silver sheen under the electric light, flowed over her petticoat in a cloud of iridescent blue that complemented the brilliance of Leilani's eyes.

"Thank you," Leilani managed, humbled by the masterpiece the kind woman had created. "I—I can't believe it's me." Her eyes met Esther's. "I couldn't have looked like this without your help."

"Nonsense," Esther replied, but she was also pleased by the overall result. "And I'm not finished." She stepped to the bed where she'd placed a small jewelry box. "My family had means," she began, and popped open the lid. "I was given these on my eighteenth birthday because my father said they matched my eyes." She smiled, remembering. "But the blue of my eyes is nothing compared to yours, my dear." She held up a sapphire and diamond necklace before she moved back to Leilani and clasped it around her neck.

"But I can't wear something so valuable," Leilani protested.

"Of course you can, dear," she said, brushing aside protests. Then she took out matching earrings, which she proceeded to clip onto Leilani's ears. "Now, that's better." Esther stepped back, examining her handiwork. "You'll be the most beautiful girl there, Leilani, and don't you forget it when you walk into the palace, with your head high."

Tears threatened, and Leilani blinked quickly. "I don't know what to say. No one has ever been kinder to me than you and Dr. Pete." She hesitated, gathering her composure. "I love you both very much."

Esther's eyes glistened and she, too, blinked. "And we love you, Leilani, we always have. Remember," she began softly, and hesitated. "Today begins a new era, and you are the symbol of the new Hawaii. You are what being Hawaiian will mean one day—having Hawaiian, Chinese and *haole* blood in your veins."

Then Esther left her alone to step into her matching satin slippers, check her silver-mounted chatelaine bag for her handkerchief and eau de cologne and find her lace shawl. Finally it was time to go downstairs. Leilani was sure Rand would be waiting.

"That's it!" someone in the crowd cried.

The final display of fireworks splashed a pattern of dramatic light across the sky above the palace, and Leilani, caught up in the historic moment, knew the dying dazzle of color symbolized the dawning of a new Hawaii. It's sad, she thought, and sensed that Rand felt the same, for his arm had tightened around her as they stood within the pressing crowd of spectators. It was common knowledge that Queen Liliuokalani wasn't present for the passing of her monarchy. She, and the heir apparent, Princess Kaiulani, together with other prominent *alii*, were gathered at her private residence, in their grief unable to accept invitations to the ceremonies.

"Are you all right?" Rand whispered next to her ear.

She nodded mutely, somehow beyond words at that moment. He pulled her closer, sheltering her within the circle of his arm, her side pressed into his. And then all she could think of was him.

Dressed in black formal attire, his white pleated shirt with stand-up collar accented by a black bow tie, he looked more handsome than ever. From the moment she'd seen him in the Peterson hall, her heart had fluttered erratically each time her eyes met his. And now she was suddenly more aware of his lean body under his finery than of the celebration all around them.

"It's okay, darling," he said softly. "Hawaii will only grow stronger." He bent his head and brushed his lips across her cheek. "Are you ready to go inside?"

She raised her lashes, and instantly her eyes were caught by his. Her cheek burned from the touch of his mouth, and her mind whirled from his endearment. Leilani could only nod, hoping he mistook her uncertainty for the drama of the history unfolding around them. But she'd never been more aware of him, of his strong brown fingers on her bare elbow, the long hard body of the most attractive man present. She willed herself to take her emotions in hand. It wouldn't do to enter the elegant palace, which now belonged to the United States, trembling and hesitant as a schoolgirl.

"Say! Is that you, Rand?" a man said nearby.

Both Rand and Leilani turned toward the voice, just as a wiry Chinese man and young woman came out of the crowd to pause before them. The man, around Rand's age, was dressed in formal attire and the young woman in a high-necked red silk gown, her hair piled up in an elaborate Oriental style.

"I didn't expect to see you here, Lee," Rand said, his tone warm. He turned to Leilani. "This is my law partner and friend, Lee Chun," he told her.

"We only came to watch the fireworks," Lee explained, his round face creased into a friendly smile, his voice sounding as cultured as Rand's. He glanced at Leilani. "Of course I know who you are," he added. "Everyone in Chinatown knows you." He gave a brief formal bow. "I'm pleased to meet you."

Leilani was intrigued. She, too, had heard of Lee Chun, although he wasn't as well-known as Rand for his success in helping the Chinese, and she supposed that was because Lee was Chinese himself, without much legal clout.

She smiled and held out her hand. "The pleasure is mine, Mr. Chun." She was aware of Rand's eyes on her, and a glance told her his expression was pleased, and warm with—what? she wondered. If she hadn't known better Leilani would have thought—*love.*

"And this is my fiancée, Annie Quong," Lee went on, indicating the young woman at his side. "Annie is an English version of her name," he added with a laugh.

The girl smiled, then put out her hand for Leilani to shake. "I, too, hear of you," she said in broken English. "Kini is cousin. Family appreciate you saving Kini from *haole.*"

Surprised, Leilani shook her hand, taking an instant liking to the slight young woman. Lee looked on, pleased, then went on to explain that Annie and her family had recently arrived from San Francisco, that their marriage had been arranged since birth.

"I see," Leilani replied, and tried not to show her disapproval of that tradition. Even if she'd been raised Chinese, she would have rebelled against such a marriage. She must love the man she married—if she ever married, she corrected herself.

"We'll see you again," Lee said, as the crowd around them began to move, the fireworks being over. "I must see Annie back to her family." He indicated a cluster of Chinese people standing off to themselves, watching.

With final grins and bows, the two moved away, leaving Leilani aware that she was the focus of Rand's amused gaze, not the retreating Chinese couple. She glanced, annoyed that he always seemed to find something funny about her. This time she decided to be direct.

"Did I say something to amuse you?" she asked, more tartly than she intended.

He grinned then, unable to help himself. He turned them toward the steps to the palace, and as they walked, he explained. "I was tickled by your reaction to Lee. I gathered that you don't approve of arranged marriages, eh, Leilani?"

"No, I don't." She paused, glancing up into his face. "How did you know?"

"Your expression," he drawled smoothly. "Your reaction showed."

"Oh Lord!" she cried, stopping in her tracks. "I hope I didn't insult them."

"They didn't notice," he said, his gaze moving over her face to rest on her lips. "And even if Lee did, he would agree with you. Believe me, had he not fallen in love with Annie, he wouldn't marry her. He's more Western than Eastern in that regard."

Leilani licked her lips, aware of his eyes, and the little embers that glowed in their dark depths. She suddenly wondered if he were remembering when he'd kissed her. And then his gaze locked with hers, and the banked-down embers flared into fire, as though they'd captured all the energy from the brilliantly illuminated palace behind him. He still held her arm, and suddenly he took hold of the other, as though he meant to embrace her, crowd or not.

"Rand?" she said, her voice so low it seemed to vibrate on the fragrant night air. "Isn't it time to go inside?"

He stared into her delicate face, hearing her words while he struggled to quell the urge to pull her back to the buggy and take her away from the crowd . . . and make love to her. He'd been fighting his desire for her ever since she'd swept down the steps to meet him, so beautiful was she that his breath stopped in his chest. She was a queen, a creation of exquisite femininity. She'd smiled, composed, yet somehow vulnerable. And in that moment nothing else had mattered but possessing her. Rand wondered about her mystique, her ability to attract him, how each time he saw her he wanted her even more than the last time.

He took himself under control. He'd stayed away from her these past weeks, believing his attraction would wane, so that when he saw her again he could trust himself to not make love to her. He was drawn to her, wanted to be with her, but he knew he couldn't compromise her without a commitment. And he wasn't ready for that, not when his wife's death still haunted him with feelings of guilt, that somehow he might have prevented her accident.

Finally he managed a grin. "Yes it is," he told her. And at that moment he knew he would eventually get over his feelings of the past. But he still had his father-in-law's loss to consider, and he couldn't do anything too quickly, not until the man began to recover from his grief.

But I will have Leilani, he told himself. Because he couldn't bear the thought of her belonging to anyone else. She would be his.

Then they went into the palace.

"You're the most beautiful woman at the ball." A familiar male voice came from behind Leilani as she waited outside the throne room in the wide hall for Rand to return with something cool to drink.

She turned quickly, and met the appraising stare of the man she'd once believed she loved. "Elwood Benton," she said, surprised because she hadn't seen him earlier during the reception when Rand had introduced her to President Dole and other dignitaries.

She had danced the first dance with Rand, but had been asked to partner so many other men that she'd been unable to manage another dance with him. He'd only grinned, and whispered in her ear that it would be an insult to refuse the prominent men who asked, and added that he would dance with their wives. Somehow their little conspiracy had given her a good feeling. Instead of being shunned as she'd feared, she was accepted, and she knew it was because she had come with Rand. No one would dare insult the woman Rand chose to escort.

Elwood gave a mocking bow. He was shorter than Rand and had gained weight with the years, and although he wasn't fat, his face was plump. His hair had receded, his mouth looked too thick, and Leilani wondered how she'd ever imagined herself in love with him. Now she could easily read him as weak, a man of no real substance.

"It's amazing we haven't met in these past five years," he went on. "But I haven't forgotten you, Leilani. I've thought of you often."

She smoothed her gown, and wished she'd gone upstairs to the powder room. "I've been in the city the whole time," she replied, her tone cool. She wished he'd move on. They had nothing in common now, and she didn't like the way his eyes traveled up and down her figure, resting on her breasts.

"Is that so?" He brushed a hand over his hair, as though he were nervous. His formal suit wasn't a good fit, being too tight around the waist so that it emphasized his extra pounds. "I suppose I should have called on you, after my parents calmed down."

"You did the proper thing, Elwood. Your parents were right." She hesitated, wishing him gone. "In any case you would only have upset them again if you had."

"Oh come now, Leilani." His voice wasn't deep, and for the first time she noticed his whine. "I hope you aren't still mad."

"Of course not, Elwood," she said primly. "To tell the truth I haven't thought about you in years."

Anger glinted in his eyes at her insult. But before he could say more, she picked up her skirts, bade him good-evening and then moved around him to meet Rand, who'd come into view.

"Do you know Elwood?" he asked, glancing at the man who watched from down the hall. He handed her a cup of punch.

"Did," she replied, and met his eyes. "Years ago when I was still a schoolgirl. We were . . . friends."

"I see." He suddenly put down his cup so he could tip her chin and look into her eyes. "Is that all?"

His tone had an edge, as though he were—jealous? she wondered. But she kept her gaze level, unwavering. "Yes, Rand, that's all. There was a short time when I imagined there was more, but it was only a crush, after all." Her long lashes fluttered, but she smiled and he saw her sincerity. "His parents didn't approve."

Their gazes seemed to intensify, blue fire and black glowing coals. The notes of a dreamy waltz flowed out of the throne room, where the dancers, in all their color and glitter, swirled

over the floor like paints on an artist's palette. Voices and
laughter and music blended into one sound that faded into the
Hawaiian night. And something unspoken passed between
them, something more intimate, more binding, than all the
kisses and touches they'd experienced together. Then Rand
took her cup and placed it with his, and, grabbing her hand,
he led her back to the dance floor, where he pulled her into his
arms.

He held her close but not against his body, and they moved
in perfect rhythm over the floor. Ever so slowly his grip tightened, until her breasts were pressed to his chest, his breath a
soft tickle in her hair. They were alone even as they danced
among the other couples. Their legs touched with each step,
and Leilani felt his muscles ripple even with their clothing between them. It was as though they floated over the polished
surface, swirling and dipping in a dance apart from anyone
else.

Abruptly the music ended, but for a moment longer they
clung to each other, unable to speak of the need clamoring
within them. Leilani, aware of several curious glances, was the
first to step back.

"Thank you, Rand," she whispered, still tingling from the
sensations he'd tantalized to life, that screamed silently for her
to be in his arms again.

A slow smile touched his lips. "Thank you, my darling."
Then he shook his head, his eyes catching the light, so that
they branded her with fire. "You're a sensational dancer."

The music began again, but before Rand could claim her
once more, Elwood cut in with a polite request for the next
dance. About to refuse, Leilani wasn't able to when Rand
stepped back, giving the other man his place.

Momentarily disconcerted, she allowed Elwood to escort her
onto the floor. When he pulled her into his arms, and began
the dance holding her too close, Leilani strained backward.
"Please loosen your hold on my waist," she told him curtly.

"You didn't seem to mind being held close a few minutes
ago," he retorted. But he relaxed his grip and they continued
the waltz, Leilani hoping it would be short so she could make

her escape. She no longer even liked Elwood. With a start she realized he was talking to her.

"I've never gotten over you, Leilani. I'd like to see you again, maybe start over with our relationship."

She looked him straight in the eyes and was blunt. "That's no longer possible, Elwood."

"Why not? Once you were crazy about me."

"I was a young girl then, not a woman," she retorted, unable to hide her annoyance.

"And you're a woman now?" he asked peevishly. "Are you involved with Rand Walsh?"

"None of your damn business!" Leilani drew back but his hold had tightened again, and she was a captive, at least for the waltz. "How dare you ask improper questions!"

"I'll dare much more!" he snarled, his hazel eyes filled with sudden anger. "Rand isn't for you, my sweet. He's vowed never to remarry, and if he did it wouldn't be to you, I assure you."

The music stopped at that precise moment, and Leilani stepped back, her cheeks hot with indignation. Without a word, she left him standing on the floor.

But when she reached the sidelines, she couldn't locate Rand anywhere in the room. Deciding he was probably still out on the dance floor, Leilani took the opportunity to go to the powder room, hurrying up the steps before someone stopped her. Shaken, she needed to compose herself before she faced Rand again. Somehow Elwood's hateful words had struck home. She knew Rand desired her, but did he love her? A great shudder went through her, but she would not allow herself to face the truth. To do so would mean more hurt. *I'm not in love with Rand.*

After a few minutes she was calmer, having decided that Elwood was just being cruel because he was jealous. By the time she went back to the ballroom she was anxious to be in Rand's arms again, having decided not to worry about whether or not he would remarry. Time would take care of that, she told herself. He saw her the moment she stepped into the room, and she realized he'd missed her, was in fact looking for her— and she felt better.

Just as she reached his side, another man, accompanied by two elegantly gowned women, strode up to Rand and slapped him playfully on the back.

"Hey, old man! You forget your own brother so soon?" The man stepped aside so the women could move forward. "Look who's with me."

"Stella! For heaven's sake! When did you arrive in Hawaii? Last time I saw you was in New York."

Then Rand remembered his manners, and, dropping an arm around Leilani's waist, drew her into the family circle. "Leilani, I'd like you to meet my older brother, Louis, his wife, Nancy, and Nancy's sister, Stella Young from the United States." He indicated each one as he introduced the three people, and Leilani felt their questions, and their interest about her involvement with Rand. "And this is Leilani Kauwe, who graciously accepted my invitation to the ball," he ended with a quick smile at her.

"I'm happy to meet all of you," Leilani said, pleased that she sounded gracious and educated, as the women before her looked sophisticated and vaguely disapproving.

Then the conversation started up again, Stella explaining that she'd planned the trip to visit her sister and brother-in-law for a year—that she was delighted to be in Hawaii at such an exciting time.

"I didn't know you'd be here tonight, or I'd have made arrangements," Rand told his brother. "But of course you're welcome to stay at my house."

"Of course." Louis, a handsome man who resembled Rand, although he was slightly shorter, grinned. "We've already deposited our baggage there. I knew you wouldn't mind, and Stella wanted to surprise you."

Rand cocked a dark brow at Stella. "Still the prankster I see," he drawled.

A flattering pink blush stole into Stella's face, giving her blond, green-eyed looks an even prettier cast. Leilani knew in that moment why Stella had really come to Hawaii. *She wanted Rand.* Then one of the men Rand had been talking to asked Nancy for a dance. She accepted, and Louis turned to Leilani.

"Would you do me the honor?"

His smile was genuine and Leilani sensed he was a nice person, if curious about her. She glanced at Rand, saw that he was about to ask Stella. She nodded at Louis and smiled her acceptance.

They all moved onto the floor, and as the music began, Leilani found herself in a conversation with Rand's brother. She managed to evade talk about herself, as he filled her in about their steamer being late from Maui, and then about Stella, who'd known Rand during the years he attended Harvard. Leilani smiled and offered comments when appropriate, and knew he didn't suspect her sudden feelings of being the extra person in the group.

She found her eyes lingering on Rand and Stella, who laughed and talked while they danced. It was apparent that they were fond of each other, and Leilani could understand if Rand found Stella attractive, because she was—extremely so. From her brilliant green velvet gown to her emerald jewels to her coiffured hair, the tall slender woman was a perfect foil to Rand's dark looks. And her honest evaluation of Stella was the last straw for Leilani. With crystal clarity, she knew that if Rand ever remarried, it would be to a woman like Stella.

The wonder and promise of the evening, of being with Rand, dancing in his arms, went flat for Leilani. Later, when he drove her home, he didn't linger, as he'd done on past occasions, as though he couldn't bear to let her go. Instead, he walked her to the Petersons' front door, saw that it was unlocked and then said his good-night.

"I had a wonderful time, Leilani," He stood in the shadows, a hand on each of her arms, and simply looked into her face. His expression was unreadable, unlike when they'd danced and he'd held her so close.

"Thank you, Rand. It was a day I'll never forget. A memorable time, and I can't think of anyone nicer to have shared it with."

She willed herself to turn into the house, because she felt he was anxious to return to his family, who'd already said they'd wait up for him. "We have lots to talk about, darling," Stella had said as Rand helped Leilani into the buggy.

Still Rand hesitated, and she wondered what he was thinking. Perhaps how he could end the evening in a friendly manner? she thought suddenly. So she took matters into her own hands to end it for him. On tiptoes she leaned forward and kissed him lightly on the cheek.

"Good night, Rand," she said softly, and before he could respond, went into the house and closed the door behind her. Then, quietly so as not to awaken the Petersons, she went to her room, tears trembling on her lashes.

Chapter Six

Once the sovereignty of Hawaii was transferred to the United States, Honolulu underwent many changes. Citizens of the republic of Hawaii automatically became citizens of the new territory and of the United States. Since most Orientals hadn't been citizens before annexation, they were excluded under territorial status, much to Leilani's disappointment.

But that can change now that we're American, she reminded herself as she went about her work in Chinatown. Yet she was disturbed by the new policy. There were rumors that the Chinese settled their own grievances within their community, as the courts weren't interested in the plight of the *Celestials* unless a *haole* was involved. Leilani knew Chinatown didn't have the criminal element of tong lords as San Francisco did. But she also knew that could happen if the Chinese didn't gain equality under the law.

Representing the sugar planter on Maui under the new political regime, Rand spent most of the autumn months at his branch office in Lahaina, leaving his Honolulu clients in Lee's capable hands. Even though he came by Dr. Peterson's office when he was in town, and once accompanied Leilani and the doctor to a local community meeting concerning law and order in Chinatown, Leilani was rarely alone with him. Often she wondered if his reason for spending so much time on Maui was Stella.

"I'll be away most of the time until after the first of the year," he told Leilani one afternoon when he stopped by the doctor's office. "It's business and unavoidable," he added when she only nodded, careful to hide her feelings.

"I understand, Rand." She continued to fold bandages. "I know you have an office in Lahaina. Besides—" she glanced at him, pleased that her voice sounded completely normal "—it's nice that you're able to spend the holidays with your family."

He lowered his lashes, hooding his eyes as he studied her. She's so goddamned in control, he thought, irritated because he was trying to say something important. He knew her well enough by now to understand that she retreated behind her expressionless facade when she wanted to hide her real feelings. To protect herself? he wondered suddenly. It was only at times like this that he saw her Oriental heritage, and something about her features reminded him of someone, but he couldn't think of who.

Unable to help himself, Rand moved to her and took her into his arms. With her body pressed to his, her face tilted upward in surprise, he kissed her, claiming her mouth as thoroughly as a branding iron burned its mark to prove possession. Abruptly he released her, satisfied by what he read on her face now. For a second he'd doubted she cared about him at all.

"I'll stop by each time I'm in town," he told her, his tone low and edged with banked-down passion he couldn't keep from his eyes as he looked at her. A strand of her long hair had loosened from its pins, and her lips were bright pink from the pressure of his mouth, but her eyes were still wide and questioning. "And we'll talk then," he added. He wished he could make love to her until she had no questions left. Yet even as he thought about it, he knew he had to go slowly with her, make sure he was doing the right thing.

She was about to reply when the doctor came into the room. Instead she resumed her work, and contrived a friendly tone of voice usually reserved for patients. "Please give my best to your brother and sister-in-law," she said, and managed to keep her poise as well.

This time he nodded, but his eyes narrowed, and she wondered what was going on in his head now. She was just glad the doctor hadn't burst through the door a minute sooner. Then Rand plopped his top hat over his thick black hair, and after a salute that took in both Leilani and the doctor, strode out into the November afternoon.

Unsettled for the rest of the day, Leilani was relieved when it was time to go home. But later, when she thought about Rand's visit, her hopes soared again. He didn't have to come to the office and say what he had—unless he cared about her. And that thought sustained her through Thanksgiving and into December.

Although Leilani was busier than ever seeing to her nursing duties, her thoughts often drifted to Rand. Knowing she had to be sensible, she would force herself to concentrate on other things, like her patients, and her young brothers, who often needed big-sister advice. Mama Kauwe stopped asking about Rand when Leilani was noncommittal, but Leilani saw her mother's puzzlement.

It was hard when she went to bed and the night splashed its shadows across her bedroom walls, and brought back mental images of Rand's handsome Polynesian face. She didn't understand him, yet she realized that he hadn't promised her anything either, except a talk sometime in the future. He'd only taken her to social events, never expressed anything about deeper feelings. Maybe all men wanted to make love to the women they escorted, she thought finally. Maybe his "talk" meant revealing feelings for Stella, not her. When time went by and she didn't hear from him, she vowed to put Rand Walsh into perspective.

While Leilani rarely saw Rand, she often ran into Elwood, much to her annoyance, for she suspected he made a point of accidentally meeting her. He worked in the family shipping office near the waterfront and would turn up at Dr. Pete's about the time she was done for the day. The first couple of times she had no option but to allow him to walk her home. As he was there more often, Leilani changed her schedule, so that she saw some of her patients on the way home, and wasn't in the office when Elwood came by. But he soon caught on, and managed to find out the location of her appointments, so he could waylay her. Finally, she asked him to stop doing so, told him that she didn't desire his company. Although he tried to convince her of his good intentions, he did finally comply with her wishes and stopped bothering her. But she was afraid he hadn't been put off by her words and was only considering another tactic.

Then she forgot about Elwood completely when Rand came into the office one afternoon in mid-December and invited her to a Christmas party. It had been an especially hectic day. She felt in disarray, having given up on her hair, which had loosened from her chignon so much that she'd brushed it out in her haste to finish her work. She heard the office door open, but as there were still patients waiting, she assumed it was only another one. When she glanced up and saw Rand, framed in the doorway, a half smile curving his well-defined lips, one black brow arched to give him a rakish expression, Leilani's heart stopped pumping.

"Hello, Rand," she said calmly enough once she was over the first shock. But she was suddenly conscious of her hair, her rumpled cotton dress and the heat she knew flooded color into her cheeks. She blinked nervously, and willed herself to remain outwardly composed, because his dark, suddenly hooded eyes missed nothing. Leilani was reminded of the day he'd found her at the falls—when he'd looked at her in exactly the same way, as though he wanted to make love to her.

The thought only disconcerted her more, and she reminded herself that she had work to do, patients to direct into the doctor's examining room. Abruptly he stepped farther into the room and closed the door. A couple more steps and he stood before her, his eyes warm—and glad to see her.

"Have you missed me, Leilani?" he asked, his tone so in command that she was even more unnerved.

Shaking her head, Leilani smiled, suddenly determined that he would not take control of every conversation she ever had with him. "I've been so busy working that I haven't had time to think of anything else." She hesitated, as though considering. "But yes, I suppose I have missed seeing you." She raised her own brows. "And I know my two little brothers have missed your visits. They've both asked after you and I told them that you were on Maui with your family." Her words gave her pause. She wanted to add—Stella.

Their eyes locked, hers carefully innocent, his abruptly uncertain about her feelings after all. Again he was brought up against the barrier that was so Oriental he couldn't see beyond it to whatever was the truth.

"Are you back in Honolulu now?" she asked, the first to break the silence that filled the space around them.

He shook his head. "Only for a few days. I'm going back for Christmas."

"Of course," she replied, and tried not to feel so hurt. Why shouldn't he spend Christmas with his family? she argued mentally. But she knew why she felt so bad. His answer had only pointed out where she stood with him. She wasn't a part of his life, the important part . . . family.

Lifting her chin, she forced another smile. "I'm looking forward to Christmas, too. We have so much planned, there are so many parties to attend, programs, and of course we cook a feast for all the Kauwe relatives." She knew she was babbling but didn't care. "Our Christmas is a Hawaiian version, with a little Eastern influence thrown in," she added with a laugh. "But it's always a great celebration of fun."

His smile had gone stiff, and it occurred to her that he might be feeling what she'd felt when he'd explained about his Christmas.

"Well since Christmas is almost upon us, I was hoping you'd attend a party with me," he drawled, his voice abruptly lower.

His request took her by surprise, again putting her at a disadvantage.

"A party! Sounds like a great time!" Dr. Pete had opened the door to usher a patient from the examining room, and overheard Rand's last remark. "Of course Leilani will go," he added after nodding a greeting to Rand. "Christmas is a time for parties." Then, his eyes crinkling from a wide grin, he shifted his gaze to Leilani. "Tell this young man you'll go with him, so we can get on with our work."

Rand's mouth quirked at the corners, and she knew he held back a grin. As she hesitated, uncertain, knowing she might be saving herself from future grief by simply refusing, the doctor prodded her again.

"Do you good, Leilani. You work too much for a young woman." He looked Rand in the eye, his expression sobering. "Besides, she needs a strong hand. Even I don't approve of all she's involved with now." And then he motioned to a young man who'd injured his leg to follow him into the other room. About to close the door, Dr. Pete glanced back to Leilani. "Bring some of the bandages right away."

Gathering a handful, she was about to follow, when Rand put a hand on her arm, stopping her. "What's this you've been doing that the doctor doesn't approve of?" he asked. His eyes were no longer warm, but cool and demanding an answer.

"Oh, he's just teasing," Leilani evaded, knowing very well that the doctor meant her interference when several Chinese men, recently arrived from San Francisco, had threatened shopkeepers who wouldn't pay for protection.

When his reply was to tighten his hold—because he guessed she was avoiding an answer—she could no longer meet his eyes. She said the first thing that came to mind—her acceptance of his invitation.

Then the doctor called again, and Rand had to let her go, although he still looked unconvinced. But he told her that he'd come to get her on Friday night at six, that dress was formal, and they'd talk further at that time. He strode to the door, then turned to watch her disappear into the examining room, determined that he would find out just what she was up to. If the doctor didn't approve, then Rand was certain she was involved in something dangerous.

Damn! he thought angrily as he hurried toward his office. Leilani did need someone to take her in hand—and make her obey the rules of safety. But he knew she wouldn't be easy to convince, especially when she thought she was helping the Chinese.

Rand kicked a pebble out of his way. He would make her see reason, he vowed. Someone had to. Before she got hurt.

Going to the party at an elegant oceanfront mansion was a disappointment, and Leilani wished, almost from the start, that she hadn't agreed to go. Rand came to get her, again at the Petersons.

He was taken aback when he saw Leilani come down the steps, gowned in crimson velvet, her hair in a casual style that fell in soft waves around her face and down her back. The gown was long-sleeved and high-necked, but it molded her full breasts and fell from her tiny waist into a wide sweep that flattered her slender figure. She had never looked more exotic, more mysterious and more sexually desirable to him. He saw the expectancy on her face and hated what he had to tell her.

"I'm afraid we won't be going alone," he told Leilani as he helped her into her long matching cape.

Something in his tone alerted her. Whatever he was about to say she knew she wouldn't like. Meeting his gaze, Leilani waited for him to go on, and tried not to think about how devastatingly handsome he looked in his black formal suit.

"My sister-in-law came over to Honolulu for some final Christmas shopping, and brought Stella with her." He hesitated, choosing his words carefully, aware that Leilani's whole body had stilled. "Nancy is at my house resting, but Stella wanted to come with us. So I couldn't refuse."

For a second Leilani stood in stunned silence, feeling humiliated in a strange way she couldn't define. Then anger hit her, but she concealed it, knowing she would be the one who looked bad—no, jealous—if she expressed it. Instead, she pulled free as he was about to direct her out the door.

"You should have sent a message, Rand," she said, pleased that her voice didn't give away her feelings. "It's Christmas and these things happen. I would have understood you having to change plans." She started to unfasten her cape, determined that she wouldn't accompany him now. *How dare he!* she fumed.

Taken aback, Rand suddenly knew he'd insulted her, and he felt awful. He'd been put in an awkward position, and Stella, although nice, was pushy. She'd brushed aside proprieties, that it wouldn't be right to accompany him on a date with Leilani. Goddamn it! he thought. It was his fault, allowing himself to be manipulated by Stella. But he was determined that Leilani was going, Stella or not.

"Nonsense," he said, quickly overriding her objections. But he noted that Esther Peterson, who'd answered the door, looked askance, as though she couldn't believe his nerve. He suddenly was even more annoyed with Stella, and vowed that she'd never take advantage of him again.

His jaw set determinedly, he took Leilani's arm, depending on her good manners to avoid a scene in the Peterson house, and guided her out to the two-seat buggy. When Stella would have remained on the front seat, he asked her, politely but firmly, to move to the back seat, as Leilani would be sitting next to him.

She complied without protest, but Leilani felt the woman's malicious stare all the way to the party, and wished herself anywhere else but in that buggy. Believe me, she told Stella mentally. Next time you can sit next to Rand—because I won't be here.

They pulled up to a brilliantly lighted house, a low elegant building sheltered among flowering shrubs and graceful palms, its sloping roofs covering a long veranda with wide double doors open to the jasmine-scented night.

"Oh, lovely!" Stella cried as Rand helped her from the buggy after Leilani. But when they walked up the steps to the front entrance, it was Stella who clung to Rand's arm, while Leilani walked sedately at his side. And once more she felt the outsider and wondered what she was doing with such people.

To make matters worse, Elwood was also among the guests, and although she could hardly stand him now, it was a relief when he attached himself to her. Leilani struggled through the meal, having been seated opposite Rand by the hostess, while Stella was placed next to him. Once the many courses of dinner were over, the group retired to the parlor, and after coffee was served, they listened to Christmas music sung by a local church group. Leilani found herself counting the minutes until she could leave.

Elwood, seated next to her, had watched her all night and wondered why she was with Rand and Stella, and when Leilani didn't explain he came to his own conclusion—that they'd had the date before Stella came on the scene. He smiled secretly. He suddenly felt he had a second chance with her.

When the program was almost over, he bent to whisper in her ear. "I'll come by your office soon. I'd like to invite you to a New Year's ball at my parents' house."

Leilani stiffened as he spoke. How dare he invite her out when she was with another man! It was terribly disrespectful of him. Even if she wanted to go with him, which she didn't, she wasn't going to be humiliated again. Although everyone present had been nice to her, they were also aware of the unusual arrangement of Rand escorting two women.

Turning to Elwood, she told him in no uncertain terms not to bother—that as she'd explained in the past, she wasn't interested in an alliance with him. Her words were meant for only his ears, but his instant anger was apparent by the tightening of his features.

"If you think Rand is serious about you, Leilani, think again." His return whisper was little more than a hiss. "If he marries anyone, it'll be Stella!"

And then he stood up, excused himself just as the music ended and stalked from the room. Aside from her high color, Leilani stayed composed, as though nothing untoward had happened. Let them think what they want! she fumed behind her calm facade, not for one second letting her humiliation show.

But one person had noticed the entire scene, and was angered, both at Elwood and at himself. Rand knew Leilani was furious, that she probably would never speak to him after tonight, and he didn't blame her. It was all his fault. But her damnable pride hadn't allowed him to make it clear to everyone that she was his date, not Stella. Even though he'd explained to their hosts how it had happened that he was escorting two women, he saw that they all favored Stella. And Leilani's aloofness—*her allowing Stella to take her place*—hadn't helped matters. He, too, was relieved that the party was ending, so he could explain.

As their buggy was brought for them, Leilani noticed Elwood also waiting for his. Rand stepped forward to help Stella first, as she was to sit on the back seat. "I'll drop you off straightaway, as I'm sure you're tired, Stella," he said, and his voice sounded stiff and strained.

"But darling," she protested. "Leilani's house is closest. Taking me home before her will take you out of your way."

It was the final humiliation. Even Elwood had hesitated, listening to the exchange before stepping into his two-seater. Leilani moved forward, her eyes blazing even though her voice was steady. "I can solve this problem quite easily," she told Rand coldly. "You both go home together." She glanced at Elwood, who was still watching. "I'm sure Elwood will see me home instead."

For a second her gaze met Rand's shocked eyes, and even as she watched, his brow darkened with anger. In fact, she'd never seen him look more upset. The hell with his feelings! she fumed. He hadn't considered hers. The last thing she could do at that moment was sit in that buggy with Stella, and struggle with the tears that threatened to overwhelm her.

After her hastily spoken thanks to her hosts, and a final glance at Rand, she spun around and let Elwood help her into his buggy. A moment later they were off down the driveway, leaving the others staring after her.

I don't care, she chanted over and over under her breath. How could Rand have humiliated her like this? Because he doesn't love me, she thought suddenly. And the next thought devastated her. She loved him.

Somewhere in the back of her mind Leilani had entertained a hope that Rand would seek her out and explain, but as Christmas came and went she knew it was a futile expectation. Even though he'd placed her in an awkward position, she had insulted him before his friends when she left the party with Elwood.

Elwood had been another mistake, but he'd behaved like a gentleman and taken her straight home, although he'd started pressing her to accept his New Year's invitation. She'd finally convinced him that she was too uncomfortable to attend a party his parents were giving.

Leilani saw in the new year of 1899 with her family and little brothers, and then went to bed to lie sleepless until morning.

Upon returning to work in January, Leilani was told by a Chinese seamstress that dark-coated men had demanded money from her, threatening bodily harm if she didn't pay.

"What?" Leilani cried, glancing up from the woman's little girl, who was recovering from an upset stomach.

The small Punti woman nodded, anger touching her face as she went on in broken English. "Work hard, can't afford pay bad men." She shook her head vigorously. "Not just me, missy. Bad men want money from dry-goods emporium, laundry and vegetable seller." she spread her hands. "Husband said maybe bad men are highbinders, maybe work for tong lord. We must pay, or get hurt."

Leilani's anger was instant. "There are no tong lords in Hawaii—or highbinders—and we don't want them, either!" She forced herself to be calm, so she wouldn't frighten the woman further. "Don't pay anything," Leilani told her, realizing that the "bad men" the seamstress referred to must be the newcomers from San Francisco who'd tried the same scheme before. "And I'll find out who these men are and put a stop to this—this robbery!"

The woman nodded, but she didn't promise. It was obvious that she was badly frightened. As Leilani went back to the doctor's office, her anger grew, until she decided she must call on the storekeepers and merchants herself and inform them of their rights. Criminals mustn't get a stranglehold on people already unprotected by the *haole* law. If only the Chinese had been offered citizenship, she thought for the hundredth time. Then thugs wouldn't believe they could get away with preying on their own people.

During the day she made her plans, and after she left work early she made the rounds of the businesses, telling the owners not to succumb to the black-coated extortioners, convincing the fearful, hardworking Chinese that the demands were not those of a tong lord. She reminded them that there were no tongs in Honolulu, that they must band together and as a unit refuse to be intimidated, because one day soon the law would change and they would be citizens.

Several days later Leilani heard that the people had decided to stand up to the thugs, mostly because they couldn't afford to give their precious pennies to someone else. As she went among them, she felt their good wishes as never before, and was pleased, and proud of them. They were good people, and she knew they'd make their place in Hawaii yet.

Life settled back into the rhythm of Chinatown, and Leilani hoped the thugs had been stopped for good, because their tactics hadn't worked. By Chinese New Year, celebrated the night of the second new moon after the winter solstice, she was convinced that they'd seen the last of the black-coated men. Alone, she watched the end of the fireworks show from the street in front of Dr. Pete's office, for her parents and brothers had already gone home. It had been a wonderful day of parades and song and celebration, and the dazzling display in the sky was a fitting climax.

About to go into the Peterson house, Leilani was suddenly aware of a man's cries in a darkened alley across the street. Horrified, she watched as he was dragged out of sight by two men dressed completely in black. Without hesitation, she ran after them, having recognized the victim as the husband of the seamstress who'd first told her about the suspected highbinders.

But once inside the alley, away from the crowd, Leilani knew she was in trouble. One of the men held the trembling victim against a clapboard wall, while the other man, a long knife gleaming in the moonlight, advanced on Leilani. She'd walked into a trap!

Then a shot rang out, and the man with the knife jerked to a stop, his gaze darting behind Leilani where a buggy had turned into the narrow alley. Instantly, the two assailants whirled around and ran the other way, disappearing into the clutter of shacks that lined the passageway. The victim, shaking uncontrollably, managed a bow of gratitude before darting around Leilani, and then fled past the buggy that had jerked to a rocking stop next to her. She turned, and her gaze collided with Rand's.

He stuffed the pistol into an inside pocket of his frock coat, muttered an oath, then jumped to the ground beside her. She stepped back, more frightened by the grim set of his features than by the two who'd accosted her. She'd never seen Rand look so determined, so upset and angry. She was suddenly reminded of his Polynesian ancestors, who would fight to their deaths if they believed they were right.

Without a word of greeting, he grabbed her and lifted her into the buggy, leaping up next to her so that she couldn't escape on the other side.

"Rand!" she cried. "What's the meaning of this?"

"For God's sake!" he retorted harshly. "Need you ask?"

He glanced at her once before he jerked the reins. With one hand on her arm to hold her against him and the other controlling the horse, he soon had them out of the alley and moving down the street toward the waterfront. He looked so forbidding that Leilani held her tongue. But as they headed toward Diamond Head she protested. His reply was to set his jaw more determinedly, and urge the horse to a faster gait. As they reached the beach, he reined in the animal so abruptly that the buggy rocked alarmingly as it came to a jolting stop.

The moon hung in the sky, casting long, shimmering silver ribbons across the surface of the Pacific Ocean. A few other people were strolling along the beach, as it was early and the strip of sand was near the city. It wasn't a private spot and for that Leilani was grateful. In the face of Rand's anger she didn't want to be alone with him.

He twisted on the seat, bringing up his other hand to grasp her in an even tighter hold, so she had no option but to look at him. To her chagrin, she found it hard to hold his gaze when his face was only inches away. The moonlight seemed caught in his black eyes, giving him an even more sinister expression. This was a Rand she'd never seen before.

"What in the hell did you think you were doing, Leilani?" he asked sharply, suddenly breaking the silence.

She licked her lips, as annoyed with him as she was aware of his lean body so close to hers. Beyond them the surf was like the rhythm of endless pagan drums, above them a coconut palm swayed as the wind rustled its fronds, and nearby she could hear the faint chatter from a group of people.

He shook her, and his touch wasn't gentle. "Answer me!" he commanded harshly. "Didn't it occur to you that the man might have killed you?"

"I saw them drag a man I know into the alley. I tried to stop them, that's all," she retorted crisply, not liking his tone one bit, even though she did recognize that her action had been foolish. She'd acted before she thought. She should have called for help instead. But she didn't admit that to Rand, and as she thought about him, she became angry herself. How dare he chastise her after that fiasco of a party he took her to—and then he hadn't talked to her since.

"You need to *think* before you act in such a rash manner," he began, his tone cutting, and before he could continue, she interrupted.

"You think I should have left him to ruthless criminals? Perhaps men who are controlled by a vicious tong lord?" She gulped a ragged breath. "You don't care what might have happened to that poor man, do you?" Her accusation sounded shrill, but she went on, too angry to consider the possibility that his fear was for her, and that he might be even more upset by the overall implications of the incident. "If I hadn't run after them the man would be dead right now!"

He sucked in a sharp breath, as though he could barely control himself. He knew these were probably the same men she'd crossed before—the very involvement the doctor had disapproved of. "I forbid you to be embroiled in this, Leilani. These men are dangerous, and we don't know what or who is behind their actions."

"But we do know that you're more intimidated by terrible men who are out to gain control of their poor countrymen, than by the helpless victims!"

The absolute silence that fell between them was like the split second before a cobra strikes with fatal consequences. Fear rippled down Leilani's spine. She'd gone too far. And from the dangerous set of Rand's features, the bruising grip of his hands on her arms, she knew that only the presence of the others on the beach saved her from his own vengeance.

Abruptly he grabbed the reins, then signaled the horse so hard that it reared up before leaping into motion, back down the road toward town. They rode in grim silence all the way to Dr. Pete's house, where Rand gave the reins another yank, stopping the animal so fast that the buggy again rocked dangerously. In seconds Rand was on the ground, lifting Leilani down before she could protest and climb out herself. Then he walked her to the door, his forbidding expression precluding protests.

Abruptly, before she could escape, he twisted her around, and after a meaningful stare, pulled her to him and kissed her, a bruising kiss that left no doubt about the magnitude of his anger. As his mouth lingered, her lips parted of their own volition, and instantly his tongue was inside her mouth. His arms tightened, until she thought she couldn't take a breath, until her senses reeled from the sensations he wrought in her.

When he released her, Leilani would have stumbled backward but for the sturdy door behind her. She brushed the back of her hand over her trembling lips, and her lashes swept down to hide how deeply his touch had affected her.

"Think about that, Leilani," he told her harshly. "Then consider what it is I care about. And in the meantime, stay out of criminal activities that are beyond your ability to deal with—because I'm already taking care of them."

Then he was gone and she went into the quiet house, suddenly trembling so that she had to grasp the banister as she walked up the steps to the bedroom the Petersons always reserved for her.

But mostly she longed for Rand to finish what he had begun . . . making love to her.

Again Leilani went about her work, and she heard through the seamstress that her husband was grateful, that the leaders in Chinatown were working with Rand and his partner, Lee, to stop any criminal activity that would prey on its citizens. But she didn't see Rand herself, and wished she hadn't accused him unfairly. She knew her words had sprung from her own fear of the two men who'd threatened her, and of her uncertainty about Rand's feelings.

When she returned to the office one afternoon a week later, Dr. Pete looked up and grinned at her.

"Your—uh—friend, Rand, was here and missed you, Leilani. Said he was on his way to Maui again. He didn't mention when he'd be back, but said to give you his best—that he was pleased that you'd been staying out of trouble." The doctor grinned knowingly at her, an impish glint in his blue eyes. "Whatever that means."

Leilani shrugged, contriving a casual manner. "I'm sure I don't know," she replied. "Rand is an enigma at times."

"That he is," the doctor agreed, and then they both became busy with the next patient, who'd walked in the door after Leilani.

But Leilani was thoughtful. She'd run into Kini and Kini's cousin, Annie, Lee's fiancée. They'd talked a minute and Annie had mentioned Rand's family, that Nancy's sister, Stella, had extended her visit indefinitely.

And now Rand is back on Maui, Leilani thought as she tried to concentrate on her work. She knew that Stella meant to manipulate Rand into a betrothal. But maybe Stella wasn't manipulating; maybe Rand was a willing participant. Didn't he go to the plantation willingly? she asked herself, feeling even more confused.

Sighing as she led the patient into the examining room, she tried to banish thoughts of Rand—because they were upsetting. She knew he was attracted to her, wanted to make love to her, and she was finding him harder and harder to resist despite all their conflicts. But when it came to commitment, if he even would commit again, would it be to a woman with unknown origins?

Or to Stella?

Chapter Seven

At first Leilani didn't believe it. But then she started paying more attention as she hurried through the narrow streets and alleys of Chinatown. She finally had to face what was happening. She was being followed.

But she could never catch anything more than a glimpse of her stalker—a shadow in a doorway, a movement from the corner of her eye. It was the very way the figure vanished and then reappeared in another doorway that alarmed her. Even though she had turned on occasion and run after the person, all she ever found were empty alleys and closed doors, the clutter of shacks that was Chinatown. Her elusive shadow was a coward, she thought, at first angry, then gradually fearful. Finally she began to wonder if she was imagining things, because she'd been so frightened by the two men who'd accosted the seamstress's husband—the night Rand rescued her.

One evening as she walked home along the road to the farm, a man's voice came from the wild shrubbery that lined the path. The whispered words were harsh and stilted, and they desecrated the beauty of the peaceful evening. "Stay out of Chinese business—or suffer consequences!"

Startled, Leilani stopped in her tracks. "Who's there?" she demanded, despite the ripple of fear that spread gooseflesh all over her body. There was no answer, but she was suddenly aware of the remoteness of the road, that there wasn't a house in sight. A stillness seemed to hover over the land, as though it were waiting—for what? she wondered, her body poised for flight. But which direction was the safe way to run?

Then the sound of a twig snapping and movement beyond the wall of foliage put wings to her feet. Leilani was flying over the ground before her mind even registered her action, her footsteps keeping time to her wildly beating heart. She didn't stop until she reached the clearing where the last rays of sunshine still illuminated the Kauwe cottage. Only then did she glance behind her. As she suspected, no one was in sight. But now she knew the phantom was real; she'd heard his voice.

There was no point in scaring her family. But she knew she must tell Dr. Pete now. Surely someone was only threatening her, she rationalized. She couldn't be in danger, for she'd always been safe no matter where her job took her.

Her anger was slow to creep up on her fears, building an intense resolve within her. No faceless man would scare her from her work, even if her work meant encouraging poor field hands and shopkeepers to stand up to criminals. She must be succeeding, Leilani thought with a flash of satisfaction, or the thugs wouldn't be threatening her. Yet as she went into the house to join her family, her apprehension lingered. She could very well be in danger.

Then, the next morning, after letting herself into the doctor's office, she hung up her wrap and was about to begin her work when her gaze fell on a sheet of paper that lay on her chair. Thinking Dr. Pete had left her a note, she picked it up and was shocked to read the scrawl in black ink: Obey or Die.

Fear was an icy touch on her flesh, a flutter in her chest and prickles down her spine. Leilani was suddenly aware of the deathly quiet in the office. The examining room beyond the half-closed door looked shadowy and ominous. The doctor hadn't come in yet, which was unusual. She was alone.

She stood frozen, fearful that someone was lurking in the next room, watching her. Leilani forced herself to stay calm, and knew she must get out of there. She backed toward the front door, her eyes fastened on the opening to Dr. Pete's surgery. Her thoughts spun with questions. How had the intruder entered the office? It had been locked, and there was no back entrance.

Leilani's hand was on the knob, about to twist it when it turned in her hand. The door suddenly burst open behind her, propelling her into the middle of the room. A cry of sheer terror tore from her throat unbidden.

"My dear!" Esther cried, rushing into the room, her arms filled with linen. "I'm so sorry to have frightened you."

"Esther!" Leilani gasped, and tired to take deep breaths so that she could speak coherently. Oh God! she thought. There was still the surgery—where an intruder might be hiding. She had to get them out of there.

But it was too late. Esther was already pushing the door wider and a moment later was inside the room, talking all the while. "I'd hoped to be here before you arrived, Leilani," she said as Leilani followed her into the room, her gaze everywhere at once in her fear for Esther's safety.

No one was there. The room was empty. Then how had the note been placed on her chair? *How had anyone entered the office?*

She took slow deep breaths, her relief tremendous. She only half listened to Esther, her thoughts spinning with questions. She wondered if she should inform Esther that someone had been in the office. But Esther would immediately decide that Leilani was in danger and shouldn't be alone there. Then Esther's chattering finally registered, and Leilani forced her mind to stop racing and concentrate on what was being said.

"Dr. Pete was called out to one of the plantations in the middle of the night," Esther was saying, oblivious to Leilani's state of nerves. "The planter's wife is in labor and having problems. Pete said for you to do your best today, because he might not make it back until late." She faced Leilani after depositing the stack of clean towels on the shelf. "I'll be home all day if you need me. Otherwise just reschedule the patients who need to see the doctor. Pete said he'd start early and work late tomorrow."

Leilani merely nodded, so relieved there was no immediate danger that her limbs shook. It was an anticlimax, but she decided not to tell Esther. She wanted to get on with the day, not have another crisis because of the note. But she resolved to tell Dr. Pete everything as soon as she had the opportunity.

So she saw Esther out, just as a woman with two small children came into the office. They were the first patients, children with the croup, and then there was a steady stream of others. She only stopped once when Esther brought lunch, then continued throughout the afternoon, seeing to simple remedies she could handle without the doctor.

All thought of someone watching her was forgotten. Except for a couple of times during the day when she felt her neck prickle, as though someone were indeed watching...everything.

It was late when Leilani finished for the day, and Dr. Pete still hadn't returned. Esther had popped in to insist Leilani spend the night, then sent a rider out to the Kauwe farm to let them know. Since there was no longer a rush to start home before dark, Leilani cleaned up the daily clutter. Almost finished, she suddenly heard a rustle of movement at the front door. Instantly all her fears rushed back.

She stared at the door, horrified to see she'd forgotten to lock it, knowing she'd never reach it before it opened. Dear God! Leilani prayed. Right after Esther left that morning, she'd discovered a window had been left open overnight, thus explaining how the intruder had entered the office. She'd immediately locked it, but not the door after the last patient.

Now as it slowly opened, Leilani braced herself, fear almost stopping her heart as she raised a straight-backed chair to defend herself.

"Rand!" she gasped, her gaze fastening on the man who was suddenly framed in the open doorway, looking so different in casual, formfitting cream pants and a blue cotton print shirt that was open at the neck. His hair was windblown and his eyes startled at the unexpected vision of Leilani, about to strike him with a chair.

"What's going on here?" he demanded, and with a quick motion stepped into the room and closed the door. As she hesitated, momentarily frozen with relief, he took the chair and placed it on the floor. "Who were you expecting, for God's sake?"

"Oh, Rand," she managed. "I'm so glad to see you." Her words trailed off, and she was horrified to hear that her voice shook, and to feel a sudden sinking sensation that robbed her limbs of strength. She felt like a rag doll that had lost its stuffing.

For a second longer he studied her pale face, the delicate features that were tense with fear, the nervous flutter of her long lashes. He wondered what had happened, then he remembered why he was there. Lord! he thought angrily. She was obviously already in danger!

Before she even had time to reply, Rand took her into his arms, holding her close against his chest. When he'd returned from Maui, Lee had told him more about the Chinese men from San Francisco, criminal types who wanted to gain a foothold in Honolulu. Rand had given himself a mental kick, because he'd believed he and Lee had discouraged such an attempt before he left the city last time. But now both he and Lee were concerned that a tong lord might find the city fertile ground for crime. Lee was also upset because he suspected his future father-in-law of being behind the whole thing. Mr. Quong had made it clear that Rand must prevent Leilani from interfering, or Lee would not marry his daughter, Annie.

Leilani's body relaxed against Rand, and she felt his arms tighten. The shadows were deepening as night approached, and she thought in passing that she needed to turn on the electric light. But somehow she couldn't stir herself from the long hard strength of Rand. For the first time in many days Leilani felt safe.

Horses trotted along the street, and two men walked down the sidewalk, their voices fading as they passed. From a tree beside the building, night birds began to sing. But the familiar sounds seemed far away to Leilani, who could think of nothing but Rand, who held her so tenderly.

"I wasn't expecting anyone," she murmured, finally able to answer. "But I'd forgotten to lock the door and—" She broke off, uncertain of what to tell him. It all sounded so elusive, so intangible.

"And you thought I was the bogeyman?" His words were low, almost as though they caressed as they soothed. "Don't worry, sweetheart, I won't let him get you." He tilted her chin with two fingers, so that he was looking directly into her face. When his lips curved into a slow seductive smile, Leilani knew her knees would have buckled had he not held her so firmly to him. He was so darkly handsome, looked so pagan with devilish lights dancing in his eyes. "Believe me," he drawled wickedly, "I'm not giving up my hold without a fight."

Before she could do more than open her mouth to reply, his lips closed over hers, drowning her words in a sea of sudden ecstasy, a need that canceled all other thoughts from her mind. At first tender, his kiss suddenly deepened, and his tongue was tickling her lips, tantalizing her so that she was kissing him back, silently begging for more.

"My darling," he murmured as he lifted his lips briefly. "My brave little foolish darling." Then he feathered her face with kisses, tracing a line of fire across her cheeks to first one ear, then the other. Her eyelids were next, and as his warm breath tickled her skin, little sensations of desire made themselves known in her stomach, and in the most private part of her between her thighs. Her body strained closer, seeking something more, something that was as yet unfulfilled.

Then his hand moved slightly so that he was stroking her breast. Instantly her nipples swelled beneath her bodice, responding to his touch. She moaned softly, her mouth opening under his as he once more claimed her lips. Somewhere in the back of her mind Leilani knew she should stop him, that his touch wasn't proper, but at that moment, after all that had happened, she only wanted more. Proprieties were the last thing on her mind.

"You're so beautiful, so sweet," he whispered between kisses. "And you must be careful, my Leilani. You can no longer confront criminals." His mouth closed over hers, passionately, as though punctuating his soft murmuring. "It's not a job for a young woman," he went on, his breath ragged as his excitement grew.

Her own senses reeling, Leilani nevertheless heard him, and the words jolted her from the lethargy of his lovemaking. She suddenly realized his words were a warning, not just endearments. She twisted her face so that her lips were free, then she struggled until she was able to step back, although he still held her within the circle of his arms.

"What did you say?" she managed shakily, intensely aware of his slumberous eyes, the strange hypnotic fires burning in their depths.

He tried to pull her back to him but she resisted. His words had shattered the spell, and brought her back to her recent fears so abruptly that her emotions were still spinning. She licked her lips, and tried not to think of his. When she spoke, her words had no volume. She began again.

"How did you know that the—the awful, evil men are still trying to intimidate poor people? You've been gone."

He saw how concerned she was, and then he remembered how she had greeted him. Rand suddenly knew much more was happening than even Lee knew. He put his desire for her aside for the moment and directed her onto the chair she'd used as a weapon. Then he sat down next to her.

"Lee told me about these guys," he began, and hesitated, wanting to hear what she knew first. "And what they've been trying to do—gain control over the illiterate Chinese."

Raising her lashes, she looked him in the eyes, her fears suddenly reflected in the wide-eyed brilliance of her stare. Then her deepest concerns flowed from her, all on one long breath. "Do you think a tong lord is behind it, Rand? We've never had one in Honolulu, or their highbinders who kidnap and murder for them. Now that we're part of the United States, and the Chinese have a chance of citizenship in the future, we can't allow that kind of criminal here." She hesitated, feeling overwhelmed by her feelings all at once. "Or people in Chinatown will suffer because of those thugs." She took a shuddering breath. "I've tried to influence people to stand up to them, not pay them."

He took hold of her again, but this time his hands on her shoulders were not caressing, nor did his hard expression resemble the one he'd worn only seconds earlier. "I heard that too, Leilani." He hesitated, wondering if he should be blunt. Abruptly he decided scaring her might be the only way of keeping her out of the problem. "You're in danger of being kidnapped yourself, Leilani. Sold into slavery, or worse."

Her eyes widened even more. "Then this is a tong lord?"

"I don't think so, but perhaps he sees himself as one. This man and his henchmen are new to Hawaii, and we'll put a stop to their aspirations of power and control, but we have to catch them first, and convict them." His eyes glinted like sun on black stone. "You're right about one thing. We've never had that type of criminal here, and we won't stand for one moving in on us now."

"Do you know who's behind this?"

Rand glanced away, as though considering how much he would tell her, then again decided to be direct. "We think it's Mr. Quong, Annie's father. He was involved in such activities in San Francisco—and was forced to leave there under threat of his life."

"The father of Lee's fiancée?"

"That's right, Leilani." He stood abruptly and strode to the window, beyond which the night was enfolding the city. "We can't prove anything at the moment. And this is hell on Lee, as Mr. Quong has given him an ultimatum."

Leilani stood too, fascination blending with fear, but overpowered by a need to hear everything. At least she knew that her own phantom was real—and dangerous, she thought with a shiver of apprehension.

"What is the ultimatum?"

He turned back, his eyes burning into hers. "That I put a stop to your interfering, or Lee will never marry Annie."

"My God! That old bastard!" She didn't even register her own use of profanity. "I'm sorry for Lee, but I hope he told *Mr. Quong* to go to hell!"

"No, he didn't, Leilani." Rand hesitated, and despite his own deep concern, humor at her choice of words flashed momentarily in his eyes. A moment later it was replaced by an even more determined look than before. "I'm here to tell you to stay out of this whole mess."

"What?" Anger added color to her face, already flushed from his kisses. "Surely you aren't telling me to let them bully people I care about, are you?" She stared, unblinking and horrified. Why would Rand allow himself to be their pawn, to relay yet another warning to her? To help Lee? Surely Rand wasn't involved in some way himself, she told herself.

But she also knew such an ultimatum wouldn't have been given, not to mention the scare tactics, had she not been successful in encouraging a rebellion against such thievery. Maybe Lee was involved, too. Hadn't she first seen Rand with Madam Silk Stockings? She backed away from him, too angry to think things out, or realize that Rand was only worried about her.

"And do you also know about the black-coated men who follow me everywhere?" she flung at him. "And the coward who threatened me from his hiding place in the bushes, or the burglar who left the note that said *obey or die?*" She gulped a quick breath, and disregarded the growing shock on his face. "But you just tell them that they aren't scaring me off, because I—unlike others I could mention—care about these Chinese people who work from dawn to dark for next to nothing! And I won't see them giving those hard-earned pennies to anyone, whatever the threats!"

And to her horror, she burst into tears.

The next second she was in his arms again, sheltered against him, as though she were his most precious possession in the world. And that made matters worse for Leilani. She didn't belong to him, and she was probably only imagining his tenderness. She couldn't stop the flow of tears no matter how hard she tried. Leilani knew they sprang not just from her feelings for Rand but from the accumulation of frightening events.

She lay against Rand, spent. Slowly, but with growing realization Leilani was stricken with another truth. She loved Rand despite everything, even though she knew that love was hopeless, for many reasons, one of which was Stella.

Suddenly fearful that she was too vulnerable, that her face might reveal her feelings, she tried to break free, to get away from him. She couldn't have him guess. It would be her final humiliation.

"You're coming home with me," Rand stated grimly. "There are some things we need to get straight—immediately."

And then he led her out to his buggy. Too shattered to argue, Leilani went with him, knowing she'd probably regret it. She didn't need one more sorrow in her life.

Chapter Eight

Leilani had never been to Rand's house, and now, as the horse turned into a long driveway lined with flowering hibiscus, jasmine and oleander, she had qualms. But the perfumed air was like a drug, numbing her already fragile state, and she didn't give voice to her feelings. She could see the two-story house, which had been built at the crest of a slope with a sweeping view of the Pacific Ocean, truly a location in paradise. Night was almost upon them, poised at that moment when the world was suspended in silhouette, caught between light and darkness. As though time had stopped, pausing between what was and what would be.

Nonsense, she told herself, and wished she'd had the willpower to resist going with Rand. Even when they were in the buggy and Esther came from the house to see if she'd finished for the day, she'd had the chance to change her mind, and hadn't. Instead she'd agreed when Rand had said he was taking Leilani out for supper, that he'd see her back at a respectable hour. Esther had only smiled and nodded and gone back to the house. And Leilani had been committed for the evening.

Committed to what? she wondered, watching while Rand reined in, jumped from the buggy and tied up the horse. Then he helped her down, holding her for a moment longer than was necessary, his expression, guarded perhaps?

The trade wind blew in from the ocean, bringing the fragrance of the sea, and faraway places beyond the horizon. A strange feeling of unreality took hold of Leilani as she walked with Rand onto the veranda, waited while he opened the door, then stepped into a wide elegant hall with a sweeping staircase that curved upward to the second floor. The koa walls and floor gleamed like polished mahogany while the huge crystal chandelier cast prisms of light over everything. Double doors were open to the parlor on one side of the hall, and she could see it was beautifully appointed with French furniture, cream papered walls and crimson-upholstered settee and chairs that matched the velvet drapes on the windows. An open door on the opposite side of the hall revealed Rand's study, a room with book-lined walls and a massive desk cluttered with papers. Completely masculine, Leilani thought in passing.

During the ride from town to the outskirts along the ocean, Rand had hardly spoken, and his silence had given Leilani time to compose herself. But now, as he welcomed her into his house, she was suddenly shy, and found herself looking away from his direct gaze.

"Do you like my house?" he asked, as he ushered her into the parlor, where the long windows opened on a garden of exotic flowers. "I had this place built after my wife died, and I sold my other house." He strode to the windows to look beyond the bluff to the darkening sea, above which night was fast falling. "I wanted a place to start over," he added, and suddenly turned to her, his eyes looking black in the shadowy room.

Beyond him Leilani could see lightning flash far out on the ocean. Even though the moon was already mounting the sky, she knew a storm was on the way. But her thoughts were on matters closer at hand. Why had Rand brought her to his house? And why had she come?

"I promised Esther I'd see to your supper," he said suddenly. "But I'm afraid I only have daily help." He spread his hands, grinning. "My housekeeper has already gone to her quarters and there's no one here to cook." He cocked one black brow rakishly. "Think you can trust me to put something together for us to eat?"

Feeling on safer ground, Leilani grinned back. "Or I can fix something, while you start the fire." She indicated the fireplace where kindling had been arranged, and where he'd moved as he spoke. "Although I don't spend much time in the kitchen, my Hawaiian mother taught me how to cook—and you know she prepares a great meal," she added, injecting a lighter note into their conversation.

He stood in the shadow of the light from the hall, a tall Polynesian, somehow misplaced in such civilized surroundings. For a second Leilani again felt the sensation of time standing still, as though the old gods were waiting for the inevitable, a union preordained. She gave herself a mental shake, because she often found herself thinking about the ancient ways and beliefs—since meeting Rand.

"Right this way, madam," he said suddenly, a rich thread of humor edging his voice. Taking her arm, he directed her back to the hall, past the staircase to an archway that led to the back of the house. He switched on a light to reveal a gleaming white kitchen, then waved a hand, indicating it was all hers.

"Sure you don't mind?" He faced her, his eyes questioning. "I did invite you to eat, not prepare the meal." As she merely shook her head, suddenly too conscious of the task usually reserved for a wife, he went on, his tone abruptly serious. "After we eat, then we'll talk."

Before she could respond, he glanced away quickly, as though he didn't want to spoil their congenial mood, and walked to the stove where a pot of soup had been left simmering. "Compliments of my housekeeper," he told her, his words carefully casual. "There's bread in the pantry, and—" He waved an arm. "Everything's here, you just have to find it." His dark eyes met hers, and she was suddenly aware that they were alone in the house, and that he, like her, was avoiding the real reason for their being there together. The strange sense of unreality touched Leilani again, and she knew they would talk—when they were ready.

He left her then, after suggesting they eat in the parlor by the fireplace. He glanced back before disappearing into the hall, his words innocent enough, but his eyes hinting otherwise. "Since it's only us we don't have to observe proprieties."

She didn't dare dwell on his meaning, and concentrated on preparing the tray of food. When it was ready, she carried it to the parlor. Rand had moved a small table before the fireplace, where leaping flames splayed flickers of light into the room. The evening chill was gone, leaving a cozy setting for their meal.

Wordlessly he moved to take the tray, which he placed on the table. Then he held out her chair, waiting as she sat down before taking his place opposite her. A quiet enfolded them, broken only by the crackling flames that licked over the logs, and the rising wind beyond the windows. Still without speaking, Rand poured red wine into their goblets, then lifted his glass up. As though mesmerized by some hidden force, Leilani followed suit.

"To the future of the Hawaiian Islands," he toasted. "And to us," he added softly, his eyes holding hers, the leaping fire from the fireplace reflected in their depths.

In silence they drank, but Leilani was unable to lower her gaze, for she felt hypnotized by him. She suddenly knew their meal was only the beginning of their evening together. But the beginning of what?

The thought jolted her. As though he understood her fears, Rand directed the conversation away from anything intimate as they ate. For the next hour she enjoyed his company, so much that she forgot to worry. He told her about his boyhood growing up on a plantation on Maui, his years at the university in Boston, and finally about his marriage and his wife.

"You remind me of her," he said, his eyes reflective. "Not in looks, but in manner and gestures." He didn't add that Leilani was far more beautiful, lovelier than any woman he'd ever met.

They finished their meal, and he lit a cheroot, sitting back in his chair, his expression obscured by smoke. Leilani hadn't eaten much, not because the food wasn't good but because she was too nervous, too aware of the man across the table.

"It must have been terrible for you when she died," Leilani said softly during a lull. She lowered her lashes, screening her eyes so that he wouldn't see how sad she felt—because he'd been deeply affected by his wife's death, and she realized he might never love another woman as much.

"It was," he replied, and took a sip of wine. "I felt responsible."

"How is that?" she asked softly, seeing his pain. Their eyes locked, and time stretched as he contemplated her question. Outside the wind strengthened, shuffling the shakes on the roof like a deck of cards, and she wondered if he would share his thoughts.

"My wife was part Hawaiian, like me," he began suddenly. "She was also the spoiled only child of a planter on Maui. When she wanted something she always got it." He pulled out another cheroot, lit it and blew smoke. "I indulged her whims as well, and gave in to her wish to own a pair of spirited horses. She'd insisted they were broken enough to pull her buggy—and I took her word for it." He drew in a shuddering breath. "They bolted and she was killed when the buggy overturned."

A log shifted lower in the fireplace, sending a shower of sparks up the chimney. Leilani didn't know what to say. Instead she covered his hand with hers, conveying her sympathy through her touch.

"To make matters even worse, my father-in-law, in his grief, began to dwell on the old Hawaiian taboos, about the *haoles* being cursed if they own land that once belonged to ancient kings."

"Surely you don't believe that, do you, Rand?" Leilani withdrew her hand, sensing he was speaking for himself as well as his father-in-law.

He tossed his cheroot into the fire, staring as it burst into flames and burned. "I don't know, Leilani. Strange things happen, have happened in my own family. My grandmother, who was Hawaiian, always feared the old beliefs, because accidents seem to happen more often to *haoles* than Hawaiians. She claimed that time will ease the wrath of the old gods, but until then one can't flout superstitions."

"But your grandmother married a *haole!*"

"Precisely," he replied softly. "As did my father-in-law's mother." He paused, and the storm gathered momentum outside, blasting the house and bending the palm fronds against the windows like hula shirts in a ritualistic dance. "And if there's any truth to the legends, then I wouldn't want to put anyone else in danger."

His final words were so low, spoken at the precise moment when a clap of thunder shook the house, that Leilani didn't know if she'd heard him right. But the storm closing in propelled Rand out of his chair. "Good God!" he cried. "I forgot to take the buggy to the stable. My horse must be out of his head with fright!"

"But I'll need to go home soon," Leilani protested.

"Not until the storm passes," he replied as he ran toward the hall. A second later she heard the front door bang shut, caught by the wind.

Uncertain, Leilani picked up the dishes, placed them back on the tray, then took them to the kitchen. Busy cleaning up, she didn't hear Rand come back into the house, didn't know he was in the kitchen until his hands came down on her arms and turned her to him.

His shirt clung wetly to his body and his hair was plastered to his head. Even a droplet of moisture clung to his lashes, half-lowered over eyes that were filled with awareness of her. Suddenly disconcerted, she couldn't hold his gaze, staring instead at his chest.

Thunder rumbled above them, somehow isolating them even more from the world outside his house. He watched her long lashes flutter nervously, concealing the brilliant blue of her eyes...and her uncertainty that he'd glimpsed. As they stood, so close, suspended in the eye of the storm, he could think of nothing other than her soft body, of taking her in his arms and finishing what he'd once begun...making love to her.

She slanted a glance upward, and it was instantly captured by his. No longer was there only fire in his eyes; the ceiling light seemed superimposed over their darkness, silvering them with molten heat. Leilani's legs suddenly felt weak, and a trembling began deep within her, seeping into her limbs so that her urge to get away was undermined by the knowledge that she lacked the strength to do so. His handsome features were set into determined lines and planes, much as his Polynesian ancestors might have looked before sacrificing a maiden to the volcano goddess, Pele. Even his mouth, those lips so practiced in the art of kissing, seemed firmed by resolve. As they stood, caught in a web of awareness, the elements beyond their shelter intensified, as though they, too, demanded their own sacrifice.

For a moment longer he hesitated, gaining control of himself. Then, turning her away from the sink, he led her back toward the parlor. He pulled the settee closer to the fire, then gently nudged her onto it. Once he'd pushed the little table and chairs away, Rand sat down next to her, his mind churning with where to begin, how to approach the subject that alarmed him so much that it had even postponed any thought of love-making.

"Are you comfortable?" he asked, his dark eyes belying the casualness of his question.

She nodded. "But I will have to be going soon," she managed, equally calm despite her own racing senses. "Esther will wonder."

"She'll know you're delayed because of the storm," he said. "No one would go out into such violent weather."

His statement took away her excuse to go, and Leilani suddenly felt as if she'd lost an important point, though she didn't know exactly what the point was. "Regardless," she went on, "if it doesn't stop soon, I'll have to go anyway."

His brows arched sardonically, as though he suspected her real fears: being alone with him. But his tone didn't indicate any such thing as he began speaking, having decided to be direct, but as gentle as possible.

"Leilani, I know what you've been doing—I can guess the rest." He took a sharp breath, his eyes compelling hers to stay level. "I want you to promise that you'll avoid dangerous situations—that you'll either come to me, or go to the authorities before taking matters into your own hands." He paused, and when she said nothing, her expression suddenly unreadable, he pushed his order even further. "In fact, whether you promise or not, I insist that you keep your activities to helping the doctor, nothing more."

For a second she digested his demand. Then a slow creeping anger took hold of her. By the time she leaped up, Leilani shook from it, harder than she'd trembled from the promise of his kisses.

"How dare you tell me what to do, Rand Walsh! The mental health of my people is as important as their physical health. I'll never promise any such thing, not as long as there is no one else to help."

She backed away as he stood, too, his expression barely containing his own anger. But somehow she kept on talking, even while she knew he was becoming more upset with each accusation.

"Are you going to help? Or is Lee, whose fiancée is related to these awful men? Or are you both in cahoots with them instead, and this is just one more attempt to stop me from influencing people to stand up for their rights?"

He grabbed her then and slammed her up against his chest, so hard that the pins fell out of her hair and the breath went out of her lungs. "You dare say such things to me?" he ground out between clenched teeth, suddenly no longer in control of his emotions. Then, one hand in her hair, he forced her face upward, and his mouth came down on hers, brutally and with all the passion he'd wanted to express gently.

She twisted in his arms, but his lips only clung tighter, demanding a response. And despite her anger, a response flickered to life within her, flaring stronger than the fire burning nearby. But still she tried to resist. He couldn't talk to her like that, and then make love to her.

"Yes, I dare!" she cried, somehow breaking free. A moment later she was in the hall, flinging the front door open, rushing outside into the raging wind and rain. The buggy was nowhere in sight, so she headed toward the stable. She'd ride bareback if need be. But she had to get away from him . . . or she'd be lost. By the time she reached the building, her hair streamed behind her, and her clothing was soaked.

He grabbed her inside the stable, just as the wind caught the door and swung it shut behind him. Instantly it was so black she couldn't see his face, only feel his warm breath on her cheeks as he fought to catch his breath. They clung together, rain dripping from their bodies, panting, both too spent for the moment to do otherwise.

"Wait," he said, catching his breath, then pulling her along as he groped for a lantern, which he lit with a match from a box next to it on the shelf. As it flickered to life, the first thing she saw was Rand's set expression, tight with resolve. She'd never seen him more angry—or more determined.

Again she tried to break free, but he was ready for her this time, for his hands tightened painfully on her icy flesh. "It won't work twice, my sweet," he drawled wickedly, and then pulled her closer still, holding her body to his by the flat of his hand on her lower back. She couldn't move even an inch away.

Fear flickered in her eyes, but Rand was past heeding it. She needed to be taught a lesson about what was truth and what wasn't. And she wasn't leaving until she admitted she'd been wrong—and agreed to heed his warning. His stomach churned at the very thought of what could happen to her. But lesson or not, Rand could no longer control his soaring desire for her, *to possess her.*

He edged her toward the empty stall behind them, and kneeling, forced her down onto the soft hay. Then, still holding her, he lay down next to her, so close that their lips almost touched. The thought of her softness, her beauty, the perfection of her body he'd once seen at the waterfall, was too much for him to resist. With a low sound deep in his throat, Rand claimed her lips.

"No, Rand, no!" Leilani cried when he began to feather her face with kisses. "You mustn't do this!" But even as she pleaded, she knew that she was lost, for that great swelling need for him was beginning between her thighs, the pleasant throbbing sensation that seemed to have a life of its own regardless of all the words of protest she could muster. Her pulse beat erratically, and she could hear it echoing in her ears, feel it pounding in her neck. Despite her resolve not to respond, she moaned softly as his tongue licked her earlobes.

The sound excited him even more, and he moved so that his stomach was against hers, her breasts heaving to his chest, their nipples hard and outlined under her wet garments, and he was reminded of how they'd looked after she'd been in the pool. His body tingled with the expectation of making her his. The thought turned him hot and hard.

"Yes, yes, my little angel of mercy—my *wahine.*"

"I'm not—I'm not your woman, Rand," she whispered brokenly, but his lips stopped more words. She felt his manhood straining to her, drawn by the ancient ritual of a man claiming his woman. The thought excited her, even while it scared her. They couldn't do this. It was wrong, because he wasn't free of his wife's memory—because he wanted to punish her.

"Yes, Leilani. You're my woman, at least for tonight you will be mine."

"Rand, please," she pleaded, but her voice sounded faint, lacking conviction, and she knew why. She wanted him, too. Her body responded even as she denied. Leilani was suddenly aware of his muscled flesh, the strength of his limbs, his ridged chest, which her hands had begun to caress. Oh dear God! she thought. She couldn't help it, wanton as it was. Then her hand moved lower over his flat stomach, and her secret woman place constricted in a pleasurable agony. She wanted him, needed him. More than anything else in the world, she wanted Rand to make love to her.

Yet, still a tiny inner voice told her no, that she could regret what was about to happen for the rest of her life. Because she loved Rand didn't mean he loved her.

"Please what, my darling?" he murmured against her lips, his hands feathering over her breasts, cupping first one, then the other. "We can't stop now. You don't want me to stop, I can tell. You want me as much as I want you," he crooned, his voice a soft lyrical whisper in her ear. Then his hand moved lower still, and stroked her where no one had ever touched her. Even though her skirt and underthings were between his fingers and her flesh, she felt him, a hot, searing touch that branded her forever.

A low moan grew from deep within her, escaped her lips into his mouth, and she felt his excited response.

He moved again, so that his body covered hers even as one arm cradled her so that his weight didn't crush her. Neither of them was aware of being wet, and of the sprigs of hay that clung to them. His mouth returned to hers, his tongue probing until her lips parted to allow it entrance. Instantly his kiss deepened, and they moaned together as his tongue thrust deeper, demanding much more than the surrender of her mouth.

Vaguely she knew the storm raged around them, that a horse shuffled his feet in another stall, and that the lamplight flickered from a draft, creating strange images on the stable walls. But Leilani was only aware of Rand, his mouth, his touch, his words and his eyes that missed nothing. She craved him now, the soft folds between her thighs tingling and moist, building sensations that demanded a release, one she didn't understand. But she knew it had to do with the hot bulge in his crotch that strained to her. She was suddenly overpowered by pure lust to know him completely.

Yet she still hesitated, that voice within her surfacing once again with a warning. She wondered about herself—how he had the power to possess her so completely without having taken her body. Was that what love meant? she asked herself. She'd never experienced such intense feelings before, certainly not with Elwood. The thought of him almost made her smile; he had only been a girlish crush.

Then with a clarity born on a moment of pure truth she knew her feelings for Rand were right—she loved him. She wanted him because of it. And somehow her reasoning took away her fears, even if his motive wasn't love for her.

Sensing the change in her, he hesitated, lifting his head so that he could look into her eyes. She met his gaze, her own open and revealing . . . and filled with sudden trust. It was almost more than he could bear. The brilliant blue of her eyes had never been more startling against her black shimmering hair that lay around her head like a halo. Her flawless skin was flushed from the desire he read on her face, and her lips were parted, as though they begged for more kisses. But when she reached to gently stroke his face, tracing the line of his lips, then his hooded eyelids, he couldn't stand it. His lashes lowered and his breath came in short bursts, and his body was suddenly in pain, because it needed to be joined to this woman, to stake his claim on her as no other man had...or ever would, he told himself grimly.

"I'm going to love you, my darling," he whispered hoarsely, and his breath was a caress on her flesh that ached for him. "I can't let you go now, you know that, Leilani, don't you?"

She could only nod, her eyes slumberous and filled with unashamed desire for him.

"Do you want me inside you?" he went on, tantalizing himself as much as her. "Do you want me to take your maidenhood, show you how love feels?"

She licked her lips and tried to speak, but she couldn't. Her body trembled and waves of sensation shuddered through her. Her long thick lashes lowered to rest against her upper cheeks. "I'm—I love you Rand." Her voice was a soft plea, a whispery song that did something deep inside him, pierced him with the timeless knowledge that he'd never known her kind of love before.

His kiss was long and demanding, but it was also tender, as though she were the most precious woman on earth. And then Leilani was truly lost. She would deny him nothing. She arched to him with a little animal sound, and he responded with more kisses, to her ears, her neck, and then lower to her breasts. Leilani's very nerve endings jolted a response to him, her veins tingled for him and every cell in her body seemed to strain for his touch.

"Sweet Jesus! How I want you!"

And with those words Rand raised himself enough so that he could unbutton her waist and remove it. She watched, her long lashes half-lowered over eyes heavy with longing, as he pulled down her skirt and petticoat. Her chemise and underthings were next, and all the while Leilani lay against him, unresisting, while her rapid breathing gave rise and fall to her breasts. He pulled off her shoes, then gently massaged each foot, his touch so erotic somehow, that Leilani was even more on fire, sparks of sensation coursing through her veins so that her whole body seemed to crackle and burn from its heat. Finally she was naked, her body exposed to his devouring eyes, glazed by the fever of passion that inflamed her even as the cool night air caressed her hot flesh.

He couldn't help himself, he crouched over her, his mouth on her nipple, gently suckling as though to claim each inch of her as his own. Then he moved to the other breast, his tongue sliding over the hard bud for the first time. She moaned under him, her body straining and twisting with desire, her eyes closed, her lips parted. Slowly, his mouth traced a path of fire over her stomach, lower to her pubic hair, lingering to know its texture, before going lower still.

Leilani cried out, the intensity of her need too much to be borne as his tongue took that part of her, too, in a silent torment of ecstasy that drove her beyond the limits of endurance.

He lifted his head to glance at her beautiful face, and at her agonizing need for release. He felt a satisfaction such as he'd never felt before—she was *his woman*. And then he needed to be one with her; nothing else could ease his own throbbing agony and desire.

Her hands clawed at his back, her head turned from side to side, and as he moved upward once more, she pulled his face to hers, so that she could have his lips on hers. This time it was her tongue that thrust into his mouth, demanding and searching for the release she longed to have, even while her thighs strained into his. New sensations rocked through Rand. He couldn't wait any longer. He tore his mouth from hers and her eyes fluttered open.

"Love me, Rand. Love me now—because—because I can't stand the torment. Oh God! *I want you!*"

Rising to his knees, Rand tore off his wet shirt and threw it aside. He stood to remove his shoes and pants. Once he was naked his movement stopped abruptly so that he could gaze down at Leilani, who waited, seeing his manhood for the first time. The thought gave him pause, and as he drank in the vision of womanhood at his feet, her breasts even more perfect than he'd imagined, trembling under his gaze, Rand was momentarily awed. She was so beautiful, so absolutely flawless, each curve and hollow exactly as it should be. Her legs were long and shapely, all the way up to her private place that would soon enfold him. Time was momentarily suspended as they devoured each other with their eyes; he thinking he'd never seen a woman so ready for the ultimate in love; she thinking he was a pagan god about to accept the sacrifice of her maidenhood.

And then they waited no longer.

His manhood thrusting toward her, demanding her softness, Rand sank to his knees beside her, his low groan torn from his lips. His desire almost beyond control, he still delayed the moment, allowing their need to soar to the edge of their limits. He caressed her, his fingertips feathering her velvet skin, then kneading her breasts gently, stroking her stomach to trace a fiery touch lower to the cloud of black hair that protected her soft femininity. While his hands tantalized her flesh, his lips found hers, kissing her long and deep. His mouth moved over her face, his tongue licking and teasing, then sliding down over her neck to her breasts where he captured first one bud, then the other, nipping and sucking until the quivery sensations were Leilani's whole universe.

Savagely, she pulled him to her, his chest against her breasts, and kissed his lips, straining to him, female to male, somehow feeling protected by his weight, his strength. But still she was unfulfilled. She yearned—demanded—deeper gratification. Nothing but total surrender to him, to his manhood, would satisfy her now.

"My darling," he murmured, his voice ragged.

Rand's hardness, hot and throbbing, pressed into her softness, his legs entangled with hers against the hay. As one he turned them sideways, so that his free hand could tickle down her back, over her thigh to the warm folds of her womanhood. When he touched her there, an animal sound escaped her lips and she pushed herself against his hand. He felt her wetness, and knew she was ready for him. His self-control, hanging by only a thread, snapped. He had to possess her or explode.

He poised himself above her for only a second, while they gazed into each other's eyes. It was a look that held the promise of eternity within a moment. Rand nudged her legs apart, then hesitated again, even as he throbbed for entrance.

"Are you sure, my darling?" he whispered, compelled to ask, because she was so innocent yet, and so trusting.

Her mind filled with him, and every cell in her body was alive with longing for the mystic joining of man to woman. Her eyes fluttered shut and she begged him to take her. "Please, Rand," she whispered urgently. "I can't stand this agony. I want you—all of you—*now!*"

"Oh God—yes!" Then, using iron restraint, Rand lowered himself into her, aware of hurting her, that she was still a virgin.

The pain of his penetration was gone almost before she felt it. But she welcomed the sensation, for it heralded another that transported her into a higher dimension of insatiable desire. She became one with him, as his muscle and flesh joined hers. She welcomed her fulfillment, arching to meet him, matching his movement as he thrust even deeper into her.

I love him, she chanted, as each of his rhythmic plunges accelerated her in an upward spiral of exquisite, unexplainable need for release, a place unknown to her. He murmured love words even as he panted and groaned in his own ecstasy.

The storm beyond the high rafters of the stable raged unabated, charging the air with static electricity. The thunder was like the pagan drums of long ago, beating out their song of surrender to the ancient gods. But the elements couldn't compare with the rising sensation of passion between them. Leilani cried out again and again, as her body writhed into sensual oblivion.

And then, with a wet rush of heat, her body convulsed as something went free within her. The soft folds that held Rand to her contracted with involuntary spasms of pleasure, the sensations triggering Rand to his own peak. He shuddered, at that moment completely vulnerable, and spilled his climax into her.

She lay in his arms, still pressed against him, but completely spent. She would never have believed the fulfillment of love could bring such contentment. At that moment she knew she wanted to spend every night for the rest of her life with Rand. She would never tire of his love, would always want more.

When Rand moved finally to prop himself so that he could look into her face, Leilani felt bereft. She wanted the moment to go on forever, even though reason said it couldn't.

"Thank you, my darling Leilani," he whispered lovingly. "You are the most beautiful woman—in every way—that I've ever known." He bent his face and kissed her gently on the mouth. "And I've never felt this way before," he added softly and kissed her again.

Her eyes were held by his. She swallowed and licked her lips—and wanted him again. She belonged to him, even though she would never demand he observe proprieties now that he'd made love to her. Her honesty shone from her eyes as she spoke, simple words, the most beautiful in the English language. "I love you, Rand. I love every part of you." She lowered her long lashes, innocently seductive. "Thank you for loving me."

"Oh God! My darling." The words seemed torn out of him as his eyes darkened once more. And Leilani suddenly knew about the power a woman had over a man, for at that moment she was witnessing it. Yet she knew the power of love worked both ways; he, too, had that power over her.

Then his mouth was again trailing kisses of fire over her flesh, and Leilani forgot that he hadn't committed his own pledge of love. The burning desire was beginning again, for both of them, separating them from the world once more.

And as he took her, quickly this time, Rand knew the passionate woman was as fearless in love as she was in her work among the poor. The thought gave him momentary pause, as an unbidden fear pierced his pleasure. Nothing must happen to Leilani. He couldn't bear it if this woman was hurt, too, as his wife had been. "Leilani," he began.

"Shhh," she whispered against his lips. "Just love me, my darling. Talking can wait."

Then, as his passion rose to even new heights by the sensual woman beneath him, he forgot his worry. And then there was no talk. Even the turbulent weather seemed calm by comparison to their unrestrained love.

* * *

Later, after they'd dried Leilani's clothing by the fire, Rand drove her back to the doctor's house. The moon slipped out from behind the clouds, webbing the wet landscape in its silvery light. Rand held her close, and as they rode through the silence of the early morning, Leilani, in her bemused state, couldn't help but reflect that it was a moon over paradise, one made for lovers.

He reined in and saw her to the door, which Esther had left unlocked. Then Rand turned her to him, and kissed her goodnight, his mouth lingering on hers, as though he hated to let her go. Finally he voiced his fears for her, and his request.

"Will you promise not to confront those men?" he asked softly, although his tone was urgent. "They're dangerous, and I promise you I will see to putting a stop to their threats."

Still under the influence of his lovemaking, Leilani could only nod before kissing him back. The men pretending to be highbinders were the last thing on her mind as she went inside, made her way quietly to her bedroom and went to bed.

But once under the blanket she was suddenly wide-awake, her thoughts churning with the events of her evening with Rand. She realized with a start that he'd never said he loved her, for all his lovemaking and endearments. The thought haunted her. He'd made love to her without a commitment of his feelings. She remembered his conversation about his wife, that he blamed himself for her death. Maybe it was true that he had no intention of ever remarrying—even if he wasn't above making love to another woman.

She twisted and turned and couldn't sleep. By first light her thoughts had shifted to Stella. Would he have made love to her without a commitment? If he did remarry, would he finally choose Stella—because she hadn't been wanton, hadn't given up her virginity before marriage? Leilani's bloom of love wilted. But surely Rand would call on her tomorrow, and she'd know everything was all right.

She had her hope, and at that moment, only her hope.

Chapter Nine

The next morning Leilani, dressed in her typical working clothes of dark skirt and high-necked waist, went downstairs early, but Esther was already in the kitchen preparing breakfast. She glanced up as Leilani stepped into the room.

"Good morning," she said brightly, then looked closer. "You look tired, Leilani. Are you all right?"

Contriving a smile, Leilani reassured her, then at Esther's probing, went on to tell her about having supper at Rand's house, and that she was delayed in returning home because of the storm. As she poured herself coffee, Leilani listened to Esther's chatter, and allowed her to believe that Rand's housekeeper had also been present. Her own feelings too fragile, she didn't want to explain anything else. Then Dr. Pete came into the room, and the conversation switched to his patients.

Esther put breakfast on the table, and as they ate, Leilani filled him in on the people who'd come into the office while he was gone. As she finished there was a pause in the conversation. Finally Pete put down his coffee cup, and met her eyes, his gaze direct in the manner it always was when he had something important to say.

"Leilani, I know about the men who have been threatening the shopkeepers, and you." He hesitated, his blue eyes kindly behind his spectacles. "I'd like you to fill me in on everything, because I believe this is a dangerous situation."

Esther's mouth dropped open, and as she was about to speak, Pete put up a flat silencing hand, stopping her words. He wanted Leilani to explain first.

She put down her own half-finished cup of coffee, and after taking a deep breath, began with the first incident, then of imagining she was being followed, went on to the voice in the bushes and ended with the note. "So I suppose these men are out to stop me," she ended, her voice breaking despite her resolve to stay calm.

"God almighty!" Dr. Pete cried. "This *is* serious. Why didn't you tell me, Leilani? We're going to have to take steps to protect you."

"Are they—highbinders? Assassins paid to do a tong lord's dirty work?" Esther asked, horrified.

"I doubt it, from what I hear," the doctor replied, but his eyes were troubled. "We've never had that kind of criminal here in Hawaii—and believe me—" his fist pounded the table "—we won't have it now!"

A few minutes later, Leilani accompanied Dr. Pete next door to the office. Several patients were already waiting so there was no time for more discussion. Leilani was grateful for that, too drained by the doubts that had besieged her during the night. She tried not to think that Rand might have used her because he only wanted to make love to her. Leilani had known, since that first meeting in the saloon, that there was a sexual attraction between them. Surely he'll come by today, so that I'll know he's sensitive about my feelings, she told herself.

"We'll come up with a plan later," Dr. Pete told her. "And in the meantime, be careful."

Esther called them for lunch, and there was hardly enough time to down the biscuits, cheese and fruit, before the office was full again. But Dr. Pete restrained her a minute longer, and by the serious expression, she knew he had something important to say.

"I know I can't stop you from your work, Leilani," he began. "But until these thugs are put out of business, I want you to stay with Esther and me. That way we can keep an eye on you, and you won't have to walk home alone at night."

"But what about my family?" she protested. "They—"

He waved a hand, interrupting her. "Esther has already spoken to Mama Kauwe, and it's all arranged." When he saw her stricken expression, he went on quickly. "Don't worry, we didn't alarm your parents, and besides, this whole mess should be taken care of in short order."

He went into the surgery with a patient, and she gathered up her satchel to make her house calls. She hurried outside into the brilliant afternoon, the breeze from a gentle trade wind caressing her skin with the fragrance of the sea. She blocked the instant mental image of the ocean as it had looked from Rand's house. She wouldn't think of him now. Somehow she'd believed, despite all her doubts, that he would have come to her in the morning, if only to say hello, so she wouldn't feel like one of the girls who worked for Madam Silk Stockings.

She gave herself a mental shake. Her imagination was overreacting, she decided, and realized she was being unfair to Rand. She'd give him a chance. It was only her own vulnerability, her old feelings of not belonging because of her mysterious background that made her so unsure, she reminded herself. Surely Rand wouldn't have made love to her if he didn't care.

Leilani didn't see Rand during the next few days after all. But he came to the office while she was away tending a small boy with chicken pox over on Hotel Street.

"Rand and I agreed that you must not confront these men, Leilani," Dr. Pete told her seriously. "He said he'd already told you that, that he will make sure something is done, and for you not to go out alone at night until things calm down."

She merely nodded, keeping her eyes lowered on the medicine bottles she was washing, not wanting the kindly doctor to see her upset. Why hadn't Rand waited, or come back when she was there? Why did he only leave a message? Because he regretted the other night? Perhaps her fears had been right after all: maybe their cultural differences precluded his ever committing to a girl of unknown background. Leilani fought against the sudden tightening in her throat. She wouldn't cry.

"Just what is he planning to do?" Her tone was casual, not giving away her upset.

The doctor shrugged, already turning back to his work. "I don't know, but Rand will figure it out, don't you worry. Even though he's still having to be out of town, I know he'll be in Honolulu this week at least—because he has house guests."

Leilani stiffened. Rand hadn't mentioned expected company. But then why should he? she thought. She realized the doctor was talking again as he strode into the surgery. "Seems like his sister-in-law and her sister are always over on a shopping trip." He cocked a bushy brow. "I wouldn't be surprised if that Stella is setting her cap for him—and I sure as hell hope he has the good sense to resist. The woman is poison."

And then he closed the door to the examining room, completely unaware that his words had devastated Leilani. It took a minute before she had herself in hand. Then she went outside to continue her calls, hurrying along the streets, fighting tears. She couldn't stop thinking of her night of love. And she wondered if the housekeeper was gone while Stella was there, too.

The last visit for the day was to deliver heart medicine to the proprietor of the dry goods store. The old man, called So Long by the community because he'd lived in Hawaii longer than his friends, was old and in frail health. Leilani was fond of him, because he was kind and so typical of the Chinese in having worked years in order to finally own his own humble establishment.

She hesitated in his doorway because his only customers were two black-coated men who seemed to be intimidating the old man. To one side, seemingly looking through bolts of material, was another pigtailed man in a blue high-necked smock, who watched everything. A thrill of fear touched her spine. She'd walked in on the very men who'd been stalking her.

Uncertain, Leilani's mind suddenly whirled with her options. She could turn and go, because they hadn't seen her yet. But as she watched So Long cringe and realized that he'd been pleading with them, that the men had already broken the glass on the old man's only showcase, his pride and joy, Leilani's anger was instant. How dare they bully a sick old man!

"Help! Help!" she cried into the street. She attracted the attention of other businessmen nearby who, recognizing her and wondering what was wrong, were jolted into action. But she kept her eyes glued on the men in the store, knowing they could hurt So Long, and her, too.

The bullies whirled around to face her, their whole stance threatening, their black eyes gleaming like polished ebony, clashing with her own blue ones, which she knew flashed with anger. As they moved as one toward her, Leilani stood her ground, so filled with outrage that she didn't have room to be afraid.

"You warned before!" the blue-smocked man cried. "Now you pay price for interfering!"

"You're the ones who'll pay!" she flung back. "You get the hell out of here—or I'll have you strung up to the nearest pole—you—you damn bullies!"

For a second her attack gave them pause, but the one in blue spoke rapid Chinese to the others, restoring their resolve to stop her interference.

Then So Long tried to stop them, fearful for Leilani. "I pay!" he cried. "Mr. Quong stop! No hurt Missy."

Mr. Quong? Leilani's eyes widened on the man in blue. His black eyes glinted dangerously, and she knew he meant to harm her.

Then other men burst into the store, surrounding Leilani, protecting her. It was a stalemate, but after the three thugs saw that no one was backing down, they relaxed their posture, bowed and moved around the crowd and out into the street. In seconds they were gone.

"Leilani, Leilani, bad business to interfere," So Long said, his lined face crinkled with worry. "They not forget. You must be careful."

She assured him that she could take care of herself, that the men threatening him were only cowards who preyed on the fears of honest people. Then she turned to the other men who'd gathered, and although she was thoroughly shaken by the incident, she didn't let it show.

"No one should pay those men! They're criminals! They came from San Francisco and they want to cause you trouble." Her face felt hot and flushed and she wished she were safely home, but she went on with what had to be said. "They can't get a foothold here if we don't let them. You've all worked too hard to hand over your profits." She took a sharp breath, willing her racing heart to slow. "Besides, you want to be citizens of Hawaii one of these days, have your children grow up to know these islands as their homeland. That means not allowing these awful men to make trouble so that new laws in our favor are delayed."

There was absolute silence when she finished. Then someone clapped, others joined in, and then everyone was talking at once, agreeing with her. Her rush of knowing she'd succeeded in swaying them was instant. But so was her growing apprehension for her own safety. It was worth the risk, she told herself. United, they'd put down Mr. Quong's attempt to create his own secret terrorist organization, and he would ultimately fail.

After more talk, she gave So Long his medicine and turned to go. Then someone mentioned Rand's name, that he needed to be told what happened. All of a sudden Leilani felt tears well, and knew thinking of Rand was the last straw. Her nerves were frayed, her emotions spent. Quickly she said her goodbyes and left.

But the Chinese shopkeepers noticed, as they'd heard she'd been seeing Rand socially, and that there was also another woman from America in his life.

"So sad," someone said, and others nodded. They were fond of her, and so afraid for her at the same time. They agreed that they would watch out for her as she'd always done for them.

Again Leilani missed Rand when he came to the office, but she heard through the doctor that he'd been furious about her standing up to the men threatening So Long.

"What did he expect?" she retorted, although her anger wasn't directed toward Dr. Pete. "That I would just walk away and let them hurt that old man? No—never!" She flounced to the desk and dropped her things on its scuffed surface. "I won't be ruled by fear!"

"But my dear." Dr. Pete went to her and hugged her. "We're all just worried about you. Rand, too. He says he hasn't been able to get anyone to talk, because they're too afraid of reprisals. Without evidence, he's unable to have those men arrested. And there is a lack of cooperation from the authorities, who won't do anything on hearsay, especially since those involved are Chinese."

Nodding wearily, she sank onto a chair. "I know," she said. "It just doesn't seem like Rand is really doing anything." She stared at the scrubbed wood floor, not daring to face the doctor so that he could see her disappointment in her eyes . . . and her feelings of betrayal. But the doctor seemed to guess, for his next words brought her gaze to his in an instant.

"Rand also said he'd be back in the morning, and for you to be here." Pete's eyes crinkled at the corners but he managed to restrain his grin. "He was really very concerned for your safety, Leilani."

"I'll be here," she replied. "Because I want to talk to him as well. Mr. Quong and his henchmen must be stopped. I'll testify if necessary."

They discussed the situation for a few minutes longer, then they both went back to work until Esther called them for supper. As they finished, there was a frantic knock on the door, and Dr. Pete went to answer. He came back, his coat already half on. "One of my patients went into labor, and it sounds like she's about to give birth." He dropped a kiss on his wife's cheek, promising that he'd try her pudding when he returned. Because Esther was going to a church meeting in the next block, Leilani offered to clean up the dishes. A few minutes later she was alone.

It was still daylight, the sun hovering just above the horizon, when she finished putting things away. At loose ends, her mind dwelling on seeing Rand in the morning, Leilani was unsettled. The morning was her bookkeeping day, and because it would be interrupted by his visit, she decided to go next door and spend an hour working on the ledgers.

After going into the office she impulsively locked the door after her, as the sudden realization that she was alone hit her. She got started at once, trying to keep her mind occupied so that her feelings for Rand were kept in abeyance. Tomorrow she'd know how he felt about her, Leilani told herself. It would be the first time she'd seen him since he'd made such passionate love to her. Again, she put such thoughts aside and concentrated on the column of numbers.

Suddenly there was a violent knocking on the door. Startled, Leilani jumped up, all her fears rushing over her. Her legs felt shaky as she forced herself to cross to the entrance. Whoever was out there knew someone was inside, for it had gotten dark and she'd turned on the electric light.

"Who's there?" she called through the wooden barrier.

"Is that you, Leilani? This vegetable man. You and doctor treated wife when she deliver son. Now she sick. High fever. Maybe die. You come?"

She recognized his voice now, and opened the door. He was obviously terribly upset, and she knew his wife had suffered a fever after the birth. The condition must have become critical.

Leilani nodded, explained that the doctor was already out on a call, but that she'd come. She gathered her cape and medical satchel, and was about to leave a note, when he tugged at her arm.

"No time!" he cried in his singsong English. "Go now, or she die." There was no question that his concern was genuine.

For a moment longer Leilani hesitated, remembering the warnings of both the doctor and Rand. Then her pride came to her rescue, combined with rejection and anger. Rand wasn't there to protect her. If he cared so damn much, then why hadn't he made it a point to see her before now?

Because he had Stella instead, she fumed as she hurried out to the street with the man. He was busy entertaining Stella and her sister and didn't have time for her, even after the passion they'd shared.

There was no time to send word to Rand now, she thought as she rushed through the narrow streets with the slight man beside her, urging them faster.

And even if there had been time, Leilani knew she wouldn't have done it. Because she didn't belong to Rand after all.

Chapter Ten

She'd been to Ho's humble home, one of the shacks in the maze of hovels that clustered along one of Chinatown's narrowest alleys, but not at night, and Leilani became confused about direction. Clothes hung from lines tied to bamboo poles, and they danced in the wind like elusive ghosts, brushing her face as she ducked and dodged through the clutter. Many of the shacks didn't have electricity, and the lantern light that glowed from the windows hardly penetrated the darkness outside. There was no moonlight, as another storm was gathering over the ocean, and the sky had lowered, as though to protect the land, when the violence of nature was unleashed.

"Hurry!" Ho cried when she hesitated, trying to get her bearings. He grabbed her arm. "Wife in terrible danger. Hurry!" His voice sounded even more urgent, and Leilani quickened her step to keep up with him.

A dog barked, and wind quickened and Ho's wicker hat blew form his head. But still the little man didn't slow his pace. By now Leilani, who believed she knew all the hidden alleys in Chinatown, was lost. She didn't recognize anything, and wondered if Ho and his wife had moved.

Abruptly Ho turned into an opening between two shacks, and Leilani saw that it was a narrow walkway to another dwelling, more imposing than the hovels that concealed it behind their dilapidated fronts. When he reached the door, he paused, his black eyes suddenly meeting hers.

"So sorry. Please forgive. Not want wife to die."

And with those surprising words, he pushed open the door and two men stepped out. Before Leilani could do more than open her mouth, they'd each grabbed an arm, restraining her. Then a hand closed over her face, muffling her scream.

The black-coated men!

She'd been tricked! How could Ho have done this to her? But even as Leilani struggled to free herself she knew why: they probably held his wife hostage, under threat of death. Ho's fear had been real, if not the reason behind it.

Then, as she twisted and turned, someone shoved her into the shadowy interior of the house. "Do not struggle!" a man hissed in her ear. "Or be hurt!" From the corner of her eye she saw Ho take the arm of a young woman Leilani assumed was his wife, and rush outside. The door shut behind him, locking her into the musty-smelling house with men she knew were dangerous. As she continued to struggle, she was forced to the floor, a gag was stuffed into her mouth and a blindfold tied around her eyes. Then jerked to her feet once more, someone tried to bind her hands behind her, and she struck out, hitting one of them in the face.

There was a grunt of pain, followed by a jabber of muffled Chinese. Then footsteps left the hall, hesitated in the next room, only to hurry back and stop next to Leilani. Fear engulfed her, and she sensed the hand a moment before it grabbed her arm to hold it steady. She couldn't escape them, and when the needle sank into her vein, she would have cried out but for the gag. Panic filled her. They'd given her a hypodermic shot—*of what?* When the blackness behind her blindfold seemed to intensify, to press into her head, as though it were being compressed, she knew the needle contained poison. They were killing her!

And then she felt nothing at all.

Leilani had no sense of time or place when she woke up to find herself lying on the floor in a tiny cell-like room. There was no light, but a sudden flash of lightning from a window high up on the wall momentarily illuminated her stark prison. She saw that she was alone, and realized her gag and blindfold had been removed, and her hands were no longer tied.

Quickly, she tried to stand, only to discover her legs were numb and wouldn't hold her. Her head pounded from the aftereffects of the drug. She swallowed back sudden panic, and forced herself to move slowly, to allow the strength to prickle back into her limbs.

Finally Leilani was able to stand, and aware that her captors could be nearby, she waited for another flash of lightning to gain her bearings before tiptoeing to the door. The deafening clap of thunder that followed swallowed the sound of creaking floorboards underfoot. Slowly she tried the knob, only to find it locked. Tears of frustration and disappointment welled in her eyes, and again she tried to quell her terror, reminding herself that she must remain calm to escape.

But her body trembled from reaction, and from knowing her extreme danger. Remembered stories of girls being sold into slavery or prostitution surfaced in her mind, and it was all she could do to keep from crying out for help. But she knew her cries would only bring attention to the fact that she'd regained consciousness.

Again she forced back her fears, holding on to her composure by sheer willpower. She waited for each flash of lightning to allow her to scan the tiny room. There was no furniture aside from a wooden crate that had been used as a stand for a burned-down candle. In the inky blackness, Leilani felt her way to the crate and grabbed the candle. Her hand slid over the dusty crate, but there were no matches.

Disappointment swelled within her. Her prison felt airless, and the dust and grime that permeated the space stung her nostrils. Leilani wondered how long they would keep her there. The thought brought a flood of new fears. Since they hadn't killed her, what were their intentions? Did they plan to simply leave her there until she suffocated, or starved to death? Knowing she was on the verge of hysteria, she forced her mind to shift to a plan of escape.

The window! she thought. That was her only possibility. Carefully, so as not to alert anyone on the other side of the door, she moved the crate to a spot beneath the window. Then she gingerly tested it, to make sure it would hold her weight.

As she was about to step up onto it, the door opened behind her instead, sending a shaft of light into her cell, momentarily blinding her. Her heart jolted with fear and she backed against the wall, her eyes on the two men who moved quickly into the room to grab her arms. The blindfold was retied around her head, so tightly that its pressure made lights dance behind her eyes.

"Come quietly," one of the men said in his singsong English. "Or you have gag."

She nodded at once, horrified to think of the dirty rag in her mouth—or the drug they'd used to put her out. She needed all of her senses now. If she were to escape, she must stay unbound and not gagged. She vowed to find a way to freedom. *She had to.* No one knew where she was.

They led Leilani out of her cell into what she sensed was a hallway. She had no way of knowing if she was still in the same house, or if they'd taken her somewhere else. She didn't even know the time of day—how long she'd been unconscious—minutes or hours.

They walked several feet, the two men pulling her along by their painful grip on her arms. Then a door was opened and they stepped into another room. Leilani sensed it was much larger, for there had been a murmur of voices that stopped abruptly upon their entrance. Once they were inside, the door closed again, and Leilani felt the eyes of everyone in the room on her, even though her blindfold prevented her from knowing how many people there were. The air was musty and stale, and she caught the whiff of opium smoke blending with perfume. Were there women in the room? she wondered. But she wasn't left wondering for long.

"You have caused much trouble," a man stated, his flat tone edged with malevolence. As he went on, Leilani thought there was something familiar about his voice. "Women must know place." She heard a collective sigh of agreement. "You did not know place, missy. Now you will be sold—to madam who pay highest price."

Leilani suddenly recognized the voice—*Mr. Quong!* But the shock that flashed through her was nothing compared to what he was saying.

"You can no longer influence Chinese to revolt against their master. Now you pay price."

"You can't do this!" Leilani cried, anger suddenly over-powering her fear. "You'll be caught and sent to jail!" She jerked, trying to free herself so she could yank the blindfold away and face the little tyrant. But her arms were only twisted behind her, and she bit back a cry of pain. She wouldn't give them the satisfaction.

"Ha!" Mr. Quong gave a sharp laugh. "No one find you. You be gone soon. To San Francisco, maybe even China. You go with highest bidder."

His words struck absolute terror in her, but somehow she managed to conceal it. She knew it wouldn't help. She must stay calm, fool them into believing she'd accepted her fate, and then find a way to elude them.

But it took all of Leilani's store of control to manage it, as the next few minutes passed in a blur of humiliation. She was touched on the face, in her hair, even her breasts and thighs. Then, with a suddenness that disoriented her even further, her blindfold was torn from her eyes, a bright lamp held up to her face, while Mr. Quong pointed out the brilliance of her blue eyes.

"Clients will like," he stated in his monotone. "She is prize woman. Whoever owns, makes much dollars."

"How dare you!" Leilani cried, unable to contain her up-set. "No one owns me—and no one ever will!" She blinked against the light, trying to see beyond it, but was unable to distinguish the figures in the shadowy room, although she could see that several were women.

Mr. Quong raised a hand and instantly the blindfold was replaced over her eyes. "Take away," he ordered her two cap-tors, who still held her. "Then I take bids for this girl. She make fine saloon girl in San Francisco—or maybe mandarin pay high price in China. We see—eh?"

Then, held securely, Leilani was forced to move back the way they'd come. The smells of opium faded, replaced by the putrid, dust-filled air of her cell. A chill touched her spine and she was struck with the hopelessness of her situation. Why hadn't she listened to Dr. Pete?—to Rand? And why hadn't she left a note to indicate where she'd gone? I was stupid! stupid! she chanted silently, knowing she'd made it easy for the men to kidnap her. She just hadn't thought that an honest Chinese worker would have been in on the conspiracy. But she should have known. Because now she was trapped.

But her disparagement of herself brought her up short. She'd be damned if she'd go meekly. Let them kill her now. With a quick motion, Leilani tried to shake free of them. "You let me go!" she cried, and would have kicked and bitten them if she'd been able. But her hope of forcing their hand died quickly.

Instantly, their fingers tightened painfully on her flesh, relentlessly digging in so that she was half dragged back to the tiny room. A door opened, her blindfold was yanked off, and she was shoved inside.

She stumbled and fell to her knees as the blackness settled around her, plucking at her final reserve of courage like icy talons. Then one of the men grabbed the crate, remembering that she'd moved it under the high window, and took it with him. The door swung shut with the finality of a death knell. And Leilani was left in silence, one that waited with her for the verdict of her fate.

Tears flowed from her eyes, dropping onto her soiled waist and skirt, and great gulping shudders shook her as she cried. For the first time in her life she was truly helpless, at the mercy of the very people she'd always tried to help. Leilani knew that the terrible Mr. Quong would carry out his threat. She couldn't bear to consider what it all meant. But somehow, someway, she meant to find a way out—even if it meant her death.

"I'm going to retire early," Nancy said, and stood up. She smiled at Rand, who sat in a high-backed chair across from the two women on the sofa, the coffee tray on the table between them. "Stella can keep you company." She gave an attractive laugh. "My sister always was the night owl."

"Gladly," Stella replied, lowering her lashes ever so slightly over her green eyes as she glanced at the man she'd come around the world to marry—one way or another. When Rand returned to the Islands she'd vowed to follow, because she'd always wanted him. When she heard he'd married a local girl, she'd kicked herself for not wangling a proposal from him before he left Boston. Now that he was a widower she didn't intend to let him slip through her grasp a second time, certainly not to another island girl of mixed blood. Handsome, rich men were hard to find. Besides, she was attracted to him, even if she didn't love him. That will come later, she told herself.

Rand stood up, too. They'd had their coffee in the parlor after supper, and although he was attempting to be a good host, his patience was running short. The last thing he wanted to do was entertain two women. Although he was fond of his sister-in-law, Stella was beginning to wear on him. He wasn't interested in an alliance with her, and he suddenly decided he must be frank with her about his intentions. He'd liked her well enough when he lived in Boston, but he'd never entertained thoughts of marrying her, not then and not now.

"I believe I'll turn in too," he drawled, deciding that tomorrow would be time enough to have that talk with Stella. Right now he simply wanted to be alone. Leilani was in his thoughts and he couldn't help his worry about her safety, even though he and Lee were working behind the scenes to stop Mr. Quong and his henchmen.

"Ohhh, Rand. It's early." Stella stood, too, and going round the table snuggled against his chest. "I'll be lonesome down here all by myself." Her voice was a soft croon, seductive and filled with promise.

"I'm off," Nancy said with a laugh, and her whole demeanor indicated that she wanted to leave the two alone. "See you in the morning." With a swirl of silk skirts, she left the room to go upstairs.

"Come, I'll pour more coffee." Stella led Rand back to the sofa, sat down and then patted the seat next to her.

With a sigh, Rand sat, but waved the coffee aside. "I think we do need to talk," he began, seeing that he could no longer delay clarifying his position. Stella had to be put straight about his future intentions.

Her smile broadened, her lashes swept lower, and the lamplight gave her blond hair the sheen of spun gold. She was lovely, Rand conceded, but not for him. Taking a deep breath, he began.

"I don't know how you feel about me, Stella, but—" He broke off when she interrupted.

"I'm very fond of you, Rand," she said, her tone husky. "I feel that we have a lot in common—family and background. And I would like nothing better than—" She hesitated, not wanting to seem brazen. But she did want things settled, and impulsively decided that she shouldn't let the moment pass. "Than to have our relationship deepen . . . perhaps . . ." Her voice trailed off, but her inference was clear. She meant *marriage*.

"That's just it, Stella," he said kindly, and placed a hand over hers on her knee. "I'm very fond of you, but that's all." He paused, aware of not wanting to hurt her feelings. "I'm pleased to know you're my friend as well as being connected by family. But that's the extent of my intentions." This time his hesitation was softened with a smile. "I don't want to misrepresent myself, because you're a beautiful woman who must have many beaus, many men who'd be proud to have you as their wife."

Anger stung Stella's cheeks with fire, but she lowered her eyes, letting him believe she was hurt rather than angry. It took several seconds before she had her emotions in hand. She had no intention of accepting his words as final, but she knew better than to pursue the topic further now. So she merely smiled again, with contrived sweetness, and agreed that they'd always been good friends, and would remain so.

Rand searched her face for subterfuge and saw none. "I knew you'd understand, that you felt just as I do," he explained, relieved. "But just in case, I wanted to be open and honest."

"I understand," she said, and her smile seemed sincere. "And I appreciate honesty." She lifted the silver coffeepot. "Would you join me?" Stella poured for herself, and when he agreed that a cup would taste good after all, she poured his, too.

"Honesty is ever so important." She sipped innocently, then glanced casually at the burning log in the fireplace. "Why just this afternoon when I ran into Elwood Benton he said that very thing." Again she sipped and went on in her chatty voice, as though she were simply exchanging innocent gossip.

"Elwood had exciting news." She put down her cup, careful to not even glance at Rand.

"What's that?" Rand asked, anxious to end their conversation when politeness deemed it proper.

"Oh, he's betrothed to his old flame, Leilani Kauwe." She met his eyes directly then. "Seems they've always carried the torch for each other, and decided to make the leap into matrimony."

Rand was speechless for long seconds. Once over the first shock, he managed to pull himself together and stand up. *It couldn't be true!* In as normal a tone as he could muster, he went through the proprieties of saying good-night. Then, without a backward glance, he left her.

For a long time Stella sat on by the fire, sipping coffee. She was satisfied. And she hadn't really lied. Elwood had said he intended to marry Leilani. Things would work out for her after all. She meant to be Mrs. Rand Walsh.

Chapter Eleven

"Hasn't Leilani come down yet?" Dr. Pete glanced up from his breakfast.

Esther turned from the stove, her expression suddenly concerned. "No, she hasn't." She had the coffeepot in her hand, but instead of filling the cups, she put it down. "Stopping to think of it, I haven't seen her since I went to the meeting last night. When I returned I assumed she was already in bed."

The doctor stood up quickly. "This isn't like Leilani. She's usually the first one up." He started toward the door. "I think I'll just go up and check on her, make sure she isn't sick. There's been lots of flu lately."

He was gone almost before he completed his sentence. Once upstairs, Dr. Pete knocked on Leilani's bedroom door, but there was no answer. Pushing it open, he hesitated, his gaze quickly taking in the fact that the bed hadn't been slept in, that indeed, it appeared she hadn't been there at all since yesterday. Alarmed, he rushed back downstairs, meeting Esther in the front hall.

"She's not been there all night!" he cried. "I'm going over to the office. Maybe she worked late and fell asleep."

Esther only nodded, grabbed her shawl from the coatrack and followed him out to the building in front of their house. Dr. Pete grabbed the doorknob, about to insert his key in the lock, when the door opened instead. He glanced at his wife, and although neither spoke, they both knew the other's thoughts: Leilani would have locked the door.

"She might not have been here," Esther offered, trying to calm her growing apprehension. "I left her in the house and I thought she was going to bed early." She paused, thoughtful. "Maybe Rand came by and took her somewhere. There was a bad storm last night, and she might have had to stay with him—that happened once before during a storm."

Pete didn't answer. Instead he braced himself for whatever he might find inside. "I want you to wait out here," he told Esther tersely.

"Why?" Fear edged her question. "You often forget to lock the door, Pete. And it's even possible that she was needed at home—that one of the Kauwes came by for her."

He didn't bother to answer. They both knew Leilani wouldn't just go without leaving a note. Something was very wrong, and he didn't know what would meet his eyes beyond the door. "Just do as I say!" he said sharply, a note of authority in his tone, one she rarely heard, and when she did, she obeyed it.

He disappeared inside. Seconds later he opened the door wide so Esther could join him. "She's not here. No one is here, and everything is in its rightful place."

"Wait," Esther said, her gaze moving to the desk where the ledgers were open, the pen lying beside the ink bottle, which was still open. "Leilani must have been working on the books, because—" She broke off, leaning lower. "She didn't even finish the last entry."

Pete was beside her in an instant, peering through his glasses at the sheet. "You're right. She must have been interrupted—but by whom?"

Neither spoke of their worst fears—the black-coated men who'd threatened and followed Leilani. But they both knew Leilani was missing, and prayed it wasn't because of those men. Then Dr. Pete resumed command, taking Esther's arm to lead her back outside.

"You stay at the house in case Leilani returns. I'm going out to the Kauwe farm, and if she's not there I'll go on to Rand's."

Esther merely nodded and then did as he asked. She wouldn't allow herself to think the worst—that even if Leilani had gone to either of those places, she still would have returned to work by now.

When she watched her husband saddle the horse instead of hitching it to the buggy, she knew he thought the same. But when he mounted and sent the animal down the street in a gallop, Esther's heart sank.

Something terrible had happened to Leilani, the young woman who was like a daughter to her. Then, despite her resolve, she couldn't stop the tears.

"Leilani is missing?" Rand threw down his pen, jumped up and came around his desk, his dark brows lowered in sudden alarm. "Please explain at once!"

For a second Pete thought Rand was about to grab him, as though it were somehow his fault. Quickly he related what he knew, that she hadn't gone to the Kauwe farm, that it was as though she'd vanished into the night without a trace.

As he listened, Rand paced his office, at first angry that Leilani hadn't heeded his words of warning—that she hadn't been more careful. "God almighty!" He stopped short as Pete finished, and the doctor thought he'd never seen a more formidable expression on a man's face, like the wrath of a pagan god.

Pete spread his hands. "That's all we know, Rand. I wish it was more, but everyone I've questioned says they don't know anything. I suspect they wouldn't tell me a damn thing even if they knew—because they're scared of those bastards."

"So you think *they* got her?" The fury went out of Rand in a rush, leaving a hollow feeling in the pit of his stomach. The thought struck terror in his heart. Leilani was no match for those thugs, and what they represented. She could simply disappear without a trace.

"I don't know what to think, Rand," Pete said, evading a direct answer.

Grabbing his jacket from the corner rack, Rand strode to the door. "We have to find her," he stated flatly. "Let's go back to your place and start from there."

Rand locked his office behind him, and taking the lead, he made his way through the vendors and workers already on the streets even though it was still early. Once back at the doctor's, they tried to reconstruct what might have happened, but it was hopeless. All they could determine was that Leilani had been interrupted, and had gone, willingly or not, without a struggle. There were no clues at all.

Rand went to each neighbor, asking questions, but no one had seen anything amiss. By noon he was tracking all of her house calls during the past several weeks. Still no one seemed to know what could have happened, and Rand began to suspect that they were afraid, that they were waiting to see what happened, who would gain control in Chinatown. Finally the man who owned the dry goods emporium, someone Leilani had helped in the past, hesitated when Rand questioned him.

"If you know something, for God's sake tell me!" Rand cried. "Leilani has helped everyone, now it's time for someone to help her. She could be in terrible danger."

The little man's black eyes flickered momentarily with emotion, then he glanced away quickly as a man entered his store. "I know nothing," he said in a voice loud enough to be heard by the newcomer.

The proprietor was holding a pencil over his ledger, and when the other shopper browsed—too casually, Rand thought—he quickly jotted down something, then scratched it out. But not before Rand had seen the name *Quong*.

Without even a flicker of expression, Rand thanked the proprietor and strode to the door where he turned briefly. "If you hear anything, please let either me or Dr. Pete know."

The little Chinese proprietor nodded politely, noncommittally, as though he hadn't just told Rand everything.

As Rand hurried back to his office, his mind spun with thoughts of what to do next. It was obvious that Mr. Quong, the self-appointed tong lord who was trying to establish a criminal network in Honolulu, was responsible. But how to approach him, and influence him to release Leilani? Rand knew it was next to impossible. For the man to admit he had abducted Leilani meant admitting why, which would lead to failure in gaining power in Chinatown.

Rand's brow was furrowed with worry as he entered his law office. Lee glanced up from his own desk, his eyes questioning. As Rand explained, Lee got up, concerned.

"I heard that your future father-in-law is behind this," Rand said tersely. "That bastard has to be stopped, before he really gets a foothold and introduces a whole new criminal element to the Islands and undermines the future for the Chinese people, not to mention Leilani's safety."

"I agree," Lee said at once. "God! I just wish this man wasn't Annie's father—that he'd gone back to China as he intended when he left San Francisco." Lee paused, his eyes troubled. "Of course, then he would have taken Annie with him."

Rand went to his desk and opened a drawer, taking out a pistol. "I'm going to pay Mr. Quong a visit."

"Rand, be careful. The man's dangerous, even more so because I suspect he's really a coward." Lee stepped between his friend and the door. "Listen, before you go let me give you a few facts that might help."

Standing a full head shorter than Rand, Lee nevertheless was an imposing man in his black tailored suit and white shirt. His black eyes sparkled with intelligence and honesty. Rand trusted Lee completely, and had since they were small boys. So now when Lee asked him to listen to advice, Rand nodded, waiting.

"Don't let Quong see weakness," Lee began. "And don't out-and-out threaten him, because that will play into his hands. Ask if he knows what happened to Leilani, and then listen as though you believe his answer. When he finishes, remind him that whoever is responsible will be harshly punished by the law. Tell him that kidnapping a woman will carry an even more severe punishment than importing opium, which is against the law. And finally let him know that the authorities already know who the opium smugglers are, and if one of those men is also suspected of something worse, the *haoles* won't hesitate to arrest that man, even without proof." Lee's tone hardened. "Tell him in no uncertain terms that there will be no mercy in such a situation."

For long seconds the two men looked each other in the eyes, as Lee gave directions to his fiancée's house. Rand realized what Lee was saying—that Quong was trafficking in opium, even though he couldn't prove it. And he knew Lee was placing himself in danger of losing Annie by telling him.

His face set in hard lines, Rand nodded and thanked Lee, then went back into the brilliance of another perfect day. He wondered where Leilani was at that moment. He dared not believe she wasn't all right.

The house was a surprise, hidden in a back alley among hovels and shacks of other poor Chinese. Rand had lost his way several times in the maze of walkways and dwellings, and had had to ask directions more than once. As he hesitated on the porch he was suddenly aware of being watched, although a quick glance around revealed no one in sight. Setting his lips in a stern line, Rand gave a sharp knock on the door.

Without hesitation, it swung open to reveal the very person he had come to see—Mr. Quong, who bowed politely, his print kimono swaying against his legs as he straightened.

"Please," he said, his whole demeanor that of a kindly Chinese husband and father. "How can I help you?"

Not fooled by his benign appearance, Rand decided to be direct, to show the would-be tong lord that he wasn't in the least intimidated. "I've come to you for assistance in locating Leilani Kauwe. I understand you might be of help."

Little lights glinted in Mr. Quong's eyes, and they narrowed ever so slightly, but his smile didn't waver. "I not know whereabouts," he replied, his cadence singsong.

"I'll pay for her release," Rand went on, his tone dismissing the other man's denial.

"Not able to help," Mr. Quong stated flatly, and Rand was suddenly aware of a black-coated, pigtailed man who watched in a threatening manner from a nearby doorway.

Anger tightened every muscle in his body; he had an urge to grab the little man and shake a confession out of him. Quong was even more dangerous than he thought, in that he'd gained control over others who, afraid of refusing, did his bidding. The bastard was ruthless and had to be stopped, he thought again. Fear for Leilani pierced him, reminding him that he'd gain nothing from inciting these Chinese. Remembering Lee's advice, Rand went on more carefully, but he intended to make his point nevertheless.

"Of course the police have been contacted and are watching the ships in port. If they even suspect someone of anything illegal, that person will be arrested on the spot." Rand held the man's gaze, willing the Chinese man to tell the truth, even though he knew it was a feeble hope. "Sure you don't know anything about this at all?"

The glint in Mr. Quong's eyes intensified, and Rand felt the pure malevolence of the man. Then Quong shook his head. "Know nothing. You go now." He stepped back, bowed again and closed the door.

Frustrated, Rand stared at the rough board surface that now separated him from the man he knew to be his enemy. He realized he had only one option at that point—to be patient and wait. But not for long, he told himself grimly, and turned back to the alley. The black-coated man had disappeared.

Intimidation! Rand thought. That damn little tyrant was a master at it, and he vowed to see him removed from Hawaii— after he had Leilani safely back in his arms.

As he hurried back the way he'd come, his fears weighted his mind. Abruptly he stopped short, as the truth he'd been suppressing for so long surfaced to take precedence over all other thoughts. *He loved Leilani.* His future would have no meaning without her. Then another realization hit him. She was in the hands of slavers, drug smugglers, the most evil type of men there were anywhere on earth. Even now she could be trapped in a situation where another man was using her.

His instant rage was the most intense he'd ever experienced—and he was completely helpless to do anything about it. The mental image of her loveliness—her naked body and the innocent eyes that had looked at him with such trust when he'd made love to her—haunted him. She belonged to him. No other man must ever touch her as he had done. She must never be sold in a brothel.

And then he was reminded of Madam Silk Stockings. Why hadn't he thought of her before, as she had more power in

Chinatown than almost anyone? Without hesitation Rand altered course. He would ask the madam for help, he told himself grimly, determined to use any means available to find Leilani—threats, blackmail, whatever.

The door swung open, surprising Leilani, who sat in the corner, her back propped against the wall. She knew it was evening because the sunlight that had shone in through the window during the day had gone, leaving her room in deep shadows. The floor was filthy and she suspected there were rats in the walls, having heard their scratching during the long hours of darkness. Now she dreaded another night in the hovel, even as she feared leaving it, because she didn't know where they'd take her next.

"Female devil," her jailer said. "You come. No trouble."

Then the two black-coated men she'd come to recognize were suddenly on either side of her, pulling her upright. Again a blindfold was placed over her eyes. "You scream, we gag," one of them said, and she nodded. Screaming wouldn't help at this point anyway, she decided.

Again she was led through the hall, then through the room that smelled of opium smoke, but she sensed it was now empty. The sudden feeling of wind against her skin told her she was outside, and she guessed she was being taken down an alley when she tripped over some rubbish. Abruptly the men stopped her, a door creaked open and then they were again in a building. But this time the smell was rank, of garbage and dampness. When they came to the steps, the unexpected drop would have sent her falling but for the tight grip of the men.

Then everything seemed to happen at once. A door, straining against its hinges, was pushed open, her blindfold was removed, and she was shoved into a room even smaller than the cell, falling onto its dirt floor. The place reeked with the putrid smell of sour earth, and Leilani gagged as one of the men lit a single candle on a wooden box.

"You stay here now!" one of them ordered. "Candle burn for little while."

With that they left her, slamming shut the door so hard that the candle flame almost blew out.

Wildly, Leilani glanced around. It was like a tomb—even the walls were dirt. She ran to the door and banged on it, pounding with her fists until they ached.

"Let me out!" she cried, her panic complete.

Suddenly there was a sharp scraping sound, as a narrow slat in the door was slid to the side. Then two black eyes stared at her through the opening.

"You stop, female devil!" the guard ordered. "Or pay consequences now!" Then the slat shut on her with a finality that sobered her, driving her panic into the wings of her mind.

"I won't give up!" she chanted. "They won't win! I won't let them!"

Somehow she would escape.

Chapter Twelve

Knowing that Madam Silk Stockings saw people only in conjunction with her schedule, that she rarely invited anyone into her private quarters, Rand was surprised that his request for a visit was honored at once. He'd gone to her establishment and made his wishes known, then waited. But he'd only just found a seat and sat down when her elderly Chinese maid appeared at his table, her wizened face inscrutable.

Her green silk kimono rustled as she bowed. "Please, Madam see you now." She indicated he follow her, then winding her way among the patrons, she led him to the door behind the dais where Rand usually met the proprietress when they discussed business.

Once in the back hall Rand was shown through several doorways and finally into the madam's residence. Then, after another bow, the powdered and coiffured maid left him. The room, obviously a parlor, was unexpected in its splendor, and Rand glanced around with interest. Deep-crimson velvet drapes shrouded the windows, the tables were ebony black, the porcelain lamps hand-painted, and the sofas and chairs were covered in a floral silk that blended with the drapes and furniture. The total effect was elegant, understated and completely Oriental. Even the paintings that hung on the walls, and the art pieces that had been tastefully placed on the tables depicted early Chinese dynasties, and Rand suspected they were priceless.

So preoccupied in the beautifully appointed parlor, fascinated because it was the first time he'd been invited into the madam's home, he didn't hear her enter the room. But some-how the air currents shifted, the quiet intensified, and he knew he wasn't alone even before he turned and saw her watching him, her eyes black and piercing in contrast to her white, rice-powdered face. Her high-necked black and white silk kimono emphasized her small frame and regal posture. Combined with her elaborate coiffure, swept up and held in place with pearl combs, the ageless Madam Silk Stockings was as regal as a queen.

Inclining his head forward in a slight bow, he waited while she moved farther into the room before speaking. Rand found himself wondering about her, as he had many times in the past. She was a woman of mystery; no one knew anything about her, aside from the fact that she'd come from China many years ago, that she'd once had a daughter who died. No one knew if she'd ever had a husband. Nor did anyone know her real name, or why she was called Silk Stockings. He'd always sus-pected she wasn't a peasant, and her choice of art and furni-ture added to that belief. She had excellent taste, which came from breeding, not just having money.

"Good afternoon, Rand," she said finally in her stilted English. "My servant said you have urgent business."

He nodded. But before he could say more, the madam held up her hand in a gesture of silence. Gracefully she moved to a nearby table, where she picked up a china bell and shook it. The tingle had hardly sounded when the green-clad maid reappeared at the door and was told to bring the tea tray. Then Madam Silk Stockings motioned Rand to one of the silk so-fas. As he sat, she made herself comfortable on the one op-posite, a small table between them.

"Your work goes well?" she asked, making small talk, and he knew that her good manners precluded a serious conver-sation until proprieties were observed and tea was poured. Another suggestion of her cultured background.

"Very well," he replied, going along with her protocol. "Lee and I have almost too much work since annexation, and I find myself away from Honolulu far more than I like."

She clucked her tongue and shook her head. "Progress comes even to Hawaii. Perhaps it will be for the good. We shall see."

He knew she referred to the question of the Chinese gaining citizenship and a voice in government. Then the maid came back with the tea and he was saved from a reply. Trying to control his fear for Leilani, he waited in silence as the tea was poured into dainty cups and one was handed to him by the madam. Still she was silent until her tea had been sipped and his also.

Abruptly she was direct.

"So-o-o," she began slowly. "What worries you, my friend, that you are so upset?"

Despite his concern, he gave a brief grin at her discernment. Nothing escaped the woman's sharp eyes. But he sobered the next second, his mind going at once to Leilani's being kidnapped. "I need a favor, Madam Silk Stockings. I believe you are the only person in Hawaii who can help me now."

Curiosity flickered momentarily in her eyes, but her lashes came down quickly as she once more raised her cup to her lips. "Yes? How so?"

"A young woman—a beautiful young woman—has been kidnapped by a man named Quong, a newcomer to Honolulu, who wants to establish his own criminal network here in the islands. This man has been trying to intimidate poor people, to extort money under threat of their lives. When Leilani Kauwe stood up to him, she was threatened and followed. Now she's been abducted—and everyone is too afraid to speak up—if they even know where she's been taken." He'd glanced away from the old woman, his feelings suddenly raw from speaking his fears aloud. After a pause during which he regained his bearing, Rand returned his gaze to hers. "I'm afraid she'll be sold into prostitution, maybe even shipped abroad, unless I can stop it."

Something flashed in her eyes. Anger? Or fear? At him or at Quong? Rand wondered. "You say the girl is Leilani Kauwe?"

"You might remember her," Rand said, hopeful that she'd help. "She came into your saloon to rescue the girl Kini from a *haole* out to have fun, and had to stand up to drunken men who accosted her." He couldn't help his worried frown. "You see, Leilani helps everyone in Chinatown, and it was her nature to confront Quong."

"Yes, Chinatown's angel of mercy is well-known to me," she replied, her unreadable expression back in place. Her words trailed off into a silence while she took another sip of tea, and even though she was the picture of calm, Rand had a strange impression that her mind whirled with his information.

"Can you help?" he asked, unable to contain himself. "Time is of the essence. She could be put on a ship at any moment."

"I have heard of Mr. Quong, and his hope of becoming a tong lord, but I have not been told of this—this abduction," she replied, avoiding a direct answer for the moment. Her mouth pursed, and again Rand sensed that she was furious behind her serene facade. Then, for a fraction of a second, the old woman's expression—or lack of it in the face of strong emotion—reminded him of Leilani. "Of course they would not tell me," she added, a note of disgust in her voice. "I do not traffic in slavery."

"But will you help me?" He put down his cup, took a sharp breath and willed her to agree.

"I will look into this," she replied. "And contact you when I learn something about this young woman you are in love with."

Again her perception was startling, but he didn't contradict her. When she stood up abruptly, indicating their meeting was over, he got to his feet immediately.

"We will be in touch...soon," she told him, and for the first time her voice revealed a determination as strong as his.

He had no option but to go, and trust that she could use her influence to stop the dangerous Mr. Quong. Rand knew it would do no good to question her further. She would never reveal her methods. But if she discovered where Leilani was being held, then he'd take care of the bastard Quong himself—*with great pleasure!*

As he stepped from her apartment, he suspected she had her own reasons for upset—maybe Quong had even tried to threaten her. Because Rand definitely sensed that Madam Silk Stockings was troubled, even fearful. He just hoped she could do something in time.

She had to!

By evening Rand hadn't heard from the madam, and feeling like a caged animal, he paced his office. Lee, very concerned about the situation, Leilani's safety and how Quong's criminal daring would affect his relationship with Annie, nevertheless took the afternoon steamer to the north end of the island in Rand's place. "One of us has to go," Lee had said on his way out the door. "But while I'm gone don't take matters into your own hands, Rand. You'll only make the situation worse."

Rand had nodded, but he hadn't promised. Now, as he paused to glance out the window at the spectacle of the dying day, the splash of pink and crimson and purple that was darkening the sky, he was even more alarmed. Nothing had changed. The madam hadn't contacted him and time was running out. Night was coming again and Leilani was still missing.

"I'll be damned if I'm just going to sit here and wait!" he cried into the silent room. Then, grabbing his hat, he plopped it on his head, patted his pistol holstered under his coat, and after going out the door, locked it after him. Then he strode purposefully down the sidewalk, crossed King Street and headed toward Hotel Street, the heart of Chinatown. Quong would talk—or else!

His headlong rush only slowed as he approached the alley where Quong lived, his glance darting everywhere. If one of Quong's thugs was hiding in the shadows, Rand meant to see him first. He strode right up to the door and knocked.

As though the Chinese gangster had seen his approach, the door was opened almost at once by Quong himself. Surprise flashed over his features for a fleeting second, and Rand wondered whom the little man was expecting—obviously not him.

But Quong recovered his demeanor in the next instant, his face suddenly glowering at Rand.

"What you want? I busy now. You go!"

"Not on your life!" Rand retorted sharply. Then he proceeded to shove the smaller man back into the tiny hall and step in himself. "I've come for Leilani Kauwe, and I won't listen to excuses. I know you have her, Quong."

The man shook his head, and instead of looking intimidated, his expression tightened fiercely. "Not true. You go before you get hurt."

Rand grabbed the front of Quong's smock, pulling him up on his tiptoes. "Let me put it this way," he ground out between clenched teeth. "Either I get what I want or I'm exposing your illegal opium smuggling—and your intention to expand into slave trafficking." He tightened his hold, so that the neckline choked off Quong's air. "And I can prove it, you bastard! If Leilani isn't released, I'll have you strung up, and your thugs deported." Abruptly, Rand let him go, and the little man stumbled backward, clutching at his neck.

"I know nothing!" he cried hoarsely. "Show me your proof!" Although his face was suffused with color and he looked shaken by the attack, his gaze was malevolent. Rand didn't fool himself; he'd made a dangerous enemy.

"You'll see my proof soon enough!" Rand retorted. "If Leilani isn't brought at once, I'll have a noose around your neck in nothing flat!"

"Hah!" Quong cried. "You have no proof! You bluff!" Although he looked enraged, and even more deadly, respect glinted briefly in the black eyes. The tall *haole* had courage, even if he'd foolishly walked into a situation from which he would never be allowed to leave. He poised himself for what would happen next, after he called his men to him.

A slight noise sounded behind Rand from the open doorway, and by reflex, he pulled his pistol as he whirled around to face the threat. Expecting the black-coated hired assassins, he was startled to come face-to-face with Madam Silk Stockings and her two burly Chinese bodyguards. Instantly, he lowered his gun.

At first her expression was inscrutable, then, for a moment he saw a sparkle of humor—approval?—in her ebony eyes, and he wondered how long she'd been listening. "So, you did not wait for word from me before you took matters into your own hands. That was a dangerous thing to do, Rand." She lifted a hand in a signal, and then stepped inside the hall. A moment later another bodyguard nudged Quong's two henchmen, their hands tied behind them, into the hall.

His own surprise was nothing compared to the incredulous expression Quong couldn't mask. He was at a disadvantage—and knew it. But before he could utter one word of protest, Madam Silk Stockings stepped forward and spoke instead.

"Whether Rand can prove his accusations is not at stake here," she stated calmly, every inch the reigning queen of Chinatown in her silk and pearls and rice powder. "Because I can prove them. *And will if necessary.*"

For the first time Mr. Quong was intimidated, knowing his bluff had been called, that she would have proof. He knew all about the power the madam wielded among the Chinese, even among the *haoles;* he knew that although she was fair and honest, she could also be ruthless with those who weren't. She had her own code and lived by it. He knew she would never make false threats. But Quong wouldn't give up easily, not if there was a small chance he didn't have to.

"She is here, in this house," Madam Silk Stockings stated flatly. "Bring her at once."

"She is not here," Mr. Quong retorted immediately, suddenly hopeful that she wasn't as powerful as he'd believed. If he gave in now, he would be finished in Honolulu, as everyone would hear that a woman had brought him to his knees.

"Then you have moved her." The madam's eyes hardened, and her tone was a threat. "I will not play games." She stepped closer. "Believe me, I will not tolerate lies."

It was no use. Quong knew she was as relentless as he'd heard she was. But he couldn't stop one last gibe. He gave a formal bow, one that was just short of being scornful. "Your sources aren't so good. They can be fooled. Remember that in future." Then, with no other choice he proceeded to tell them where Leilani was being held.

* * *

Huddled in the corner, her back against the wall, her feet tucked under her skirt, Leilani couldn't stop shivering. She had no idea what time it was, or even if it was day or night. Her candle had burned out long ago, and aside from the narrow shaft of light from the slit in the door, it was utterly black.

The earth under her was damp, and although she'd gotten used to the putrid stench, the scratching in the walls terrified her, and jolted her awake each time she fell asleep. For the first time in her life she felt weakness from lack of food and rest. Leilani knew she was in terrible danger, that at any moment the door could open and she would be taken away. She had no idea where, except that it would be to a fate worse than dying where she was. The thought sparked a new sense of urgency within her. She mustn't give up, mustn't allow herself to drift into a lethargic state. Somehow she had to fight back.

The first thing is to stand up, she told herself. Keep her strength in her limbs. Only once since she'd been brought to the tomblike room had the door opened, although she suspected eyes watched her from time to time, peering at her through the slit. The guard had come in hours ago with a bowl of broth, greasy liquid that was too sickening to drink. But she'd demanded to know why she'd been moved to such a horrible place.

"Master said to," the huge, bald man had told her in halting English. "Too dangerous to keep at his house." He'd waved a thick, muscled arm. "You safe here from interfering *haoles*."

"You bastards!" she'd cried, and flung the soup at him, only to have the wooden bowl hit the door as it clanked shut in her face. Frustrated by being so helpless, and terrified by thoughts of her fate, Leilani had given in to tears and cried until she had none left. When she'd subsided in the corner, a voice had come through the door slit.

"You not be here long now. Madam come for you soon. Then you give pleasure to many men." The words were followed by a harsh laugh.

Now, as she tried to conquer her fear, Leilani forced herself to consider a plan of escape. But she knew that as long as the door was locked, she was trapped. Her only chance was to make a move when the door opened, perhaps use the element of surprise to get around her captors and gain a head start. But how could she do that? she wondered, frantic for an answer. Then she thought of the only item at her disposal—the wooden box.

For once grateful for the blackness, she groped through the darkness to where she knew it was. Then she lifted it over next to the door, placing it at the ready. When the guard stepped into the room, she'd hit him over the head. The thought terrified her, even as it excited her. Timing would be everything. She must be ready, the box poised to strike the moment she heard the bolt sliding to unlock the door.

She waited, straining her ears, hoping she could maintain her position without exhausting her last shred of strength. Then she heard the bolt. Instantly, she raised the box, stepping behind the door as it slowly swung open. As the man entered the room, she brought the box down on his back with every ounce of strength she possessed. He staggered forward as the thin wooden slats shattered over him from the blow. But he was only stunned.

Tossing what was left of the box aside, Leilani rushed around the door to take flight in whichever direction presented itself. Then a woman, her lined Oriental face startled by the unexpected spectacle, stepped in front of her, bringing her to an abrupt stop.

Panting, Leilani's gaze darted wildly for another avenue of escape, but there was only one way out—past the woman and the tall man standing behind her in the deep shadows. Her heart seemed to leap out of her chest in fear. Her attempt to escape was too late. The woman was Madam Silk Stockings. The evil Mr. Quong had made good his threat. She'd been sold into prostitution. Please, dear God, help me! she prayed silently. But she knew she'd never escape now.

Then the man stepped into the pool of light from a lantern that hung from the low ceiling. *It was Rand.* Oh God! Rand *did* work for Madam Silk Stockings after all.

And then the velvety blackness she'd been fighting against for all those hours finally took her.

Chapter Thirteen

Arms reached out, catching Leilani before she fell, holding her secure against a broad male chest. The blackness that edged her mind faltered, denying her blessed oblivion. From far away she still heard the Oriental cadence of the madam's voice, and the deeper notes of Rand's, and there was a dangerous edge to his that she'd never heard before. Then the words, "Better you marry her... keep her out of trouble next time..." filtered down into Leilani's semiconscious state. Or maybe I'm dreaming, she thought vaguely, and abruptly became more alert to her surroundings.

"Leilani! Leilani! It's all right. You're safe now." Rand's voice sounded urgent and soothing at the same time.

The fog lifted a little more from Leilani's mind; she was suddenly aware of her icy flesh, the trembling that seemed to originate from the very core of her being. She knew that she was on the verge of nervous collapse as well, and fought to regain her equilibrium, fearful of sinking back into the blackness that still threatened to overpower her. Everything seemed removed from her, and strangely unreal.

She sensed other men pushing past them to grab her jailer, men obeying the terse orders of the madam. There were sounds of a slight scuffle, thuds and groans and oaths. Then she was suddenly lifted into Rand's arms, her head cradled against his chest, and it occurred to her that his heart, under her ear, was beating erratically—as though he were terribly agitated—or frightened.

Nonsense, she told herself, as her reasoning began to assert itself. Rand was in control; he wouldn't be frightened, only angry that Mr. Quong could flout the rules of the law-abiding community of Chinatown. He began to walk, and she felt his muscles tense as he started up the wooden steps. Still her lashes seemed too heavy to open her eyes, and although she was more aware, she felt as limp as a stringless puppet. But somewhere in the back of her brain she realized that the madam wasn't buying her, that she and Rand were rescuing her...that she was safe.

Rand was appalled by the condition of the place. That Leilani had actually been locked up in such an airless, black hole enraged him. It took iron restraint to keep himself from strangling the self-appointed tong lord, Quong. But his anger was curtailed by one look at Leilani, whose eyes had fluttered open, brilliant blue in her bloodless face. He'd glimpsed her desperation in the instant before she struck her guard with the wooden box, then her terror when her way was blocked by the madam. Her face had gone as white as parchment, and he'd guessed that she believed the madam had come for her, that she'd been sold into prostitution. God only knew what the thugs had told her.

But all that could wait. She was in shock, and even though Quong had stated emphatically that she wasn't "damaged goods," Rand knew she was in bad shape. He could feel the tremors that shook her body, how her breathing was shallow and uneven.

In only seconds they reached the upper level of the building, and from the stale smell of the smoke in the air, Rand guessed it was an opium den, an extremely dangerous place for a young woman. Once they were on the street, the night air, fresh with the fragrance of the ocean, was a welcome relief from the dead, putrid odor of the cellar.

He held Leilani closer. Thank God he'd gotten to her in time. He'd found out from the madam that Quong had already made a deal to send Leilani to San Francisco, that Rand's earlier warning that the ships were being watched was the only reason that she wasn't already on the high seas.

"Take her home," the madam told Rand. "Give her whiskey." She indicated Leilani's state, that she still shivered even though Rand held her close to this chest, willing his body heat to warm her.

Then Madam Silk Stockings was helped into a buggy by one of her men. She gave orders to her bodyguards in Chinese, and Leilani caught a word here and there. It seemed that the matter of Quong's criminal activities would be reviewed by a group of his countrymen, headed by the madam, and the law would not be informed of the kidnapping. Leilani just hoped that the madam could really put a stop to Mr. Quong. Her earlier perception of him said the opposite—yet she'd also suspected he was a coward. When the truth got out, as it always did in Chinatown, his brief reign of terror might be over. She hoped so.

After paying one of the madam's men to take a message to Dr. Pete that Leilani was all right, that he was taking her to his house, Rand lifted her into his buggy and tucked a lap robe around her shoulders and over her legs and feet. Then he jumped up beside her, took the reins and soon had the horse moving down the street.

He had another thing to be thankful for, he reminded himself grimly. Stella and Nancy had taken the steamer back to Maui. He'd made it clear that he had no time for entertaining.

But the thought of Stella brought back her words of the night before—that Leilani was seeing Elwood again—that they were betrothed. Remembering brought back all his anger and frustration. He glanced down at her head, which lay against his shoulder, her hair a tangle of silky black threads against the lighter material of his jacket. She looked so helpless, so utterly beautiful, even in her state of dishevelment and rumpled dirty clothes. His anger receded again. Now was not the time to discuss whom she belonged to. She needed immediate care first.

The wheels on the road had a hypnotic effect on Leilani. All at once she couldn't keep her eyes open, and her head slipped lower on Rand's shoulder. Instantly his arm was around her, supporting her body. I'm safe, she thought. I'm really safe.

For the first time in more than twenty-four hours she dropped into a peaceful sleep.

Leilani was only vaguely aware when the buggy stopped, when Rand lifted her out and carried her into his elegant front hall. It was his Hawaiian housekeeper's lilting voice answering Rand's burst of orders that finally opened her eyes.

"Please—please," she managed, rousing herself out of her stupor. "I can walk. You don't have to carry me, Rand." When he still didn't put her down, she squirmed in his arms, feeling foolish all at once in front of the heavyset woman whose curious but kindly stare disconcerted her.

"You sure?" His body stilled as he searched her face.

For the first time she noticed how drawn and pale Rand looked under his bronze skin. His eyes burned with a feverish glaze, and she suddenly knew he hadn't slept for a long time, either. Their eyes met and held. Vaguely, Leilani was aware of the housekeeper fluttering around them, her oohs and aahs about the state of Leilani's clothing and health fading away as Rand's gaze intensified, speaking to her with a message all its own. It was almost as if he'd said aloud, *I love you.*

Instantly, a flash of heat touched her face, and new sensations trembled through her. Misreading her shaking for delayed reaction, Rand reined in his feelings, and managed to cool his sudden surge to possess her—to make love to her. With firm resolve, he placed Leilani on her feet, although he kept a tight hold around her waist.

But her legs buckled. Appalled by her weakness, she grabbed on to him to steady herself. That was all Rand needed to see. He swooped her back into his arms and strode up the stairs. "Prepare a hot bath," he told the astounded housekeeper he called Kama. "But first bring glasses and whiskey to the front bedroom. And a tray of food."

"To your room?" Kama asked, hesitating, and her tone denoted her sense of proprieties.

"That's right," he retorted over his shoulder. "It's the one with the connecting bathroom." He hesitated at the top of the steps to glance back. "Hurry, Kama!" he cried. "She needs attention at once!"

Upon reaching the bedroom, he nudged open the door and strode inside to place Leilani in a comfortable overstuffed chair. As he went to the fireplace and lit the kindling that had been arranged in readiness for the next fire, Kama came in with a silver tray containing a crystal container of whiskey and two glasses. With each hurried step her pinned-up gray hair bounced, and she explained that she'd return immediately with the food, then see to the tub. Leilani managed a smile of thanks, abruptly aware that this was the room where Rand slept. She pushed back thoughts of Rand naked, of the night he made love to her, knowing she was too emotionally fragile to dwell on those feelings now.

Suddenly aware of her soiled clothing, that the dank smell of her cell clung to her, she started to get out of the chair, fearful that she'd ruin it. But Rand was there at once, gently nudging her back.

"You'll sit here until your bath is ready," he told her firmly, his eyes hooded and unreadable.

With a flash of intuition, Leilani knew that he too was aware of her being in his bedroom. But she subsided back onto the soft cushions, only too conscious of her bone-weary fatigue, something she'd never experienced before in her life.

"You didn't sleep while they had you, did you?" he asked, looking down at her with an odd expression, his words picking up on her thoughts.

She shook her head, and her long lashes swooped downward, graceful half-moons on the upper curve of her cheeks. "I was afraid to, once I woke up."

"You slept at first?" His tone was sharp, incredulous.

She glanced before returning her gaze to her knotted hands in her lap. "No, I fought them," she replied softly. "And made them mad. They gave me a hypodermic shot in the arm—and I blacked out."

The ensuing silence was almost palpable. "Morphine. Those bastards! It could have killed you." Rand's whole body tightened, and the lines and hollows of his face seemed suddenly more pronounced. "I ought to kill them!"

"They aren't worth it, Rand." Leilani met his eyes, loving him even more because of his anger for her. "And I think Mr.

Quong's aspirations for becoming a tong lord in Honolulu could be finished.'' She took a deep breath, hating how weak she felt. ''And if that's the case, then it was worth all I went through.'' Her words faded off into another silence.

''Let's hope you're right about Quong,'' he replied in a low throbbing voice, and added something under his breath that she couldn't quite hear. Rand's eyelids lowered, hooding whatever else she might have seen in his eyes. Abruptly he diverted his attention to the whiskey, pouring the liquor into both glasses. Then he handed one to her. ''Drink it all, Leilani. It'll calm your nerves.''

She held the drink in both hands, for seconds swirling the liquid in the glass before she raised it to her lips. Unused to alcohol, Leilani only sipped, because it burned her mouth and throat.

He squatted in front of her, his fingers covering hers on the glass. ''Go ahead, sweetheart, drink up.'' He guided her hand to bring the glass to her lips, his eyes never releasing her gaze, and she did as he requested, as though mesmerized by both his look and his voice.

Tipping the glass, Leilani drank it all, swallowing without tasting. She put down the empty glass, coughing and choking as the liquor took her breath away.

But Rand was satisfied, as her color was better, not the parchment white that had scared him. He stood just as Kama returned with the food tray and placed it on the table next to Leilani.

''Once you fill the tub I won't need you further tonight,'' Rand told the housekeeper.

Kama nodded, then moved quickly to the bathroom and turned on the water, Leilani stared at the food, feeling more sleepy than hungry, although the soup smelled good and the buttered bread looked fresh. They both seemed aware of the woman in the other room, and the running water combined with the crackling fire to fill the quiet that lay between them. Then Kama came out of the bathroom, wiping her hands on her huge apron as she moved across the bedroom to the door.

''Good night, Mr. Rand,'' she said, her dark eyes darting between them, and Leilani knew she was wondering about

their sleeping arrangements. But she also knew the woman
wasn't malicious, and wouldn't spread gossip, as Rand had
often commented in the past about how fond his housekeeper
was of him, and he of her.

Kama's sudden smile transformed her round face into the
friendly countenance typical of the Hawaiian people. "Sleep
well, Leilani. You'll be a new girl in the morning."

Then she closed the door and Leilani was left alone with
Rand, too tired to worry about the proprieties of being in his
bedroom. She just wanted to bathe and then go to sleep.

"Go ahead, eat," he urged when she only stirred the soup
with her spoon.

She lifted her long lashes to meet his eyes. "I'm not really
hungry," she said. "Just sleepy."

He seemed to consider her words, and when he came to a
decision it was reflected in his expression. "You have to eat a
little—to regain your strength," he said, his tone low and
coaxing. "Come on, I'll help you."

When he would have taken the spoon—and fed her—Leilani began eating herself. She managed half of the soup and a
couple of bites of bread, then pushed it away. The whiskey was
already affecting her, numbing her senses even more, and as
her mind slowed down, so did her resistance.

But she shook her head when he insisted she have more, and
Rand didn't push when he noted the way her whole body
drooped. Leilani was spent, and only rest would revitalize her
to the energetic young woman he loved. He quelled another
jolt of anger, but he vowed to make sure Quong never in-
flicted such havoc on another girl.

"All right then, I'll let you off the hook," Rand drawled, his
tone soothing. He took her hands and pulled her out of the
chair. "We'll get you into your bath." He walked her toward
the bathroom, and Leilani went with him, somehow feeling so
numb that resistance didn't enter her head. Not until they were
in the bathroom and he made no move to leave her.

Despite her weakened state Leilani was suddenly shy, uncertain of his intentions. She held on to the edge of the sink,
not trusting her legs to hold her. Oh God, she thought, she
should never have swallowed the whiskey. Although she was

mentally calmer, and was no longer icy cold, her body was as limp as a rag doll. Never in her life had she been so at the mercy of another person. And that thought alarmed her—because that person was Rand.

The room was steamed up from the hot water, and as Rand watched her, he became even more concerned. She'd gone through an ordeal, fearing for her life. But she was safe now, and her continued lethargy made him wonder if he should send for the doctor after all. But he dismissed the thought, knowing she was suffering from lack of sleep, and the aftereffects of her terrifying experience, and perhaps even the drug she'd been given, a dose strong enough to put her out.

My God! he thought. Even the drug could have killed her. That possibility brought him back to the task at hand. He was determined to get her bathed and in bed, and to forget about how desperately he wanted to make love to her, how his manhood throbbed even now at the very thought of possessing her loveliness.

"We'll make this quick," he said, contriving a matter-of-fact tone.

"We?" Her eyes widened in alarm. "I'll manage fine. I don't need help." She knew she was rambling, that her face had gone scarlet, but she was pleased that her voice was stronger. That he'd once explored her body completely didn't occur to her at that moment. All she knew was how vulnerable she felt. She pretended a strength she didn't have and stepped away from the sink, indicating that he could go. Instead, she staggered, to her horror.

"That settles it," Rand stated flatly, his face showing only his concern, not the awareness of her exquisite femininity.

He sat her down on a stool and proceeded to unbutton her waist, take off her shoes and skirt, and all the while she protested. He ignored her, raising his brows when she again seemed too weak to stand unaided as he removed her underthings. His fingers skimmed her flesh as he worked.

"Please, Rand! I'm really able to do this myself. It's only the whiskey that's affecting me now." Her words didn't deter him. In fact he seemed completely oblivious that his fingers were leaving a wake of fire on her flesh, that her nipples had

hardened as he loosened her chemise, that her breathing had
accelerated as exquisite sensations of longing shuddered deep
within her. All at once she was on fire. His touch was taking
away the past twenty-four hours of hell. She moaned softly,
her need of rest second to her rising desire. Leilani wanted him
more than any bath.

Glancing at her, Rand saw her eyes were closed, that her
parted lips and flushed cheeks denoted she was very near the
end of her endurance. Hardening his heart, he hurried faster,
because the heat in his loins was almost unbearable. Finally she
stood before him, naked, a vision of perfection.

"Now," he began gruffly. "Into the tub."

Her lashes flew open but he looked away, not meeting her
eyes. From somewhere in her drugged brain, reason reasserted itself. He was completely unaffected by her even while
every cell in her body screamed for his touch.

And then he did touch her, as a father would touch a child.
He picked her up, and for a long lingering second cuddled her
in his arms, her softness against his chest. Then, almost reluc-
tantly, Rand placed her in the tub. When he grabbed for the
washcloth, she stopped him.

"I can manage—don't embarrass me further—please."

He was on his knees, bent toward her, his face only inches
away. Their eyes caught—and locked—black and blue. Little
bubble sounds from the water seemed to swirl around them,
and for a long time neither spoke. Leilani couldn't have ut-
tered a sound at that moment if her life had depended on it;
her breath had stopped in her throat. She knew intuitively that
he shared her feelings at that moment—raw, throbbing passion that clamored for release.

He more than shared it; he was inflamed with it, consumed
by a need greater than he'd ever felt. Rand knew if he stayed
with her for a minute longer he couldn't control his primitive
urge to take his woman—in the tub or on the floor.

God! he thought, aware he was reacting like his pagan ancestors, who'd taken their women when and where they
wished. How could he have such thoughts?—after she'd suffered such an ordeal? Fearful of the passion building within
him, that was ready to explode with the force of one of the

Hawaiian volcanoes, he forced himself to stand up and step back.

"I'll be right outside then," he said, surprising her with his sudden acquiescence. "But the door will be ajar and I'll check on you." Then he left her.

It was an anticlimax. The air seemed to go out of Leilani with his unspoken rejection of her. She'd glimpsed his mounting desire, rising with hers. So why had he left so abruptly? she wondered, confused. Had her fragile state distorted her perceptions? Maybe she only thought he'd been aroused. Although she'd wanted her privacy, now that he'd gone so quickly she was deflated. Even as she realized her rationale was contradictory, it didn't help her new hurt.

Then Stella's face surfaced in her mind, and she suspected why he'd gone—because he was committed to another woman. She fought against tears, the tightening in her throat. On top of everything else she didn't need to think of Stella.

Yet her thoughts brought a flash of anger, and it was that jolt of adrenaline that enabled Leilani to bathe quickly, conscious of Rand beyond the door. Quietly she stepped from the tub, dried herself and put on the nightshirt he'd left on the stool. Then she stepped from the bathroom, surprising him as he grimly contemplated the glowing embers in the fireplace.

Without a word, Rand came to her, his black eyes reflecting the flames that flickered light into the shadowy room. His arm around her, he guided her to the bed, helped her under the quilt, then straightened to look down at her. Again their eyes met, and held. As the electricity between them again crackled with renewed energy, he suddenly smiled, his expression tender. He bent and kissed her gently on the mouth.

"Sleep well, my Leilani," he murmured. "When you're strong again we'll tend to—other matters."

It was just the right touch for her at that moment. Her worries fled, she relaxed, and then she slept.

Rand waited by the bed until her breathing slowed and he was certain she was asleep. Then he went back to his chair by the fireplace and resumed his contemplation of the embers. Now that she was safe, *in his bed,* his concern shifted to Stella's ugly words—that Elwood intended to marry Leilani, that they'd never stopped loving each other, that she'd never gotten over his leaving her when she was eighteen. And now she wanted him back.

A grim resolve took hold of Rand in the deathly silence of the room. He meant to find out the truth from Leilani, before she left his house. He meant to show her what love meant . . . and whom she belonged to.

The place was so filled with blackness that she could feel its malevolent presence pressing in on her, sense the evil things creeping toward her from where they'd hidden in the walls. Paralyzed, her eyes wouldn't open, and her scream couldn't free itself from her throat. She was trapped, because there was no door, no window, no escape. She would be devoured by the horror about to pounce on her. Her heart beat wildly; she fought the invisible vise of terror that gripped her body, bathing it in sweat. Suddenly she broke free, and her scream pierced the darkness, echoing off the cold walls like a chorus of demons.

The shrill scream brought Rand out of the chair where he'd finally dozed. In a second he was beside Leilani, cradling her in his arms, soothing her with reassuring words that she was safe, gently bringing her out of the nightmare.

Her eyes were wide open, staring at something only she could see. Gradually, reason asserted itself, her eyes cleared and she was suddenly aware of her surroundings, that she was safe in Rand's arms.

"I—I had a bad dream," she whispered shakily. "That I was still—"

He put a finger over her lips, stopping her words. "Shhh," he murmured. "It's all right, sweetheart. You're safe here. Nothing will harm you."

She nodded slightly, snuggling into his chest, warmed by knowing he was there. But her delicate face, framed by the silky cloud of black hair, seemed too pale, too fragile to Rand. He could feel her fears hadn't been completely banished, for her slender body trembled under his flowing nightshirt. His decision was instantaneous.

Gently, he set her aside onto the pillow. Then as she watched wide-eyed, he undressed, tossing his clothing onto a nearby chair. When he climbed in beside her and pulled her close, Leilani didn't protest. With all the feminine wisdom of the ages, she knew she needed him beside her.

Leilani snuggled against him, her head on his arm, her back against his chest, her legs entangled with his. A great sigh of relief escaped her, as her lashes fluttered closed. Lulled by his hand that caressed her cheek and neck, that smoothed her hair, she drifted back to sleep.

But Rand couldn't even close his eyes. He savored the softness of her in his arms, and banked down his desire for her, which never completely went away. For a long time he stared into the quiet room, listening to her soft breathing, and recognized how important she'd become to him. Beyond their fire-lit room he wondered if the night marchers walked in the mountains tonight, ghosts looking for unsuspecting *haoles* who'd flouted the old laws of the Polynesian gods. He wondered what would happen to Leilani if she married him, a man who'd already lost a wife tragically—perhaps because his own family had ignored the ancient taboos.

He gave himself a mental shake. He'd never really subscribed to the superstitions, although he was proud of his ancestry. It was his former father-in-law, Richard Drew, also part Hawaiian, who'd almost convinced him that the old taboos were responsible for his daughter dying, for his being left with wealth and land and no one to inherit it. Rand had come to see that Richard was sad and lonely, and needed something to blame for his terrible loss.

Time passed, and Leilani moved in Rand's arms, snuggling deeper against him, at the same time conscious of not being alone in the bed. Gradually, as she surfaced toward wakefulness, she became aware of new sensations—the sound of the ocean beyond the windows—the heat of the male body next to hers—the breath that was a steady ripple over her hair—the fingers that still stroked her skin with a light, tickling touch that sent a tantalizing message into the part of her known only to one man . . . Rand.

Somehow he sensed she was awake. "Are you better, Leilani?" he whispered, and she felt his mouth on her hair.

She nodded, ever so slightly, and heard his breath catch. His arm, which lay around her waist, pulled her even closer. Then Rand gently tilted her chin, and she turned slightly, so that he could look into her face.

Their eyes caught, and Leilani couldn't look away, even though her lashes fluttered, because he was so close. His firm lips, so practiced in the art of kissing, were only inches away, and his dark gaze, so filled with mysterious lights, seemed to portend his intention to make love to her.

The lingering night outside stilled around them, the dying embers in the fireplace flared a finger of light occasionally, and the waves moved in and out, as if even nature waited with them for what was inevitable.

"It'll soon be daylight," he whispered finally. "You've slept soundly for a couple of hours."

"I know," she murmured, her lashes fluttering nervously. "I'll be fine now. I was—"

"Shhh,' he whispered, his lips brushing hers. "I'm going to make love to you. You know that, don't you?"

Even as he spoke she felt his hardness against her, and then something primitive and instinctive responded within herself. His words tingled along her veins, surging hotly to the warm, soft place between her legs. Leilani strained to him even while her mind tried to reject him. She recognized the passion that was always ready to explode between them, but she was uncertain of his feelings, even as she knew her own for him. Could Rand make love to her even as he planned marriage to Stella?

"We—we can't," she managed faintly. "It wouldn't be proper." Even as she gave her stilted excuse, Leilani knew how inane it sounded when their bodies were pressed together—when they wanted it so much.

"Not proper?" His hands stilled on her flesh, and a sharp note had crept into his tone. He propped himself on an elbow, and his eyes looked suddenly forbidding. "Because of whom? Elwood? Your long-lost beau?" All his fears—and his resolve—came flooding back.

"Elwood?" She tried to twist away but he held her fast. "How dare you say such a thing—when—when you're involved with Stella, your own long-lost love!"

Good intentions flew up the chimney with the smoke, and Rand was beyond control of his rising passion. He lowered his mouth to just above hers. "Will you tell me now—as you lie in my arms—in my bed—that you aren't planning to marry Elwood?" His words were harsh, and his breath came in ragged gulps, as though his restraint hung by only a thread.

Momentarily stunned by his accusing words, Leilani was struck dumb. Her eyes widened with disbelief, and her cheeks flushed with instant anger. How dare he bring up such a painful reminder of the past! Surely she'd done nothing to give him such an idea.

Watching her, Rand read her astonishment—because he knew her secret? Or because it wasn't true? It didn't occur to him that even while she'd regained strength from sleeping, he hadn't slept and his fatigue hadn't been relieved; he might not be thinking rationally. All he knew was that she was his woman, and if she had any doubts, he was about to banish them for good.

Unable to wait for her answer, his lips came down on hers, possessively, almost brutally, stopping her own words of anger. She couldn't escape him, and as his kiss deepened, and the remembered sensations of his lovemaking swept through her, she no longer wanted to be anywhere but in his arms.

Lifting his mouth briefly, he met her suddenly slumberous eyes, seeing her desire reflected in their depths. Her lips were parted, swollen from the assault of his. But still he wasn't satisfied. He kissed her again, his tongue probing, thrusting into her mouth, electrifying her so that she responded by doing the same. A low moan escaped him, and she felt his hardness strain against her nightshirt.

But Rand was already removing the garment, no longer concerned with thoughts that she would resist, for their mouths were locked as they tasted each other, savoring the moment, prolonging the foreplay. Then she lay naked under him, the soft mounds of her breasts heaving, their nipples hard against his bare chest.

Still he didn't take her, and as she writhed in exquisite agony, he feathered her face with kisses as his fingers stroked and tickled and kneaded her breasts. Then his mouth was on her throat, moving lower to capture first one hard bud, licking it until Leilani's head fell back from sheer lustful need of him. When he took the other bud, she could stand it no longer.

"Rand—Rand." Her words were a plea. "Take me now—please!"

Despite his own tormenting need, he continued his scorching journey down her body, his tongue a fiery brand on her flesh. When he reached her secret place, warm and moist from its craving for the ultimate union with him, she cried out. But that only intensified his movements, for he was drunk from the power of being her master now.

As his mouth came back to claim her lips, Leilani couldn't stand it any longer. Her hands moved over his muscled flesh, stroking him, tracing the ridges of his back, the lines of his arms. But when she touched his manhood, his body stilled, as though an intense sensation jolted him with paralyzing intensity. He lifted his face to see all of his feelings reflected on hers. He'd never known her eyes to look so brilliantly blue, so filled with passion for him.

"I love you, Rand," she said simply, holding him tenderly. "I want you—all of you—" Her voice broke, as though the power of her words were more than she could bear.

His eyelids lowered, and she saw how deeply her revelation affected him. "My darling," he crooned. "Oh my precious darling."

Lowering his body as he spoke, Rand positioned himself over her. Then he took her, his earlier desperate need to possess her, to show her that she belonged only to him, tempered now by the loving light in her eyes. Together they soared into the beginning of a new day, sensation after sensation rocking them both. They moved together in the ancient rhythm of love, until he spilled himself into her. And she shuddered with her own climax to their shared passion. When it was over they lay spent, their bodies entwined. And it was a long time before Leilani's throbbing sensations subsided deep within her.

"Do you know who you belong to now, sweetheart?" he whispered against her hair, again nibbling at her earlobe.

"Who?" she teased, sated but somehow back to her old self.

"You still need to ask?" His voice was gruff with contrived disbelief. He shifted himself into a more dominant position. And proceeded to show her again.

Leilani forgot her questions. Her passion was enough for now . . . for the night. As was Rand's.

Chapter Fourteen

It was well past dawn before Leilani fell asleep in Rand's arms, tired for a good reason this time. She came awake slowly, listening to birds singing in the flowering trees beyond the windows and the tumultuous ocean breaking over the beach. There was a faint smell of Rand on the sheets, and the thought of last night brought warmth to her cheeks. Opening her eyes, she saw at once that she was alone in the bed, that the drapes had been closed against the sun and that the day was well advanced.

"Good Lord!" she cried aloud, and sat up.

For the first time she took in the elegance of the beautifully appointed bedroom. Although the walls were paneled with the rich splendor of koa wood, lush carpeting covered the floor, a deeper green than the velvet draperies, bedspread and high-backed chairs near the fireplace. Even the fringed lamp-shades were a pale green. She recognized the wallpaper as being French, as was the furniture. A seascape hung above the mantel, and she guessed it portrayed the Maui coastline near the Walsh plantation.

The evidence of Rand's excellent taste suddenly intimi-dated her. He was so cultured in his way, so much a man of the world, whereas she had never traveled farther than the other Hawaiian islands.

As Leilani found the nightshirt and pulled it on, her earlier joy began to slip away. She glanced at the bed, her gaze rest-ing on the dent in the pillow where Rand had slept next to her. She tried not to feel disappointed because he wasn't there. He hadn't abandoned her, she told herself, only let her sleep. It was a weekday after all, and he needed to work. But still, she felt awkward, out of place, and as she glanced around it struck her that her clothes were gone.

Then the door opened quietly behind her, and she turned to see Kama peek around the door. When she saw Leilani was up, her round face beamed with a big smile and she strode into the room, a breakfast tray in her hands.

"It's lunchtime, but I made you breakfast," the woman chattered, as she placed the food on the little table by the fireplace. "I always like breakfast as my first meal of the day—and I thought you might, too."

She was wearing a flowing dress, much like the floral prints Mama Kauwe wore, and she was friendly, now that she'd gotten used to Leilani in Rand's bedroom. *She doesn't know we slept together,* Leilani suddenly realized. Kama believed she'd been asleep during all the hours since arriving in the house. Leilani didn't know if that pleased her or not. One part of her wanted the whole world to know, the other side warned her to be careful—because she still didn't know where she stood with Rand—*where she wanted to stand with him.*

"Oh, Esther Peterson came by this morning with other clothing, and she said to tell you that your family knows you're safe."

"Thank you, Kama," Leilani replied sincerely. She'd only just thought of her parents and that she needed to send word. Apparently Rand had seen to that, too. "And thank you for everything." She waved a hand. "Last night and today. I'm afraid I was pretty upset and forgot my manners." She managed a smile.

"You're welcome, child. But manners aren't important at such times. The important thing is you've recovered, eh?" She poured coffee into the cup for Leilani. "And Mr. Rand said you are to rest all day."

"But I'm much better now, and I'd appreciate my clothes, so I can return to Dr. Pete's." She hesitated, not wanting to appear abrupt or ungracious. "I know they've been anxious about me, and I need to explain what happened." She gave a little laugh. "Not to mention all the work waiting for me."

"Sure you don't want to stay in bed, as Mr. Rand said?"

Leilani shook her head. "I think I'm all slept out, and need to move around now, get back to normal."

Kama nodded and walked to the door where she turned back. "I understand," she said. "It's healthy to put this behind you, be with your family."

Leilani smiled again, a little sadly. "Yes, that's exactly what I was thinking, Kama."

Then Kama left her, returning a short time later with Leilani's things. Once more Leilani thanked her, and when the housekeeper was gone again, she finished her coffee, washing down the toast and fruit she'd eaten from the tray. Keeping herself busy with her ablutions, and putting on the clean underthings, she didn't allow herself to think about her immediate future—or Stella—or Rand's not being there when she awoke, so she wouldn't feel so—*separate from his real life.*

Going to the windows, Leilani opened the drapes, and the French doors to the upper veranda. The ocean breeze wafted the salty fragrance inland, cooled her hot cheeks and dried the tears that had welled in her eyes. Even the immaculate lawns and garden below her spoke of Rand's privileged life-style, so different from her own. She swallowed hard, and composed herself, and tried to tell herself that she was still emotionally fragile from all that had happened. Then she turned back into the room and put on her blue muslin waist and matching skirt, both work garments.

"You're all ready, I see," Kama said when she came back for the tray. "You're certainly quicker than any of the other women guests who visit us."

Hearing the casually spoken comment, Leilani stiffened. She quickly lowered her lashes so that Kama wouldn't see how deeply hurtful the words were to her. Instead she indulged in small talk, to hide behind and to hear whatever it was Kama was about to reveal.

"Is that so?" Leilani said lightly as she fidgeted with her buttons.

"I believe Stella is even worse than Nancy when it comes to primping." Kama giggled, but Leilani heard a faint note of censure and wondered if she wasn't overly fond of Stella. "But then she always wants to look her best for Mr. Rand," she added dryly. The dishes rattled as she stacked them. "Nancy says Stella will probably marry into the family by the end of the year."

Unaware that Leilani was stunned into silence, Kama waddled back to the door with the tray. "You come on downstairs when you're ready," she called over her shoulder, and disappeared into the hall.

Leilani waited until she'd mastered another urge to cry. Then, without a glance at the bed where Rand had made love to her, where she'd been blissfully happy in his arms, she followed Kama down to the kitchen. She forced her mind to the problem at hand: how she would get back to Chinatown.

Before she solved her dilemma, Rand strode into the house, looking tall and bronze and fit in his cream morning coat and trousers, and oh-so-much the Polynesian god in modern clothing. His eyes were on her the moment he stepped into the room, and for a second something flickered on his face—and she knew he was remembering last night.

He glanced at his housekeeper, and behind her back, cocked a black slanting brow at Leilani, as if they were conspirators, sharing a priceless secret. His grin was rakish, almost boyish in his pleasure at seeing her.

Oh God! she thought, smiling back before lowering her long lashes. How could she doubt him? But Leilani couldn't allow herself to succumb to his undeniable charm, or be fooled. She needed to remember Kama's words. And she needed to go home to the privacy of her own room before she allowed herself to think about what last night meant to her future.

"I was just going to ask Kama about transportation." She managed another smile, pride coming to her rescue. When he would have protested, she went on quickly, explaining her reasons for having to go—Esther and Pete, and her family.

There was something different about her, Rand thought, although what she said sounded logical. She's still shaken by what happened, he told himself, studying her, trying to read past her Oriental veneer, which was suddenly between them. He remembered how she retreated behind that barrier when terribly upset and unwilling to show her fears. He stepped back, realizing now was not the time for their talk. He'd wait until she was stronger. It didn't occur to him that she might be upset by something other than Quong and his thugs.

He resisted the urge to take her back upstairs, and wished that Kama wasn't there. He'd never seen Leilani look so strangely beautiful—flushed by his presence, yet so unapproachable. Her eyes, bright as sapphires, were steady, even as they pleaded for understanding, and her black hair, silvered by a shaft of sunlight, gave her the look of Pele, mythical fire goddess of the volcanoes. She was innocence, yet she was an enchantress. And she was his, he thought with satisfaction.

Because she was determined to go, he agreed to take her. They drove into town under a faded denim sky, while a flock of white terns rode the air currents above them, their plaintive cries somehow echoing Leilani's depressed feelings. Neither found words to mention their night together. As they reached the crowded streets of Chinatown, Leilani sighed, remembering how easy it had been to talk to Rand after they'd made love.

He looked at her, sensing her feelings, suddenly realizing that she might have been uncertain when she woke up and found him gone. Once he reined the horse to a stop, Rand turned to her. "We didn't have our chance to talk, did we, sweetheart?"

His low deep voice rekindled her feelings, and she only shook her head without looking at him.

"But we will, soon—about a change to both of our lives." He tipped up her chin, and gently forced her eyes to his. "When you're up to it." His teeth flashed white against his dark skin as he grinned knowingly. "You'll need your strength, my sweet, so it's just as well to postpone it—because I want all of you."

He jumped down then, taking her agreement for granted, and turned to lift her to the ground. But he kept her in his arms, her breasts crushed against his cotton chest, for seconds longer than necessary, as though he were hesitant to let her go. Without a thought for onlookers, he lowered his mouth to hers and kissed her.

"Until next time," he whispered, his eyes darkening in a way she'd come to know. "And in the meantime, be careful." He didn't add that he'd already had a talk with the doctor and they'd agreed on a procedure to protect Leilani until they saw how Quong reacted to the turn of events.

She went into the house, strangely relieved that the talk was postponed. She didn't want to hear the truth from him; she didn't want to know she'd never be his wife. Nothing was changed, she told herself. She was still the foundling without a background.

Hesitating before she stepped into the house, Leilani felt confused about everything. She didn't even know for sure if Rand had ever gotten over his wife's death. He'd never said so, and never said if his future plans included Stella. Just as he'd never told Leilani he loved her. She shook her head, trying to clear it. All of his actions said that he did love her. But for all she knew, Stella might think the same.

Why did I have to love him? Leilani thought sadly. Taking her fragile emotions in hand, she composed herself and went into the house.

"It seems Mr. Quong believes I coached you, Rand."

Lee had come from behind his desk when Rand came into the office. He paused to light a cigar, and as he blew smoke, Lee's manner was completely Chinese, inscrutable even to Rand, who'd known him since they were children. Then he suddenly knew his partner was terribly upset.

"He's lost face, he's angry, and he's blaming me," Lee went on in a low tone. "He's now saying that he has to reconsider whether I will be allowed to marry Annie."

"That bastard!" Rand cried, tossing his hat onto a chair. "He's just mad, trying to maintain some sort of control, even if it's just over his family."

"Perhaps," Lee replied, but Rand saw that his partner wasn't convinced, that he believed his marriage plans were up in the air. "In any case, this isn't easy for me," Lee went on. "You may have gotten Leilani back, Rand, but I may have lost my future wife, the woman I love."

"Good Lord! Quong is a madman! Surely he wouldn't stop a marriage between you and Annie. It would give him status in Honolulu."

"You have to understand." Lee's control suddenly slipped, and Rand saw how upset he was. "He doesn't necessarily want that kind of status—respectability and living within the boundaries of law. *He wants power!*"

Moving to his own desk, Rand was thoughtful. He turned back to face Lee. "Don't be upset by what I'm about to ask— it's meant well." He hesitated in an attempt to ask his questions tactfully. "Just what did Quong do in San Francisco? Was he a tong? A highbinder? Involved in criminal activities? Or what? And why did he leave there under threat of his life? I understand he was on his way back to China when he decided to stay in Honolulu."

Lee snuffed out his cigar and began pacing the room. Then he stopped in midstep to face Rand. "I gather from Annie— and others—that he was only a shopkeeper. He saw the amount of money being paid to the tong lords and imagined he, too, could make money by threatening and coercing. When he tried it he came up against the tongs and their paid assassins, the highbinders, and fled America to avoid being murdered."

"My God!" Rand cried. "And then he saw that Honolulu was free of such criminal tyranny and saw his chance."

Lee nodded. "That's about it as far as I can tell." He hesitated, and then nervously lit another cigar. "Except that Quong believes I might have overheard things when I was in his house visiting Annie, and then repeated the family secrets to you." He paused to inhale smoke. "The fact that you and I have been so involved in using the law to free the poor Chinese from criminal brutality—legal or illegal—only lends credence to Quong's suspicions about both of us."

"That's insane!"

"I know. But that's Annie's father, blaming others." Lee went to the window and looked out over the harbor. "I believe his dream of becoming a tong lord is over, but that's not the question now."

"What is?" Rand asked, curious to know what the Chinese community thought.

Lee turned from the window, his expression troubled. "What Quong will do next is the question. He will feel compelled to show his intentions—to stay in Honolulu after losing face, or return with his family to China." Lee gave a tired sigh. "In either case, I'm the loser."

"How so?" Rand thought Lee's revelation about Quong was the best news he'd heard in a long time.

"If he stays, he might feel he must forbid my betrothal to his daughter. If he leaves, he takes Annie with him." Again he paused, his gaze intensifying. "There is one other option he might choose—if he's truly crazy."

"Which is?" Rand stiffened, anticipating Lee's next words.

"He might choose to go on with his campaign to gain power and control, and that would mean retribution against those who opposed him. Whether he does will depend largely upon the Chinese community, and how they perceive his strength now."

When Rand only stared, digesting Lee's evaluation, Lee went on. "You went further than I expected, Rand, when confronting him." He hesitated, contemplating the burning tip of his cigar. "Not that I blame you. I probably would have done the same if the woman involved had been Annie." His eyes were suddenly direct and a wry smile touched his lips briefly. "What I'm trying to say is that I understand why you did it. I just hope it all turns out to our advantage." He went back to his desk and sat down, and Rand knew the topic was closed . . . for now.

Disturbed and worried, especially about Leilani, he tried to start the work that was stacked on his desk. He knew Quong and his "secret society" would decide soon about their course of action, and the thought was chilling. Then, thinking about how Quong had been stopped, his contemplation went to Madam Silk Stockings. If it hadn't been for her, and her behind-the-scenes power, Rand was convinced that everything would have turned out differently. And she would have her say about Quong's future. Maybe it would all turn out differently than any of them thought. Maybe Quong would even go back to being a shopkeeper, and become honest—because he had no choice. The madam's influence was often surprising.

Abruptly, his head came up as a random thought struck him. In that way Leilani was like the madam. He shook his head, trying to clear it so that he could get on with his work. He just had Leilani on his mind, he told himself.

"Oh my dear!" Esther kept saying over and over as Leilani related what had happened, why she'd gone and how she'd been rescued—but not that she'd spent the night in Rand's arms. For the time being she wouldn't allow herself even to think of him. That would come later.

"Madam Silk Stockings, eh?" Dr. Pete remarked, his expression suddenly closed. "It just proves what I've always thought—the woman could well be the most powerful person in Chinatown."

Once they were satisfied that they'd heard everything, Leilani announced that she could go back to work.

"Nonsense!" the doctor retorted. "You're taking the next couple of days off, and I'm going to drive you out to the farm so you can be with your family."

When she would have protested, he put up a silencing hand. "It's all settled, my dear. Esther and I value you too much to allow you back to work before you've completely recovered from your ordeal. Monday is soon enough—and that's final." Although his tone indicated he would brook no argument, his smile softened his words.

Within the hour he drove her home, made sure she was settled, then left to see more patients. Mama Kauwe hugged her every once in a while at odd moments during the day. "We love you," she said. "We were so frightened. Quong is an evil man." Then she would smile, her round face beaming. "But you're safe now. Rand and the doctor will make sure."

Leilani was relieved when she was finally alone in her bedroom for the night. As much as she loved her family, it had been exhausting to explain her story again when the boys arrived from school, and once more to her father when he came from the fields. But she also felt fortunate to have such a loving family.

So why am I always trying to find out who I am? she asked herself, as she sat by her open window and stared out at the night. Why can't I just be thankful for who I am, and what I have? But she knew why, as Rand's strong face surfaced in her mind, and all her old fears came back to haunt her.

The woods were black and mysterious beyond the house, the treetops gilded by silvery moonlight. Night birds sang in the fragrant shrubbery, but other than that, the darkness was silent. Contrary to her earlier belief that she'd burst into tears the moment she was alone, Leilani sat dry-eyed, no longer feeling so fragile. She'd regained her equanimity.

She smiled, and realized just how distraught she'd been. All she'd needed was to be home, and to know that nothing had really changed. She hadn't been permanently hurt after all.

Shifting on the cushion, her gaze followed the outline of the distant mountains, etched against the luminous, moon-haunted sky. Now that reason had reasserted itself, Leilani reconsidered Kama's conversation. The kindly housekeeper had only expressed an opinion about Stella's motives, not Rand's. It was my mind that made that leap, and I was unfair, she told herself. The realization made her feel better, more positive about her relationship with Rand. She must trust that he shared her feelings, perhaps was even falling in love with her. Hadn't he told her that their talk would change both their lives? Maybe he was through grieving for his wife, maybe he wasn't in love with Stella, and just maybe he wouldn't care that Leilani was a foundling.

A peace settled over her, an affirmation that she would eventually find her place in the world. She sat on, allowing the tranquillity of the Hawaiian night to soak into her soul. It was as though the moonlight were magic, a mystical light that bathed her in its beauty—and perhaps even made wishes come true.

Silly, she told herself as she finally went to bed. Only children believe in fairies and magic and happily-ever-after.

But she fell asleep with a smile on her lips, and hope in her heart.

Chapter Fifteen

By Monday Leilani was more than ready to resume her work. She was surprised when Dr. Pete sent the buggy for her, which he'd never done before. Again she packed her bags to stay with him and Esther till Friday. She realized these were safety precautions, and she didn't argue about them, as she would have before being kidnapped. Mr. Quong's power to hurt people was all too real to her. She never wanted to be at his mercy again.

During the next few days she saw Rand often, although when he dropped into the office she was always busy, and unable to do more than say a few words. But he reminded her that they needed to talk, and promised to set a date for dinner with her soon, when he wasn't working half the night to finish up important legal work for the island planters.

"I'll look forward to that, Rand," Leilani said, aware that Dr. Pete was looking on, curious. "But you get your work done first."

He grinned, and when the doctor turned away, winked. Then with a jaunty tip of his hat, he left them to their patients.

The pattern continued over the days that followed, and Leilani began to feel more secure about Rand. Even the doctor and Esther hinted that they believed something serious was happening between the young couple.

The news of her abduction had spread like a plague through the community, and as a result the Chinese people treated her with more respect. Even Ho came to her, and in faltering

English apologized for his role in the kidnapping. Leilani was surprised by the overall reaction, and simply shook her head at how no one could keep a secret in Chinatown. She'd become a champion to the Chinese who hoped to become independent citizens of Hawaii, so that they, too, could stand up to dangerous bullies like Mr. Quong. She couldn't help but wonder what Quong thought of the current situation, or what he'd do next. Even Lee didn't know, because Quong wasn't allowing him to visit Annie.

Dr. Pete continued to be cautious about Leilani's activities, and rather than leave her alone, he took her with him on visits to patients he'd previously avoided exposing her to. That was a bonus for her—even though it was sometimes upsetting—for it allowed her to see more complicated cases and their treatment.

"I don't know if you should really have come along this time, Leilani," Dr. Pete said, as they rushed to the bedside of a young pregnant woman, led through a maze of alleys by her frantic husband. "This woman has attempted to abort herself, and it sounds like she's bungled it badly," he added grimly.

Leilani was silent when they were finally ushered into a shack not fit for farm animals, with a sleeping mat in a corner. There the woman writhed in agony on a blood-soaked blanket. Appalled, Leilani swallowed back an urge to gag, and quickly set a pot of water on the stove to boil. Then, obeying the doctor's terse commands, she spent the next couple of hours helping to save the woman's life, although they lost the baby.

"Why did she do it?" Leilani asked later, as they went back to the office.

"Desperate," Dr. Pete replied, his round face etched with lines of fatigue. He glanced at Leilani, his blue eyes candid behind his spectacles. "They already have four kids and no money to feed them. She took the only out she knew."

They walked in silence, and the thought occurred to Leilani that she'd been lucky to not be pregnant after her night with Rand. *What would she have done?* Although Rand was attentive, they hadn't been alone since, and she realized that it was just as well—because they couldn't control their passion.

By the time she and the doctor reached the office the day was over and she went into the house instead. Esther had asked Rand for supper, and Leilani wanted to freshen up before he arrived.

When she entered the front hall, Leilani called a hello to Esther, then continued on to her room upstairs. She quickly busied herself with a bath, selecting what she'd wear, doing her hair—all in an attempt to put the woman they'd saved out of her mind. Somehow the situation had pointed up Leilani's uncertainty about Rand.

When she was ready Leilani hesitated at the mirror for a final look at herself. She'd pinned her hair into a confection of curls and rolls, and had applied powder, lip rouge and even a dab of charcoal on her eyelids; the result pleased her. Her cheeks were flushed—from hurrying, she told herself, unwilling to admit how much she looked forward to being with Rand. Her dress was an off-white organdy with short sleeves and a scooped neckline, its bell-shaped skirt falling in soft folds to the floor. The fabric for the garment had been an extravagance—and the sewing project had kept her occupied during the long evenings.

Her eyes met their reflected image in the mirror, and Leilani smiled, not really seeing their startling blueness under her long black lashes, or that they matched the ribbon trim exactly. She was too pleased by how well the dress had turned out, and hoped that Rand would think it pretty, too.

As nice as anything Stella might have brought from New York? she wondered suddenly. The question had come unbidden, and Leilani whirled away from the glass and swept to the door. I won't allow *that woman* to ruin my evening with Rand, she told herself firmly, not liking the idea that she might be jealous.

Upon reaching the lower floor, Leilani again hesitated, hearing her name mentioned in the conversation that drifted into the hall from the parlor. Rand had just stated that he and Lee had heard that Quong had dropped his grudge against them. "He had to after the abduction became common knowledge. But Leilani still needs to be careful, as men like Quong can't be trusted."

Dr. Pete and Esther must have nodded because Rand changed the subject then to explain that he was leaving for Maui in the morning to attend a meeting of the planters he represented. Leilani hardly heard Dr. Pete's reply, suddenly so disappointed that she only wanted to run back upstairs. Would there ever be a time for her and Rand? Couldn't Rand make time if he really wanted to? And was Stella his real reason for going? Lingering for a moment longer, she managed to compose herself. Then with her chin up and a smile on her face, she went into the room to join them.

Rand stood up at once, unable to take his eyes off her. She possessed such innate dignity, such elegance despite having grown up in a humble Hawaiian family. For a moment he wondered about her background, and who in Honolulu some twenty years ago would have given up their baby. But the thought was only in passing, for as she swept into the room, her blue eyes mysterious under her half-lowered lashes, her full lips lifting in a smile, the lamplight shimmering on her lustrous hair, all he could think of was making love to her. He quelled the jolt of desire within him, and instead took her elbow, to make sure she sat next to him on the settee.

Esther excused herself to see to dinner, and Dr. Pete followed his wife, with a smile and a promise to return shortly. But Leilani knew they left to give her a few minutes alone with Rand.

Suddenly shy, Leilani found herself momentarily tongue-tied. She felt his gaze, and wished she weren't sitting so close to him on the small settee.

"You're looking even more beautiful, sweetheart," he drawled in a husky tone, and turned her face to him.

Their eyes locked, and she was suddenly unable to look away, caught by what she read in his. In that moment all her doubts about his motives, her fears for the future, vanished. *He wanted her!*

Then he pulled her close, so that he could feel her breasts against him, and kissed her, a long satisfying kiss that left her breathless.

"Just so you won't forget who you belong to while I'm gone," he said, and then sat back just as the doctor entered the room.

Leilani tried not to look like a woman who'd just been kissed. And who wanted more, much more.

No longer feeling as if she were being watched, Leilani began to breathe easier about Mr. Quong seeking revenge. But the lesson she'd learned at his hands ensured she'd never be foolhardy again.

It was soon after Rand left town that Leilani ran into Madam Silk Stockings at a meeting for plantation workers. Leilani wouldn't even have been there but for accompanying the doctor, who wanted to speak to the Chinese about recognizing childhood illnesses before they became serious. To Leilani's surprise, the elegantly gowned madam spoke to the group about sending their children to the school she was funding.

"Important that children be educated," she explained as the meeting adjourned, her unreadable gaze on Leilani.

"I agree," Leilani said warmly, realizing that she'd misjudged the old woman.

As they walked toward the door together, the madam suddenly placed her hand on Leilani's arm, stopping her. For a second all she could think was that the madam's fingernails were the longest she'd ever seen.

"You're safe now, Leilani. Mr. Quong won't hurt you again." With those startling words, the madam walked on to where her bodyguards helped her into the buggy. A moment later they were gone, and Leilani was still staring after them. But one thing stood out above all others. She believed Madam Silk Stockings's words.

She went home with the doctor, her thoughts lingering on her impression that the madam liked her. Over the following weeks and into the summer, that feeling was strengthened when Leilani ran into her at other meetings. For some reason Leilani was now allowed to attend these, to represent the workers and the poor to Chinatown's leaders. She believed it was the madam's influence that had brought about the change, as well as her own reputation for standing up to men like Quong.

The summer days were busy for everyone, and she and Rand were never alone, although the sexual tension was building between them. Leilani began to believe that marriage to him might be possible, even though his work often took him to Maui, where Stella was still visiting.

When Leilani learned that it was Madam Silk Stockings who funded many of the projects to better the lives of the poor, she wasn't surprised. Since she'd been allowed into some of the policy-making meetings, and heard how the madam supplied food and medicine to help desperate families, her respect for the enigmatic Chinese woman grew. The madam even helped workers who had fulfilled their plantation contracts and weren't returning to China, to start small businesses. And her legal adviser for her philanthropy was Rand.

Leilani only smiled when she heard, so proud of him. She suddenly knew she'd never really believed he was involved in illegal matters, though she'd briefly suspected it shortly after meeting him.

When she discovered the madam had even been funding her own small project to create a school-like environment for child care so mothers could work and help the family, she was grateful. On impulse, Leilani decided to thank Madam Silk Stockings in person.

Tomorrow afternoon, she decided. After I finish for the day.

It was late afternoon before Leilani made her last house call and headed for the madam's establishment. To avoid the saloon, she went to a side door and knocked, believing it was the entrance to the private quarters. When no one answered she contemplated entering through the saloon after all, even though it was crowded with patrons. But the side door was unlocked, and opened when she tried the knob. Leilani stepped into a narrow hall, thinking there must be an inside entrance to the madam's private apartment, for the building itself was deeper than others along the street.

As she passed several closed doors, Leilani began to suspect that she was in the wrong place. The hall appeared to lead back to the saloon at the front of the building. She stopped short, suddenly realizing that she was in a section of bedrooms, and that the outside door was for the convenience of patrons. *This was where "the girls" entertained their "clients"!* She whirled around to get out of there. She'd rather brave the saloon.

It was too late. A door opened and a bearded man, garbed in sailor trousers and a striped shirt, stepped into the hall, pausing when he saw Leilani. He had a wiry build and though he was only of average height, muscles rippled under his formfitting clothing. He suddenly blocked her way.

"Please," she said crisply. "Let me pass!"

His face broke into a leering grin. She was appalled to see how rotten his teeth were—and that he was drunk. "C'mon, gimme a little kiss, sweetie," he said, his words slurred, his pale eyes lingering on her breasts. Then he lunged forward and grabbed her arms in a painful grip, yanking her to him so hard that some of her hair came loose from its pins and fell into her eyes. He lowered his face and tried to kiss her.

"Release me at once!" she cried. Twisting her face away, she struggled to escape his lips, and his hands, which were moving knowingly over her body. But it was hopeless; his hold only tightened. Then he edged her backward toward the room he'd just left.

"Old Silk Stockings really knows how to pick 'em!" he said hoarsely somewhere above her head.

Oh God! she thought. He thinks I'm a prostitute! Knowing she had to do something quick, Leilani brought her knee up into his groin. His cry of pain was instant, but before she could make her escape, he'd tightened his grasp, and his expression had turned ugly.

"You little bitch!" he snarled. "I'll show you what happens to uppity sluts!"

She kicked his ankles, scratched his face, but he didn't release her. Instead he edged her toward the doorway of one of the rooms.

"You release me, you—you low-down gutter rat!" she cried, and then screamed for help.

He slapped her hard across the face, stunning her, and her body went limp momentarily. As he was about to push her across the threshold, a woman's voice stopped him in his tracks.

"Let her go at once!"

He jerked his head toward the voice, ready to defend himself, and then he saw who had spoken. He let Leilani go so quickly that she had to grab the wall to prevent herself from falling.

"I'm only having some fun," the sailor whined, his excuse having no effect on the inscrutable Madam Silk Stockings, or her two bodyguards. "And I already paid for the woman," he went on, his words giving him courage. "Ain't that what you're so all-fired worried 'bout—the money?"

The madam didn't bother to answer, and her men knew what to do. They moved forward, one on each side of the sailor, and manhandled him to the back door.

"Come around in front," the madam said after him. "Your money will be refunded." She hesitated, then added, her tone icy, "We don't want your kind here."

When they were gone, her gaze shifted to Leilani, and for a second something like humor flickered in her black eyes. "You seem to have a talent for finding trouble, Leilani. How is it that you happen to be in—in my—uh—back hall?"

"I came to see you, Madam Silk Stockings," she replied in her most proper tone, suppressing any lingering upset in her voice. "And I came in the wrong door, thinking it was the entrance to your apartment."

The madam held her gaze for a long moment, her rice-powdered face almost garish in the light from one electric bulb on the ceiling. "I see," she replied finally. "You should have sent a note, made appointment." The censure in the Oriental voice brought a flush to Leilani's cheeks. "Those who love you would not want you here, I assure you."

Before Leilani could respond, the madam indicated that she was to follow her. Before the hall ended at the door to the saloon, another corridor veered in the opposite direction, and they walked along it toward double doors at its end. The madam knocked once, and a second later an old Chinese woman opened up for them.

The elegance of the entry hall took Leilani's breath away, and she could see that the parlor to one side of it was equally splendid. She hesitated, again uncertain. In her wildest dreams, she'd never thought such a place existed in Chinatown.

Madam Silk Stockings spoke in Chinese to the servant, then shifted her gaze to Leilani. "You wait in the parlor. We'll have tea...and talk." Then she moved away, back toward the saloon, a slender, elderly woman who might have been the empress of China for all her innate dignity and pride.

Following the servant, Leilani entered the parlor and was shown to a floral silk sofa. As she seated herself, the woman bowed slightly, then left the room, her slippered feet silent on the Oriental carpet. When she was gone, Leilani glanced around the beautifully appointed room, noting the crimson drapes, ebony furniture and hand-painted lamps. Unable to resist, she stood to admire the art pieces, and walked from painting to painting, then to the figurines. As she sat back down, she noticed the small jewelry box that had been left on the table between the two sofas.

Stiffening, she bent closer, seeing that it contained a collection of cloisonné. The objects were painted in a design that closely resembled the pin left on her baby blanket.

Her heart was suddenly racing, and her hand shook as she picked up a pair of earrings that looked exactly like her pin. Of their own volition, her fingers groped under her bodice and pulled out the pin she always wore on a chain—her link to her mysterious roots.

Holding the three pieces together, Leilani studied them. There was no mistake. They were exactly the same—a perfect match. Confusing thoughts whirled in her head. How could it be so?

And what did it mean?

Chapter Sixteen

"They're from the Ming dynasty," Madam Silk Stockings said behind her, having come quietly into the room.

Startled, Leilani whirled around to face her, and she knew her eyes were wide with all the questions that had come to her mind. But before she could speak, the madam took the earrings from her and placed them back into the jewelry box.

"My maid forgot to put them away," she said. Her words were casually spoken, but Leilani sensed—what? she asked herself. Upset? Shock? Annoyance that a guest would handle personal property without permission?

At that moment the maid, her bright floral kimono swishing against her legs, came into the room with a tea tray. The jewelry box was in the way, so Madam Silk Stockings snapped the lid closed and picked it up. She nodded to the maid, who placed the tray on the smooth ebony tabletop. Then the madam spoke in rapid Chinese and handed the box to the maid. In seconds the maid and the earrings were gone.

"She will put away," Madam Silk Stockings said, her gaze lowered on the tray. "Now we have tea, eh?" She completely ignored the cloisonné pin, which now hung on the outside of Leilani's high-necked, white shirtwaist, and poured the steaming brew into the first cup.

Politeness kept Leilani from continuing the conversation until the tea had been poured and sampled. But she wasn't going to let the matter rest, because she might have stumbled onto a connection to her own background, the first one she'd ever uncovered. The madam handed her the delicate china cup and saucer, then poured for herself. She offered a cookie from a matching china plate, but Leilani declined.

"Thanks, tea will be fine," Leilani said, making small talk. "I never eat between meals."

The dark eyes watching her suddenly crinkled as the madam smiled. "Nor do I."

But the smile didn't disarm Leilani. On the contrary, she began to feel as though she were under a microscope, being assessed feature by feature. She was sure that a great deal was going on behind the madam's placid demeanor. But she sipped her tea, as if she hadn't noticed, and then replaced the cup on its saucer. When she again met the unreadable eyes across the table, Leilani's gaze was as direct as any the madam had ever encountered.

In silence, Leilani pulled the chain over her head, then handed the pin to Madam Silk Stockings. She watched the madam's expression, looking for a twitch, or a flutter of her lashes, or even a movement of her scarlet lips. But no expression revealed itself on the painted and powdered face. For the seconds she seemed to study the pin, Madam Silk Stockings was so still she could have been a Chinese doll dressed up in all its finery. Finally she handed it back.

"It's a cheap imitation." The madam shook her head, and in passing Leilani noted that her piled-up hair was larger than her face. "So sorry."

Disappointment welled up in Leilani, as she replaced the chain around her neck, using those seconds to compose herself. But something about the tone the madam used, or her contrived indifference, wouldn't let her drop the subject.

The madam sipped her tea, peering at Leilani over the cup. "You came to see me, Leilani? Perhaps need help for one of your many projects?"

She'd changed the subject completely, again regaining lost ground. The old woman was clever, Leilani thought wryly. She would never allow herself to be trapped in a conversation, or in business, if Leilani was any judge of character. She was a woman of mystery, yet she'd created her own little empire, such as it was. A powerful woman, Leilani decided, and not one to have as an enemy. Yet she vowed that the old lady wasn't going to evade her, no matter what the cost.

But Leilani answered the madam's question before she asked more of her own. "I came to thank you. I just learned that it was you who put up the money for child care so those mothers could work." Leilani smiled sincerely, for this was a subject different from her other concern. "Those families will benefit by having more income, however small. I appreciate your help—and your willingness to do so."

The usually unreadable face of the madam suddenly shone with pleasure. "I thank you as well, Leilani. As we both know, women *can* work." She paused. "It pleases me that we share an interest in our people—as well as not eating between meals."

The final comment almost made Leilani grin, but because it was a sincere compliment, she restrained herself. She drank the last of her tea, gathered her wits and put down the cup.

"A moment ago you said my pin was only an imitation," Leilani began, bringing back the subject the madam believed she'd avoided. Despite the old woman's control, Leilani saw her features tighten, but she went on anyway. "It looked like an exact match to me. I'm sorry if I upset you, Madam Silk Stockings, but I'm afraid I can't let this matter pass so quickly. I need to know who owned the pin to match your earrings—the pin that now belongs to me."

The room went absolutely silent but for the ticking of the cabinet clock. If Leilani hadn't been so eager to know the truth, she might have apologized and given up the subject, but when the madam only stared, stony-faced, she was suddenly annoyed. Why couldn't she answer a simple question if she had nothing to hide? Leilani asked herself.

"Why won't you answer?" Leilani prompted, leaning forward on her chair. Still the madam said nothing—as though she were groping for words? "Even I know that my pin is not an imitation, and I assume your earrings aren't, either," Leilani went on, pressing her point. "That makes it quite a coincidence, don't you think?" She willed the old woman to respond.

"I know nothing about your pin!" the madam retorted sharply. "Now drop subject."

"I won't—because you're lying!"

Leilani jumped up just as the madam stood and clapped her hands for the maid, who appeared so fast that she must have been right outside the door.

Frustrated, Leilani was now convinced that the madam knew something. She blurted the next thought that came into her head. "Did you know my mother?" She stepped around the table to confront the woman. "If you did, why won't you admit it?"

For a moment shock flickered in the madam's eyes, and her face seemed to go gray under her rice powder. Then she sat back down in her chair, suddenly looking sick. "You go—now!" she cried, and her lashes swept down, black half-moons on her white cheeks.

Instantly, the maid took Leilani's arm, tugging at it, pushing her toward the door. "Mistress—bad heart," she said in singsong broken English. "Go—no trouble, please. Come back later!"

Oh God! Leilani thought, suddenly drained. How could her questions have been so upsetting? The old madam had slumped lower in her chair, as though she really were ill, and her maid was bent over her, rubbing her arms, soothing, giving her something from a bottle.

Leilani managed to go through the saloon and out to the street without a mishap. Once on her way back to the office, she was stricken with many emotions all at once: guilt for upsetting an old woman, disbelief that her well-meaning visit had ended so badly—and sudden shame.

Her mother might have been a fallen woman, might have been from "the floating world," as the Japanese called such an occupation. But the shock of that revelation was nothing compared to her next thought. Was it possible she was related to Madam Silk Stockings herself? Disturbing as her thoughts were, she dismissed the last one because the madam was too old to be her mother.

She moved through the streets, oblivious to the vendors and the traffic, the admiring glances and greetings. For her whole life she'd believed that learning the truth about her birth would change her life. Never once had the thought occurred to her that the truth might be even more shameful, and less acceptable to polite society, than being a foundling without a past.

The tears blurred her eyes when the final, agonizing realization came to her. If what she suspected was true, then she could never marry Rand after all.

Almost back to the office, Leilani stopped in midstride. She wiped away her tears on her sleeve. And when she started off again, it was in the opposite direction. She was walking home, Quong or no Quong threat. If Mama and Papa Kauwe knew the truth, then they must tell her—whatever the truth was.

Papa Kauwe and the boys had just come from the fields, and Mama Kauwe was already preparing supper when Leilani stepped into the kitchen. Since it was midweek, she took them by surprise, but the hugs were instantaneous.

"I can't stay," Leilani said, when Mama Kauwe started to take another plate from the cupboard. "I finished early today, and decided on impulse to come out, because I forgot a pair of shoes I need for a special occasion." Leilani had contrived a reason during her walk to the farm, having calmed down enough to realize she had to get back to Esther's for supper, or the Petersons would be alarmed and think she'd come to harm again.

"Aw gee!" Paulo cried. "I thought maybe we could go swimming."

"Yeah," Willy chimed in. "Since school is out for summer vacation, we don't have much fun."

"You had fun at school?" Leilani was curious, although she knew things had gone better for the boys since Rand's intervention.

Willy nodded at once. "And I miss my friends. Me and Paulo can't wait for school to start again in September."

Leilani only grinned back at their enthusiasm, and marveled at how things had changed...because of Rand. As Mama shooed them away to wash up, Papa Kauwe peered at her, as he'd often done when he suspected there was something on her mind.

"Daughter," he began, and settled his huge bulk into the chair opposite the one Leilani had chosen, "what's troubling you?"

She glanced away from his kind dark eyes, gathering her thoughts. She should have remembered. Her father, although a simple man, had always known when she was upset. Her mother was the dominant personality in the family, but it was her father who had the innate wisdom of his ancient Polynesian ancestors. He, like them, was a man of the volcanic land, in tune with all its ancient vibrations, whether concerning nature or people. And now he waited for her reply.

Motioning for her mother to sit down, too, Leilani struggled with how she would begin. Finally she decided to simply relate what had happened, and proceeded to do so. When she finished there was absolute silence in the kitchen, and Leilani was momentarily bemused. She was getting accustomed to a sudden quiet descending upon people when they were shocked by her questions and at a loss how to answer them.

"So I'm asking you if there's something you know about my birth that you haven't told me," she added, breaking the utter stillness. She glanced from one to the other, but neither parent met her gaze, both looking down at their hands on the table. When they didn't respond, she went on quickly, suddenly knowing that they, in their own way, were devastated.

"I love you both," she reminded them. "And I always will. You're the only parents I've ever had—wonderful, loving parents—and nothing will ever take that away." She hesitated, sensing their hurt. "But I must know the truth, for my own sake." She didn't go into the social aspects of being a foundling, and how that might impact her future concerning marriage to a man like Rand.

"Leilani, Leilani," her mother crooned, her voice soothing, loving. She shook her head, and her large brown eyes were filled with tears—and hurt. "We love you. *We* are your family, no one else. What does it matter who gave birth?"

Her father nodded agreement. "You were a gift to us. And we thank God—even the old gods—that you were given to us." He paused, placing his big hand over hers. "What can be more important than that?"

"Nothing is," she agreed, and searched for words to reassure them, even as frustration pressed down on her. She should have known how they'd react. They meant well because they loved her unconditionally, but they would never understand her insecurities. And for her to mention them would only be more upsetting to them.

She stood, and when they did as well, she hugged and kissed them both. "I love you both so much," she began. "No daughter ever loved parents more." Then as more tears threatened, she left them to get her shoes.

When she returned they were waiting for her. "We understand," her father said unexpectedly. "We know you are truly our daughter, given in love."

"And we don't know who other parents are. That's truth," her mother added, her musical lilt more pronounced. She went to Leilani and placed a hand on each shoulder, her massive bulk overshadowing her daughter's slender figure. "But we have old suspicion—that Dr. Pete might know."

Her revelation took Leilani aback, but she managed to hide her first reaction, instead thanking and kissing her parents one more time. Then she left with the promise to return on Friday for the weekend.

It was only when she was on the trail back to town that she fully realized how upset they had been. They'd forgotten to have one of them accompany her, a practice they'd begun after her abduction.

But the thought was fleeting. She was already bracing herself for her confrontation with Dr. Pete.

Leilani dropped off her shoes at the house and spoke with Esther, who told her that the doctor was still working and that supper would be a little late because of that. Leilani only nodded, and went out to the office to help with the last patient. She'd decided to speak to Dr. Pete alone, as she suspected that Esther wouldn't be in on the secret, if there really was one.

He glanced up and smiled when she came in, nodding when she offered to help clean up while he finished with a patient. Once the boy who'd sprained his ankle left with his mother,

Leilani waited until she and Pete were ready to leave for the house.

"Wait just a minute," Leilani said as he moved toward the door. "There's something I need to discuss with you, and I'd rather do it here than in front of Esther."

Pete turned back to her, his expression questioning. As he waited for her to begin, he took off his spectacles and wiped the smudges away with his shirtsleeve. He was suddenly aware that Leilani was troubled, and gave her time to gather her thoughts. As he replaced his glasses on his nose, she started to talk, relating how she had gone to the madam's establishment to thank her and been accosted.

"For God's sake!" he interrupted. "It wasn't one of Quong's thugs, was it?"

"Oh no!" she cried, her flow of thought suddenly diverted to the other issue. "It has nothing to do with them!"

Grabbing his pipe, he lit up as Leilani resumed her story, listening intently as she related the part about the cloisonné jewelry. She paused, aware that she had his rapt attention, that he was now biting on the pipe stem, not smoking. But he said nothing, waiting for her to continue.

She ended her recitation with her feeling that Madam Silk Stockings had avoided the topic, and, when Leilani pursued her inquiry, had lied outright.

"I believe the madam knows who my mother was," she stated flatly, her words soaring into the room, which almost throbbed with unspoken emotion. She watched his face closely, and his expression went, however fleetingly, from patience to alarm, and when she related the exchange between herself and the madam, from being stricken to tight control. And she knew.

"You know, don't you?" Leilani whispered, suddenly so shaken she had to sit down. Maybe her background was even more shameful than she'd first suspected. Maybe her birth mother was still alive—maybe she was diseased—was afflicted with *mai pake* and was at the leper colony on Molokai.

She forced herself to close off such disturbing thoughts, and stiffening her resolve, waited for Dr. Pete's answer, knowing she would face whatever the past presented. It would be better than what her imagination conjured up, and at least she'd know whether she could ever marry. Yet, even as she thought of marriage, she knew it was probably out of the question now. She loved Rand, would never love anyone else. And she would never shame him.

"The past doesn't matter, Leilani, only the future," he said finally, and placed his pipe in an ashtray. Then he gently pulled her up from the chair and into his arms, soothing her, as a father would soothe a precious child. "The Kauwes love you, Esther and I love you. We've known you for your whole life. No other parents matter, you know that."

"But I need to know. Can't you see that?" she pleaded, aware that he, too, was avoiding a direct answer. "I'm asking you, please, tell me if you know."

He drew in a sharp breath, as though he had come to a decision and was about to answer, when the door burst open and two field hands rushed in, their words a jumble of Chinese interspersed with English.

"Come quick!" one cried. "Knife cut—bad!"

The worker pantomimed a slashing movement to his upper leg, and before he'd even finished Dr. Pete had rushed to grab his bag. They both knew a cane knife was sharp enough to cut off a limb.

"We'll talk soon, Leilani," he promised from the door. "And believe me, honey, you have nothing to be ashamed of." Then his expression altered away from his concern for her, into the professional mode of doctor. "Tell Esther to keep my supper warm." Then he was gone, and she knew he was relieved at the interruption.

After locking up, she went back to the house, related the message to Esther and went to her room to freshen up. But she stood by her open window for a long time, gazing out over the ocean. The sun had descended beneath a bank of clouds on the western horizon, illuminating its strata with feathery fingers of flame, and suffusing the water with a golden opalescence of color.

It had been a startling day. Her life was altered forever, even if no one, aside from herself, would admit it. Dr. Pete had promised to talk again, but she realized her edge was gone.

Now he had time to come up with a plausible story to avoid the truth. But why would he? she asked herself. Unless the truth was too shameful to hear.

Dry-eyed, she stared at the spectacle of changing light as the sun began to disappear for the night. Had he known all along? she wondered. And felt betrayed. By everyone who loved her.

Chapter Seventeen

"I can't help but wish things had gone differently." Richard Drew got up from the overstuffed chair to lean on the fireplace mantel, his gaze holding Rand's. He took a long drag on his pipe, and his blue eyes, still bright despite his being middle-aged, reflected the sorrows he'd endured during his life.

Nodding, Rand was silent in the magnitude of the other man's grief. Although the Drew sugar plantation was one of the largest and most productive in the islands, and Richard's house rivaled the Hawaiian palace in its magnificence, the older man had lost his zest for life. But Rand was resolute; as much as he admired and respected his former father-in-law, he meant to say what needed to be said.

"I, too, wish our lives had gone in the direction we expected," Rand agreed. He swirled the whiskey in his glass, and realized it was going to be even harder to express his feelings than he'd expected. "I'll never get over the death of Nolina, and a part of me will always love her."

Richard smiled sadly. "That's my problem, son. A part of me will always love my daughter, Nolina, and my wife, and my parents." He shook his head, the sheen of his black hair dulled by heavy swatches of gray. Even his hunched posture was indicative of what he was about to say. "And I have no parts left for anything else." He spread his hands. "But it's not in me to give up completely. There are still my workers to consider, my crops to occupy my thoughts."

Glancing away, Rand looked out through the long glass doors that were open to the garden, a riot of flowering plants and shrubs. Birds sang in the leafy branches, and beyond the sweep of lawn, a bluff dropped away to the ocean, an infinite mirror that reflected a cloudless sky. Paradise, Rand thought. But peopled only by ghosts. He shifted on the cushion, and wondered again how he could broach the subject of his own future with this man who had none.

"Come," Richard was saying, bringing Rand's thoughts and gaze back to the older man. "I want to show you something."

He led the way out of his book-lined study to the spacious entry, where the doors to the main salon and huge dining room, both unused since Nolina's death, were closed. But light streaming in through the open front doors, and the long windows from the stair landing illuminated an otherwise shadowy hall. Richard paused in the center, directly under the crystal chandelier, and gestured to indicate the paintings along the wall. "Here are my loved ones," he said, and Rand heard the note of pain in his tone, although his voice was steady.

Glancing along the wall, Rand saw that the gallery of faces included Richard's parents, his wife, Nolina and, at the far end, a young woman he didn't recognize. She was a beauty, dark and exotic, probably Hawaiian. Posed in a crimson velvet gown, hand-painted earrings on her delicate lobes and a matching pin attached to the material in the cleft of the plunging neckline, she looked out upon the world with trust and hope. Before he could ask about her, his curiosity aroused, Richard spoke instead, seeing Rand's puzzlement.

"She was my first love, long ago," he said quietly. "I loved her with all the fire of youth, but it was never to be." He met Rand's eyes. "She's dead, too, for many years now—I included the painting of her to please myself," Richard said with a wry laugh. "There's no one to tell me otherwise, eh?"

Abruptly, he took Rand's arm and led him back to his study. "Contrary to what you think, son, I didn't show you the portraits because I'm being morbid. Oh, I admit to a little sentimentalizing," he went on, as he splashed more whiskey from the decanter into their glasses. "But I've come to my senses. I realize tragedies can happen." His hand stilled for a moment after putting the decanter down. "And I really know what happened to my family isn't because of the wrath of Polynesian gods—although I'm not completely discounting them,'' he added quickly.

Taken aback by Richard's sudden change of opinion, Rand was momentarily without a response. He wondered what had happened to change his mind.

''I know what you're thinking,'' Richard continued and took the chair opposite Rand. ''The old man's gone round the bend.'' He took a quick drink. ''Fact is, hanging those portraits helped. It made me realize that I've had a good dose of life—both good and bad.''

''That's true, Richard,'' Rand agreed, and waited, uncertain about the direction of the conversation.

Richard leaned forward, his lined, still handsome face suddenly earnest. ''What I'm leading up to, Rand, in my own way, is that you're still young. I know you loved my Nolina, but I want you to go on with your life, find someone else to love, marry, have children.''

Astounded by Richard's change, relieved that he didn't have to bring up that very subject, and puzzled by what motivated the man, Rand studied him and tried to determine if he was indeed serious. ''But you were convinced that the old taboos about *haoles* owning sacred ground was responsible.''

''Yes, because I'd taken up that belief when my father blamed my mother's death on the superstition, because she was Hawaiian and had married my father despite disapproval and old traditions.'' He hesitated again, his gaze turned inward, remembering. ''A family scapegoat was established, and in my need to blame, I used it, too.'' He smiled sadly. ''Both my parents died of natural causes, as did my wife. Only Nolina's death was an accident.''

''I don't know what to say,'' Rand said softly, his admiration for the elderly man growing even more. Richard had always been a dominant force on Maui, and now Rand saw his strength of character reflected in his honest appraisal of his own actions.

''You're like a son to me,'' he told Rand, and gave an embarrassed laugh. ''I hope you feel the same about me, but in any case I don't want you to pine your days away. Like I said, find a good woman to marry and have a family. It's what life is all about.''

"I came to discuss that very thing with you," Rand began, knowing he could be nothing less than honest in the face of such generosity. As Richard nodded and waited, Rand explained that he, too, no longer blamed old taboos. Then he told him about Leilani, that he loved her, but that before declaring any intentions to her, he'd wanted to tell Richard first.

When Rand stood up to go a few minutes later, Richard saw him to the door. Then he held out his hand to the man he considered a son. "She sounds like a wonderful girl." He hesitated and Rand thought the blue eyes were brighter than usual. "I look forward to meeting her one day soon. And I'm glad, son. The real tragedy would have been for you to go on grieving."

Then Richard went back inside to the portraits of the past and Rand hurried to catch the steamer back to Honolulu.

Leilani sat in her white silk robe, sipping her tea, having bathed and gotten ready for bed early. The Petersons had gone to a church meeting, and she was enjoying a quiet evening alone. She was sitting on the bench in the tiny back garden, which was fenced and private, to watch the sunset. She welcomed the feeling of peace that settled over her, and tried not to think of how she'd deal with Rand.

But once his face surfaced in her mind it wouldn't go away. Her fears flooded back—and all her feelings of love for him. She took a ragged breath. The terror she'd known at the hands of Quong was nothing compared to her sense of loss concerning Rand. But nothing had changed. She was convinced that her parents had told her everything they knew, and the doctor had explained again that he didn't know any more than her parents had told her. She'd sensed that he was avoiding telling her the whole truth, but when she pushed, he'd only repeated what he'd already said, and very kindly told her not to worry— that the past wasn't important.

It is to me! she thought, and jumped up, leaving her cup on the bench. She began to pace, her earlier peace completely gone. She'd even gone back to see the madam, but the maid had only shaken her head with a curt "Mistress not well."

The sky slowly darkened until the moment when time was suspended in twilight. A night bird began to sing nearby, a plaintive song that was completely in tune with Leilani's melancholy. A slight breeze turned inland from the ocean, rustling the branches above her, but when she heard the creaking of hinges, she whirled around just as a man came through the gate into the enclosed garden.

Her breath stopped in her throat, as her mind leaped to that other night when she was abducted. Her scream was rising to her lips as her heart jolted back to life. Then the man stepped into the swath of lamplight from the open door, a tall man whose pants and shirt molded his lean form, whose dark eyes immediately captured hers in another heart-stopping moment.

"Rand!" she gasped, the word hardly a whisper.

"Sweetheart! Lord, I'm sorry if I frightened you." Rand took hold of her, steadying her as reaction set in. He felt her shaking, and pulled her into his arms, so that she was secured by his body against hers. Smoothing her long hair with a hand, he lowered his mouth and kissed its silky strands. "I went to the front door and knocked, but no one answered," he said softly.

"I thought you were over on Maui," she managed, her mouth against his chest.

"I just got off the boat," he replied, and his breath was warm on her hair and scalp. "And I came directly here." He tipped her chin upward, so that their faces almost touched. "I have something important to say—and I couldn't wait."

A full moon was rising over the ocean, sending its magical light into her garden, enchanting it with a silvery sprinkle of fairy dust. *A paradise moon,* she thought, suddenly so happy to be safely in Rand's arms. She fluttered her lashes nervously, and swallowed hard. But she didn't lower her gaze. The spell of the night seemed caught in Rand's dark eyes, mesmerizing her, holding her with a promise she didn't yet understand.

"I love you, Leilani." His whispered voice throbbed with passion, and his arms tightened possessively around her, aware that only a layer of silk lay between him and her bare flesh. "I love you more than I've ever loved anyone."

Her lips parted but only a soft moan escaped, her words unformed by the impact of his. After all the times she'd agonized over his not declaring his feelings, now his admission took her completely by surprise. Then his mouth was on hers, demanding, passionate, his tongue probing until it gained entrance. The kiss deepened until they clung to each other, their hands moving and seeking. He edged her backward until they were seated on the bench, and the teacup tumbled to the grass.

But reason surfaced momentarily. "We can't do this, Rand," she murmured against his lips, yet her body spoke its own language, pressing closer to him. "The Petersons could return, or someone else might come around to the garden—as you did."

Her protests went unheeded. It was almost as if Rand had suppressed his feelings too long, and now he couldn't stop. His hands cupped her breasts, his fingers tantalizing the nipples into hard buds that sent a shivery sensation throbbing into the warm folds of her femininity. She moaned, suddenly oblivious to anything else.

"It's all right, my darling, because we love each other." His hands traced fire on her flesh under her gown, skin softer than the silk that covered it. "And if anyone should come, it doesn't matter, because you're mine—and you're going to be my wife."

Her whole body was inflamed by his touch, she wanted him, was ready for him, but she pulled back, his words bringing her back to reality.

"Marry you?" she stammered.

Reflected lamplight burned in his eyes as he looked into her face, momentarily diverted. "Yes, my little angel of mercy. As soon as I can arrange it."

Her heart stopped, then raced forward, sending her fears coursing though the very veins that had been ignited by passion only seconds earlier. Her eyes widened with it, and he was suddenly uncertain.

"You do want to marry me, don't you, sweetheart?"

Oh, dear God, she thought, knowing it was what she wanted most in the world. She loved him more than she'd ever believed it possible to love anyone. Leilani sucked in her breath on a sob. Because she loved him, wanted the best for him, could never humiliate him or their future children by secrets hidden in her past, she couldn't say yes.

His expression tightened, and he looked uncertain all at once. "You have to marry me, darling, and put me out of my misery." He feathered kisses over her face and throat, willing her acquiescence. "If you're worried that I'm still living in the past, then I assure you that I'm not—that I love only you."

She reached and stroked his hair, softly, lovingly, then his face. "I wish I could say yes," she began, her voice shaking as she buried her head against his chest. "Oh God, how I wish I could. But I can't."

Under her ear his heartbeat was steady and strong, and loud in the stillness that held them each in their own torment. When he would have spoken, she put a finger over his lips. "I care too much to hurt you or disgrace you, perhaps even ruin your career," she managed.

"You could never do that," he replied at once, his tone puzzled. "Is it perhaps because of that Quong incident? Because nothing you've ever done makes any difference to me."

She shook her head, gathered her courage and blurted out her deepest fear. "It's not what I've done, it's who I am—or might be." She hesitated, struggling for control. "You've forgotten I'm a foundling," she said, her voice fading into a whisper as she glanced away.

"For heaven's sake!" he cried, but he sounded relieved. "For a second I thought something was really wrong. I don't give a damn about that."

"I do, Rand, and—"

At that moment she heard the Petersons' buggy stop in the street, then turn into the little driveway past the office to the house and stable.

"Oh my God!" Leilani whispered, abruptly aware of her undressed state, that she was flouting social convention by being with Rand when she was next to naked. "It'll embarrass them if they see us together like this, and they'll wonder."

He nodded, but his eyes were still troubled. Quickly, he pulled her back against him and kissed her long and deep. "Then I'll go out the gate before they see me," he whispered gruffly as he lifted his mouth. "But I mean to see you soon and get to the bottom of this nonsense." His look intensified. "And in the meantime, don't forget who you belong to, and who you'll always belong to."

Then he was gone, disappearing into the night. Leilani shivered as she walked to the house. The warm trade wind had suddenly gone cold.

Over the next few days Leilani made some changes to her work pattern. She had a talk with Dr. Pete to point out that the danger from Mr. Quong was passed, that rumor said even his henchmen had taken proper jobs, having realized that Honolulu wouldn't allow a tong lord to gain a foothold. There was even speculation that Quong would return to China. That pleased Leilani, even though she wondered how it would affect Lee Chun's hope to marry Annie Quong.

"I've decided it's safe to live at home now," Leilani said, careful to conceal her real feelings—that he hadn't told her the whole truth, that she needed to be with her family now because she felt even more rootless.

"I don't know," he said, his expression concerned. "Quong isn't a man to give up easily, or forget a grudge."

They discussed the matter and the doctor finally agreed, with the stipulation that she wouldn't go home after a certain hour when the road had no traffic. "If it gets late, then you stay with us."

She went home that very night, having seen to her house calls during the morning. With the doctor's approval, she took the ledgers to do in the evening. Because she felt too hesitant to accept Rand's proposal for all the reasons she'd said, or to refuse and end their relationship forever, the arrangement worked out for her. She missed Rand each time he came to the office and to the Peterson house, and she stayed away from meetings he might attend. She was even gone when he came to the Kauwe farm on the Sunday before he had to return to Maui on business, having taken her young brothers to the beach for the day.

During that time Leilani didn't allow herself to think of the future, because to do so conjured up images of always being alone, or of marrying Rand only to have the past cause a scandal and destroy their lives. In avoiding Rand, Leilani believed she was doing the best thing for both of them. But she knew the day was coming when she could no longer postpone ending their relationship.

Although she didn't see Rand, she kept running into Elwood, and finally realized he was crossing her path on purpose. When he asked her to a social function, she declined; when he offered to help fund her child-care project, she directed him to the person in charge; when he said he'd like to visit her at the farm, she told him she was busy with her family. She wondered when he'd accept that she wasn't interested in him, hadn't been for years.

Then one afternoon as she left the office for the day, Elwood fell into step with her. "Hello, Leilani," he said. "Walk you home?"

She stopped short and faced him. "Elwood, why on earth would you want to do that?"

His smile froze, but he tried to seem nonchalant. "Why does a man usually want to walk a woman home?" he replied quickly. "Because he enjoys her company."

Trying not to look as annoyed as she felt, Leilani drew in a deep breath, and knew she had no option left but to be brutally frank. Niceties simply didn't work with Elwood.

"I don't wish your company, Elwood," she began, keeping her tone level. "I'm no longer an eighteen-year-old girl with a crush on you. Long ago I realized that you were right to adhere to the wishes of your family. Now, years later, I'm not interested in your company, for my own reasons."

"I don't believe you!" he cried, his eyes narrowed with anger. Gone was his smile, and Leilani suddenly saw the spoiled boy she'd once imagined she loved. When he grabbed her and slammed her against his chest, oblivious to the people around them, she was momentarily too shocked to protest. His arms held her in a viselike grip, as his mouth came down on hers in a wet kiss that repulsed her completely. Pinned to him, she couldn't move, let alone struggle.

"Now tell me you don't care!" he whispered hoarsely, lifting his lips for only the moment it took to speak.

Before she could do more than open her mouth, he claimed it again, but not before Leilani saw that Elwood's public display had attracted a crowd, and standing to one side, looking shocked and angry, was Rand.

Horrified by what she knew he must be thinking, Leilani kicked Elwood in the leg, then stamped on his foot with her heel. With a screech of pain, he let her go. She stepped back fast, until she was stopped by the hitching post.

"You bastard!" she cried. "How dare you accost me like this!" Leilani's whole body throbbed with embarrassment and she knew her face was scarlet. The crowd, aware of her humiliation, shuffled away. But Rand was already gone, and she suddenly knew he thought her a submissive partner to Elwood. "I ought to have you arrested!" she flung at him, and to her further mortification, her voice broke on a sob.

With a swirl of her skirts against her legs, she left him, and ran across Pauahi Street, headed toward the farm, which lay in the shadow of the mountains. Although she'd been avoiding Rand for her own reasons, she knew he wouldn't keep trying to see her now. By the time she left the town behind she could no longer control her tears.

"Damn Elwood!" she murmured. "Damn him to hell!"

When the summer drifted toward fall with no further contact with Rand, Leilani knew it was for the best, although she often cried herself to sleep at night. But she kept her feelings private and went about her life. She'd heard he was on Maui more than ever, and that saved her running into him by accident. Once more she tried to see Madam Silk Stockings, but was again stopped by the maid. It was fate, she thought finally.

Or perhaps the intervention of the old Hawaiian gods, she reflected early one Saturday afternoon as she walked through the woods to the waterfall. She smiled at her own whimsy, knowing she'd grown far too introspective over the past several weeks. But she allowed the thought free rein, and projected it further. Perhaps the gods, the ones her Hawaiian parents had talked about since she could remember, knew a foundling such as herself would only bring disgrace to the Walsh family, which could trace its roots back to the early Polynesians, even though its heritage was part *haole*.

Her musing about Rand no longer brought instant tears, although Leilani knew her feelings were still close to the surface. As she walked, she allowed the utter peace of the woods to enfold her, like a benediction that would heal her broken heart. A melody of bird song added to the splendor of the perfect day, one that was hers to spend alone, her parents having taken the boys to a Hawaiian music festival. Leilani had gone each year, but this time she had begged off, fearful of running into Rand.

Mama Kauwe had only nodded, saying, "It's all right, Leilani. One day all will be fine—you see." And Leilani had known that her kind mother realized how she was suffering over Rand, even though neither of her parents had pushed her to talk about it. As always, they would wait until she was ready to tell them.

She heard the waterfalls and quickened her step, anxious for her swim. When she stepped into the tiny clearing, fragrant from the blossoms of lush tropical shrubs and trees, she paused, as always transfixed by its wild beauty. Her gaze followed the sun-dappled water from where it poured over the rim at the top of the cliff, to crash into the pool at its base before bubbling away into the stream that wound into the valley. She was alone. No one would disturb her afternoon in her own secret hideaway.

It was a heady thought, and as she changed into her bathing costume, placing her simple blue cotton dress with her underthings in the shade of a shrub, she made an instant decision. She'd swim without the bathing costume, since the pool was private, a thing she was able to do on rare occasions. Once naked, she remembered her chain and pin and quickly placed them atop her clothing as well.

Then, without hesitation, Leilani stepped to her favorite rock and dived into the pool, deep into its blue translucent depths. She swam underwater to the base of the falls, surfacing where the spray misted the air and reflected the sunlight in prisms of rainbow colors. She floated, her long hair splayed out behind her in a sun-silvered sheen of black, watching a lonesome cloud slither across the sky, like a white puff of smoke expelled from an invisible giant.

Frolicking and floating, diving and swimming, Leilani loved the sensation of the water caressing her skin. Then she dived deep, aiming herself toward the falls, swimming under them to the place she'd found accidentally when she was fourteen, a tiny grotto she'd never shared with anyone, even her brothers.

When she popped to the surface she was behind the falls, and the sun on the wall of water cast the little cave into a flickering display of rainbow light. It was possible to see though the falls where the water wasn't heavy, and as Leilani crawled onto the ledge just above the swirling pool, she stretched out, relaxing, spreading her hair to dry in the fractured sunlight. Closing her eyes, she dozed, lulled by the hypnotic sound of the waterfall.

Caught between sleep and wakefulness, Leilani gradually became more aware of her surroundings. But something niggled at the back of her mind, and she suddenly opened her eyes.

At first she didn't see him, standing at the end of the ledge, perhaps ten feet from her. For a moment she thought she'd conjured him up to indulge herself in a daydream, an ancient Polynesian god straight out of one of the old myths. He stood graceful and completely masculine in his nakedness, his manhood exposed in all the glory of love, like a magnificent bronze statue. But the fire in his dark eyes was real, as was his intention.

"Rand!"

Her use of his name brought him to her just as she scrambled to her knees, prepared to dive back into the water. In a second he'd closed the space between them, and was kneeling next to her, pulling her into his arms. Her cool breasts were pressed against his warm chest, so thickly matted with hair that even its casual brushing aroused her nipples into hard erections. He tipped her back so that he was arched over her, his face above hers, and looked into her eyes.

"Why didn't you tell me that Elwood accosted you that day?" he demanded, and although his voice was low, there was a ragged edge to it. "If it hadn't been for the doctor, I'd have gone on believing you'd kissed him."

"It was for the best, Rand, because—"

She broke off as his grip tightened around her waist, pulling her even closer. Something—anger? frustration?—ignited in his eyes, blending with the raw desire that held her gaze, even as her long lashes fluttered nervously.

"For the best?" he repeated. "How can that be so? Are you still in love with Elwood?" Even as his words tore from his throat, his hands had begun to caress her, his fingers practiced in the art of stroking and coaxing her flesh into a state of ecstasy.

"I don't love Elwood," she managed faintly. "Surely you can't believe that I do."

Already his touch was clouding her resolve. She tried not to remember how it felt to be controlled—possessed—by him, how his pulsating rhythm had taken her to heights of sensation almost beyond bearing, only to make her crave more. Unable to answer, she could only shake her head.

"Oh, Leilani!" he groaned. "Thank the good Lord that I saw your parents at the festival and they told me you were here." He paused, his hand sliding over her breast to her thigh, and his fingers so close to her soft folds brought a low moan to her lips. "Because we're settling whatever is bothering you right now—before we leave this place."

Feeling trapped by her own desire, Leilani tried to break free so she could swim back to her clothes. But his grip only tightened, and then he forced her lower onto the ledge, so that she lay under him, his body arched over hers.

"Struggling won't help you now, my darling," he whispered, a rich thread of passion coloring his voice. "Because there is no escape."

He stared into her brilliant eyes, their blue never more startling, reflecting their rainbow grotto—and her rising passion. Even if he'd wanted to, there was no way he could have stopped himself from making love to her. Seeing her clothing stacked on the grass when she wasn't in the pool had struck such terror into his heart that it had almost stopped. Then he'd seen her vague shape behind the falls, and immediately threw off his own clothes so he could join her.

A wing of black hair had fallen forward onto his forehead, blending with his thick brows. The flickering prisms of light seemed caught in his eyes, pulling Leilani into their depths, somehow making her one with him even though they were still separate. Vaguely, she knew that the enchanted grotto was a virgin place where lovers had never made love before—until now.

Rand watched her changing expression, knew her resistance was about gone. Satisfied, he lowered his mouth to her lips, his tongue moving inside her mouth, claiming her just as his manhood would thrust inside her when he could no longer control his restraint.

"We can't do this, Rand. We must talk."

He stopped her protest with more kisses. "I'm going to make love to you—love you so completely that you'll never be free of wanting me—never love another man after me," he crooned softly, so sure of himself, as he punctuated his words with kisses on her face, her ears, her closed eyelids. His fingers tickled her nipples, and the jolt of hot desire in the soft, moist folds between her thighs was instant. Her words could deny, but her body strained for his, desperate for their joining.

"You're so lovely," he said softly, and Leilani's hands crept around his back, stroking the irregular ridges, the sudden hollows, tracing the firm swell of his muscles. He caught his breath, and with a low moan, he lowered his mouth onto hers, savagely, as though he couldn't get enough of her, couldn't fill himself with her essence.

Then they clung together, exploring, smoothing limbs with searching hands, kissing and licking, until the grotto felt steamy from the lust of each for the other's body. He cupped her breasts, then sucked each nipple, until an agony of longing merged with sheer ecstasy for Leilani. She stroked his male shaft, so big and powerful, so absolutely hers. They moved to the brink of their joining, only to recede again, delaying the ultimate, seeking the thrill of sensation building upon sensation, testing themselves to higher peaks of sensual pleasure.

"Take me now!" Leilani cried finally, her voice a broken plea. "Rand!— Rand! Please take me now—before I die of you."

But he demanded even more, and lowered his mouth over her breasts, then lower still, touching her secret place, that was *his* place—her soft folds that were moist from her need of him. His tongue electrified her, peaking her with a reaction that sent instant spasms radiating from the very core of her. She cried out, clinging to him, her nails digging into his back.

Rand lifted his head, satisfied by her absolute submission to him, inflamed by her climax. His lids were lowered from the weight of his own surging need, and his eyes burned with passion he could no longer control. He wanted her—now.

Raising himself, Rand poised himself over her for only a moment. Then he slipped inside her, and for only a fraction of a second was he gentle. Unable to help himself, he plunged deep, but Leilani arched to meet him. She held him to her, as one with the gleaming body she loved so much, the muscles that rippled with each rhythmic movement. They soared higher than ever before, and the music of the waterfall was a mounting crescendo in Leilani's ears, music that climbed the scale toward a final note that encompassed the total meaning of love.

She loved him. Spiraling upward, faster and faster, Leilani welcomed the affirmation of their love, and the uncontrollable spasms that reverberated through every cell in her body. She called out his name, and begged him to give her his own climax. A moment later, he spilled himself into her, as his convulsive tremors joined hers.

They lay still in each other's arms, still joined, their legs entwined, until their passion subsided. After a while, he nuzzled her hair. She turned slightly, offering her mouth.

"I love you," she whispered sincerely.

"I love you, my little darling," he answered back, his voice still rich with passion.

And then he drew her closer, and as they hadn't pulled apart, he slowly began again, this time as they lay facing each other, their eyes locked, their faces open to each other as the sensations started once more. But as passion grew, going beyond control, there was no time to contemplate anything other than soaring into the oblivion of mutual climax.

It was a long time later that they slipped into the water, swam under the falls together and came up on the other side, their lips locked as they surfaced. The sun was lower in the sky and the pool was shadowed with leaf patterns. A faint breeze stirred the tropical foliage, whispering its secrets to the mythical *menehunes* who must live near the pool, for it was truly an enchanted paradise, Leilani mused, sated from Rand's lovemaking.

He pulled her into the shallows and they sat on a submerged ledge, so that only their shoulders and heads were above water. Rand draped an arm around her, so that she was tucked into his side. He glanced into her face, his eyes slumberous, looking more relaxed than she remembered ever having seen him. Then he smiled before dropping a light kiss onto her mouth, which felt bruised and swollen from their hours of lovemaking.

"Now my sweet," he drawled softly, "I want to know why you've been avoiding me."

Somehow, sitting naked with him in the sun-dappled pool, feeling closer to him than she'd ever felt to anyone, her old fears didn't seem so important. "It has to do with me being a foundling," she began and paused, glancing away.

"I told you how I feel about that—it doesn't matter."

"But there's more." Leilani went on quickly, for despite their intimacy, she felt a twinge of apprehension. So before she lost her courage she told him about her visit with Madam Silk Stockings, and about finding the cloisonné earrings.

"Wait here," she told him and quickly stepped from the pool, ran to her clothes and returned with her pin. Dangling it from its chain, she explained that it was clasped to her blanket when she was left on the Kauwe doorstep—and that it matched the madam's earrings.

Startled, Rand took a closer look, turning it over in his hands, recognizing it as Ming. He glanced at her, puzzled, and then something clicked into place in his mind—and he remembered where he'd seen it before. God! he thought. What did it mean? Could it be just a coincidence?

His gaze intensified, as though he were studying her face—looking for something? she wondered. Suddenly disconcerted, Leilani lowered her lashes, and couldn't finish what she'd begun to tell him. Why didn't he comment? she asked herself. Was he already making the connection between her and the madam? Perhaps he was repulsed by the ramifications of her story.

Oh God! How had she ever believed she could tell him? she cried inwardly. But she knew it was because she loved him so much, believed him when he said her past didn't matter. She took a deep breath, and forced herself to think of getting dressed and going home, so she wouldn't embarrass herself with tears. Everything else could wait until she was alone.

When he didn't ask her to continue her story, didn't protest when she took back the pin and pulled its chain over her head, Leilani stood up, suddenly conscious of her naked state. It was apparent that Rand was completely preoccupied by what she'd told him. Was he having second thoughts? she wondered. She waded to the bank and began dressing.

He followed her out of the water, went to her and nuzzled her neck. "I suppose we must go," he whispered, and with a final kiss on her wet hair, he turned to his own clothes.

The sun slipped lower, so that the pool was completely in the shade, and Leilani suddenly felt the chill of evening in the air. When she was ready, he was already waiting, and they started out immediately. He talked about other things, about his work for the planters seeking a voice in Washington, D.C., concerning sugar exports, then about the issue of the Chinese gaining citizenship in the new territory.

He sought her opinion, and she gave it, and if she hadn't noted his earlier reaction to her pin, she would have been walking on air, anticipating years at his side. But it was as she'd always known—never to be.

By the time he left her with a kiss, conscious that her family had returned, he still hadn't mentioned their earlier conversation, only that he'd see her soon.

"And remember, no more evasive tactics, sweetheart," he whispered as he mounted his horse.

Leilani watched him out of sight, then went into the house, a smile on her lips for her parents. A few minutes after that she went to her room.

Confused and upset, she lay on her bed, watching the changing patterns on the ceiling as the sunset sent brilliant streamers of color from the far horizon. Her mind went back over his reaction, and how he'd dropped the subject completely after he'd seen her pin. Yet he'd still been affectionate, and wanted to see her again. For sex? she wondered, devastated by the thought, because he hadn't mentioned marriage again, and she had believed he was leading up to that. It was one of the reasons she'd been open with him about the questions raised by the jewelry.

She squeezed her eyes shut, vowing not to cry. It never occurred to her that she was totally wrong, that Rand was shocked by something else entirely. She only knew she was still the foundling. And always would be.

Chapter Eighteen

Once home, Rand went into his study, wanting to be alone so he could think. He realized that in his absorption over the pin, Leilani hadn't clarified her relationship with Elwood, but he suspected it wasn't an important one. If being a foundling weren't such a problem to Leilani, he'd just marry her, but obviously she feared that an old scandal might ruin him, and he realized she'd stick to her decision.

Ridiculous, he thought. It didn't matter to him. But then he wasn't the one who'd never truly belonged, he reminded himself. He wasn't the little girl who'd been shunned because of being a half-breed with no background, who'd been turned down by her first love because she wasn't good enough for his family. And now it was plain that she believed she was connected to Madam Silk Stockings in some way, an even more unacceptable background to polite society. Maybe the madam knew her mother, he thought suddenly, because it was obvious that Leilani had Chinese blood as well as *haole*.

Lighting a cigar, he stared out into the night, wondering what old secret would compel a mother to give up her child. Being unmarried, he thought suddenly, and his mind again flashed on Leilani's pin. It was a mystery, and maybe the key—her father—was on Maui. As soon as he could get away from his obligations in Honolulu, he was going over to Lahaina and find out. The sooner Leilani's past saw the light of day, the sooner they could get married. Rand intended her to be his wife, and no power on earth was going to stop that from happening. If his suspicion proved true, it could restore more than

Leilani's hope of learning the truth. But he'd keep his own counsel, he decided, until his investigation was complete, in case he was wrong.

"Oh, there you are." A female voice came from the doorway.

Startled out of his contemplation, Rand jerked his head in the direction of the door just as Stella swept into the room. His brows arched when he took in the fact that she was wearing a revealing, emerald-green dressing gown—that she was dressed for bed.

"Am I disturbing you?" she asked sweetly, and he hid his annoyance.

She and Nancy were in Honolulu on one of their frequent buying trips, and to attend the festival. After he'd run into the Kauwes at the festival, he'd left the two sisters on their own, and hired a driver to take them home when the event was over. He'd seen Stella's frown and known she didn't want him to leave, but she'd quickly suppressed her anger under a veneer of understanding. And now she'd disturbed his need to be alone, and his only thought was to be rid of her.

He stood up. "No, you're not disturbing me, Stella. In fact I was about to go up to bed." He paused, his gaze flickering over her night wear. "I see you are about to do the same."

She smiled, and it suddenly occurred to him that she was being seductive. But even though the upper curves of her small breasts were exposed by the low cut of her gown, and he suspected she wore nothing under it, he felt cold to her charm. His heart belonged to a hot-blooded, headstrong woman of unknown origin, and the mental image of Leilani brought a smile to his lips.

"I thought perhaps we could have a nightcap," she suggested, and moved closer, feeling more confident when she noted his expression. "Nancy is already in bed and the housekeeper has gone to her quarters." She hesitated, letting the implications of their being alone sink in. "A sip of liquor always helps one sleep."

"Sorry," he replied, careful to keep his tone casual, knowing very well what she was up to. He'd been trying to avoid this very situation for weeks. She'd like nothing better than to be compromised—so she could manipulate him into a proposal.

"Oh, come on, Rand," she crooned seductively. "You never used to be so stuffy."

"Perhaps you never knew me, Stella," he retorted at once. Watching her, he saw that she was determined, and he suddenly knew that he was the reason she'd come to Hawaii, and then stayed on—to land a husband...him. In that moment of realization Rand also knew that he must now be frank, let her know where his feelings lay, that he was already in love with another. He had no intention of being seduced by Stella.

"Oh, I think I know you very well," she went on, choosing not to be thwarted from her goal. "And I believe we have much in common, that we should spend more time together, so we can explore the possibilities of a future—uh—our friendship," she ended boldly.

He took her elbow, his touch light and impersonal, and directed her back out to the hall. "As I've said in the past, we'll always be friends, Stella," he told her as they walked to the stairs. "You're family after all, being Nancy's sister. And I'm sure that when I marry again, my wife will feel the same way." They'd reached the landing and started up the final steps to the second floor. Rand's intention wasn't to hurt her feelings, only to make the situation perfectly clear once and for all. She was becoming a serious irritation, and she needed to forget him and get on with her own life.

She stopped abruptly, facing him. "Are you saying that you aren't interested in me being anything more than your friend?" Her tone was sharp, her words clipped.

He met her angry eyes, and felt sorry for her. But he'd never been romantically interested in her, and never would be. And he'd never led her on. "Yes, Stella, that is what I'm saying," he replied gently, trying to soften the hurt.

An angry flush started in her neck to suffuse her face. She licked her lips, started to say something and then closed them again. She whirled away and ran up the remaining steps. "Go to hell!" she tossed behind her, and a minute later he heard her bedroom door slam.

He continued on to his bedroom, a wry smile on his lips. She'd get over it. And he'd be grateful when she was no longer dogging his heels, visiting at unexpected times. As much as he hated disappointing her, he'd had no choice but to level with her.

He went into his room, his mind already on what he would do first thing in the morning. Dr. Pete must know something about Leilani's past. Back when she'd been born, he was one of the few doctors in Chinatown. Whatever he knew, Rand meant to find out. One way or another.

"For God's sake!" Rand cried, unable to control his annoyance. "I sure as hell didn't expect you to lie."

The doctor's blue eyes glinted at Rand's words, but his lips were set in a firm line, as though clamped shut to resist saying the wrong thing. He turned away to busy himself with his surgery equipment. The two men were alone in the office, and Dr. Pete suddenly wished that a patient would walk in the door, or that Leilani, the very topic of their conversation, would return early from her rounds.

"Have you ever heard of confidentiality between doctor and patient, Rand?" He shot a glance over his shoulder. "Why can't you let matters be? What does it matter who Leilani's parents were, for God's sake?" His tone hardened. "If you love her then marry her, and let the past be damned!"

Rand sucked in his breath, striving to stay calm. "Haven't you heard a damned thing I'm saying? Leilani won't marry me—anyone—with this cloud over her." He began pacing the little waiting room. "I think she would have, had she not seen those earrings, and the madam, *and you,* being so evasive. She thinks there's something so terrible surrounding her birth that she won't risk it tainting anyone else, should the real truth surface."

"Are you sure she won't marry you?"

"I couldn't be more positive," Rand stated emphatically. "Even though we love each other. And she knows I've gotten over my first marriage now."

The doctor's hands stilled. "I'll have a talk with Leilani," he said finally. "Remind her that the past doesn't matter—that—"

"That's a damn stupid thing to say, and you know it!" Rand interrupted. "You already did that once, and it had the opposite effect." Rand stopped pacing, and grabbed the doctor's arm, punctuating his words with slight shakes. "I thought you loved Leilani like a daughter, wanted her to have a good life, be happy!"

"Heavens, man, that's exactly what I do want. It's exactly why she's been protected all these years."

"Then wake up!" Rand retorted. "Times have changed, and it's too late to lock the barn door after the horse is out. In other words, Leilani's fears might be worse than reality, and in any case she's an intelligent woman who'll cope with truth far better than with everything her imagination is conjuring up at the moment." Rand dropped his hand from the doctor's arm. "The truth can't hurt her any more than what she's suffering right now."

Putting down his instruments, Dr. Pete moved to the window, his eyes on the ships in the harbor, above which dark clouds were threatening an October storm. But he was seeing another scene, one that happened more than twenty years ago. Finally he turned back to the room, his plump face serious, as though he'd come to a decision. He waved Rand into a chair, then took the one opposite. The cabinet wall clock gonged the hour, a ship in the harbor tooted a horn, and a Chinese vendor passed on the walkway beyond the door, calling his wares.

"Perhaps Leilani should hear this first," he suggested, still putting off the inevitable.

"It's best you tell me first," Rand replied at once. "I'll explain the reason after I hear your story."

"I have your word that what I say will remain confidential, should I decide not to tell Leilani after all—or should you decide not to marry her?"

Rand nodded. "But I guarantee you, one way or another, Leilani will be my wife."

His words satisfied the doctor. Slowly, he began, and almost from his first words, Rand sat transfixed. "I was the doctor who was present at Leilani's birth. It was one of my first deliveries after setting up practice." He broke off, remembering the tragedy, his round face stricken. "They waited too long before summoning me, although I don't know if it really made any difference."

"Who?" Rand leaned closer.

"The mother of the girl giving birth," Dr. Pete went on. "The girl—she was twenty—was beautiful, looked more Hawaiian than Chinese, and she had bad complications, wasn't dilating properly." He shook his head, and his gray unruly hair fell forward, but he didn't seem to notice as he went on. "By the time I got there she was weak, and probably already dying. I knew I had to do something quick, and I finally managed to deliver the baby." He hesitated, and Rand saw how desperate the young doctor must have been. "She lived long enough to hold her little girl, and I've never seen such love in any new mother's eyes as was in hers."

"What about the father?" Rand queried as the first flash of lightning flickered through the room, followed by a rumble of thunder. "Was he there also?"

Dr. Pete shook his head again. "The girl wasn't married, and to this day I don't know who the father was, although I gathered he was *haole,* and that their secret relationship was ill-fated, because of her being half Chinese."

"Half?"

Nodding, the doctor continued. "The young woman's mother was Chinese, from China, descended from the ruling class. She met a white man who'd come to China to do business with her father, to recruit peasants for the fields in Hawaii. Behind the backs of her proper parents, she'd fallen in love with the foreigner, who'd promised to return for her." The doctor paused for quick breath, then went on. "After he was gone she realized she was pregnant and fled China in disgrace, following her love to Hawaii. But she only survived the voyage by being the mistress to the captain, and when she finally reached Honolulu, she found out her lover was a married man. By then her innocence was gone."

"God!" Rand was totally involved in the story. "Did she confront him?"

"I don't know what happened, or who the man was. She bore her daughter, who could have passed for white, hoping the girl would have the future that had been denied to her." Dr. Pete pushed back his hair, his eyes clouding even more, and waited for more thunder to pass. "Then history repeated itself, the girl grew up, and although she'd led a sheltered life, met and fell in love with a Hawaiian planter and became pregnant. But her mother, believing she was saving the girl from heartache and despair, forbade the relationship and hid her daughter from the man—and I suspect had guards to make sure the girl obeyed. Finally the man gave up, the baby—Leilani—was born, and the young woman died." The doctor spread his hands. "I suspect she didn't have the will to live."

"My God! It's a tragedy." Rand's mind whirled with thoughts of the man who didn't know he'd fathered a daughter...Leilani. "How could that grandmother give Leilani away? Allow her to grow up a foundling?"

"Because the grandmother believed she'd have a better chance for future happiness without the connection to the past. And after the grandmother told me this story, and in the light of all the prejudice then, I thought so, too, and pledged to keep the secret."

Dr. Pete paused again, suddenly looking old and tired. "Neither I nor her grandmother anticipated Leilani's determination to know who she was, and why she'd been left at the Kauwe doorstep. We'd hoped that she'd get married and she'd forget about it, so she wouldn't have to be embarrassed by knowing who her grandmother really is."

"Is Madam Silk Stockings Leilani's grandmother?" Rand asked sharply, just as sudden rain hit the windows.

Dr. Pete's head jerked up, his eyes meeting Rand's. He couldn't lie, and he inclined his head. "She sold some of her jewelry to buy her property. Becoming a madam was the only way she could earn a living. She'd soon realized that white men don't marry *Celestials*, even if the *Celestial* is descended from the ruling class."

Releasing his breath in one long sigh, Rand felt his whole body relax. "That's it? The whole story?"

"That's enough, isn't it? The madam was sincere in trying to do the best for her granddaughter—she believed Leilani would have more of a chance for happiness with the Kauwes than with a Chinese madam." Pete shook his head. "Poor old woman. Too much sadness in her life. That's why she helps the poor and homeless, because she's never forgotten how it felt."

Beyond the room, the rain was a steady downpour, but the quiet that fell over the men was like a final benediction to the tragic story. The despair of an innocent, sheltered girl, seduced by a lover and cast out by her family, her suffering perpetuated into future generations.

But this is where it ends, Rand thought, and stood up to go. He offered his hand for the doctor to shake, but his gaze was suddenly direct. "Dr. Pete, do you know if Leilani's father knew about her?"

"I don't know, but I assumed he, like the man before him, wouldn't take responsibility for a bastard daughter—even if she was only a quarter Chinese."

"You might be wrong this time," Rand told him.

"What do you mean?"

"I'm not sure yet." Rand hesitated. "But I'd like you to promise not to mention this conversation to Leilani until I can get over to Maui and back. I'd like to be present when she hears the truth—and maybe I'll have news about her father. Is that agreeable with you?"

"Of course." Now it was Dr. Pete's turn to be curious. "I'll leave this in your hands, until I hear from you, because I don't relish going up against Madam Silk Stockings when she finds out I broke my promise."

"Maybe that, too, will turn out fine," Rand said, and with those final ambiguous words, went out into the torrential rain.

Standing on the corner waiting for several wagons to pass, Leilani was startled by the sound of a loud sputtering engine. Her gaze darted to the automobile that turned from King Street and headed up Maunakea toward the corner of Hotel Street where she stood. There was a flurry of movement as people and horses got out of the way. The first automobile had only arrived in Honolulu recently, owned by a Mr. Baldwin, and Leilani, like everyone else, was in awe of the horseless carriage.

To her surprise the vehicle pulled over to the edge of the walk and stopped, its idling motor shaking the gleaming metal frame that sat on four spoked wheels, its round headlights perched out in front like giant bug eyes. Leilani jumped backward, fearful that the thing would suddenly bounce forward.

"Want a ride?" the driver shouted above the din.

Her gaze flew to Rand, who sat behind the wheel, one black brow cocked rakishly, his eyes dancing with fun, his hair windblown over his forehead. Their eyes caught, hers in surprise, his in admiration of the girl, who wore a brilliant blue percale dress the exact color of her eyes.

"I—I don't know," she evaded, for two reasons—fear of the contraption, and fear of being alone with Rand.

Over the past few days reason had reasserted itself, and she knew that it was madness to go on seeing him. Nothing had changed. She was still a Chinese girl without a family history, and she loved him too much to subject him to whatever that could mean. Besides, Dr. Pete had mentioned that Stella had been his guest again, and had only just left with her sister for Maui.

"Come on!" he coaxed. "It's fun!"

But he saw her reservations weren't just over the automobile. Pulling on the brake, he jumped out and ran to her, his eyes filled with such feeling that she found it hard to refuse. As she hesitated, he edged her to the passenger side and boosted her up onto the leather seat. He ran around to the driver's side, fearful that she'd jump out. Once beside her behind the wheel, he shot her a completely boyish grin, disarming her completely.

Then with a blast on the horn, they were off down the street, headed toward the ocean. For a couple of blocks they rode in silence, jostled by the bumpy street while the wind streamed past their ears. He glanced at her and was pleased to have her grin back, seduced by the pleasure of the ride. For a second he was thoughtful, glad he was leaving for Maui tomorrow where he hoped to find the final truth of her background. He vowed that before he left her, she would have no doubts about his intentions for their future, but he decided not to tell her what he was up to yet—in case he failed, and had to dash her hopes.

"Is this yours?" she called over the loud engine.

He shot her a grin. "It belongs to a friend. I'm just trying it out. You like it?"

She nodded, and the wind caught her hair, pulling it from its pins so that it streamed out behind her. Her light musical laughter floated on the air currents around her, and he was jolted with a sudden urge to stop the automobile and take her in his arms. But he resisted, knowing there was time for that in a little while. Instead he turned onto the road that led to the beach.

"I ordered one!" he told her. "I'll take delivery sometime after the first of the year." He hesitated, his eyes on her rather than the road. "So this is only the first of many adventures," he added, and somehow she got the feeling he meant more than just motoring along the oceanfront.

Giving herself up to the pleasure of speed—they were hurtling over the road at fourteen miles per hour—and to the sense of freedom it gave her, sitting next to him, under the fabric top, their bodies touching—it made her feel as though she and Rand were the only people in the world.

"I love it!" she cried, gulping in the fragrant sea air that was flowing inland by a quirk of the wind. And suddenly she was nestled to him, having been drawn there by his arm, which now rested around her shoulders.

Once beyond the town, Rand turned off the road, the big, white-rimmed wheels forging their own path to a grove of palms and flowering trees at the top of the sandy beach. He stopped, turned off the engine and then took her into both arms, his fingers dangerously close to her breasts.

She meant to resist, knew she should, but his first kiss melted her resolve. As always, her body obeyed Rand and not her own feeble mental commands. His touch sent her heartbeats into a nervous flutter and her blood coursing through her veins, hotter than molten lava. She tried to stop the trembling that had begun deep inside her, anticipating his lovemaking.

He lifted his mouth long enough to look into her eyes, and she was mesmerized by the infinite darkness of his, dark coals of passion that told her how much he wanted her.

"My darling," he whispered, his warm breath tantalizing her mouth with the promise of more kisses, "I can't get enough of you—can't stop wanting more."

She pushed back the long strands of silky hair that had fallen forward—like a little girl, he thought, and a surge of hot, throbbing fire touched his groin with a need so strong that he almost groaned from the exquisite pain of it. And when she licked her lips, he remembered licking her flesh, all the way down to where he'd tasted the muskiness of her femininity.

Leilani swallowed, suddenly too moved by the way his eyes had darkened, the way his lashes had lowered, reminding her of the rainbow grotto behind the falls—and their passion fulfilled. In that moment she knew she was lost once more. She loved him despite everything. *She wanted him!*

A seabird floated along on an invisible air current over the ocean, and low-flying clouds scuttled above it. Another bird joined the first, and its cry above the wind and surf seemed to call to its mate for their joining. The sun, moving in and out of the clouds, shimmered the ocean with a fairy dusting of magical gems. Bemused from the sensations of desire tickling at every cell in her body, Leilani was startled when Rand moved away.

He reached for a blanket on the back seat, then jumped to the ground and came around the automobile to help her down beside him. Wordless, he led her to a grassy place under the fragrant flowers that weighted down leafy branches. After he spread the cover, Rand pulled her down beside him.

"I'm going to make love to you, my little angel of mercy," he drawled lazily. His arm was around her, and with his other hand, he began to unbutton her bodice, all the while lowering her under him. In seconds her breasts were exposed to his hungry gaze.

"Rand, no," she whispered, wanting him, but knowing each time they made love would be one more time to remember in her loneliness later.

"Yes, my sweet. You know you want me as much as I want you." Tiny sparks of passion flared in his eyes, as his mouth descended close to hers, tempting and seducing her with memories of what his lips, his tongue could do to her. And then he proceeded to do it again, arousing her nipples to hardness, her breath to mere gasps, until her desire was out of control.

"It's all right," he whispered, feathering her mouth with his kisses as he spoke. "We belong together, you know that. I love you, you love me, no one else." He lifted his face suddenly. "You don't love anyone else, do you?" And when she didn't answer at once, too overwhelmed by the quivery vibrations deep within her private place, the sudden surge of liquid heat that was readying her for him, his voice took on a note of urgency. "Surely not Elwood, because I'll make you forget him."

With a low moan, she pulled him to her, her hands raking his crisp black hair, then the ridges and muscles of his wonderfully toned body. "I only love you, Rand. You're the only man I'll ever love—you know that." She kissed him passionately, as though the feel of him had to last a lifetime. When she moved her mouth enough to speak again, she went on in a whispery, shaky voice, "And because of loving you more than my own life, I'll never ruin yours—and I know you understand what I'm saying." She hesitated, gathering her courage. "I've sensed my—uh—position is unacceptable to you."

He went still, as her meaning sunk in. She believed he shared her feelings about her past. For a second he wanted to tell her what he knew—and what he suspected. But he suppressed the impulse, because if what he hoped wasn't true, he had to be sure that telling her about the madam was the right thing, that it wouldn't only cause her more shame.

"Sweetheart," he whispered softly, no longer stroking her with passion, but holding her with tenderness. "I'm going to Maui tomorrow, and when I return I may have something important to tell you that will make all the difference in the world to you." He traced the delicate curve of her face with a finger. "But I want you to remember, that however things turn out makes no difference to my feelings, or my intentions, toward you." He snuggled her even closer, and watched as her long, thick lashes lowered over the brilliance of her eyes. "I love you, only you. And I will until I die."

His words took her breath away. For a moment she forgot everything else. Did he mean he would marry her despite everything? She took his hand to her mouth and kissed it, and somehow the gesture brought all the passion back to Rand.

"And now I'm going to prove my words, even though I won't ask you to marry me again because—"

Abruptly, he lifted his head, listening. Above the sound of the endless waves, and the wind shuffling the palm fronds, came the voices of young boys. When Rand got up on his knees he could see them approaching along the road, fishing poles in hand and pedaling their bicycles, as they talked and laughed. They hadn't seen the lovers yet.

Quickly Rand explained, and Leilani straightened her clothing. By the time the boys came into view, Rand and Leilani were already on their way back to the automobile. They were delayed when the boys saw the vehicle and had to examine it. Then they moved on to fish in the ocean near the cluster of palms.

"So much for privacy," Rand drawled sardonically after he'd cranked the motor, jumped into the automobile and steered it back onto the road. "But there'll be other times...and soon," he added and shot her a grin charged with sexual promise.

He didn't seem to notice her quiet, didn't realize that his words that were cut off—*I won't ask you to marry me again because*—had gone straight to her heart, to her soul, and she was devastated, after all. Each time she felt hope it was crushed in the next second.

They rode back to town in silence. Leilani had never been more miserable. But Rand was unaware, pointing out the functions of the horseless carriage, and why it would soon make any other form of ground transportation outmoded. He felt secure that he'd finally convinced Leilani that his intentions were honorable, if not pure when it came to her body.

He kissed her goodbye after she asked him to let her off at the Peterson house. And when he drove away he still had no idea that he'd given her a completely opposite impression than he'd intended.

She watched him out of sight with tears in her eyes.

Chapter Nineteen

Later the doctor drove Leilani to the Kauwe farm, and as she stood to step from the buggy, he restrained her with a hand on her arm. "Is everything all right?" he asked, his round face anxious. "You're not coming down with the flu? You're looking pale."

She shook her head and managed a smile. "I'm just fine. I'm thinking about my day, that's all."

He let her go, but he was thoughtful as he drove away, wondering if Rand had said anything about their conversation, for Leilani looked too damned upset. He didn't dare bring up the subject, feeling too uncertain about the whole situation. Besides, maybe she was only thinking about patients and work, and Rand hadn't told her his suspicions. I can't interfere, he told himself, and signaled the horse into a gallop. He didn't want to be a party to any more secrets. They always came back to haunt you, he thought grimly.

Leilani watched him go and then went to join her family for supper. Later, after the others were asleep, she sat alone on the veranda, wrapped in her long wool robe, and watched the quarter-moon, misty and far away, blink in and out of clouds that trailed across the sky like witch fingers, heralding a storm by morning.

Her deep sigh was ragged from suppressed tears, from the hollow feeling in her stomach each time she thought of Rand, tall, muscular and darkly handsome, like his Hawaiian forebears. *The man she'd love forever, whom she wanted to marry and bear his children.* Her hands knotted in her lap, and Lei-

lani knew her wishes could never be. Hadn't he as much as told
her that, even as he'd told her he loved her and would always
want her? Perhaps only sexually, she told herself, knowing that
haoles didn't believe they had to marry a *Celestial*.

The turbulent thoughts only brought back her other fears
concerning Madam Silk Stockings, and her past that was
shrouded in mystery. As Leilani pictured the madam's stricken
expression when she'd confronted her, she suddenly came to
a decision. Maybe she couldn't change Rand's intentions, but
she could demand the truth from the madam, stand firm despite the old woman's show of dramatics to avoid answering
painful questions.

The wind quickened, a flowing stream of cool air that
smelled of rain. Leilani shivered and stood up. She would see
Madam Silk Stockings tomorrow, one way or another. She'd
found a link to her past, and she'd be damned if she'd ignore
it. Besides, she needed to overcome the mental struggle she'd
had since childhood, needed to know her heritage, know the
worst, whoever her mother was. *And no one was stopping her
this time!*

Leilani's hooded cape sheltered her from the worst of the
downpour, but the mud underfoot was ruining her shoes.
Nevertheless, she didn't regret her decision to approach the
madam's saloon through a maze of alleys and walkways so
that her arrival wasn't anticipated. She'd decided on the back
entrance again, hoping the door would still be unlocked. She
intended to let herself in quietly, to both the back hall and the
madam's apartment. She wasn't going to announce herself
again, knowing she'd be turned away.

It was a bold plan, and she didn't allow herself to think
about being accosted, as she'd been during her two previous
visits. Hesitating, Leilani glanced around to gain her bearings. It was easy to be lost, and today there were few people
outside, the weather being so bad. As she decided on direction, she was struck by the obvious poverty of the area, how
the rickety, board buildings, some three stories tall, with flimsy
porches that hung over walkways, leaned against one another
for support. It's a firetrap, she thought with a shudder, and

hated to think what would happen if one of the shacks went up in flames.

The thought was fleeting as she started out once more. Beyond the next corner was a main street, and the walkway that led to the side entrance of the saloon. Once she reached the door, Leilani hesitated, her hand on the knob. Finding it unlocked, she braced herself and went inside. Satisfied that the hall was empty, she headed for the madam's apartment. Again she gained entrance without anyone seeing her. Her heart hammering, she approached the parlor, her feet soundless on the Oriental carpet.

Madam Silk Stockings sat in a high-backed, silk-covered chair near the fireplace, her feet on a footstool, staring into the flames, a cup of tea on the ebony table beside her. Momentarily uncertain, Leilani stared at the elegant little woman, her elaborate hair, rice-powdered face and painted mouth as perfect as those of a china doll. In repose, the madam appeared pensive, even sad, and Leilani knew she was glimpsing a private moment.

Suddenly uncertain, Leilani had an urge to return to the door and knock. Somehow the old woman looked too fragile, too vulnerable all at once, and not at all the fearsome proprietress of an infamous brothel. Her impulse was arrested when the madam, sensing she wasn't alone, looked up and saw Leilani. Their eyes locked, the madam's reflecting surprise, Leilani's uncertainty. For long seconds neither spoke.

Then Madam Silk Stockings, having quickly composed herself, motioned Leilani into the room and waved her into the opposite chair. Herself wordless for the moment, Leilani obeyed her bidding.

"I've been expecting you," the madam said, and Leilani was taken aback. But before she could reply, the old woman continued. "Please, take off your wet cloak."

Instantly Leilani jumped up, aware that her wrap was staining the silk chair. As she was about to apologize, the madam again waved her to silence. She clapped her hands and the maid appeared, her expression astounded when she saw Leilani. But she complied with her mistress's request that she take Leilani's cloak, and then bring more tea.

"You knew I was coming?" Leilani couldn't help but ask, and wondered if the woman had spies everywhere.

She inclined her head, her black eyes examining Leilani's face. "I knew you would come, if not today, then one day soon." She paused, letting her words sink in. "That is another way you are like me. You will not give up."

The meeting was going in a different way than Leilani had expected. She wasn't being thrown out; there was no scene; it was all very civilized. She suddenly wondered what the old woman was up to, and stiffened on her chair, braced for any eventuality.

Her body language was not lost on Madam Silk Stockings, who hid a smile. As much as she'd dreaded this hour, she admired the girl for her courage, and suddenly wondered if her decision long ago had been the right one. But she shook off such thoughts. It was much too late for regrets.

The tea was served, but Leilani left hers untouched on the table. She was too emotionally charged to calmly drink tea—and be disarmed from saying what she'd come to say. So she took a deep breath and plunged in, abruptly direct.

"I know that you know who my mother was, Madam Silk Stockings, and I'm not leaving here until you tell me."

Placing her china cup into its saucer, the madam was prepared this time for Leilani's question. "Why would I know such a thing, child? Why—"

"Because of my pin—and your earrings," Leilani retorted, interrupting. She wasn't going to worry about manners now, and she pulled her pin from beneath her dress. "And because of your reaction to seeing this pin the last time I was here."

"The pin is only a coincidence."

"I'm not a child and I won't be fooled!" Leilani leaned toward her, waving the pin. "Do you know what it's like to have only one connection to your background, your parents, the history of past generations—all the things that everyone takes for granted as their right?"

She drew in a shuddering breath, and when the madam only stared passively, she went on, her tone sharper, edged with anger. "I've been shunned because I'm part Chinese, not good enough to marry into a proper family. And now I'll never marry because my past could be an embarrassment." Her words came faster. "If there's a way to find my mother, then I must, because I have nothing left to lose."

"But you have the Kauwes, good parents."

"And I love them, but I still must know who I really am, so I can face the future, even if I'm alone." Leilani knew she was the one sounding dramatic now, but she didn't care. A lifetime of yearning for the truth was manifest in this meeting. Somehow she knew that the key was with the madam, and this was her last chance to know.

"I believed you would marry Rand Walsh," the madam stated, her voice still as controlled as when she'd first spoken.

Leilani shook her head, gathering her composure, fearful that she was close to tears. "He—he loves me," she admitted honestly. "And I love him. But we will not marry," she added, her voice breaking. "Even if he hadn't told me that, I would not have married him anyway."

Her explanation was the last thing Madam Silk Stockings had expected to hear, but she managed to conceal her shock. Never had she believed things would turn out this way. She read the hurt of the years on Leilani's face, and suddenly thought of her own life. All during the decades since she fled China, her background had sustained her. When people spit on her, she remembered her noble parents, and could lift her head. When she wasn't invited to the rich homes, she saw again the house she grew up in, with its priceless art and far more elegant than any place in Hawaii. Her background had been the rock upon which she had built a new future. Why hadn't she thought of that for this girl?

"Knowing is so important?" she asked, but already knew the answer. In Leilani's place I would do the same, she thought suddenly.

Leilani didn't reply, only waited with growing hope. The madam's tone had softened somehow, and her lashes trembled ever so slightly, giving away that she was more upset than she let on.

"I am Hakka, and my family were rulers in China," she began slowly. Her black eyes intensified, and her Chinese accent was more pronounced. "One day a white man came to my father's house, to discuss taking workers to the Sandwich Islands—Hawaii—to work in cane fields. He was tall, a handsome man with blond hair and blue eyes, so different, and we fell in love—behind my father's back. The man left with workers finally, but promised to come back for me."

The madam's gaze had shifted to the flames leaping and dancing around a log, and Leilani knew she was seeing again those golden days of hope and love.

"I learned I would have a baby." She suddenly met Leilani's eyes, and remembered pain was etched on the usually unreadable face. "My father blamed me for shaming the family, and himself because he'd left my feet unbound—because he abhorred the practice, and didn't want a daughter disabled like her mother, who had to be carried everywhere. I left China, because I had no choice, to follow the man I loved to Honolulu." Her sigh left a huge gap in the story but Leilani could guess what had happened. She'd disgraced an honored family, and the sin was unforgivable.

"I soon learned that unprotected girls, however innocent in the ways of the world, are easy prey." She waved her hand, as though to push back emotion so she could continue. "If not for the captain taking me as his mistress during the voyage—which I paid for with a piece of priceless jewelry—I would have died at the hands of the peasants on board. But when I arrived in Honolulu, the man I loved wouldn't have wanted me, even if he hadn't been a married man!"

"The bastard!" Leilani cried, unable to help herself. "He was married and never had any intention of returning to China for you."

Despite her own upset, the madam felt a flash of pleasure at Leilani's response. But she went on, while she still could. "He's dead now for many years, died without having children to carry on the name of one of the old missionary families." She shook her head. "Once I thought it fitting punishment, but I even got over that after his death—because I had his daughter, a beautiful girl who looked more like him than me, aside from having black hair and brown eyes. I sheltered her, saw that she was educated and kept her innocent of the business I started so we could survive."

She seemed to crumple all at once, her gaze lowered and her hands trembling on her lap. But she maintained control over her voice. "At twenty, my daughter Senni met a rich sugar planter, and fell in love. I knew that what had happened to me was about to happen to her, and I forbade them to see each other, sent Senni away to get over him." Madam Silk Stockings blinked quickly, and Leilani thought she saw a sparkle of tears on her lashes. "You see, we Chinese were even more discriminated against then." Her breathing had quickened and her voice had faded into a whisper as she went on. "She, too, was with child, and she died in childbirth."

The log shifted lower in the fireplace, shooting sparks up the chimney, and the clock gonged the hour. When the final sound slid away into the shadowy corners, swallowed up like the madam's words, the old woman suddenly looked up. Her eyes glistened with moisture, but tears were already running down Leilani's cheeks from the tragic story.

"The child lived." The words seemed to soar into the vacuum between them that waited for the final denouement. "You were that child, Leilani—my granddaughter."

And then tears streamed from the black eyes, streaking down her rice-powdered face to stain her silk kimono. "I gave you to the Kauwes to allow you a different life, so that you wouldn't be influenced by my business—so you would have the chance my daughter didn't have."

The madam's lips trembled, and Leilani was so shaken she sat motionless, speechless, trying to take it all in. For a moment their roles were reversed: Leilani the stoic, the old woman shattered.

"I'm not asking forgiveness," the madam said, her voice thinner still. "But I want you to believe that I gave you up out of love, not because I didn't want you. Please understand that I would not have done it if I'd anticipated your sorrow over being a foundling." She paused for a shallow breath. "And know that I've always watched over you, paid for your schooling, made sure you were safe. I left the pin because it was a favorite of your mother's, and I wanted you to have that remembrance."

Madam Silk Stockings was her grandmother! Her mother's name had been Senni. Thoughts spun so fast in Leilani's mind that it was hard to separate them. Whatever she'd expected to hear, she'd never dreamed the mystery would be unraveled so quickly. She was numb from the madam's revelations—but she believed her. And although sad, the truth wasn't shameful, at least not to Leilani, who could understand loving a man as much as her mother and grandmother had loved. Didn't she love Rand with equal passion? She was just lucky that she, too, hadn't gotten pregnant.

Gradually she became aware that the madam—*her grandmother*—looked even more upset, because Leilani hadn't responded, and the old woman was riddled with guilt. Leilani suddenly knew how terribly she must have suffered, and even though she was a madam, she'd had no choice—*and she was an honest madam.* An intense feeling of love overwhelmed Leilani all at once.

Going to her grandmother she pulled her into her arms. And in silence, they wept together.

The meeting was the first of many over the next two weeks. For as much as it was a healing time for Leilani, she began to see that it was even more so for her grandmother.

"My real name is Hsi Shen," she told Leilani, and smiled. "It sounds strange on my lips, for I haven't said it aloud for many years." She hesitated, her gaze suddenly turned inward, remembering. "It was the captain who first called me Silk Stockings, and when I opened my business, I kept the name."

They were having afternoon tea, which had become a daily habit since the old secret had been exorcised. With each visit Leilani learned more about her mother, how gentle and kind she'd been.

"Like my own mother," the madam said, and went on to tell another story of her girlhood in China. "I, on the other hand, am like my father, who was always determined and fearless, even though he was honest and fair." Her eyes, no longer inscrutable to Leilani, warmed as she looked at her granddaughter. "You are more like me than like your mother." She smiled thoughtfully. "I've observed from afar since you were an infant, and it gave me pleasure to see family traits in you, even though you were being brought up by others."

Pride in family, a new feeling for Leilani, was growing within her as she listened to her grandmother. Her mother had become a real person, and she'd realized that she wasn't descended from peasants, that her grandmother's family was rich and cultured.

"How terrible it all was for you," she commented softly at a break in the conversation. "You gave up too much for the sake of loving a man."

The old woman nodded, lowering her lashes, but Leilani still glimpsed the emotional pain that had never gone away. "But it was all fate," she said finally, once more meeting Leilani's eyes. "If I hadn't loved, your mother would not have been born and you would not be here today."

It was a profound thought, and Leilani had no quick response. "Did you ever contact your parents after you left China? Surely they would have wanted to know—"

Her grandmother interrupted. "No, never possible to do so. They would have grieved for me after I was gone, as if I had died." She hesitated, her words so final that they brought goose bumps to Leilani's flesh. "Their daughter was dead to them. But they still had three sons."

"I see now why you believed it best for me to be raised by the Kauwes," Leilani said, only beginning to understand how her grandmother had suffered, and how strong she was to have survived. "Especially after my mother seemed to be in the same predicament."

Their visit was about over and Leilani hesitated before getting to her feet to put on her cloak. There was something else she needed to know. It was obvious that her grandmother had avoided the subject, so she'd put off asking, waiting until they'd established a grandmother-granddaughter relationship.

Deciding to be frank now, Leilani simply asked the question. "Grandmother, you've never told me the name of my father. Is there any reason why you shouldn't?"

Her grandmother was equally direct. "I have avoided that, Leilani, and I'm not ready to reveal him to you yet, until I'm more sure of how you'll react." She hesitated, gathering the right words. "There are several reasons, the first being he doesn't even know you exist. I'm not sure you should know, or he should know."

"But you can at least trust me with his name!"

"Perhaps. We shall see."

They both stood, and Leilani knew her grandmother would say no more on the issue. She gave an inward smile despite her disappointment. The old woman was completely Oriental in some ways.

She kissed the soft powdered cheek, and again the incredulity of having the elegant little madam as her grandmother struck her. After promising to return the next afternoon, Leilani left to see her last patient of the day.

But as she hurried along the crowded street her thoughts turned to Rand, and she wondered if her love for him would also end sadly. The November wind off the ocean was cool, and it whipped at her cloak. Whatever happened she wouldn't allow the past to repeat itself in her. She'd been lucky so far—only because she hadn't gotten pregnant, like her mother and grandmother before her.

I must not be seduced by love, she vowed.

Chapter Twenty

"Damn it anyway!" Rand cried, having met the boat from the Big Island. Richard Drew, whom he'd been trying to see since his arrival on Maui, wasn't on it, as expected.

"He'll be on the next one later in the afternoon," the captain said.

Turning back to his buggy, Rand soon had the horse moving away from the Lahaina waterfront, headed toward the Walsh plantation. Some planters, like Richard, had several plantations on more than one island, and periodically had to visit them, as he'd been doing the past two weeks.

While waiting for Richard's return, Rand had occupied himself with plenty of work; his law practice on Maui was quickly surpassing his Honolulu business. During this visit he'd realized he should take over in Lahaina permanently and let Lee handle the Honolulu office. It had been a relief to both him and Lee when Mr. Quong had allowed Lee to resume seeing Annie, thus allowing his partner to return his concentration to his legal obligations.

But Rand's work was second to his impatience. He needed to get back to Honolulu, but he wasn't going until he'd talked to Richard, the man he believed was Leilani's father. Although he meant to find out if Richard's first love—the woman in the painting—was the daughter of Madam Silk Stockings, he had no intention of telling him that he had a daughter—not yet. Leilani deserved to be told first, Rand thought.

Signaling with the reins, Rand urged the horse into a gallop, suddenly anxious. He'd have his talk with Richard this evening and take tomorrow's steamer, he decided. He hoped to hell his former father-in-law really got back as planned. This time of year the weather sometimes delayed crossings, and a storm had been threatening for several days now.

Thank goodness! he thought, as the horse turned into the long driveway that divided the cane fields, approaching the house where his brother and Nancy lived. Tonight would be the last time he'd have to put up with Stella's pique. Although he was usually away from the family, spending most nights in Lahaina, Rand had come to dread being in the same room with Stella, who was still trying to manipulate their relationship. He wondered how he'd ever thought she was attractive, although for the sake of the family he managed to keep his distaste from showing. It had been a relief when she announced she would return to New York after Christmas.

As he reined in near the front entrance, Rand's thoughts had reverted to Leilani. He knew she'd love Maui, and the Walsh mansion, which was surrounded by flower gardens and lawns, and commanded a spectacular view of the ocean. But he'd build her their own house, he mused, missing her dreadfully.

He knew she'd be waiting for his return, and he felt secure that she was now clear about his intentions, that he meant to propose, and that he'd never thought of Stella in terms of marriage. The thought didn't occur to him that because he'd stayed here several weeks instead of days, Leilani might believe the worst. If he had he would have returned at once.

No one was in the entry hall when he went inside, so Rand went directly to his bedroom and packed his bag. After goodbyes, he meant to drive over to the Drew plantation, then spend the night in Lahaina close to the boat. Once back in the hall again, he placed his bag by the door, then went into the main salon where Nancy, Stella and his brother were having drinks before supper.

"I won't be staying to eat," he told them, but accepted a whiskey from his brother.

"I expect I'll see you before I go," Stella said coyly, and he had a sudden impression that her decision to go was only another ploy—so that he'd suddenly come to his senses and beg her to stay.

"Maybe, maybe not," he replied, noncommittal. "But if I don't, have a good crossing."

He finished his drink, set down his glass and strode to the door, where he turned to look back into the room. "I'll be taking the boat tomorrow, and as I have a few things to finish up in the office, I'm spending the night in Lahaina." Then with a salute that included all of them, he went into the hall, picked up his bag and went out to where he'd left the buggy.

Suddenly he felt exhilarated. The next time he came to Maui, Leilani would be with him.

"You've told me about some of your assets, Grandmother," Leilani said, liking the sound of the name on her lips more and more. It meant so much to have roots, family and the special bond that comes from a blood tie. "And you've hinted at others," she went on, then hesitated. But knowing the old madam respected honesty gave Leilani the courage to be direct. "So you're financially secure and could retire."

They'd had their afternoon tea and Leilani was about to leave when she blurted out her feelings. "I would like to see you away from business—so you could relax and enjoy a good life."

"Are you ashamed of me, Leilani?" the old woman asked sharply, her eyes alert to any subterfuge.

Looking her straight in the eyes, Leilani gave an instant answer. "No, I'm not. In fact, I'm very proud to have you as my grandmother," she went on honestly. "Not many women could have done what you have, let alone survive."

Madam Silk Stockings glanced away, not wanting to shame herself with more tears. This granddaughter was an unexpected blessing to her in her old age, she thought. Leilani, although influenced by other cultures, and only a quarter Chinese, was as Oriental in some ways as she was.

"I will consider it," she said, more briskly than she intended—because she didn't trust her voice, either.

"Good." Leilani bent to kiss her, then taking her wrap, readied herself to go.

"But one last thing, Leilani." As her granddaughter glanced up from buttoning her cloak, the madam went on. "I'm a rich woman, and I must be honest. Had the secret of your birth never been revealed, I would have left all my wealth to charity. Because to do otherwise would have exposed the truth, and I never had any intention of doing that, for your sake."

"I think you should still leave it to charity," Leilani answered at once, again surprising the old woman. She grinned. "But only after you've enjoyed all the pleasures money can buy for you." She moved to the door. "Because you deserve pleasure more than anyone I know."

Then she was gone, leaving Madam Silk Stockings feeling happier than she had since her daughter died. Already she was thinking about the best deal she could make to sell her establishment.

Leilani, too, felt happy as she made her way through the saloon to the street entrance, her thoughts on Christmas, which was only three weeks away. She meant to include her grandmother in the Kauwe family celebration. As she walked, Leilani no longer feared being accosted, as the patrons knew to leave her alone, not like that first time when Rand had rescued her. But when the sudden image of Rand appeared in her mind, her joy of the moment was shattered.

Dear God, she prayed. Don't let my happiness be marred because of his rejection. And then she closed her mind to Rand and what he'd said that last time about not marrying her, and stepped out to the street—and straight into the solid frame of a man.

"God almighty!" Elwood cried, shocked. "What are you doing in a hellhole like this saloon?"

Instantly annoyed, Leilani tried to be civil, but it was next to impossible for her to do so since he'd kissed her on the street. He still dogged her steps, appearing at inopportune times to walk with her, and to ask her out. He wouldn't take no for an answer, and nothing seemed to deter him, including her reminder that her background was still the same one that hadn't met with Benton family approval in the past.

Now, as she didn't reply at once, he stopped her with a hand on her arm. "I asked you a question, Leilani."

"Unhand me at once!" she retorted, her glance scathing, ignoring his order.

His face flushed with his sense of impropriety, and anger at her response. His hand tightened painfully. "Proper women don't go into brothels. So what in hell were you doing there?"

"None of your damned business!" she cried, and tried to jerk away.

"It is my business," he said between clenched teeth. *"You're my business!"*

All at once Leilani was struck with inspiration. "Did you say a proper woman wouldn't have any connection with a brothel?" she asked, her tone deceptively soft.

"That's right." His grip loosened. "I'm surprised you have to ask that, Leilani," he added in the pious tone she hated.

"Then in that case I need to confide something important, because I'm sure it'll affect your future actions—at least toward me." She contrived a smile and demurely lowered her lashes, affecting an attitude of sharing a secret. "I've learned the truth, Elwood—about my oh-so improper background."

"What do you mean?" His eyes narrowed, but she had his complete attention.

Allowing the suspense to build, Leilani shook her head. "Life is strange, Elwood. Never, for the life of me, would I ever have dreamed that Madam Silk Stockings was my grandmother."

"What?" He laughed suddenly. "You're joking!"

Shaking her head, she went on. "That's why I'm at her place, to visit." She ignored his incredulous expression. "And it's a miracle, Elwood. You can't imagine how it feels to suddenly find a grandmother—a wonderful grandmother." She yawned behind her hand. "And now the truth has freed me— I can consider becoming betrothed—because I'm no longer just a foundling." She gazed up at him in wide-eyed innocence. "Isn't it wonderful?"

He dropped his hand, releasing her. "You aren't joking, are you?"

"No, Elwood, I'm not." She hesitated. "But enough about my good news, what were you about to ask me? If you're inviting me to accompany you socially, I'd be delighted to accept."

"No, no, I wasn't." He backed away, not able to hide the horror on his face. "I only wanted to say hello."

Then he tipped his hat, turned on his heel and headed in the opposite direction. Leilani watched him go, for a second so angry she had to fight the urge to call him a damnable hypocrite. But a moment later she only felt sorry for him, a man of weak character. She knew he'd never bother her again.

Straightening her shoulders, Leilani set off toward the office just as it started to rain. The gossip would begin, she knew. But having a grandmother was worth it, she told herself. Even if Rand reacted just as Elwood had to the news.

"God help us, it's bubonic plague!" Dr. Pete cried as Leilani stepped into the office. "By Christmas hundreds of people could be dead if it's not stopped."

Frozen by his words, Leilani stood horrified. "So it is the plague, after all."

He nodded, his round face creased with worry. Shortly after Thanksgiving another doctor had been called to treat a deathly sick Chinese man, and had suspected the plague. He'd reported his findings, but others had disagreed with his diagnosis. Then more cases were discovered, all in Chinatown. But still they'd hoped it wasn't the deadly disease that was caused by infected fleas on brown rats.

"Most of the cases are confined to the crowded section of shacks back toward the mountains," the doctor added.

"It's really the plague, and not just measles or the flu with a high fever?"

"The purplish nodules in the groin and armpits are unmistakable." He mopped his forehead with a handkerchief, sweating despite the cool December day. His gaze suddenly intensified. "You won't be working now, Leilani. I can't let you take the risk of getting it yourself."

"What about you? And Esther?"

"Esther will stay in the house, out of harm's way. You'll go home to the Kauwes, away from Chinatown altogether."

As he spoke, she shook her head. "If this is truly the plague, you're going to need every hand you can get, especially one who is already trained as a nurse." Leilani paused to take a breath, knowing she was making a life-and-death decision. "I'm going to continue with my work." When he tried to protest, she rushed on. "I know these people, my grandmother lives here, and I won't abandon them when I can help."

"I can't stop you, Leilani, but I want you to sleep on it before you make a final decision." He turned away. "God knows I can use your help."

"It's settled then," she said quietly, and went to ready her satchel, and his. "Besides, it may be stopped before it really gets a hold on the city. There's never been plague in Hawaii before."

"It won't be stopped easily," he replied, his tone edged with fear. "The only way is to burn each house that is stricken with it, isolate the sections of Chinatown where the known victims live."

"But that'll cause terrible hardship to those poor people— if not a riot!" Leilani protested. "They have so little as it is."

"I know, but if that decision isn't made some time soon, those people will lose their lives, and all of Honolulu will be infected."

He went into his surgery and closed the door, and she knew he was marshaling his strength, for if it was as he said, they'd both need more than just strength. They'd need the hand of God to protect them from dying as well.

She worked in silence, reflecting on the strange twists and turns of life. She'd found her grandmother, the doctor had substantiated her story of her birth and explained why he'd agreed to the madam's plan, and the Kauwes had been delighted for her. Mama Kauwe had only said, "Now we have bigger family—we all have new grandma." Everything in Leilani's life was out in the open now, except her feelings for Rand, who'd stayed on in Maui . . . with Stella.

The doctor was called out almost at once, and Leilani accompanied him. Finally he didn't protest, because he needed her help. The first victim she saw was dying, and the sight was hideous. The full ramifications of the disease hit her like a shock wave, but she managed to control her shaking enough to help the doctor. Later he reported the case to the Department of Health, and recommended that the house be burned, and Leilani agreed that fire was the only hope of the city.

The next few days became a blur of hurrying through the filthy maze of alleys to shacks so flimsy that some were propped upright by poles, then into windowless rooms that smelled of death. She and Dr. Pete frequently bathed and washed with antiseptic, and each day burned their clothing.

Then one evening as they rushed from the area of many new cases, they found that section cordoned off, guarded by panic-stricken *haoles*. They weren't allowed to leave.

"I was afraid of this," Dr. Pete said grimly.

She only nodded. The worst had happened . . . for them.

Rand stepped off the boat, having decided to go past his office before seeing Leilani to make plans for that night. He wanted everything just right when he told her his good news. It had been a turbulent voyage from Maui, the storm having brought gale-force winds. The departure had been delayed in the first place because of the storm. He was just relieved to finally be back in Honolulu.

We'll have dinner at my house, he decided, his thoughts far away from the excited chatter on the wharf. But two words brought him up short—*bubonic plague.*

"What did you say?" Rand demanded of the group of longshoremen on the dock.

"We got the plague, man! Right here in Honolulu!" a stocky worker answered.

"Yeah! Brought here by them damned *Celestials!* Serves them right that the disease is confined to Chinatown!" a second man chimed in.

"But for how long?" the first man added. "I say we gotta burn 'em out—torch Chinatown. Ain't no other way to kill those rats."

"Jesus Christ!" Rand cried, and was already running toward the street. Since his office was nearby, he went there first, but his thoughts were on Leilani. "Let her be safe," he chanted, his words in time with his footsteps.

Bursting in through the front door, he surprised Lee, who was about to leave the office. The two men stared at each other in shocked silence, and Rand knew the news was true.

"How bad is it?" he asked tersely.

"Real bad," Lee answered. "I can't tell you not to worry, because we've got one hell of a problem, worse than you know."

"Is Leilani safe?" Rand could see that Lee knew something, and that he was trying to think of a way to soften whatever it was he needed to say.

"She's not sick, if that's what you mean," Lee began, his usually calm expression stricken with fear. "But she's behind the cordon."

"What in hell are you talking about man?" Rand demanded, and restrained himself from shaking an answer out of his friend.

Quickly Lee explained what had happened since the news got out about the plague. "Leilani and the doctor are caught behind the lines, and they won't let them out—and if they tried to cross anyway, they might be shot."

"Lord! It's sheer panic!" Rand clenched his fists, completely frustrated and angry. "I believed the doctor had more sense. What possessed him to take Leilani with him in the first place?"

"She went of her own free will," Lee explained quietly, suddenly fearful of what his partner would do. "You know Leilani when people need help."

"Damn! Damn!" Rand punched the wall, but even his anger couldn't blot out the icy fear that was creeping over him. "She could die."

Lee nodded. "And so could Annie." His voice broke and he cleared his throat. "Her father is truly a madman. He didn't even tell his family, just kept them in the house where he believed they'd be safe. Now they're trapped, with him on the outside of the cordon, because he'd gone to a meeting.

"Come on," Lee said, his arm around his friend, knowing exactly how Rand felt. "I'll take you so you can see for yourself."

They went outside into the gray afternoon. Rand had never felt so helpless in his life. His good news no longer mattered, only Leilani. He suddenly stiffened his back, and with jutting chin, hurried along with Lee.

He'd get her out somehow, or die trying.

Chapter Twenty-One

"**D**amn it!" Lee cried, his face flushed with anger. "You must allow those two women out of the restricted area. They aren't sick, but they will be if they don't leave at once!"

Rand and Lee had gone to the emergency meeting of cabinet members and doctors representing the Department of Health, intending to persuade the city leaders to allow Leilani and Annie to cross the cordon. But as they stood facing the exhausted frightened men, Rand saw his mission was hopeless even before one of the doctors spoke up.

"Impossible! We can't make exceptions, or there'll be a stampede."

The others nodded agreement, and one of the cabinet members added his regret. "We're sorry, because each of us can identify with how you feel. It's how we'll feel if the plague spreads from Chinatown into the general population of Honolulu—and wipes out most of the people."

"Our only hope is to contain it," another man added. "We may even have to burn the whole infected section of the city, not just the houses of plague victims."

Accompanied by Lee, Rand left the meeting with a sense of hopelessness. The business area of Chinatown, the half near the ocean, had few cases of plague, while the other half closer to the mountains, where the people lived, was reporting an epidemic. It was tragic . . . and terrifying.

"I'm not giving up, Lee." He glanced at his partner. "Leilani is my future, and I'm not going to let fleas take it away." He didn't add that he couldn't face Leilani dying, as his wife had. Or allow fears of ancient Polynesian taboos to overwhelm him with panic. He'd just gotten past such superstitious beliefs. He meant to take matters into his own hands if necessary, but he still had to figure out how to do that.

"What can we do? Our hands are tied."

"There's one person who might find a way, and that's where I'm going right now." They'd hesitated at the corner to wait for traffic. "Madam Silk Stockings controls more than her own establishment in Chinatown. If anyone can do something it's her."

"Why would she?"

"I'll explain later," Rand told him, already headed in the opposite direction, glad that the madam's building wasn't behind the cordon—yet. God only knew when all of Chinatown would be closed. Already schools and churches and public functions had been canceled.

"I'll be at the office waiting," Lee called after him.

The saloon was almost empty when Rand stepped through the swinging front doors a short time later. Without hesitation, he strode to the back hall, then on to the entrance of the madam's private apartment, where he knocked. Seconds later the elderly maid opened the door, and Rand explained he was there to see her mistress.

"Please, step inside," she said in heavily accented English. When she had shown him to the parlor, she went to inform the madam that she had a visitor.

"So, Rand," the madam said from the doorway, startling him from his contemplation of his fears. He jerked his head in her direction and then stood up. "It seems our Leilani has gotten herself in another dangerous situation."

As she moved into the room, gowned in silk and elaborately made-up, he wondered at her composure when Leilani was in such danger. But then he was suddenly reminded that this woman didn't let her fears show, just as Leilani hid hers behind a veneer of calm. There was definitely a family resemblance, if not in looks then in mannerisms, he thought.

He nodded. "And this time it might be an even worse situation." He hesitated. "She will probably die if she isn't allowed out of the restricted area."

Pain flickered momentarily in the madam's eyes, and she quickly sat down in the nearest chair. "You are right, my friend," she agreed. "And there's nothing I can do to prevent it."

"Can't you use your influence, under the table if necessary?" He took the chair near her, and grabbed one of her hands. *"You must!"*

She moved her hand and patted his. "Do you think I haven't tried? I even attempted to bribe the city fathers with a promise to donate a fortune to help fight this plague." Her lashes fluttered, giving away her fears and frustration. "But they refused, said money is no good if everyone is dead." She took a deep shuddering breath. "Their fear of the Black Death supersedes everything . . . or anyone."

He stood and began pacing the distance between the chair and fireplace. "I just came from their meeting—with the same results." He stopped abruptly, and his dark eyes looked feverish as they met the madam's. "What in hell are we going to do?" He dropped back into his chair. "We'll just have to smuggle her out of there somehow."

Slowly she shook her head. "Not possible. I looked into that, too." Her gaze intensified, and her tone hardened. "You could have prevented this, Rand, and I wonder why you didn't."

"How?" Surprise edged his word. "I was over on Maui."

"When we rescued Leilani from Mr. Quong I was under the impression that you meant to marry her, that you loved her."

"Your impression was correct," he retorted, unable to control his irritation. "But she wasn't agreeable and I had to convince her." He hesitated, wondering if he should confess what he knew. Then deciding it was stupid to keep secrets at such a time, to dance around the issue just because she'd given up her granddaughter, he blurted out what he knew. "Leilani is the reason I went to Maui in the first place, and then—damn it!— I was delayed."

For long seconds she was silent, considering his words, realizing how Leilani had misunderstood his intentions. They'd each been trying to protect the other, and the result was unneeded heartache. Finally she responded, another kind of fear tightening her features. "Did you tell Leilani about her father? Or him about her?"

"That was my intention, but she's beyond my reach—and I didn't tell him about her, because I felt that decision should belong to Leilani."

While he spoke, she'd lowered her head to stare at the floor, and he suddenly knew that she was terribly upset. Rand felt awful, remembering how tragic her life had been, how she must have suffered. And now he was adding a further burden. But it couldn't be helped, he reminded himself. Leilani was all that mattered at the moment.

"Yes, that decision is not mine. It belongs to my granddaughter." Then, meeting his gaze once more, she began to talk, telling him about Leilani's coming to demand the truth, how they'd finally gotten past the old lie, exorcising it forever to reunite as grandmother and granddaughter. "I love her," she said, and despite her Oriental sense of propriety, tears welled in her eyes. "I've been a fool, made wrong decisions, even though I believed it was for the good of everyone." She paused, striving to control the deep shuddering sobs that threatened to break free of her throat. "I can't lose her now!"

"You won't—we won't," Rand announced, his voice tight with resolve. "I'm sending for Richard Drew. He has more pull with the government than all of us put together. If anyone can have Leilani released, it will be him."

"But—"

"Yes," Rand said. "It's time. We'll tell him the truth."

"This is incredible," Leilani stated emphatically. "You want me to stay at the Quong house—the very man who had me kidnapped?"

Dr. Pete was showing the strain, his face drawn from fatigue. "It's the cleanest, best place to stay. You're less likely to get the plague there." He sighed deeply. "Don't forget you'll be with his daughter, Annie—and he's not there, stuck on the outside in the refugee camp." His tone lightened briefly. "Besides, this is Christmas week. It'll be good for you to be with Annie."

"Why can't I go with you?" Leilani insisted. "You need my help, because no one else will volunteer to nurse plague victims."

"I know, I know," he retorted, his usual good temperament edged with impatience. "But they will only let me leave because there aren't enough doctors to check out all the possible victims, so they can be isolated." He paused for breath. "And it's just as well that you stop helping. I never did like the idea of you contaminating yourself. You're still all right, and I want you to stay that way."

She knew there was no use arguing. It was irony—a twist of fate—that she would now take shelter in the very house where she had been held a prisoner. Had Quong still been there she'd have flatly refused, because she didn't trust him for all his appearance of having dropped his criminal activities. Since she'd be with Annie, Lee's fiancée, she finally agreed, secretly relieved to be away from the horror of people dying. Yet she realized that rats knew no barriers; they could move into the Quong house as easily as anywhere. But she didn't mention that. She was stuck until the epidemic was over, and it was true that the Quong house was the most sanitary, her best hope of escaping alive.

"You're sure they won't let me leave?"

"Positive."

"Then I'll stay at the Quong house," she replied, sounding far calmer than she felt. Dr. Pete was exhausted, and looked almost sick himself, and she couldn't add to his burden. "Will you send word to my parents and grandmother that I'm well, that I love them very much?"

"Of course," he replied, and for a moment he was diverted by a sudden thought. "And Rand, too?"

"Yes, Rand, too—if he's back from Maui." She lowered her lashes to hide the hurt his name invoked in her. "You can tell him that I'm doing just fine."

Then the doctor escorted her through the maze of alleys, past several houses that had been burned down, a hideous reminder of the Black Death, to the Quong door. Annie answered her knock.

"And I love you, Dr. Pete," Leilani added as he turned to go, referring to their conversation. "And Esther. You've always been my other parents." Then she kissed him goodbye and went into the house, but not before she saw the sparkle of tears in his eyes.

They both knew it could be a final goodbye.

"You don't know how difficult it was to get to Honolulu. Most of the ships are being diverted to other harbors," Richard Drew remarked, his expression perplexed. "Everyone said I was crazy to come, but knowing you, Rand, I realized it was an emergency. Your note said—" he broke off with a nervous laugh "—that it was a life-and-death situation."

"That's right," Rand agreed tersely. "And I'll explain shortly. There are—uh—others involved."

They were walking by the waterfront, headed into Chinatown, when Richard put out a hand, stopping the man he considered his son. "That's where the plague is, isn't it?"

Nodding, Rand explained briefly. "But up until now, the epidemic has been confined largely to the residential area of Chinatown."

It was all mysterious to Richard and he still hesitated, his worry surfacing. "What's going on, Rand? Are you sick? Because you've lost weight and you look god-awful." As Rand shook his head, Richard went on. "By George, that's what I thought at first. Why else would you send for me?"

"Just be patient, Richard," Rand said as they started walking again. "You'll soon know everything, and I'm just sorry you have to learn about it under these circumstances." He glanced at the older man he'd always admired, and wondered how he would take knowing the truth.

Sensing that something important was about to happen, Richard fell silent, but he was surprised when Rand led him into the establishment of the notorious Madam Silk Stockings, his old nemesis, and straight to her private apartment. The maid let them in after the first knock, and then they were in the parlor, facing the madam herself.

She stood, as unreadable as ever to Richard, and he felt the old anger flame to life. Enough was enough, he decided, and refused her offer of a chair.

"What in the hell is going on?" he demanded, his gaze flickering between Rand and the madam. "And it better be good, because I don't appreciate being brought here."

"I apologize for what I did long ago, Richard," the madam said, breaking the sudden silence that had fallen at his words. "I was wrong."

Her words took Richard aback, but they didn't lessen his anger. "Surely you didn't bring me here to tell me that—not after all this time."

"You loved my daughter," the madam went on. "And I sent her away because I believed it for the best. Then she died." Her voice faltered, and she quickly sat down, suddenly overcome with emotion.

Again the room went quiet, and Rand saw Richard's puzzlement. Thinking the man was about to turn and leave, Rand spoke up. "Do you remember our talk, when I told you about Leilani, the girl I wanted to marry, and you showed me the paintings in your hall?"

"Of course. I showed you the painting of the girl I loved . . . the daughter of the madam here," Richard added crisply, looking even more bewildered.

"She was wearing a cloisonné pin and matching earrings," Rand went on.

"They were her favorites. Ming. She always wore them," Richard added, still waiting to find out what all that had to do with him now.

"And when I came back to Honolulu, I saw that pin, worn by a young woman—a foundling—who'd grown up not knowing where she belonged, and because of that she wouldn't marry me."

"Leilani?" he asked. "But—"

"She's your daughter," Madam Silk Stockings whispered, her voice breaking.

Her revelation seemed to paralyze Richard. His face drained of color, his lips formed words that wouldn't come forth, and he suddenly staggered.

Rand rushed forward and helped him into a chair, alarmed, realizing the man was no longer young and the shock might have been too much for him. "I'm sorry, Richard. I didn't mean it to be like this—didn't know if you'd appreciate learning this now." He paused until Richard recovered from the initial shock. "But we need your help—to save Leilani."

"Dear God," Richard whispered hoarsely. "Of course I want to know about my daughter—my Senni's baby." His eyes shifted to the madam. "Why in hell did you wait all this time to tell me?" he asked angrily. But his face was stricken by the magnitude of his loss.

"Wait," Rand said, sitting next to him, "until we tell you the whole story, so you can understand, just as I've tried to understand."

Then, as Richard listened, both the madam and Rand took turns relating the events that led up to the present. When they finished, Richard was no longer angry, but a sad old man, regretful of all the lost years. "But I won't lose her again," he told them. "I know the cabinet members. I'll get her out, or die trying."

"I was wrong, Richard," the madam repeated. "Please forgive me because . . . because I love Leilani too."

Before he could respond, the parlor door was suddenly flung open and the maid stood in its arch. "So sorry to interrupt," she began, obviously flustered. Then Mr. Quong pushed past the old Chinese woman.

"You must help," he cried, running to the madam. "You have power. You pay *haoles*. I give money. My family will die Black Death without your help." He flung himself at her feet. "So sorry for past."

"Get up!" Rand pulled the man to his feet. "How did you get out of the refugee camp?"

"Had to save family!" he cried, but didn't explain. "Please help."

Rand and the madam exchanged glances, and then Rand told Quong that they would try. The horrible disease had done what they hadn't been able to do: humble the man who'd envisioned himself a mighty tong lord. The Black Death was truly in control of everyone and everything in Honolulu.

But together they'd stop it and save Leilani and Annie, Rand told himself. Because they had to.

The city was paralyzed, and no one knew if Honolulu would survive. Richard's attempts to use his influence to gain his daughter's freedom fell on deaf ears. Security was tightened, and as the number of those coming down with the deadly symptoms grew, so did the panic. Christmas came and went without anyone taking notice, as did the turn into a new century. By early January, when the authorities decided that burning entire infected sections of the city must begin at once, Leilani's grandmother, her Hawaiian parents, Rand and the father she'd never met were united in their fear for her. Old grievances were forgotten . . . and forgiven.

Leilani watched the fire from an upstairs window of Mr. Quong's house, and although it was much bigger than any of the others, she decided it was just another controlled burning. She and Annie had become good friends, and to her surprise, she'd become fond of Mrs. Quong, a kind woman who spoke little English and who worshiped her bully of a husband.

When Annie took to her bed with a fever, they were terrified, believing it was the plague. But it turned out to be only the flu. At dawn Leilani had sent Annie's mother to the cordon with a note for Dr. Pete, requesting cough medicine. And Mrs. Quong hadn't returned.

Going to Annie's bed, Leilani was glad to see that the patient's fever had broken during the night, that she now was sleeping peacefully. Exhausted because she'd stayed up to watch over her friend, Leilani sat down beside the bed, then dozed in the chair, though she had not intended to sleep because she was worried about Mrs. Quong.

"Leilani! Leilani!"

She came awake with a start, and realized Annie was shaking her. Then her gaze fastened on the window. "Oh dear God!" she cried, and leaped to her feet.

The room was bright with fire. Wisps of smoke curled past outside, and the acrid smell of smoke made her feel like coughing. One glance told Leilani that the whole city was aflame.

Grabbing Annie's hand, she yanked her toward the door. There was no time to lose. There was only one way out of the Quong house, and one narrow alley crowded with shacks and sheds that led to the main street. She prayed it wasn't too late to escape.

Or they would die after all.

Chapter Twenty-Two

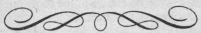

To her horror, Leilani saw that the downstairs was already filling with smoke.

"We're trapped!" Annie cried, her black eyes wide with terror. "The whole street is on fire!"

"Stay calm!" Leilani cried. "We'll make it."

But when she opened the door, it was all she could do to control her own rising panic. Annie cringed behind her, fearful to step from their shelter into the inferno that was hungrily eating up the dilapidated shacks that lined the alley.

"What have they done?" Annie whispered, her voice shaking. "Why would they burn all of Chinatown?"

It was Leilani's very thought. Had the city fathers decided that the Chinese were expendable—that it was worth their dying to wipe out the plague once and for all? But even as her anger blended with her fear, Leilani knew they would die if she allowed such thoughts to cloud her reasoning. She needed all her mental and physical reserves to escape the flames that raged all around them.

Leilani looked everywhere for a way through the wall of fire before them because their only chance was to make the street beyond the maze of alleys. It looked hopeless. Even as her gaze lingered on the narrow passage, a three-story building quivered like crimson tissue paper, then collapsed, sending fireworks of sparks into the clear midday sky.

Abruptly, firecrackers went off beyond the flames, and rockets soared skyward with the smoke, some pinwheeling across the dry wood roofs, others star-bursting against the blue above the billowing thick haze, only to drop back and start new fires. It was worse than any hell the teacher at the mission school had ever described. *It was the end of Honolulu!*

"Mr. Chang's shed where he stores fireworks," Annie said faintly at her side. "Oh my God, Leilani. We're going to burn up!" Her words caught on a sob.

"No!" Leilani cried. "There has to be a way out. The fire isn't behind us. Maybe we can go to the roof, jump to the next building . . . until we reach a street."

But even as she spoke the capricious wind strengthened, and the fire snaked to the roof of the house next to the Quongs. A glance upward told Leilani that their house was already on fire. *Oh, dear God,* she prayed, *please help us find a way.*

"I know a path between buildings," Annie said suddenly, her voice under tight control. "It was my secret route to meet Lee, when Papa wouldn't let me see him."

"Show me!" Leilani cried, because already flames were shooting from the window of Annie's bedroom from which they'd fled, on the upper floor of the Quong house.

They ran from the house into the tiny open area that was surrounded by buildings, most of them burning. The path that led to the alley, which emptied into the street, was completely ablaze. So much for Mr. Quong's need to live where no one could find him, Leilani thought, remembering when she'd been brought along that very route—to be kidnapped. Now it was only a trap. The rats would die, but so would she and Annie—unless the path Annie knew of wasn't closed off by the fire.

Annie shouted something but Leilani couldn't hear her because the roar of the fire shut out any other sound. She could no longer see the blue sky as heavy black smoke was poised above them, like a giant fist about to squeeze the life from their bodies. She motioned for Annie to lead the way, and to run!

But running wasn't possible, for chunks of burning buildings kept falling around them and they had to be watchful to avoid being hit. Annie's path led along a fence, behind which was a building already burning, and overhead the flames formed a tunnel. At any moment the walls could collapse and bury them.

Abruptly, they turned a corner to come up against a sheet of fire. They were cut off.

"Oh no!" Annie cried, tears steaming down her face. "We can't get out here!"

Then, panicked, she saw an open door to a house that wasn't burning, and ran into it. "Come on, Leilani. This is a neighbor. I know they have a cellar where we'll be safe."

"No, Annie!" Leilani cried, trying to stop her.

It was too late. Annie had already disappeared into the smoke-filled shack, and as Leilani followed, hoping to grab her, she was suddenly engulfed in the suffocating haze. But she caught a glimpse of Annie, trying to pull open the door to the cellar.

Instantly Leilani sprang to grab her. When she saw Annie's wide-eyed terror, Leilani knew she'd panicked completely. Her scream was a high, keening shrill that rose up the scale into hysteria. Without hesitation, Leilani slapped her face, then slapped her again, until Annie's scream subsided into sobs.

"Come on," she soothed, although her voice was raised above the crackling fire and the thunderous roar of the smoke. "I know we'll get out. Come with me, Annie. We can't stay here—the house is about to burst into flames!"

Gradually Annie was calmed enough that she didn't fight when Leilani hurriedly led her from the house. Leilani swallowed back her own terror when she saw how quickly the fire had spread in those few seconds. Grasping Annie's hand, she pulled her back the way they'd come. Leilani braced herself, knowing they'd have to make a run for it down the alley, even though the buildings on both sides were burning.

The situation had worsened. The Quong house was fully ablaze, but the wall that had fallen into the alley was now a mass of smoking embers. Without breaking stride, Leilani forced Annie into the alley. Smoke scorched her throat and burned her eyes. Burning debris fell all around, but Leilani only paused once, quickly tearing strips from her petticoat to tie around their noses and mouths, in order to breathe better. Then she was off again, pulling the sobbing Annie behind her.

Abruptly, they burst into the street, and Leilani brought them to an abrupt stop so that she could get her bearings. Behind them, the alley suddenly exploded into flames as two buildings fell into it at the same time.

Annie crumpled to her knees, shaking so hard that Leilani wondered if she would faint. But there was no time to stop now. They had to keep on, or perish. The street, a tunnel through smoke and flames, was utter pandemonium. People ran to and fro, trying to salvage their prized possessions, loading them onto carts or bamboo carrying poles, then racing away as the fire licked at their heels.

Blue-smocked women carried babies and pulled children after them, and each person looked stricken by a sense of doom. Everything they owned was being destroyed.

The noise was deafening. The combination of fire storm and fireworks, shouts and cries, was a cacophony Leilani would never forget. Her dress was torn and filthy, smudged from dirt and cinders, and her hair hung in her face. Annie, still in her nightgown, was in worse shape, having fallen to the ground several times. Her smudged face was streaked with tears, and Leilani suspected her own face looked no better.

When Annie fell again, she was too weak to get up. "Go on without me, Leilani," she whimpered. "I haven't the strength to stand."

A glance at the crumbling buildings, the sudden explosion of shacks that sent fountains of sparks into the sky to blossom like giant poppies, told Leilani that the danger was even greater than before. She didn't even know if her route would take them deeper into the fire. But she knew they had to keep going, had to stay ahead of the fire-breathing dragon of death.

Conserving her own strength, Leilani didn't reply, but instead pulled Annie back onto her feet, realizing she was still weak from her fever. Then, her arm around Annie, Leilani half dragged the girl along, her own legs trembling from the exertion.

Her breath came in painful gulps, as she went first one way, then another, each time blocked and forced to try a different direction. Finally she only kept going by sheer willpower, praying that she'd ultimately find a path out of the maze. When she could no longer go on, she slumped to the ground in the middle of the street, Annie in a heap beside her. Neither spoke, for talking took too much breath. When two rats ran past, squeaking and nosing the ground, Leilani didn't even bother to jerk away. At least the plague would be stopped by the fire, she thought. But she and Annie would die.

The fire raged, and each ragged breath burned Leilani's throat; the cloths no longer helped. Sweat ran down her back from the heat—*the devil's breath,* she thought hysterically. The smoke was a dense swirling cloud that precluded determining which direction led out of the fire...if they could even get past it. Somehow the people they had seen had been left behind, and she wished that she'd thought to follow them, even if they had appeared to be headed in the wrong direction. Now a numbing lethargy pressed down on her. Her strength to help Annie was gone—and she couldn't leave her.

She pulled Annie to her, and they huddled together, their eyes squeezed shut. Leilani just hoped the end would be quick. Gradually, she sank deeper into the heat, and everything became vague and shadowy. The numbness intensified, and try as she would, Leilani couldn't fight it. Beside her, Annie had gone still.

Then strong hands were tugging at her, forcing her to her feet. "Leilani! Snap out of it. I'm here—and I'll get you out of this!" The hands shook her with frenetic urgency.

Her lashes lifted slowly. It was Rand! His hair was mussed, the hollows and planes of his face were set in tight, hard lines, his white shirt and black pants were streaked with dirt and sweat—*but it was really him.* She licked her dry lips, and felt a surge of hope.

He didn't waste time dwelling on his relief as he helped her stand. Then he lifted the limp Annie into his arms, his eyes filled with dread, fearful that the girl was dying.

"She had a fever, was weak," Leilani managed in a croaky whisper.

"Plague?"

Leilani shook her head. "Flu."

Without wasting another moment on talk, he started back the way he'd come, taking them into what appeared to be the heart of the fire. But within another block they'd moved beyond the holocaust, into an area of black cinders, all that remained after the fire storm. When they reached the cordon, crowded with Chinese people trying to escape, they were brought to an abrupt halt.

"Stop! There's another way out—a safe way to the refugee camp!" one of the guards cried, including them with the Chinese.

As the pigtailed men in dirty smocks and trousers tried to push through, someone fired a shot, forcing them back. But Rand didn't move with the others.

"Let us pass," he told them, his voice a harsh command.

When they refused, he was about to stride forward when a man Leilani recognized as a doctor rushed forward. "Dear God, Leilani! Let me help," he cried.

"You can't let them cross here!" the first guard insisted. "The Chinese girl looks sick—could be plague."

"It's not," Leilani told the doctor, having gained strength once the air was fresher. She explained quickly, as Annie opened her eyes.

"I'll take her," the doctor said, and lifted Annie's slight form into his arms. "But she'll have to go to the camp where the doctors can watch her. Precautions," he added.

"My mother," Annie whispered weakly, and again Leilani explained.

"You'll probably find her in the camp, because she wouldn't have been allowed back once the fires were out of control."

The doctor started off and the guards didn't stop him. But when Rand followed, his arm still around Leilani, they leveled their guns on him. Rand only raised his black brows in a scowl. Instead of heeding their command, he swept Leilani up into his arms and strode off.

"Go ahead, shoot!" Rand told them tersely, knowing they wouldn't dare. Then he walked briskly to his buggy in the next block. He was taking Leilani to his house, the quarantine be damned!

Once they left the business area behind, Leilani didn't look back, too emotionally fragile to watch the full destruction of the fire. Rand urged the horse into a gallop, heading out the road to his house. They rode in silence, his arm around her so that she stayed against him, as though he couldn't release her now that she was safe. When they reached his driveway, Rand didn't turn in, but veered onto a track that led to the beach.

"What?" Leilani straightened, her gaze darting to his face, which was set in determined lines.

He glanced at her, his black hair flying in the wind, his dark eyes alight with all the fire she remembered, and never before had he looked so like his pagan ancestors. A sudden grin brought a flash of white teeth, and Leilani felt a whole different sensation—the kindling of desire deep within her, a trembly jolt to her secret, feminine place between her thighs.

Once the horse reached the sand, Rand urged it down the beach until they were directly below his house. He was suddenly on his feet as he cracked the whip over the horse's flank, turning the animal directly into the surf.

"What are you doing?" Leilani cried, astounded by his action. He was driving them right into the ocean!

He shot her another grin, but she saw that he was completely serious. "Precautions, sweetheart!" he cried above the crashing waves, and urged the horse into the breakers, until the buggy wheels were also in the water. "Stay here!" he told her as if she would have jumped out. Then he climbed into the foam and bubbles and freed the horse from the harness to lead it even farther into the ocean, until they were both soaked. Bringing the horse back, he slapped its rump and sent it galloping back to the beach, to head up a path toward the stable.

"Come on!" He held out his arms to her. "It's your turn."

She suddenly knew what he was up to. They'd been in the restricted area, and in the event that a stray flea had hopped onto their clothing, he was about to let the surf drown the plague carriers. Again he surprised her, for once she was in the water, he immediately began undressing her.

"Rand—stop!" She pulled her unbuttoned bodice together, her gaze darting to the expanse of beach. But no other person was in sight to witness their strange actions.

"Trust me, Leilani," he said, having to shout above the thunderous breakers. "I love you! And your false modesty isn't going to stop me from throwing your infected clothes away." He crushed her to him, his eyes suddenly filled with all the fear he'd felt when he'd believed she was trapped in the fire. "I can't lose you ever again," he said grimly.

Her smile was tremulous, and filled with love for him. "I understand," she whispered, and pulling his head down, kissed him on the mouth. Because she'd escaped the fire didn't guarantee they'd escape the plague if Rand's house became infected. And she would die if he came down with the horrible symptoms because of her. She just hoped they'd both be safe.

Instantly, his arms tightened, and as the waves crashed over them with the cool touch of the ocean, he kissed her, too, hotly, passionately. Then he lifted his mouth. "Later, my darling," he murmured, and proceeded to undress her, his movements hurried, as though he wanted *later* to happen soon.

As each garment was discarded, Rand threw it out into the breakers. "When the tide turns in an hour or so it'll take everything out, and wash my buggy in the process," he said as he worked, as though words would distract him from the soft curves of her body. Once she was naked he undressed quickly, throwing his clothing out with hers. Then, hand in hand, they walked out to their shoulders, letting the waves crash over them, so that every inch of their flesh was scrubbed by the powerful hand of the sea.

Emerging from the breakers into the shallows a short time later, they stepped onto dry sand, leaving the buggy to its bath. In the distance a haze of black smoke hung over the city—a glimpse of hell—but above them the sun was warm and renewing. Leilani hesitated, suddenly uncertain about what to do next. She was naked, completely exposed except where her long hair clung to her breasts, like wet silk.

"What will people think?" she said, unable to meet his amused gaze, too aware of his bronze body, so strong and powerful—and so capable of taking hers into ecstasy.

"Probably that I've compromised you completely," he drawled casually. There was a meaningful pause. "That we should get married at once."

She didn't lift her gaze, too uncertain about his motives, whether he was serious or teasing. In either case, she was still too emotionally fragile to cope.

When she didn't respond, Rand took her hand. Sensing her state, he pushed back his rising need for her perfectly formed body, which gleamed wetly in the sunlight, her high, full breasts with their rosy nipples. Instead he led her to the path that went up the bluff to his house. Once near the top, Leilani pulled free, her eyes wide with another worry.

"What about Kama, your housekeeper?" she asked anxiously, her voice hardly above a whisper. "I can't let her see me—like this."

"Relax, sweetheart," he told her, his tone carefully controlled to hide his sudden urge to make love to her right there, on the grassy ledge of the path. "She's not here. The house is empty. I gave her time off to be with her family during the epidemic." He hesitated, his eyes warm as they swept over her curves. "And don't worry about our state of undress. Drastic times require drastic measures."

Rand forced himself to forgo the urgency of his manhood—for the moment. He took her hand again, running with her over the lawn to the back entrance. Leilani just prayed no one saw them. She wondered if the buggy would still be there after the tide went out. One thing had happened since he'd driven into the ocean; she'd begun to regain her strength, and her hope.

The house was peaceful, so quiet, Leilani thought as he led her through the kitchen to the back hall, and on to the stairs. And so spacious when compared to the small rooms she'd gotten used to at the Quongs'. In the past several weeks her whole life had been Chinatown—and now it was being destroyed, she thought sadly. Many poor people would be destitute.

But she couldn't think of that now. For now it was all she could do to remain composed, because being naked in the company of the naked Rand, the man she loved and needed, was almost more than she could endure.

Leilani dried herself with the fluffy white towel, then slipped into the robe Rand had left for her. Once in his bedroom, he'd become brisk, and quickly readied her bath. She'd been grateful to soak away the weeks in the fragrantly scented water, and didn't dwell on his abrupt change of manner. He'd made sure she had everything she needed, that she was strong enough to be left alone, and then he'd gone to see to his own bath somewhere else.

Now, ready to leave his bathroom, she hesitated, uncertain about facing him—because he'd said *I love you* when she'd resisted being undressed on the beach. A tremor went through her, as she realized they were alone in the house. She wasn't afraid of Rand; she was afraid of her own feelings. She couldn't end up like her mother and grandmother, pregnant without a husband.

Ridiculous! she chided herself. She was safe now. Rand had only seen to her well-being . . . even if that meant discarding their clothes. Now that she was safe, she'd ask him to take her to the Kauwe farm, perhaps even to her grandmother, who Rand had said was safe when she'd asked after others, and casually included the madam.

Glancing at herself in the mirror, Leilani saw that her cheeks were as flushed as they felt, giving the blue of her eyes an even more startling brilliance. Her hair, gleaming clean, lay in soft waves down her back, a black cloud against the burgundy color of Rand's satin robe. Turning back to the door, which she quietly opened, Leilani knew there was no reason to delay.

Barefoot, she stepped into the bedroom, then paused again, her eyes on Rand, who sat before the fire he'd built in the fireplace. The ebbing day had cast the room into shadows, and the flames licking over the logs sent flickering light dancing over the carpet at Rand's feet.

He glanced up, saw her and was immediately on his feet, long and lean in a robe as black as his hair and eyes. Their glances locked, each aware of the other's nakedness under the wraps, and neither could move for a heart-shattering moment. Their need throbbed in the silence between them, and Leilani suddenly knew she was lost. She loved him and could deny him nothing, even if history *did* repeat itself.

As though drawn by the hypnotic power of his gaze, she moved to him, caught by the reflected firelight in his eyes that spoke of passion barely controlled. She was helpless before it, awaiting his searing touch that would send her desire soaring into the oblivion of ecstasy in his arms.

"Leilani," he murmured hoarsely, and then he could restrain himself no longer. He reached to pull her against him, where he could hold her close to his heart and never let her go. He needed to possess her, know that the flesh-and-blood Leilani was really safe, was really his forever.

Then she was in his arms, his mouth on hers, gentle at first, as though she were more precious than life itself. With a low groan deep in his throat, Rand deepened his kiss. His tongue thrust into her mouth, and she received it with a thrill of passion that rippled its quivering heat into the secret areas of her body.

"Oh Rand," she whispered against his lips. Her arm moved around him so that she stroked the muscled ridges of his back under the soft fabric of his robe, and felt them tense from her feathery touch. Her other hand slid upward, her fingers tickling over the strong column of his bronze throat, to comb the thick crispness of his black hair. Only material lay between their naked flesh, and she felt the tautness of his long legs against hers, his hardness pressing into her satin robe.

His fingers began their own search, sliding under her loosely tied garment, seeking the swell of her breasts, which tingled for his touch. Her nipples, which hardened in exquisite anticipation, sent sparks of fire into her veins and a rich rise of sensation into the soft folds between her thighs. Leilani arched to him, her long silky lashes fluttering against the top curve of her cheeks. A low moan of surrender escaped her lips.

She felt his rising passion in the tightening of his arms, the urgency of his kisses as he feathered her face, her ears, her neck and lower still. "Dear God. Oh, dear God," she whispered, her words a plea for fulfillment.

As Rand seared a trail of fire across her flesh, his tongue licking and tickling back to her mouth, Leilani's lashes flew open to reveal her slumberous eyes, their pupils dilated with passion. A sheen gave her heated skin a luminous glaze, and he saw her desperate need of him in her whole bearing.

With sure hands, Rand untied the cord that held her robe together, then slipped it from her shoulders where it rustled to the floor like a great burgundy pool on the Oriental carpet. A moment later his fell next to it. They stood, each taking in the nakedness of the other—a Polynesian god and a beautiful porcelain doll. Then he swooped her up into his arms and strode to the bed he'd readied for them while she bathed. Gently, he placed her on the soft feather mattress, then stood gazing at her...his woman.

He drank in her beauty, her perfectly formed limbs, her high pointed breasts that seemed to strain for him, her long silky hair that framed her flushed face, and her bright sapphire eyes, their lashes half-lowered to screen the blooming need within her. He couldn't wait a moment longer, and lowered himself to her, holding the softness of her flesh to his own muscled body.

"My darling—my angel of mercy—be merciful to me now." Then his mouth came down on hers once more in a searing kiss that molded their bodies together, so that their racing hearts beat as one. "I love you," he told her between kisses.

At that moment a horrible thought gave her pause, and she blurted it out in the next second. "More than any other woman? More than Stella?"

Instantly he lifted his head, his dark eyes darkening even more at such a question. "I don't love Stella. I've never loved that woman." He hesitated, examining her face, wondering why she thought such a thing. "Do you doubt me, sweetheart—or are you jealous?" A slow smile curved his lips, the lips so experienced in the art of kissing. "You *are* jealous, I can tell."

Her lashes swept down, and she felt suddenly uncertain again. She looked so upset that Rand was pricked with guilt for teasing at such a time, when his answer was obviously so important to her. When Leilani met his eyes, her own eyes so open and honest, he was almost overwhelmed with his love for her.

"Yes," she admitted softly. "I have been jealous. And so very hurt when you told me that last time—" she took a shaky breath and went on "—when we went for a ride in the automobile, that you couldn't marry me."

His eyes widened in surprise. "Oh, my darling," he whispered, wanting her more than ever. "I'm so sorry to have given you that impression, because I was only waiting to ask you properly, until I could give you a wonderful wedding gift, your birthright—*your father.*"

Then he explained everything. Leilani listened incredulously, her wonderment growing with each thing he said. As Rand finished, his last words slid into a silence pregnant with the promise of a whole new life for them both.

"Rand, Rand. How I love you. You have given me everything in the world I ever dreamed of having. Thank you, my darling." And she pulled him to her, kissing him tenderly, then passionately.

The depth of her passion, her love for him, shook Rand to the core. He held her, wanted to hold her longer, but it was impossible. The demands of their bodies, the hot, aching agony of being separate when they each craved the other could not be denied.

"Take me now, Rand. I love you—want you—will always want only you!"

And he made them one in the timelessness of love fulfilled.

Chapter Twenty-Three

A week later it began to look as though the plague had been eradicated. But the price was high, for more than forty-five hundred people were left destitute and homeless, although, miraculously, no one had died as a result of the fire.

"Property loss will probably be more than three million dollars," Dr. Pete said when Leilani went to his temporary office on King Street, just beyond the heart of Chinatown, which had been obliterated forever. "But the bubonic plague has lost its breeding ground."

Leilani only nodded, feeling sad, because even the doctor and Esther had lost everything.

He sensed how she felt, and tried to reassure her. "It could have been so much worse," he said. "All of Honolulu could have burned, or, if the plague hadn't been stopped, then most of the population—Chinese, Hawaiian and *haole* alike—would have died." He hesitated. "It was hard to lose our house and office, but it was worth it, Leilani, worth all the lives that were saved because of the fire. We'll rebuild, and this time our office will be constructed of bricks."

"I know," she agreed. "But it's tragic, because again the Chinese are the ones who suffer."

"They'll need our help more than ever now," he agreed, and she fell silent, reflecting on the plight of the homeless people.

She'd gone to the farm of her Hawaiian parents the day after Rand rescued her from the fire, and Mama Kauwe had insisted she rest for several days, despite her wanting to help in the city. "Let fires go out," her mother had said in her musical voice. "Let rats be gone—no new plague."

Having so much on her mind, Leilani had been relieved that her mother took the decision out of her hands. And over those days she'd sorted out all the things Rand had told her about her real father. Finally, she'd been able to discuss everything with her Hawaiian parents, who'd listened solemnly. When she told them all she knew, that Rand was arranging a meeting with her father, that she wanted them with her at that meeting, they'd suddenly broke into big smiles.

"Then we'll still be your parents, too?" Mama Kauwe had asked, her brown eyes large with worry.

Leilani had reassured them, kissing them both. "No one in the world will ever replace the two of you," she'd said with tears in her eyes. "I couldn't love you more if you were my birth parents. And I'll always love you and Paulo and Willy."

Now, as she examined Dr. Pete's office, which was hardly more than a shack, she hesitated, her gaze suddenly level, holding his. "I found out who my father was, Dr. Pete," she told him.

He didn't look surprised, only inclined his head waiting for her to go on.

"Rand told me."

"So that's what he was up to." He shook his head and his unruly hair fell forward over his round spectacles.

"What do you mean?"

"Well, before he went to Maui—before this damnable plague hit, Rand and I had a talk." He smiled wryly. "I should say Rand had a talk with me, demanded information about your birth." Then he went on to explain. "But I didn't know he knew your father. I didn't even know who the man was."

She digested his information, then decided she couldn't hold a grudge against him for keeping such a secret. After all, she'd loved the doctor all her life, and he, like her grandmother, had believed that he was doing the right thing back then. So she went on to invite him to the family meeting at Rand's house the next night. "And bring Esther," she added.

"We'll be there, Leilani." He paused, trying to put words to his feelings—and his guilt. "I'm sorry about everything," he began slowly. "I hope you'll forgive an old man his misguided attempt to right the wrongs of the world."

"I understand why you helped my grandmother," she said quietly. "And in this past week I let go of any lingering anger at not being told, because everything is so wonderful now." A smile brightened her face. "Besides, I could never wish my Hawaiian parents away. They've always loved me unconditionally, and I know how very lucky I am to have had them raise me." She went to him and kissed him on the cheek. "So you and my grandmother made a wise decision, after all. Things would have been very different for me if I'd been raised in a brothel. I realize that now."

She left him then to return to the farm, her mind already preoccupied with thoughts about tomorrow night. It would be the first time she'd seen Rand since the night of the fire—her face flushed even to think about it. And it would be her first meeting with her father. Leilani's heart fluttered nervously. She was looking forward to meeting him . . . and dreading it.

But everyone I love will be there, too, she reminded herself. I won't be alone. And in any case I'm an adult. I don't have to do more than meet him, and if I don't like him, I never have to see him again.

With new resolve, she quickened her step, and forced her thoughts into concentrating on what she'd wear. Yet her apprehension lingered.

Gowned in a deep blue velvet dress, its bell-shaped skirt dropping away from a tiny waist to a wide hem, Leilani felt she looked her best. The matching jacket, with its wide revers lying on top of the puffed sleeves, added a touch of fashion, and her feathered hat perched on her upswept hair gave her the air of a confident woman, an effect she'd sought to achieve.

Her grandmother had come for Leilani and the Kauwes in a double-seated buggy driven by her Chinese houseboy. Although elaborately gowned, jeweled and coiffured, and looking every inch the descendant of Chinese rulers, the madam was without her rice powder for the first time. Leilani kissed the pale cheek, then sat down beside her, the Kauwes across from them, their massive bulk weighting down the vehicle. She smiled reassuringly at her father, who was uncomfortable in his black suit, and her mother, who kept fidgeting with her straw hat, only worn because of the occasion. They looked out of place in their finery, but Leilani admired them nevertheless. Now, as always, they didn't put on airs. They accepted others as they were and expected similar treatment.

After small talk they rode in silence to Rand's house, the driver taking them around the devastation of Chinatown, and Leilani knew he did so on her grandmother's orders. Already apprehensive about the upcoming meeting, they didn't need other worrisome reminders to add to their state of nervousness. But Leilani's thoughts did linger for a moment with the fire. Her grandmother had also lost her building and apartment, although she'd had the foresight to remove her priceless art to a safe place once the city fathers had decided to burn individual homes. "I knew it would get out of hand at some point," she'd told Leilani after the fire was out. "Everyone knew Chinatown was a firetrap."

Now, as they turned into the driveway that led to the stately house overlooking the ocean, her grandmother suddenly patted Leilani's knee and smiled. "It'll be fine, Leilani," she said, her tone encouraging. "And whatever happens, you already have a family."

Both the Kauwes nodded agreement, big smiles on their faces for their beloved daughter. Then the carriage came to a gentle stop, and Rand, looking incredibly handsome in his black suit and white shirt, ran down the veranda steps to greet them, his eyes hardly leaving Leilani.

He helped the madam down first, then Leilani, lifting her from the step and holding her a moment longer than was necessary. "You're beautiful, sweetheart," he murmured for her ears only. "I love you."

Then, carefully banking down the little fires Leilani had glimpsed in his eyes, he helped the Kauwes from the carriage. "Please come inside," he told them, and walking between the madam and Leilani, he strode to the open front doors, her parents following behind. Once inside, they went directly to the parlor, where Dr. Pete and Esther sat talking with a tall, middle-aged man, who stood up at once, his bright blue eyes going immediately to Leilani.

For a moment it was as though time was suspended; everyone hesitated and no one spoke. Finally, Rand stepped into the vacuum, sensing that no one knew where to start, what to say.

"Richard, you already know Madam Silk Stockings," he began, his tone friendly, as though he were welcoming guests, not bringing people together who shared a tragic past. "But I'd like you to meet Mr. and Mrs. Kauwe, Leilani's adopted parents." As they all smiled acknowledgments, Rand's arm was suddenly around Leilani's shoulders, and as he spoke, his fingers gave her arm a slight squeeze of encouragement. "And this is Leilani, Richard . . . your daughter."

Brilliant blue eyes met identical brilliant blue eyes. Leilani swallowed hard, suddenly unable to speak. He was a tall man, still strikingly handsome, and she had no doubt *he was her father*.

He, too, seemed choked up, too overwhelmed to respond. Then she saw his lips tremble, and the sparkle of tears, and all her own fears vanished in her compassion for him. *He'd been denied his daughter all these years*. Without a word Leilani went to him, hesitated, her eyes blurring from her own tears, and then placed her arms around him in a gentle hug.

They stood in silence for long seconds, gathering their ragged emotions into a semblance of calm, so that they could speak. Finally Richard managed his first words to his daughter.

"You're as beautiful as your mother was, Leilani," he said softly, and held her at arm's length so that he could look into her face. "I didn't know my darling Senni gave me a daughter." His voice broke. "I'm so sorry I didn't know." He hesitated, looking so sad and lonely that Leilani thought her heart would break. "But I know now," he whispered, pausing again to take a deep breath. "And I know you have other parents—good people—" He broke off, too emotional to continue.

Tears streamed from Leilani's eyes. Rand had told her about Richard Drew's life—how he'd lost everyone he'd loved. And how he'd blamed the old Polynesian taboos, because he was part Hawaiian—and how he'd finally come to believe that they weren't responsible. He'd suffered greatly, and Leilani saw how much it meant to him to know he still had a family after all.

"I would be honored to have you for my *other* father," she managed, her voice shaking. "And I would love to know my mother, Senni, through your eyes, Father," she ended hopefully.

Then they embraced, holding each other in the eternal bond of blood, father and daughter. Gradually, Leilani became aware of other arms holding them both, small dainty hands that patted her back.

"Please forgive an old woman who was wrong, a mother who was trying to protect her only daughter, a grandmother who thought her only grandchild would be better off with strangers." The madam's voice sounded even sadder than Richard's or Leilani's, faint and tremulous and regretful, and it broke on a long shuddering sob.

And then the old woman, so proud and determined and strong, collapsed into a chair to bury her face in her hands, crying for all that she'd lost, crying because she couldn't help it, for there was no longer a compartment to hide her sorrows. Now, for the first time since fleeing China, a frightened, innocent girl who'd been seduced by love, she'd come face-to-face with her life. Her own actions had brought her to this moment of reckoning.

"Grandmother!" Leilani cried, going down on her knees before the little woman. "It's all right. I understand. And I forgive you." She held her grandmother's hands in hers. "Please don't cry. I love you and I'm so very proud of you, proud that you're my grandmother."

Richard knelt beside her. "I, too, forgive you. Senni wouldn't have wanted us to do anything less." He took out a handkerchief and handed it to the old lady, who couldn't seem to get hold of her emotions. "You see, even though I lost Senni and my baby daughter, I married and had another daughter, and now I couldn't forgo having my memories of them—because I loved them, too." He hesitated, drawing on his own emotional reserves. "Don't the Chinese believe fate is preordained, Hsi Shen?" he asked, calling her by her rightful name for the first time.

She managed a nod, and finally more faint words to explain. "I wanted to tell you about Leilani when you lost your family, Richard. But I couldn't, because Leilani didn't know about either of us, and I believed it was too late to disrupt her life." She was beset by more choking sobs. "And now fate, as you say, has intervened."

"Then so be it," Richard said softly. "For all the sorrows each of us has suffered, this day was coming. And now we need to rejoice, for it's here." He tipped her chin so that she had to look at him. "I have a suggestion," he said softly. "Why don't we all forget the past, and be one big family?"

"You forgive me, Richard?" the old madam whispered, her voice as wispy as falling leaves.

"Yes," he replied softly. "How could I not?"

And then they wept together, all the tears that had gathered within them because of all they'd lost . . . and now found. Beyond them Esther cried softly and the doctor stared out the window at the ebbing afternoon, its splendor blurred by his tear-filled eyes. Papa Kauwe looked inward, knowing the scene before him was truly the will of the old gods, while Mama Kauwe sobbed loudly, her big heart almost bursting with compassion for all of them. Rand only stared at Leilani, so filled with love that he could hardly stand it. How had the gods—or whoever—decided he was worthy of such a forgiving, gentle, beautiful woman? All he could think of was holding her, keeping her safe for the rest of his life.

During the whole healing experience, Leilani was conscious of one thing in the back of her mind. Her mother, *Senni,* was an innocent, had become pregnant before marriage only because she loved and trusted—she might well have died of a broken heart rather than from childbirth. Leilani understood how her mother must have felt—*because she loved Rand that much.*

Finally her grandmother wiped her tears. Then her father stood up, pulling Leilani with him. "We have many years ahead of us," he told her. "And there's room for forgiveness—because now all of us are family."

Leilani nodded, her gaze shifting to Rand, who watched from his position by the fireplace. They exchanged a look that held a promise of when they'd be alone, and then she met her father's eyes once more, knowing how much this moment meant to him. She suddenly felt blessed, because she had a Hawaiian family, a Chinese family and a *haole* family. And one day she and Rand would have their own family, which would be a blending of all of their backgrounds.

"In Hawaii there are many superstitions," Richard began, breaking the quiet in the parlor. "But if there are old taboos, then they have been satisfied, because I have been given a new family after I believed my life was over except to live out my years."

His words seemed to break the tension in the room, and everyone seemed to talk all at once. Finally, in a lull of talk, Leilani asked Rand a question that had been on her mind but that she'd forgotten to bring up.

"How did you know Richard Drew was my father?"

Rand was thoughtful, considering his answer. "Remember when you showed me your pin?" he began. When she nodded, looking down because she recalled the circumstances, he went on. "I recognized it because I'd seen it before—in my father-in-law's house—in the painting of a woman he'd loved before he married the mother of my deceased wife."

"I married after I'd given up hope of ever finding Senni," Richard added. "And my daughter—my second daughter," he amended, "was born two years after you, Leilani. Nolina was Rand's first wife, and now I couldn't be happier than to know he'll be my son-in-law again."

Rand barely had time to nod before Dr. Pete interjected his own view. "Enough sadness!" he cried. "Bring out the whiskey, or brandy—or whatever! It's time we forgot the past and toasted the future."

And they did—they toasted the future of their new family, and the new century that had arrived unnoticed by Honolulu because of the plague.

By the end of the following week Leilani had agreed to visit her father on Maui, and her grandmother had given her a trunk of her mother's belongings. After the meeting at Rand's, she hadn't seen him, as he, like everyone in Honolulu, still worked from dawn far into the night, in the aftermath of the plague and the fire. But he'd sent a note that he missed her, would see her soon, and then they'd set their wedding date.

"I'm retiring," her grandmother said one day when Leilani visited her at her rented house on the outskirts of Honolulu. "And I've decided to move off this island, to make a new life and become a respectable woman in my old age."

Leilani stared, wide-eyed, instantly upset. "You're going away?" She tried to hide her distress. She'd grown to love the old woman, and the thought of her going away brought her close to tears. "Where?" she managed in a faint voice.

Seeing that Leilani misunderstood, she immediately clarified. "I'm only going as far as Maui—if I can find a suitable house." She hesitated, her eyes gentling, pleased by Leilani's show of affection even as she wanted to reassure her. "Richard—your father—has offered to help me find a cottage near Lahaina where I'll be close to everyone."

Relieved, Leilani knew she was referring to Rand's statement that he intended to live on Maui permanently in the future, while his partner, Lee, would handle the Honolulu half of their practice. When her grandmother invited Leilani to stay in her house with the cook while she was away, Leilani accepted.

Several days later Leilani moved from the farm to her grandmother's house, saw her and her maid to the boat and then settled into the bedroom assigned her for the next week. She welcomed the time alone to go through her mother's trunk, and as she opened the lid one evening, she wondered if that was one of the reasons her grandmother had asked her to stay—so she would have privacy when looking at Senni's treasures.

The cook was in her quarters above the stable, and Leilani had lit a fire in the stone fireplace to ward off the chill of the winter night. She'd already bathed and put on a flame silk robe over its matching gown, both gifts from her grandmother. They were exquisite garments, and she suspected they were also expensive. She sighed, thinking how drastically her life had changed, and then bent forward to examine her dead mother's things. But her hand stilled on the tissue paper covering the contents, and her gaze went to the painting above the fire-place.

"Oh, Mother," she whispered to the lovely dark-haired girl, whose lips were curved into a sweet smile, whose eyes seemed to hold a secret meant only for her lover, a pose forever frozen in time. Leilani knew the painting had been completed shortly before Senni announced her love for Richard Drew. Unknown to the madam, the artist had painted two portraits, the other for the man Senni intended to marry.

Leilani stood up, moved around the trunk and stood under the canvas. "I'm so sorry that I never knew you, Mother. So sorry that you had to die."

The lamplight shone on her long black hair, and outlined the perfect profile of her face. Reflected fire seemed to catch in the crimson sheen of her gown, and for a moment she could have been the girl in the painting, Rand thought from where he hesitated in the doorway, his gaze fastened on the woman he loved. She hadn't heard his knock or his approaching footsteps, and now he saw why. Her mind was deep in the past, and he'd intruded on her privacy.

As though she sensed his presence, she turned suddenly, her long lashes wet from the tears brimming in her eyes. It was too late for him to slip away unnoticed. "Rand," she gasped, startled to see him.

In a second he'd closed the space between them, his fingers gently wiping away the drops of moisture. "Oh, my darling," he murmured as he embraced her. "I hate seeing you look so sad."

"But I'm not really sad," she said against his coat. "Only sorry that I never knew her." She glanced at the painting, and the dark eyes of her mother seemed to look back, her smile somehow meant for her daughter now. "She was so beautiful and—it was all so tragic."

"I know, sweetheart," he soothed. "But she would be happy to know everything turned out fine in the end."

Leilani tipped back her head so that she could meet his eyes. "Do you think she knows, Rand? Wherever she is now?"

He hesitated, searching her face. "I'm sure she knows," he agreed softly. And then he could resist her no longer. He bent his head, and his mouth found her lips. Instantly, the kiss deepened, and Leilani was suddenly straining against him, her filmy garment a flame against the blackness of his clothing.

Then he feathered her face with kisses, his tongue tracing a line of fire over her cheek and into her neck, and lower to the full curve of her breasts. A low moan sounded from Leilani's throat as they sank back onto the settee, and the loose wrap slipped from her shoulders.

"No," Rand whispered, and reined in his desire, remembering that he was in the madam's parlor, not his. "We can't do this. Someone could come at any moment." He managed a crooked grin and sat up. "I came to talk, to set our wedding date with you and your grandmother—not make love to you."

For long moments she seemed to consider what he said. Then she stood, backing away from him so that her body was backlighted by the fire, showing her nakedness under the gauzy silk.

"My grandmother has gone to Maui," she told him softly. "To look for a house to buy." She untied the cord to her robe. "The cook is in her own quarters." Leilani's long hair fell forward over her cheeks as she allowed the robe to slither down her limbs to the floor. "No one is here—except us." She lowered her lashes seductively as she slipped the straps of her gown from her shoulders. "I want you to make love to me, because I need you more than I can say." Her whispered words were hardly distinguishable, yet they soared into the quiet room like a benediction to all that the woman in the painting had lost. And then her gown fell around her bare feet, and she stood before him, completely his for the taking.

"I love you! I love you!" he cried, humbled by what she was giving him, not just her body, not just her love, but the essence of herself. He took her back to him. And as quickly as the constraints of his clothing could be removed, he did as she asked. He made love to her, without foreplay, almost savagely, because his manhood wouldn't wait, his hardness needed to feel her around him. There was time enough to taste her later, to lick and tickle and tantalize after their first passion was spent. For now only the ultimate would satisfy them, only their joining.

And he didn't leave until morning.

Chapter Twenty-Four

Once back from Maui, Leilani's grandmother announced that she'd bought a house overlooking the ocean near Lahaina, and that she was selling her property in Honolulu. "But first things first," she told Leilani. "We have a wedding to plan."

The date was set for late March, and Leilani left most of the arrangements in her grandmother's hands, as she saw how much it meant to the old woman. She'd missed her own wedding and her daughter's, and now she could hardly hide her mounting excitement as she orchestrated the whole affair, which was to be held in Richard Drew's home on Maui.

Often Leilani paused in her work with the doctor to reflect on how different her life had become. Everyone was involved in the wedding; it was as though the family's coming together had given each one new hope for the future. The rebuilding of Chinatown had already begun, and Rand and Lee worked long days seeing to the construction of their new office, and sorting through their files, which they'd managed to save just ahead of the fire. That Leilani had no time alone with Rand was bearable to her—because they'd soon be together every night.

Even Lee was in high spirits. Mr. Quong was so grateful that his daughter's life had been saved, he'd given permission for Annie to marry Lee in the summer. Rand reported Mr. Quong as saying he was sorry for what he'd done to Leilani in the past, that he was in her debt—and would not forget. "I decide not to be tong lord," he told Lee and Rand. "Honolulu good place, much opportunity—make money here without being bad. Get rich honestly."

"He's even saying he's going to help his people get established, maybe lend money for them to start a business," Rand told Leilani while they visited in her grandmother's parlor.

"And charge interest," Leilani added. "You wait, in a few years he'll be president of a Chinese bank."

They laughed, and her grandmother chimed in. "It's a new beginning for the Chinese. Hawaii is a new territory, it's a new century, there will be a new Chinatown, and one day they will even be citizens."

For a moment they sat in silence, because what she'd said was true. It was an exciting time for Hawaii, Leilani thought, and for the Chinese, although there was much work ahead of them before it all came true.

Then Rand stood to go, and took leave of the madam. Leilani walked him into the front hall to the door.

"I won't see you again until Maui," he said, pulling her into his arms.

"I know," she whispered back. "But that's only ten days away, and I can wait because it will be my dream come true."

"Oh, sweetheart," he murmured, his mouth almost touching hers. "I can't wait to hold you, to know that you're mine forever."

He kissed her then, a deep, probing kiss that jolted her heart with fluttery sensations, and sent the remembered fire into the moist folds of her secret place that was reserved for only him. Her body strained to him, as for a second she forgot where they were.

"I love you, my little angel of mercy," he whispered as he lifted his mouth. "I've never loved anyone this much."

"Not even Nolina?" she asked, finally daring to express what she'd thought about so often.

His dark eyes, hooded by their moment of passion, were suddenly reflective. "No, my darling, not even Nolina. I got over her long ago, after I met you." He tipped her chin so that she had to lift her lashes, which had lowered as he spoke. "She was your half sister, and you resemble each other slightly, and I'll always be sad about her death." He hesitated, the light in his eyes intensifying. "But I never knew such profound love . . . until you."

"Oh, Rand, I love you, too." She stood on her tiptoes and kissed him then. "Until our wedding day," she told him.

"You look so beautiful." Leilani's grandmother came into the upstairs bedroom where Leilani was just stepping into her wedding dress, with the help of the madam's maid. "You look like my Senni today," she said, walking farther into the room. The elegant Chinese woman was gowned in a dark floral oriental silk with dramatic jade jewelry, her black hair as stunningly coiffured as always, complete with Chinese combs. But she wore no rice powder and only a dab of rouge on her cheeks and lips, a proper grandmother of the bride, Leilani thought.

"Thank you." Leilani smiled at her grandmother's image in the mirror. "The dress is exquisite, as is everything you've done for my wedding." She turned and kissed the woman's cheek. "You've made everything perfect."

"Your father helped," the madam said at once, honesty not allowing herself to take full credit. "He insisted on paying for everything." She smiled suddenly, and Leilani saw how much the compliment pleased her.

"Very nice!" Mama Kauwe added with a big smile. "My boys say they never want to leave Maui. Everyone is so good to me and Papa and Willy and Paulo." Dressed in a flowing pink silk gown, another gift from Leilani's grandmother, Mama Kauwe had never looked more grand. "We all see our daughter marry good man. Rand will make fine son-in-law for us."

Leilani hid a smile. Mama Kauwe had adopted everyone, her generosity of spirit never so evident. Neither she nor Papa Kauwe felt in the least upstaged by the advent of Leilani's real family. They'd simply fit themselves into the larger group, welcoming more relatives. Papa Kauwe had even suggested it be Richard Drew who escort *their* daughter down the aisle. "I was at all important events in Leilani's life," he'd stated with a wide smile. "Time you had turn." The Kauwes' unselfishness was so typical of old Hawaii, Leilani thought, and realized again how blessed she'd been to be raised by them.

Her gown was finally fastened, and the maid turned Leilani back to the mirror. Leilani caught her breath, and her long silky lashes flew open over the brilliance of her blue eyes. She couldn't believe the pink-cheeked girl in the glass was really she. Her wedding dress was made of white shimmery satin, trimmed with Brussels lace and white ribbons, the skirt falling away from a tiny waist to the wide sweep of skirt. It was cut low in front, and even with the lace inset, the top curve of her breasts were bare. The lacy puffed sleeves narrowed at her wrists, and her veil was fastened to her hair, styled in long soft curls and waves, by a wreath of fragrant white tropical flowers, with a touch of blue to match her eyes.

"Beautiful!" Mama Kauwe breathed. "So beautiful!"

"As beautiful as her mother before her," Richard said from the doorway. Downstairs, someone had begun to play the piano, and as he stepped into the room, Leilani knew there were only seconds before he would escort her down to the main salon where she would become Rand's wife.

She smiled at her father, who looked so handsome in his black formal suit. She had gotten to know him during the days they'd been together before the wedding. His stories about her mother had brought the beautiful Senni to life for Leilani. It was the final piece to the puzzle of her background, she reflected. She was finally whole, free to love—and marry the man of her dreams.

Papa Kauwe followed Richard into the room. "I wish you as much happiness as your mother has given me," he told her, and kissed her on the cheek. Then Mama Kauwe did the same, and with tears in their eyes, they went downstairs to find their seats.

"I'm blessed in my old age," Leilani's grandmother said, and held out a tiny box for her to open. "These belonged to your mother and now they are yours."

Blinking quickly so as not to shed a tear, Leilani took the cloisonné earrings from their bed of velvet. Because her hand trembled, her grandmother helped her fasten them to her ears.

"To match your pin," she said, tears brightening her black eyes. "It's the perfect touch on your wedding dress." As Leilani nodded her thanks, too overcome at the moment to speak, her grandmother moved forward and kissed her. "I love you, Leilani. And I'm looking forward to being a part of your life now."

Then she, too, went downstairs.

"Are you ready, my dear?" her father asked gently, his own eyes looking suspiciously bright.

She nodded, took his arm, and they swept out to the hall, hesitating at the top of the staircase. Downstairs her family, the doctor and Esther, Lee and Annie, all awaited her entrance. For a moment Leilani glanced down at the maile and floral decorations that outlined the banister all the way to the lower floor, beyond which clusters of flowers perfumed the air and lighted candles added magic to the tropical night. She knew that the driveway and outside entrance had been carpeted with rushes and marsh grass, Mama and Papa Kauwe's suggestion to bring luck to the marriage. And she'd glimpsed the lighted torches from the upstairs veranda, their flickering flames an exotic touch to the backdrop of coconut palms and crashing ocean breakers.

"Thank you, father, for all of this," she whispered to the man who'd just found his daughter, and was about to give her away in marriage.

"Thank you, Leilani, for giving me a new life."

Then the first notes of Mendelssohn's "Wedding March" floated up to them on soft air currents. It was time. Leilani went down the steps to meet the only man she'd ever love.

He watched her approach, tall and darkly handsome in his formal black suit and white ruffled shirt. *Her pagan god,* she thought, and smiled into his eyes.

Seconds later she stood next to Rand and repeated her marriage vows, watching the love for her in his eyes as he said his. Then they were pronounced man and wife, and Rand's lips were on hers, kissing her with passion despite family and friends who watched.

Oh, dear God, thank you for Rand, and for my new family. Her senses swam with emotion, but one thought superseded everything else. *She was Rand's wife!*

"I love you, sweetheart," he whispered against her lips.

"I love you, Rand," she whispered, and contrary to wedding tradition, kissed him back. "Forever."

"And even beyond that," he said, his eyes filled with all the fire that would be hers again.

Leilani knew she had roots now. Rand knew the old taboos were gone forever. His family, a combination of *haole* and Hawaiian, now included Leilani, who would add Chinese to the Walsh bloodline. He pulled her close as they turned to receive their guests. They both knew that the intermingling of cultures and blood would be the true meaning of being Hawaiian in the new century.

Epilogue

Six months later Leilani stood on the veranda of their house in Lahaina, her gaze on the wide expanse of sand between their lawn and the ocean, where her two Hawaiian brothers played. Down the beach she could see the roof of her grandmother's house among the palms, and smiled to herself. Her grandmother, now known by her rightful name, Hsi Shen, was fast becoming a respected member of social circles on Maui, thanks to Richard.

"You're looking mighty thoughtful, sweetheart," Rand said, coming up behind her to kiss her neck. "Not having second thoughts about going over to Honolulu, I trust," he drawled, his voice lower, and she recognized a rich thread of passion in its tone.

She turned so that he could claim her lips. After he'd kissed her, she murmured against his mouth, "Not at all. I'm looking forward to seeing Lee marry Annie."

He lifted his head, sensing something on her mind, although she didn't look upset. "You aren't missing your brothers already, before they're even gone, are you?"

"No, Rand," she said, and hid a smile. "They've been here for a month, and they have to go home and start school." She stepped back, so that she could see his face better. "And I'm looking forward to seeing the doctor and Esther, and my parents. No, I don't miss living in Honolulu now that you've moved us here permanently. I believe it's wonderful, in fact, that Lee will handle the Honolulu office and you the Lahaina practice."

"Then what's wrong, Leilani?" Rand's eyes expressed puzzlement, then concern. He loved her so much that he sometimes couldn't believe she really belonged to him. Now, as he watched her long lashes flutter, he knew she was about to say something important.

"Do you remember what it is that my father—Richard—wants so badly? What my grandmother is looking forward to with great anticipation?"

"I know they, like Lee and ourselves, are involved in helping to set up opportunities for the Chinese now that Chinatown is being rebuilt."

"Yes, that's true," Leilani answered, a secret smile on her lips. "And of course, helping poor Hawaiians, too. As I've said many times, I want my two brothers to have the best education they can get, so they can become what they want in the future."

"Leilani, what is it, for God's sake?" He pulled her back into his arms, his eyes clouding with worry. "You're not sick, are you?"

"Well, no, that is, I don't have anything fatal." Her eyes were suddenly filled with love for him. "Next spring I'm going to give you something very special, Rand." She smiled her sweet smile that was reserved for him alone. "We're going to have a baby."

It took a few seconds for her news to sink in. Then he swooped her up into his arms and danced across the veranda, suddenly putting her back down on her feet, aware of her delicate condition. "I love you, oh, how I love you, my darling. Thank you!"

But he couldn't contain his joy. He let out a whoop of pure excitement. "You're right, Leilani. Your grandmother anticipates many great-grandchildren, and somewhere among our future brood, Richard hopes for an heir to his empire."

Abruptly, he paused. "Leilani...does that mean you can't—uh—we can't..."

She shook her head. "I'd almost forgo having a baby if it meant that," she teased.

"In that case," he said, but didn't finish his sentence. Instead he swooped her back into his arms and strode toward the bedroom.

She snuggled to him as he climbed the stairs to the upper floor, secure in her happiness. She and Rand were the lucky ones, because they were so much in love. And their children would be lucky too, because they would know what love meant. *And we'll bring them up to respect all people,* she reminded herself, knowing that was the way of the future for Hawaii as well as their family.

And then Rand took her inside their bedroom, and closed the door on the world.

* * * * *

presents
MARCH MADNESS!

Come March, we're lining up four wonderful stories by four dazzling newcomers—and we guarantee you won't be disappointed! From the stark beauty of Medieval Wales to marauding *bandidos* in Chihuahua, Mexico, return to the days of enchantment and high adventure with characters who will touch your heart.

So rev up for spring with a bit of March Madness . . . only from
Harlequin Historicals!

MM92

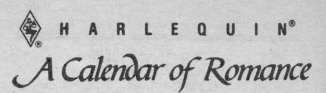

HARLEQUIN®

A Calendar of Romance

Be a part of American Romance's year-long celebration of love and the holidays of 1992. Celebrate those special times each month with your favorite authors.

Next month, live out a St. Patrick's Day fantasy in

#429 FLANNERY'S RAINBOW
by Julie Kistler

Read all the books in *A Calendar of Romance*, coming to you one per month, all year, only in American Romance.

Harlequin Regency®
Romance™

WHO SAYS ROMANCE IS A THING OF THE PAST?

We do! At Harlequin Regency Romance, we offer you romance the way it was always meant to be.

What could be more romantic than to follow the adventures of a duchess or duke through the glittering assembly rooms of Regency England? Or to cavesdrop on their witty conversations or romantic interludes? The music, the costumes, the ballrooms and the dance will sweep you away to a time when pleasure was a priority and privilege a prerequisite.

If you are longing for the good old days when falling in love still meant something very special, then come to Harlequin Regency Romance—romance with a touch of class.

HARLEQUIN Temptation

Rebels & Rogues

All men are not created equal. Some are rough around the edges. Tough-minded but tenderhearted. Incredibly sexy. The tempting fulfillment of every woman's fantasy.

When it's time to fight for what they believe in, to win that special woman, our Rebels and Rogues are heroes at heart.

Cameron: He came on a mission from light-years away... then a flesh-and-blood female changed everything.

THE OUTSIDER by *Barbara Delinsky.*
Temptation #385, March 1992.

Jake: He was a rebel with a cause... but a beautiful woman threatened it all.

THE WOLF by *Madeline Harper.*
Temptation #389, April 1992.

At Temptation, 1992 is the Year of Rebels and Rogues. Look for twelve exciting stories, one each month, about bold and courageous men.

Don't miss upcoming books by your favorite authors, including Candace Schuler, JoAnn Ross and Janice Kaiser.

AVAILABLE WHEREVER HARLEQUIN BOOKS ARE SOLD.

HARLEQUIN
PROUDLY PRESENTS
A DAZZLING NEW CONCEPT IN ROMANCE FICTION

One small town—twelve terrific love stories

Welcome to Tyler, Wisconsin—a town full of people
you'll enjoy getting to know, memorable friends and
unforgettable lovers, and a long-buried secret that
lurks beneath its serene surface....

JOIN US FOR A YEAR IN THE LIFE OF TYLER

Each book set in Tyler is a self-contained love story;
together, the twelve novels stitch the fabric of a
community.

LOSE YOUR HEART TO TYLER!

The excitement begins in March 1992, with
WHIRLWIND, by Nancy Martin. When lively, brash
Liza Baron arrives home unexpectedly, she moves
into the old family lodge, where the silent and
mysterious Cliff Forrester has been living in seclusion
for years....

WATCH FOR ALL TWELVE BOOKS
OF THE TYLER SERIES
Available wherever Harlequin books are sold

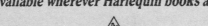

my VALENTINE 1992

Celebrate the most romantic day of the year with MY VALENTINE 1992—a sexy new collection of four romantic stories written by our famous Temptation authors:

GINA WILKINS
KRISTINE ROLOFSON
JOANN ROSS
VICKI LEWIS THOMPSON

My Valentine 1992—an exquisite escape into a romantic and sensuous world.

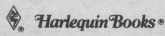

Harlequin Books ®

VAL-92-R